the STRANGERS

Native Edge
David Heska Wanbli Weiden, SERIES EDITOR

Native Edge will highlight established and emerging Native voices producing experimental and genre work in fiction and creative nonfiction: mystery, horror, science fiction, and noir sitting side by side with experimental literary fiction and creative nonfiction. Intended for general readers and classroom use, these books will offer compelling original work bearing on the Native experience in North America and worldwide, and the series will also explore past works that may have gone underappreciated in their day and are now judged to be ripe for revival.

Also Available in the Native Edge series:
The Indians Won by Martin Cruz Smith

the STRANGERS

a novel

KATHERENA VERMETTE

University of New Mexico Press | Albuquerque

First hardcover edition published by Hamish Hamilton Canada, 2021
Second hardcover edition published by Penguin, an imprint of Penguin Canada,
a division of Penguin Random House Canada Limited, 2022
First paperback edition published by the University of New Mexico Press
by arrangement with the author, 2024

ISBN 978-0-8263-6606-1 (paper)
ISBN 978-0-8263-6607-8 (ePub)

Library of Congress Control Number: 2023951265

Founded in 1889, the University of New Mexico sits on the traditional homelands of the Pueblo of Sandia. The original peoples of New Mexico—Pueblo, Navajo, and Apache—since time immemorial have deep connections to the land and have made significant contributions to the broader community statewide. We honor the land itself and those who remain stewards of this land throughout the generations and also acknowledge our committed relationship to Indigenous peoples. We gratefully recognize our history.

Cover illustration: *Green Forest* by Nicole LeClair. Courtesy of Nicole LeClair.
Cover design by Felicia Cedillos
Composed in Alegreya

For my family

Indian girls can be forgotten so well they forget themselves.

—TERESE MARIE MAILHOT

Some stories are stories and some are just facts,
facts so important that story can't mess with them.

—LEANNE BETASAMOSAKE SIMPSON

FAMILY TREE

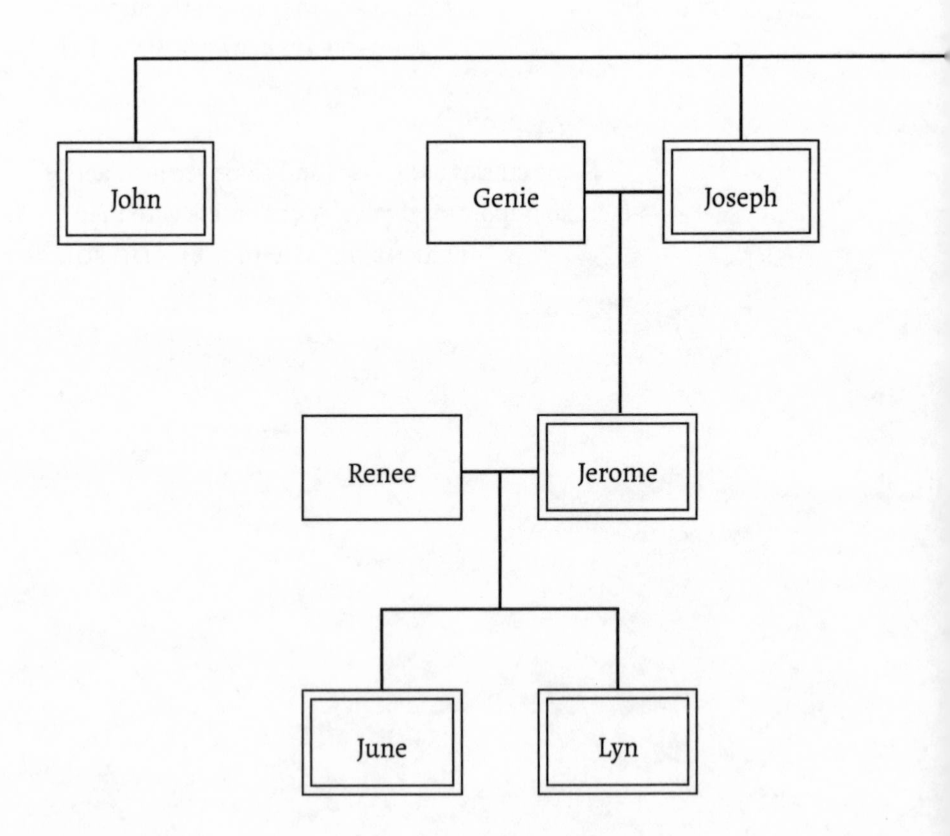

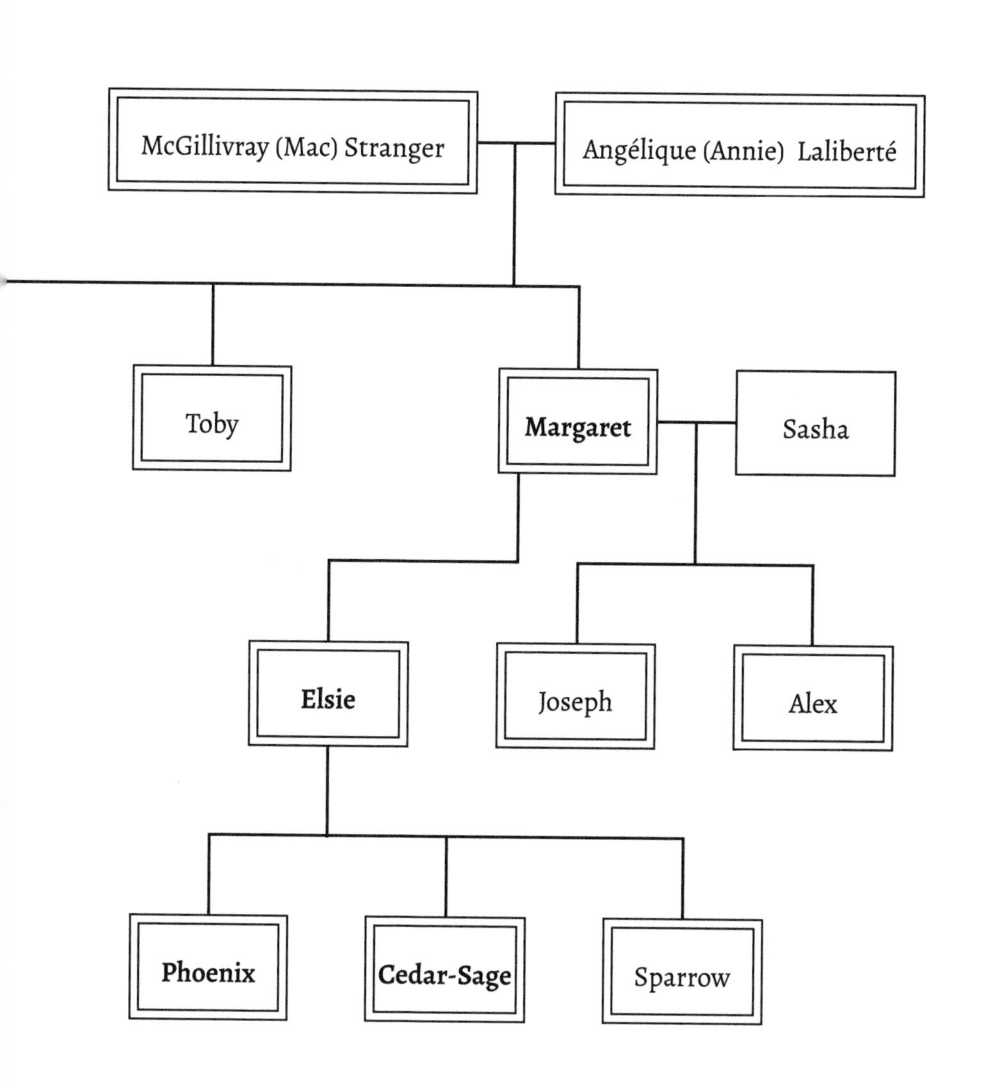

McGillivray (Mac) Stranger
Angélique (Annie) Laliberté
Toby
Margaret
Sasha
Elsie
Joseph
Alex
Phoenix
Cedar-Sage
Sparrow

TRIGGER WARNING

This book is about coping within the systems that have been imposed upon us, so there are plenty of triggers for those whose lives have been traumatically affected by them. These include depictions of child apprehension, solitary incarceration, suicide ideation, some drug use, and some physical violence. (It's not just about that, hey? And I do try to cram as much love and hope in between as possible.)

YEAR ONE

1

PHOENIX

The pain started in the middle of the night.

Woke her up, that first one, like a fucking knife going right through her. She jolted up and almost made a noise. But then it went away as quick as it must have come, so Phoenix lay back down. Rolled over on her side and tried to get comfortable again. Tried to go back to sleep, but only ended up staring up at the top bunk. At the lump that pushed down on top of her.

She hated being on the fucking bottom. Always grabbed the top as soon as she could. But big as she was now, she couldn't get up and down without grunting or even falling, so she was stuck with the fucking bottom. That bitch Winona was on the top, snoring and rolling around. It felt like she could fall on Phoenix any fucking time, fall right on her gut and hurt her baby, even. All Phoenix could do was turn over. She hated being stuck on the fucking bottom.

On the other side of the room was another bunk with an old lady, Sue, on the bottom. The top was empty, for now. This was the infirmary cell. Women came and went. Revolving fucking door. Phoenix had been here for days. Her due date was almost two fucking weeks ago. Any fucking time, was all the bitch-ass nurse said when she checked on her every morning. Any fucking time, like that was fucking helpful.

Phoenix knew about Braxton Hicks or whatever they were called, she wasn't a fucking idiot. She'd had a few, like strong cramps, for months, so she didn't freak out at that first pain. Even though it was different. Even though it felt like something different and scared the shit out of her. But she just rolled over again. Watched Sue sleep open-mouthed across the room. Every now and then the old bag would cough so fucking deep and gross, sounded like her lungs would come up her throat. But ol' Sue wouldn't even wake up all the way. She'd only readjust her nose oxygen thing and go right back to sleep.

Another pain came a bit after Sue's next coughing fit. That's how Phoenix tracked them. She knew to fucking track them, and gauged them on Sue's coughing and how bad they were. In between she tried to breathe like the book had told her. Like the nurse had told her. It didn't fucking help much. It hurt like hell. And it was only getting started. It would be over soon. That's what they told her. Soon it'd be fucking over. Like that was a good thing.

Phoenix thought of everything those first few hours. She tried to distract herself with anything she could think of. The brown house. Grandma Margaret's pancakes. Grandmère's frybread. Sitting in the old lady's lap listening to her stories. Her English broken by French words, Michif words, words Phoenix didn't always know but somehow it didn't really matter. She got stuck for a while on her uncle's music. That was always her favourite thing to think of when she needed to think of something. Trying to remember the words to old Steppenwolf or Aerosmith songs. She mostly only knew the choruses but she kept them going. "Dream On" became a chant with the pain. She didn't realize she was making any noise until Sue woke up. The light out of the small gap of a window getting brighter with morning, and the old lady still blurry across the concrete floor.

"Wah? What's going on with you?" The old lady sat up with a choking sound that brought up another wave of cough and spit. "Is it, is it your time?" It took her a while to say.

Phoenix just lay there. Breathing.

"How long you've been hurting?"

"I don't know," she managed.

Sue leaned forward to look better. "Guard!" she tried to yell but only coughed again. "Get up and, press, Winona, the button!" she choked as she called.

"Fuck!" Winona's voice mid-snore.

"She's getting her pains. Press the button!" Sue's hand to her chest like her lungs would fall out right there. "My word! You preggos will be the death of me. Guard!"

The metal coils screeched as Winona got up and climbed down. "Why are you fucking yelling? They can't fucking hear you!" She pounded on the button and the light came on right away. The glare hit Phoenix's eyes like a hammer. "Finally, fuck, hey?"

Phoenix didn't say anything, just breathed. Felt like the pain was all the time now. Her body fucking wrecked with it. Waves and waves on top of each other.

"Can you sit up? They're gonna come in and check on you." Winona was about forty, skinny as shit. She puffed up every couple days before she went to dialysis, but came back looking deflated and even skinnier. She looked super skinny now. She had a shunt in her arm and she was so thin, it stuck out of her sleeve, a plastic tube like a big open straw. It grossed Phoenix out all the time. Made her want to puke now.

She looked away and tried to sit up, but her whole middle was like a brick, hard and pushing down. Felt like the baby was going to fall out right there.

She finally managed to get her feet on the cold floor. The shock of it went right through her. She didn't want to stand up though.

The door finally fucking buzzed open.

"Is this what I think it is?" Fucking Henrietta was guard tonight. Fuck. Phoenix hated that one. Always looking at her too long. Fucking creep.

"You've got to take her, Henrietta." Sue's voice was always

somewhere between a whine and something even more annoying. "I got to get my sleep or else I'm going to just feel so bad all day."

"You're all heart, Sue." Henrietta's hands on her belt, thumbs hooked off it like she was relaxed. Phoenix knew better. She knew this chick was always fucking ready. Usually Phoenix was too, but right now she was only pain. And at this bitch's fucking mercy. "How you feeling, Phoenix? How long has it been?"

"A few, hours," Phoenix panted.

"Are they close? Getting closer?"

Phoenix nodded.

"Get her out!" Sue shouted. "Get her out of here. It's only, like, five in the morning!"

"Shut up, Sue!" Winona yelled.

"I'll call it in, Phoenix, but the nurse'll want to check you first. She doesn't get in 'til seven."

"Seven! She's got to stay here 'til seven?"

"You know how this works, Sue."

"That's two hours!"

"You took that last one in, like, right away."

"That was her sixth kid. She could have sneezed that one out." Henrietta faked a laugh. "Phoenix is overdue and it's her first. It's going to be a long one." She turned to go out.

"You don't know that!" Sue called after her as the door clanged shut. "She doesn't know that, does she? Winona!"

"How the fuck do I fucking know?" Winona looked down at Phoenix. "How, like, far apart are they?"

"I don't, fucking, know." Phoenix wanted to scream but she had no breath.

"Okay, Sue, gimme your clock."

"That's mine! You're going to break it."

The old lady's whining was really getting on Phoenix's last fucking nerve. She wanted to fucking tell her so but couldn't find the words. And then another fucking pain started. Her whole body tensed up like she was trying to fight it. But couldn't.

"You better give it back as soon as they take her."

Winona grabbed the little clock from Sue's outstretched hand. It was only a small old alarm, the kind that ticked loud and could fold up into its little case. Sue kept it under her pillow but Phoenix could still fucking hear the tick tick ticking. It was annoying as hell the first couple nights. Until she got used to it.

"Okay, let me know when the next one comes and I'll time it."

"We didn't have to do this with the other one!" Sue's whine reached a whole new pitch.

"She knew what she was fucking doing. Does this one look like she knows what she's fucking doing?"

"Fuck, fuck," Phoenix started.

"I know." Winona rubbed Phoenix's leg like it was something she had seen on TV. Something she thought she should do but didn't really want to. "It'll be okay. I was with all my sisters for most of theirs. It's all okay in the end. Just can be long."

"Can you get them to turn the lights off at least?" Fucking Sue.

"How am I going to tell the fucking time then?"

"It's almost light out," Sue said. "Oh no! I'm going to be so sore all day now." She started coughing again like she remembered she needed to be even more annoying.

Winona settled in cross-legged on the floor with the clock in her hand and turned to Phoenix. "Lie back down if you want. But don't tense up. Try to relax."

Phoenix did that and another pain came right away. She couldn't relax. How the fuck was she supposed to relax? She braced her body like she was about to get hit all over, which is kind of what it felt like. Hit from the inside. Like the baby was beating his way out. She held her breath and waited for it to be over.

"Okay, that's one. Try to sleep in between them." Winona

readjusted herself. To get comfortable on the concrete floor. Phoenix closed her eyes. Sang her song in her head.

It felt like forever before the door buzzed open again.

"Morning, Phoenix! How are you feeling?" The nurse always talking in her too-loud voice. Never looking at Phoenix's face.

How the fuck you think I'm feeling? Phoenix thought but didn't say.

"Looks like this baby is finally coming." She looked down at Winona. "Have you been timing the contractions? That's good!" Always talking down to every fucking body.

"They're all over the place still," Winona said.

"Well, we'll see about that." The nurse didn't look at Winona's face either. "Phoenix, I'm going to get you to walk to my office, okay?"

"She can't," Winona said. "She hasn't walked all night."

"She can walk. Can't you, Phoenix."

Through the pain, Phoenix glared at her. She wasn't going to let this bitch win. She sat up like she was fucking dared to. Winona took her hand to help her keep steady.

"Good," the nurse said like she was a fucking kid, and took her other hand. Hers was ice cold. Somehow Phoenix knew it'd be.

At the doorway, Winona gave Phoenix's hand a squeeze. "Good luck, Phoenix. Sue, wish her luck."

"Wah?" Sue said like she was groggy from sleep that she had been pretending to do for the last hour. Then she coughed. That's what Phoenix heard as the door slammed shut.

Her legs felt like rubber. It was all she could do to keep her feet shuffling. Fucking guard Henrietta followed behind them and through the clinic door. The nurse told Phoenix to get up on the table. No one made a move to help her so she waddled her sore body onto the high, narrow table all by herself. The stirrups were as cold as the bitch nurse's hands. Who didn't bother to tell Phoenix what she was doing, just slapped on a glove and stuck her fingers up Phoenix's twat.

"You're only about two centimetres dilated." She took the glove off and pulled up Phoenix's shirt to check her belly with her fucking cold-ass hands.

"What?!" was all she managed, sure the baby was gonna fall out of her by now.

"What do you wanna do?" Henrietta asked the nurse like she was all fucking in charge.

"She needs to walk. She needs to move around or else this is going to take forever."

"Okay," Henrietta said. Like it was normal.

"I'll check on her in a couple hours," the bitch nurse said. She wrote on a chart and then left, without giving Phoenix another anything.

"You heard her. What are you waiting for?"

Phoenix braced for more pain and tried to sit up. She felt like she was going to fall over. Fucking Henrietta made no move from the other side of the room as Phoenix stepped down slowly. Her feet still bare but at least this floor was tiled. She pulled her underwear back on, then sweats, so fucking slow. That bitch Henrietta looked up at the ceiling like Phoenix wasn't even there.

Then took her out to the hall, the sun bright and high now. "We can walk here. To the doors and back."

"I gotta, fucking, walk?" Phoenix was already panting from walking from the table.

"Yup."

"How, many?"

"As many as it takes."

Phoenix started shuffling. She wanted to lie down on the cold floor and yell until they took her to the hospital. She couldn't believe these evil bitches not letting her get the drugs like a normal person. No, she had to fucking walk, like fuck. So Phoenix fucking walked. She walked until the pain came and then she bowled over, holding her belly until it was over. Then she stood up and walked some more. She walked until she could see Winona and Sue beyond the locked door. They must have been leaving for breakfast. That meant it was eight. But she was still fucking walking. Henrietta didn't say anything, didn't do anything but walk beside her. Not touching her, just going at the same pace, however slow. She'd stop when Phoenix bent over but didn't fucking do anything to help. Phoenix thought her legs were going to give out but they didn't. She'd stop, they'd buckle, but she just stood up again and kept walking. The light of the day moved around them, and one time another guard came through and said to Henrietta, "Still at it, eh?" Henrietta must have nodded but Phoenix didn't fucking look up. She just kept at it. Until she bowed over and couldn't stand back up, and Henrietta finally fucking called the nurse.

The nurse said over Phoenix's spread-eagled legs, "Okay, you can take her now." Still not fucking looking at her, but at least not putting her fucking hands in her again.

Henrietta got Phoenix some shoes and a windbreaker. They took the elevator down to the garage, where the van was waiting. Phoenix thought it'd be an ambulance or something but what the fuck did she know. Henrietta opened the door and Phoenix could see the cuffs ready. She sat down and let the bitch guard cuff her to the seat. Like she could fucking do anything. The driver made some stupid joke Phoenix didn't catch and Henrietta laughed. Like it was a normal fucking day. And it fucking was. No one fucking cared. There was no siren. No rush. Everybody was taking their sweet-assed fucking time. No one cared if this baby fucking fell right out of her.

Everything looked like spring outside. Bright as fuck and spring. There almost wasn't even any snow anywhere anymore. They drove through downtown, busy with office people and delivery trucks. Even pulled over for an ambulance and seemed to crawl their way to the fucking hospital.

When they finally fucking got there, Henrietta opened the door and reached in to unlock her. Cuffed her other hand in front and led her through the doors. Phoenix could feel the normal people's eyes on her. How they tensed up like she was going to do something. Pulled their children closer.

Henrietta took her through the check-in and all the way to a room. No one asked her a fucking thing. Henrietta said everything anyone cared about. No one fucking cared what Phoenix thought. Or felt. She sat or walked as they told her to. Braced for each pain and never made a fucking sound.

When she finally got to her room, Henrietta cuffed her to the bed and another nurse stuck her hand up her twat. But this one finally looked at her. "You're nearly six centimetres. Good job!" Again like Phoenix was a little kid. "How's the pain?"

"B-bad." Phoenix's voice felt like it came from somewhere deep down inside her.

"Now, I can't say you can have drugs, but if you want something like an epidural, now would be the time to get one."

Phoenix looked to Henrietta, who nodded and sighed. Then, bracing for another contraction, Phoenix nodded. The nurse held her shoulder as she bent over as best she could, with her left hand stuck to one side. "Are you saying you want an epidural?" Again with the loud voice, like they taught them that in nursing school or something.

"Ye-yes," Phoenix managed.

"Okay," the nurse said but didn't let go until the pain started to fade. "Okay, I'll get that started for you."

She seemed to take forever but finally came back with an old guy pushing a cart. The nurse put a needle in her hand, attached it to a long plastic tube, and taped it up her arm with clear tape. It felt so heavy. Weird to have something metal like that inside of her. Then they rolled her on her side and it felt like they put a giant pin right into her spine. "Should kick in in five minutes or so."

Phoenix thought they had done it wrong and felt nothing but the knife wound in her back. The huge needle in her hand. She was sure they did it wrong, and she bent over for another pain but halfway through, it seemed to fade. All the way down to her toes she felt numb. Like when her foot fell asleep but this time nothing woke up. She was completely fucking numb. She felt like hollering, it felt so fucking good. She was high for a minute and then so, so fucking tired.

Before she could stop herself she smiled at Henrietta. Who kind of laughed. "Fuck, eh?"

Phoenix laughed. She could sleep. Her whole body seemed to sleep before she did.

She woke up with the nurse shaking her. "Phoenix, it's time to push now."

It took her a minute. To realize where she was. What was happening. Then it all felt like it was too fucking soon.

"The fuck?" she yelled. Slapped away the hands that were on her.

"Settle down, Phoenix." Henrietta's voice from beyond the other bodies. So many people were here now. Someone propped up her head. Someone at her feet.

It felt too soon. She remembered the hours and hours and nobody fucking caring and now it was like they were sick of her and going to pull this baby out too soon. She couldn't feel a thing. She couldn't feel the baby. What the baby needed to do. For weeks the baby had been pushing on her pussy like she was going to fall right out. But now there was nothing. Like the baby was hiding inside her. Not wanting to come out after all. She tried to wrap her hands around her belly, like she had been doing for weeks when no one was looking. But she couldn't. One hand was cuffed to the bed, the other held down by the heavy needle sticking out the back of it. She followed its tube to the bag overhead. Clear fluid dripping into her.

The nurse noticed her staring. "We'll take it out as soon as Baby is here and everything is okay. Don't worry."

Baby is coming out. When Baby comes out nothing will ever be okay again.

Phoenix wanted to cry. The nurse was telling her how to push and she sort of heard words like "bear down" and "push there" but the world was spinning. Baby coming. Another came in and looked between her legs. Fucking Henrietta at the other end of her, sort of smiling again. Like they were fucking friends. Fuck that. Phoenix pushed her chin out like she did when she didn't want to fucking cry and got fucking mad instead. Fuck these fucking assholes.

"Okay," the nurse said, "when I say so, you push down into your bum, okay . . . now! Keep going, keep going, keep going, keep going, and . . . good. Okay, rest for a minute. That was good."

Phoenix kept pushing, over and over. It was like the fucking walking. She didn't know what it was fucking doing. Only that they kept fucking harping on about it. She didn't want the baby to come out. Didn't push as hard as she could and it's not like they could notice. It's not like she could have stopped it anyway. Babies come out whether you fucking walk or push or don't do anything. They come out because they have to. Even when they're trying to hide inside of you and don't want to fucking come out ever.

After another forever, the nurse said, "Okay, Phoenix, we can almost see the head. One more good push and we can get the head out. Now really try this time. As hard as you can."

Her body betrayed her and pushed even when she told it not to. Her body pushed even when she couldn't feel anything. The people around her shouted like it was a good thing. Even fucking Henrietta cried out and put her hand over her fucking face like she had something to fucking do with this. Phoenix felt the tears fill up her eyes and fall hot to her face. The baby was coming no matter what she did. He was going to be here and then he was going to be gone. Forever. She heard the scream before she knew it was from her. She felt it through her whole throat. Until her throat burned raw and that's the only thing she felt. After keeping it all in, it all came out. She swore she could feel him go, even though she couldn't feel anything. She could feel him slip out of her like something so smooth. Like it didn't hurt at all.

"It's a boy!" the nurse announced. "A big guy."

Phoenix saw him between her open legs. Her eyes full, he blurred into the world, held up by a stranger. He opened his mouth and wailed. His lungs wide. His voice strong. She too cried out but no one seemed to notice. A small moment in time she could cry. She reached out to grab him, but they didn't see her. They took him over to a cart and washed and checked him. He kept screaming. She could feel the heat lamp over him but swore he was cold.

"Good job, mom." The nurse patted her shoulder. And then looked down and walked away. Said over her shoulder, "Eight pounds six ounces. A good size."

Phoenix gathered herself up. Breathed in and put her hand, the one heavy with the needle, on her belly. It felt loose, open and deflated. She thought it must be how Winona's skin felt after dialysis. It was a weird thought. She looked over at Henrietta, who had a goofy fucking look on her face.

The bitch guard turned to her. "I've never seen that before. It was so . . ."

"Want to hold him?" The nurse had the baby all wrapped up in the white blanket, had even put a cap on his head, and faced him to her. He was still whimpering a bit.

She did. She didn't care about anything else. She nodded and the nurse placed him in her arm. Leaned him against her right arm, and Phoenix grabbed hold even with the hard needle there. He stopped whimpering. As soon as she held him, he stopped and looked up at her.

The nurse pointed to the cuffs. "Does she really need those on now?"

"Sorry, have to," Henrietta mumbled. Still sitting like an asshole across the room. Still with that goofy fucking look on her face.

Phoenix looked down at him. His eyes were bold and big. He reminded her of Sparrow. That other ballsy baby. Only this one was a boy. Phoenix was glad he was a boy. Boys had it easier. Boys could be strong and didn't have to fight for everything. Boys could get respect just for being boys. Not like girls. Girls had to work for it all the time and never really got it. This boy could have it is easier than her. He could have anything.

"Did you call the social worker?" the nurse asked another.

"Yeh, she can be here in twenty."

"Call her in about an hour, then."

Sparrow. That's what Phoenix would call him. Sparrow Stranger. Another one. A stronger one. A boy one. This one wouldn't get sick. Or have a fucked-up Dad and a fucked-up life. This one would be luckier than the other Sparrow Stranger.

"The Grandma is here."

"Tell her to wait for a bit. Doctor needs to check the baby yet."

"Is something wrong?"

"No, I don't think so. But you know, we want to be sure."

He settled in to sleep. Leaning his little head against her chest. Phoenix wanted to curl up around him. To sleep and never let him go. She wanted to be so still the world stopped. Forever.

Phoenix jolted awake at the scream. Her hands empty. She patted around.

"Sorry, sorry. I just put him in the bassinet." The nurse pointed to the baby kicking around in the plastic bin next to her. Close enough Phoenix could reach out and touch him, so she did. "Want to feed him?"

"I— That's not a good idea," Henrietta fucking chimed in.

"We got bottles. You can use a bottle."

Phoenix nodded and took the baby again. She glared over at fucking Henrietta while the nurse leaned him to her cuffed side and stuck a little bottle in his mouth. He took it like he was starving. Phoenix fumbled but took it too and fed him.

"He'll only want a little bit."

She was right. It was over too soon.

"The social worker is here."

Everything in the room changed. The baby started crying, and Phoenix's body started to hurt. The drugs wearing off. Her back ached.

"Hi, Phoenix." She didn't remember this one's name. She was a blonde chick from who the fuck cares. When they had met she told Phoenix she was Métis too but she didn't look it. Phoenix thought she must be one of *those* Métis, the ones who only said that when there was something to get for it. "Big day. Congratulations."

Phoenix just glared at her. No energy for anything more. All the shit she wanted to do to this fucking social worker.

"How you feeling?"

Phoenix didn't look up. She looked down at her baby, Sparrow, as he cried. She bounced him gently like she used to with the other Sparrow, and he calmed. But was wide awake.

"Jesse is here. She's been waiting. She can take this little guy home right away." She was talking slow like Phoenix was stupid. "He won't spend a day in care."

There was a long-drawn-out moment when she could hear the clock on the wall tick tick.

"She wants to apply for an adoption, Phoenix. That means you sign away your rights."

"I know what that fucking means."

"It means you can't try and get him back when you get out."

"Like you people would fucking let me have him."

Phoenix could almost hear the stupid cunt trying to think.

"It could be for the— She's his family too, Phoenix. It's the best possible arrangement—" Her voice hung there like she was going to say something else. "Best thing you could ever—"

Phoenix felt the back of him, smooth and small. So very small. She forgot babies were ever this small. The first Sparrow was even smaller, only five pounds when she was born. Phoenix barely remembered that time though. This, this she wouldn't ever forget.

"I'm sorry, Phoenix. It's time. You have to—" Again she didn't know what the fuck she was saying. Trying to act like she cared but really she just wanted to be fucking gone. Wanted to get this over with and fill out her fucking paperwork so she could get on with her life. No matter what it did to fucking Phoenix. The nurse made a move closer, hesitant, like she wanted to pull back. Henrietta looked ready for her to do something. But she didn't. She wouldn't. She wouldn't do anything crazy while he was around.

Phoenix slowly leaned over and passed the baby to the nurse. She left her hands on him for as long as she could and when he was gone, the space he'd filled was cold and hollow.

"Thank you," the nurse whispered. It was a stupid fucking thing to say and Phoenix could see the bitch realized it as soon as she said it. But she looked away and passed the baby to the fucking social worker.

"He's going to be okay, Phoenix," she tried, but Phoenix had already turned over.

She could hear them in the hall. The nurse, the social worker. She could hear Jesse, Clayton's mom, cry out, "Oh what a beautiful boy!" Her boy. Phoenix's. She had no songs left in her head. No thoughts to distract her. Henrietta was saying something about staying for observation, but she didn't fucking care. It was night again. Everything looked fucking dark again. She hadn't seen it go dark. Didn't know how long it'd been so dark. She was cold, so fucking cold. She covered her head with the blanket and closed her eyes as if she could sleep.

She must have because she woke up in complete dark. Her whole body ached a sore that went through her bones. Her stomach slack and crumpled but heavy and hurt. Her pussy felt like it was cut in half. Like someone had taken a knife to it. The nurse had given her pads. Had told her to tell them when she had to go but she was still numb then. Had no idea it could hurt like this. She twisted her body slowly and pulled the blanket down so she could see. Henrietta was gone and in her place was another guard. Phoenix didn't remember his name, just some fucking creep who leered at anything under thirty. He sat upright but his mouth was open in sleep. He let out a gross deep-throated snore. Phoenix was disgusted. But at least it wasn't fucking Henrietta thinking they were all friends now.

"How we doing in here?" Another nurse with her too-loud voice. The fucking guard sprang to attention as if he was actually with it or something.

"It fucking hurts," Phoenix said. Her voice raw and dry.

"Language," the guard tried, but Phoenix and the nurse ignored him.

"I can give you some T3s for the pain. Do you have to go to the bathroom yet?"

Phoenix looked to the guard, who looked like he was back asleep, and shook her head.

"Well, don't leave it too long." The nurse leaned in and talked a bit quieter. "I'm going to give you a stool softener too, so it won't hurt as bad."

Phoenix glared quick at the guard before lying back down. She didn't know how long she'd be here. Didn't know what would happen next and didn't want to ask. She was fine to stay here as long as she could.

It all kept going too fast though. In the morning, Henrietta came back. A doctor came in and Phoenix got into the fucking stirrups again. Everything healing, everything fine. It still hurt like a motherfucker but all they gave her was regular Tylenol now. It wasn't like she was a fucking drug addict or anything. Fucking assholes.

She got Henrietta to let her out to use the bathroom. Wasn't about to use the fucking gross bedpan. Her legs were still fucking wobbly, but they felt better. Like they had been running all night but were still strong.

When she got out, she knew by the way that bitch Henrietta was standing and smirking that it was time to go. Back into her sweats that stank of institution. Back in the van that smelt like vomit. Through downtown that still looked almost spring. Back to Remand as if nothing had ever happened.

—

"So what was it, a boy or a girl?" Sue coughed as soon as Phoenix walked in.

"A boy," Phoenix said before she thought about it.

"What's his name?"

Phoenix sat on her bunk slowly and glared at the old lady.

"They didn't even let you name him? They have to let you name him."

Phoenix lay down. She didn't want to say it. The name she picked. The name that was full of pain. Both times. "Where's Winona?" was all she said.

"Hospital. All the stress from helping you, if you ask me. She got the kidney failure again." Sue's whine turned into a cough. Phoenix turned over and faced the wall. Wasn't going to get up until she had to.

Three days later she had to. They had a bed for her at youth detention. She was lucky she wasn't tried as an adult and they considered her past and trauma in sentencing. She was getting off easy and would only have to do about three years, if she behaved herself. These were all the things they had told her before. But they told her again as they sat in the counsellor's office. Sat there with that social worker who wasn't saying a goddamn thing. Phoenix waited for the officer to stop fucking talking and see what the bad news was. The social worker came with documents to sign, waivers for the officer to witness. Words spread out like a crowd in front of her, so many, too many, things like "relinquishing all rights" stood out, and "petition for adoption of."

"Sparrow. What an usual name," the social worker said like she was just making conversation. "Where did you think of it?"

Phoenix just looked away. If the lady wasn't going to bother to look at her file, she wasn't going to bother to answer her stupid questions.

"She got a new place, Jesse did, and her mom moved in. Lots of support and space. He has his own room, Phoenix." All things that should make her feel better.

The last three days she lay in that bunk. Listened to Sue cough. Waited for Winona to come back but she never did. No one told her anything about that either. She slept, mostly. Tried not to think of anything, only wanted to let old songs run in her head. But when she was really asleep and couldn't stop it, she dreamed of babies. A baby not too far away, crying. She couldn't see the baby, didn't know where it was. But could hear it. Crying like it was left alone. Crying like it needed something. Like it couldn't stop. She'd wake up with a start and listen like the baby was in real life. But she didn't hear anything. Only the tick tick of Sue's fucking clock and in time, always, her fucking coughing.

"He's in a good home, Phoenix. They love him and will take good care of him. Don't you want that for him?" She didn't have to try so fucking hard. Phoenix had already signed the fucking paper.

Lock-up looked the exact same as it did the last time she was fucking here. It had been a year or so, but everything was the same down to the guards, the posters on the walls, even the girls. It was dinner by the time she was pushed through so she went right into the dining hall. She looked around at a bunch of faces she knew and some shouted "Hey!" and "Phoens!" She nodded at them. Not ready to talk or anything. Knowing they weren't really her friends and wondered what they had heard. Then she saw Dez. Fucking Dez all high and mighty sat at the front table right in the middle. A girl she knew, Lacey, on one side and another fucking slut bitch on the other.

"Hey Phoen, how's it going?" Dez looked nervous. She should be.

Phoenix nodded and went up and got her food. She sat down across from fucking Dez and stared at her until the bitch looked away. Then she looked at the new girl.

"This is Dakota. They're good. No worries." Dez was almost shaking.

Phoenix looked at the kid. They were young, maybe fifteen. Didn't seem to be good at all. Looked like a lost cat. The kind with fur all matted and big eyes. Dez always wanted to be tough shit. And this was one way to do it, Phoenix thought. But she smiled quick. Young Dakota smiled back and looked down. Weak.

Phoenix ate her meatloaf and asked what was new and who was doing what. Dez picked up on it right away at least. Cheyenne had been jumped, ended up with broken ribs. After that her mom sent her to her rez. Roberta had been beat up and turned out. Phoenix nodded. It was better than she deserved but at least Phoenix would know where to find her when she got out.

Dez was waiting for sentencing. She was likely to get a suspended one, like the others, but had priors so it was taking a while. Oh and her and Mitchell were still in love. He was waiting for her. Wouldn't think of cheating on her.

Yeh fucking right, was all Phoenix thought and sneered a bit too much. Dez looked like she noticed.

When they'd all finished, and the girls all got up to leave, Dez turned to Phoenix. "You wanna come play cards with us? We been playing this new game these girls from Philippines know. It's a decent game."

Phoenix nodded at her and let Dez lead the way. Then took her plastic tray and broke it over the side of that stupid bitch's head. Dez didn't fall, just stumbled forward so Phoenix dropped the cracked tray and shoved her down hard. Dez tumbled over and Phoenix pinned her to the floor. Felt like she ripped the fucking stitches in her fucking pussy, but she still moved quick and got her knee on her. Then punched Dez's stupid fucking face until her lip bust open. Someone pulled her off so she started kicking. Dez started bawling, "I didn't rat, Phoen. I didn't." Phoenix felt her foot connect at her little fucking stomach and kept hoofing until someone got ahold of her arms and pulled her away.

"I didn't rat, Phoen, honest." Dez's face all bloodied and a guard pulling her up and leading her away. "Honest. I didn't, Phoen. I wouldn't."

Phoenix pulled her arms back but couldn't get loose. They pulled her down the hall. Dez's stupid, useless minions and all the other girls staring down at the broken tray and blood on the floor. Dez still yelling even though she was around the fucking corner and no one could see her. Phoenix thought she should have punched her mouth harder. Some other bitch started laughing and Phoenix glared. Bitch had blue hair all faded but the ballsy bitch stared right back at Phoenix.

"Quite a first day, Phoenix," the guard, Chris was his name, said. "Even for you." He was around last time she was here. A short little fucking muscle-head. She started walking properly, and he finally let go of her arms.

She only shrugged at him. Let the air out from between her teeth.

"You'll remember this place, hey?" He was trying to be funny. "Home sweet home."

It was. Kind of. The solitary room, or cell, whatever they wanted to call it now, was small. Big enough for a skinny bed, a table and chair, a toilet and small sink in the corner. There was a window but she had to stand on the bed to look out. Even then could only see the tops of the trees at most. She could see it getting dark now. She could see the blanket and pillow folded on the bed that wasn't a bunk.

"Better than sharing" was all she said, and slowly sat on her new bed. Careful not to hurt her sore-again body. But more careful to make it look like she was wasn't in pain at all.

2

CEDAR

"Can you believe it, Cedar-Sage?" Mama says. Her voice cracks so I can tell she's not really as happy as she's trying to seem. "You have a nephew! You're an aunty!"

I don't say anything, just push my annoying hair behind my ears and look down at my old leggings. There's a small mustard stain by my knee because I'm such a slob. I pick at it and don't look up. I want to be excited, but mostly I only feel sad. I pull the cuffs of my sweater down all awkward, pull them over my hands, and then remember to nod. Pretend I'm happy. For Mama. But I don't look up. I don't want to.

Mama sighs. Gets up and paces around the small room. I know what that means. She's getting impatient with me.

"There's no air in here," Mama says. "Don't they think to ventilate these rooms? We need air, for Christ's sakes."

She opens the old glass door and waves it back and forth like a fan. It does make a small breeze. The social worker sitting outside the door makes a face at the crazy woman waving the door around, but doesn't say anything.

Mama's been twitchy since she got here and now I know why. This big news. I wish I was excited about being an aunty, but really, what's there to be excited about? Phoenix had a baby and it got taken away. Phoenix is in jail now. Phoenix did a horrible thing and is jail for a long time. She had a baby but it went to live with its other Grandma. No one will even tell us where that is, or anything other than his name.

A sad name.

Sparrow.

After our other sister. The little one. Who died.

"Well, I can't wait to meet him. I bet he looks like my Grandpa Mac. All the boys in our family look like him. Your Uncle Alex is like his spitting image. Your Uncle Toby, too." Mama does this every time we have a visit. Goes over family members I don't even know. I have blurry memories of living in the brown house and an old Grandmère, Mama's Grandma, my Great-Grandma, and another one, our actual Grandma who was named Margaret. I remember her a bit but only know her name 'cause Mama calls her.

"Babies are gifts, Cedar baby, gifts! Yeh, I can't wait to meet him." Mama paces around the room in that unnatural way she does and picks at a big sore on her lip. We only have another half-hour before the social worker will come get me and take me to my respite worker who will drive me back to my foster home. Foster *place*. Don't know why they call them homes. Never had one that was like a home. This one's better than the last one, I guess, but still. I got a room to myself, for the first time, and the lady there's nice enough. Luzia is her name. She cooks a lot and talks to the TV like a crazy person, but there's only one other girl there. Nevaeh. She's a year older than me and acts all hard. Runs away a lot and stuff.

To be honest, I don't know how to get excited about a baby I doubt I'll ever get to meet. Another family member I'll know about only 'cause someone told me about them. Named a sad name.

If I'm really honest, I'd admit I want to go now. Mama's making me anxious and is probably going to get worse. She seemed fine when we got here, twitchy but put together enough for our first visit in almost a year. But now, who knows. She must be on something, or maybe hasn't been on something in too long. I used to be able to tell which was which, but it's been so long I don't really know her moods anymore. Or her drugs.

"Cedar-Sage, Cedar baby, don't get all attitude with me now. Just 'cause you're a teenager now doesn't mean you have to act like one. I need you to say something. I can't, I can't stand you just sitting there." Mama's voice cracks over the words. She sits down across from me and nervously puts her hand on my knee. "I— I love you so much, my girl."

I want to reach out and hug her but I wait for a minute, to be sure. I used to be really good at being what Mama wanted, needed. I was always happy when she wanted me to be. Talkative when she wanted to listen, quiet when she needed quiet. I was always that way. But can't seem to do it this time. I did feel happy when I first got here. When I first saw her, I smiled so wide I felt like a goof. Was so glad to hug and feel her arms around me. I even had a bit of that crazy little kid hope I used to, that this would be the time, finally the time that they would tell us we could go home and Mama would take me to our real home to live. Then I felt how skinny she is, how sick and wrecked she looks. And I knew. Again. Just like so many of the things I want, or used to hope for, it was never going to happen.

When I finally look up, Mama is staring at the wall, all big eyed and stoned looking. She does that when she's upset, goes far away.

"I love you, too, Mama." My voice is small and rough. I was going to say more but she looks up too quickly, sucking on her cut lip like she's trying to hide it. Like nothing is wrong at all. Then jumps up again.

"Okay? I'm just going to go grab a coffee."

I don't say anything. Don't have to.

"Be right back, Cedar baby." The door closes slowly behind her. Doors don't slam here. They just close slow, as if with a sigh.

This is her third cup of coffee in the last hour. If Mama could, she'd go down and have a smoke too, but she can't do that anymore. When we used to visit regularly, back when Sparrow was alive, the first Sparrow, Mama used to take lots of smoke breaks during visits. She said she needed them because the whole thing broke her heart so much, but they stopped all that a few years ago. For safety reasons.

For everybody. So instead, she's twitchy the whole time, needing a smoke, waiting to be able to go for one.

Maybe that's the only thing that's wrong with her, that she needs a smoke.

I know cigarettes are bad for people. I've seen so many videos at school about what happens when you smoke, a new one every year, complete with an assembly and a cancer survivor, or a cancer victim's loved one, and a warning of how we can all die. They once showed an old man's lungs all sick and black all the way through. That's probably what Mama's lungs look like now. Sick. All the way through.

But I also know there are things worse than cigarettes. They have assemblies about some of those too. They go over different drugs and warnings of how we could all die, like that's the worst thing. They never seem to know the whole story. Only a small part. Not everything.

I sit there all quiet for a while, looking around the small room. I don't like this one. It looks dirty and feels worse. The paint is chipped in the corners, and the chairs smell like sweat. The wooden arms all scratched up—someone knifed on mine: *Rita was here 1992.*

I always liked the big room down the hall better. It was cleaner. Had a couch, a TV, and a big painting of an eagle with its wings stretched out far and brown. That one's for big families though, and now it's only me and Mama.

We used to go in the big room when we first started coming here. Back when we were visiting regularly. When we were first in care, we'd visit every month. Back then, we were always so happy to see each other. It was like Christmas every time. Mama was in treatment and normal, and Phoenix was in a group home in West St. Paul. I remember missing and loving them both so much. Phoenix missed me too. She'd always give me a hug so big and so long I thought she'd never let me go. She'd hug me before she hugged anyone else. Even Sparrow who was so small she'd cling to my side for the first bit, unsure about Phoenix and Mama, as if they were strangers. Phoenix would tell us all about all the crazy kids she was living with at the group home, and before that, at the hotel. She always had lots of funny stories. Or made them funny by how she told them. Phoenix was always really good at that. Mama was usually pretty quiet. She'd go out for her smoke breaks and cry too much, but she was always calm and clean. In those days.

Now Phoenix is a mama, too. Well, she is but she isn't. Her baby. This new Sparrow is not even going to know her. Is not going to know any of us. At least with me, I always knew my mama and remembered living with her. We all lived together for a long time. For Phoenix's baby, it's worse.

Or better.

The social worker pokes her head in the door and looks around. "Where's your mom?" she asks, not really looking at me.

"Um, she went, for a coffee." I stumble over the words. "I think." I get so stupid and shy around other people, especially around new people. Especially new mean-looking people like this one.

The social worker makes a noise like a huff and stomps off.

I sit and wait some more. Only twenty minutes left now. My respite worker will be downstairs soon, ready to take me back to Luzia's. After that, I'll have nothing to do but watch TV, or if there's any chores that need to be done, I'll clean something. I could read, but all my books are old already. I need to get to the library and take out some new ones. But no one will let me go alone. I have to ask the respite girl. Chelsea. She's new, too. Just started this summer.

The door opens with a sigh as Mama comes back holding a new half-full styrofoam cup of coffee, bright with creamer. Her face looks sad again. The all the way sad. And the social worker follows her. Now I know something is up. Another something.

"Cedar, honey, we have some more news. It's good news," Mama says but doesn't look it. "Your dad, remember we were talking about your dad last time?"

Last time was almost a year ago, months and months anyway, and my dad is just this other family member I don't know but hear stories about. Your dad used to, you dad could be so, your dad would.

I don't remember him at all. Hadn't seen him since I was little, since before Sparrow was even born. I don't know much life before Sparrow, but know everything about life with her, and after.

"Remember we were talking about you maybe going to live with him?"

This was another story she told but it wasn't like I believed it. Not after a while. Mama has always said something about me going to live with my dad, maybe, if this, if that, when. When Sparrow was alive, I didn't want to go because I thought that if I had to go to my dad then Sparrow had to go to hers, and I didn't want Sparrow to have to be with her horrible dad. That or Sparrow would be alone at Tannis's house, and I didn't want that either. But it never happened anyway. It was just another story.

"Well, he got a pardon, and he's, umm, he's married now, so . . ."

The social worker cut in. "Cedar, your dad's in a good place. He recently moved back here and petitioned to get custody of you. Everything's gone through. What do you think about that, Cedar?"

I can't even remember this social worker's name. She's new, too. Doesn't matter anyway. It's not like I have to say anything.

"They have a house, in Windsor Park. That's in the south end of the city. A good neighbourhood. And his wife has a daughter your age, a bit older, I think. You have a stepsister, Cedar!"

Mama looks ready to cry but is trying to hide it. She looks ready to crawl inside her own skin and disappear, if she could. I know the feeling.

"I have to go? Now?"

The social worker laughs a bit, like I'm an idiot. "No, oh no, not right now. If you want, we can arrange a visit with them. Then maybe in a few weeks, before school starts, maybe, we can think about moving you there."

I start picking on the mustard stain again. Luzia always puts too much mustard in her sandwiches. I thought I was sitting upright at lunch. Thought I leaned over my plate like I'm supposed to but sometimes I am such an effing slob. I pick at it until it's almost gone, until it's only a small faded yellow bit on the now-frayed fabric.

"I'm going to let you two talk about that a little more. It's good news, Cedar. Best thing you could have hoped for." The worker leaves and the door sighs a long sigh.

Mama wipes her eyes. She acts like it didn't happen but I saw. I try to think of something good to say, but I don't have to, Mama does.

"That social worker's pretty uptight, hey?" Mama kind of laughs and slaps my leg, trying to be all happy again. As unpredictable as Mama is, I always like it best when she gets happy. "So, what do you think? You would be a south side girl, how about that?"

"Yeh," I say, trying not to smile. Mama's smiling sometimes makes me want to smile. Used to always.

"It's a good thing, Cedar-Sage. Your dad is a good person." Her voice light and smooth.

I frown but nod. Can't look up.

"What? What is it, honey?" Mama's hand still on my leg. Warm.

I think for a long time before I look at her, but then have to look away to say it. "What's his— What's his name?"

Mama is quiet so I look over, see the tears fill up in her eyes. The kind that stay there a minute before they fall down. I was pretty much near tears as it was anyway, but I always want to cry when I see my mama cry. Always.

No matter what.

The ride back is long and hot. It's super hot today, like record-breaking hot, but I don't take off my hoodie. Don't even push up the sleeves.

Chelsea has an old car and the air conditioning is busted. That's what she said, but it looks so old it might not have ever had air conditioning in the first place. We keep the windows rolled down all the way but it's not that much cooler than keeping them shut, only more like sitting in front of a hair dryer.

Chelsea is pretty quiet after her usual "Hey, ready to go?" and I don't feel like talking so we don't say anything. She's good like that. Doesn't make me talk, only plugs her phone into the long cord and lets me pick the music. Just always looks to make sure I'm not doing anything else. You're not allowed to go online when you're in care, and I don't have a phone. I only have an old iPod I got for Christmas last year. It was a hand-me-down from another foster parent. Foster person. She had filled it with One Direction songs because she thought that's what I'd like. I did at the time. But now it's too old to download anything new so that's all I've got. Chelsea has so much and this is my new favourite thing to do. I scroll through all the names I want to know and pick the only one I've learned so far, A Tribe Called Red. I turn it on, lean back, and close my eyes, letting the hot air blow my hair around.

Saying goodbye to Mama is always the hardest part. We had to say goodbye with the social worker right there propping the door open. Mama cries and says sorry over and over.

"I'm so sorry, baby, oh my sweet baby. You are such a good girl."

I squeeze her tight and try to ignore how bony she is. Try to ignore that stupid worker who checks her phone again. I breathe in her long, crazy hair and skin. I'm almost as tall as her now.

"I'm working so hard, Cedar baby. You've got to believe me. Please believe in me." She pushes me off her and grabs my face in her sweaty palms. "Don't get any teenage attitude and get yourself in trouble like your sister. Not you. You hear me?"

I nod frantically and try to smile. But Mama pulls me to her again.

"It's so hard to dig yourself out once you get in the hole, you know?"

I can feel her hot breath through my hoodie. Can smell the Mama smell of her. Shampoo and something else. Something she always smells like. Something I always forget when I'm away from her too long. I run my hands over her hair. Her big curly hair that's still wild but stringy-looking now, like it's weighed down. Still beautiful like it's always been, only thinner like the rest of her, and more grey. Like the rest of her. But it's the same smell. Always.

"I'm going to try and go see that baby. I'm his Grandma too, you know. I should be able to see him, right?"

"Yeh" is all I say.

"I'm gonna see you again soon, too. Once you get settled. And don't be afraid, honey. He's family. Your dad is your family, too. I love you so much, Cedar baby."

"I love you too, Mama." She has a lot of grey strands in the front, and a few more lines around her eyes and that big cut on her lip, but she's the same, really. Worse off, but still the same.

Mama pushes away one more time and cups her hand over her mouth like she's trying to keep all her words from falling out. She looks at me for a long moment before she turns and walks away.

I watch her walk down the hall. Not knowing where she's going. Or when I'll see her again.

"Your respite worker is downstairs," the social worker says. "Do you need anything before she takes you home?" It's not like she cares.

I shake my head, and don't look at her.

We stand there, like the worker is waiting for me to say something, but really she's just waiting for Mama to be gone long enough so I can leave, too. Finally she says, "I'm going to set up that visit and let you know in the next couple days. Okay, Cedar?"

I still don't look at her, just pull at my sleeves again and walk out. The same way Mama did.

The car goes down Main and turns on Selkirk. I know the way without looking. I open my eyes around Charles Street and look down to the corner of Flora Avenue. There's an old grey house, behind a big old church, and Mama said she lived in the basement. She had pointed to it when we drove by this way, on the way to Sparrow's funeral. She told me she'd take me there one day, for an overnight visit.

It never happened, but it made me hope for a while.

I always look for her there, at the grey house, when we pass this way. I've always lived around here. No matter where I've lived.

Selkirk Avenue goes on for a long time. The houses go from bigger and older to smaller but still old. Some look damaged. Some look perfect and painted. There's another pretty big church, and a few new university buildings that stand out bright and shiny. One is painted in the four colours with a Tipi built into the side.

Next is Arlington. We had an apartment down Arlington once, but further down the street near Inkster. I was really small then, but remember it had a lot of stairs and a big window that looked out into the street. I used to sit there and watch the cars pass for a long time. Phoenix always made us toasted sandwiches. Phoenix was always really good at making food for me and Sparrow.

We turn on McPhillips, then to Burrows. Our first foster place, Tannis's, was down Burrows. We lived there for a few years. Until. After that I went to stay in this place in the country, way down McPhillips. Down past the city where the open fields stretched out on either side of the road. It seemed to take forever the first time, but I got used to it. Even though I wasn't there a year.

The songs change and the beats go slower as we pass the high school and move through the development where all the houses and apartments squish together in big buildings with so many windows. They all look the same but different colours. The brown siding of Jig Town, the Yellow Houses, the White Houses, and Lego Land. Called that 'cause it's all the other colours, red, blue, and green. We lived in Lego Land for a while, too. That was my favourite but probably only 'cause I was young and we were all together for the last time. That place was big like a house and the windows were never shut. Mama likes to keep the windows open, no matter what season. She likes the fresh air. It was always so bright and clean, too. The long wall by the stairs was large cement bricks painted over white. I used to trace my finger along the in-between seams as I went up and down. Back then, before we went into care, Sparrow was a crazy, messy little kid, and Mama was there all the time. Back then, even Phoenix didn't get into much trouble.

Our house was red on the outside and there was a park right behind. I used to think it was the biggest, best park ever, but I know now it's not much of anything. Only a big open field with an old swing set in it. Still, it's a really big field.

After Keewatin, the street starts to curve and rounds a man-made lake. The houses are newer. Further apart.

"You doing all right, Cedar?" Chelsea turns down the music but not all the way.

I nod back, and watch little kids roll their scooters down the sidewalk.

"You still want to go see a movie on Saturday?"

I nod again. And clear my throat as quietly as I can, knowing I should say something soon.

"You sure you don't want to go to the beach or something? It's so hot these days." Chelsea tries but not hard.

"It's air-conditioned in the theatre."

"Very true."

"And there's Coke."

"Also true." She smiles as she turns the wheel. "You've got this all figured out, don't you, kid?"

I smile. I like when Chelsea calls me kid. It's not the most unusual nickname but it's probably the best one I've ever had.

"Could we maybe, also, um, go the library?"

"Library? In the summertime?" Chelsea laughs. "For sure, kid. I'd be happy to take you to the library."

Chelsea is okay. I hope she sticks around for a while. Respite workers seem to come and go pretty quick. Even faster than foster places. But Chelsea seems nice. And has great music.

I really miss my sister. My real one, the only one I have left. We used to talk on the phone every once in a while, back when she was at the Centre. She had phone privileges every other day. When I first came to Luzia's, Phoenix would call after supper and Luzia let me talk for a while before I did the dishes. Phoenix even wrote me a letter once. It wasn't much. A few pages of jokes she had heard that she thought I would like. She drew a little comic too, just to make me laugh. I still have it. Put it someplace safe.

I haven't seen her in person since the funeral. I got to meet Mama at the office downtown and they drove us together, but Phoenix had to be escorted and came in with handcuffs and guards. They took off the cuffs but the guards stayed at the back watching us the whole time. As soon as she could, though, Phoenix came over and hugged me. After that she held my hand the whole time. Didn't let go until she had to leave again.

That was almost two years ago. I can't remember her face, not all the way. Or know how it must have changed. It must have gotten older-looking. Not kid-like anymore, like how I remember her best. Phoenix is seventeen now. Almost aged out. Or would have, if she didn't go to jail.

I like my room here. The walls are clean and I don't have to share. In the country, I had to share a room with one girl, and there were two other girls across the hall. Here there's only Nevaeh and she's way down the hall in her own room, too. My bed is straight and high and has a thick red wool blanket on it. The blanket is itchy on its own but I also got an under-blanket and a flat sheet. I don't use all these things all the time, especially in the summer, but I always like to make them all together like that in the morning.

Luzia told me I was the cleanest girl she's ever had. It's a pretty big compliment, 'cause Luzia has had lots of girls. She's fostered for years. Used to have as much as six kids at a time. But that was when her husband was still alive and they were younger, she had told me anyway.

I lie down on the bed and think about what I want to do. I don't want to watch TV, or read, so I stare at the ceiling. I really hate summer when I have no homework or anything to do, but sometimes I like staring at ceilings and thinking. I like to think all the things I want to. Everything, everybody, like they are right here happening with me. Sometimes I can think about them so well it doesn't even hurt that none of them are with me anymore.

I think of Mama and Phoenix and imagine us all together somewhere in the country. Mama has always wanted to live in the country, where it gets super dark at night and you can actually see the stars. I like to imagine buying a big house and Phoenix getting out to come live with us, too. We'd cook big meals like Luzia does, and laugh all the time.

If I can really get into imagining everything I really want, Sparrow'd be there, too. She would fly down like a perfect little angel and then Mama would be all the way happy, all the time. The baby too, the little boy Sparrow, would be with us and Phoenix would know how to take care of him because she used to take care of the other Sparrow so well.

I think about this for a long time. I imagine running around in the grass with Sparrow while Phoenix and Mama sit in the shade with the baby, looking on at us. Laughing.

After a while, I can hear Nevaeh coming in with all her banging and heavy steps. Luzia's voice is muddled through the wall, asking questions. I can hear Nevaeh getting closer.

"I know you have to report me . . . Fuck." She only swears quietly once she's in the bedroom hall, and knocks at my door as she passes. "Hey Freak," she yells at the closed door. Nevaeh always calls me Freak. Also not the most unique nickname. And I don't like it as much as kid. But it's still nice somehow. The way she says it.

She slams her own door and turns on her music. She likes hip hop, rappers I've never heard of, and she likes them loud. Luzia lets her, most of the time. Nevaeh has her own iPhone, only they took the SIM card out. She was super mad about that, but still has her music. She also gets burners off her friends so she can keep in touch. She told me she could get me one too, but I said no. She laughed at me, thinking I was just too scared I'd get caught. I let her think that. Didn't want her to know I didn't know any of the numbers of anyone I want to call.

—

By five, I start getting hungry. Luzia likes to eat around then, so I get up to see if I should set the table or something. I'm halfway down the hall when I hear my name.

"Cedar's a good girl," Luzia is saying to her daughter Maria, who was visiting. She was always over.

"I know she's good now, Ma, but she's getting older," Maria says. "You know what they get like when they're teenagers."

Luzia makes a noise like snort or something. "You don't know this girl."

"Ma, you always say that. You always believe in them and you always get taken advantage of. Or worse!"

"You are only remembering the bad ones."

"Oh come on, Ma. You're so gullible." Maria sighs. "You have to start being realistic. You're an old lady and you're vulnerable. I wish you would just move in with me and look after your own grandchildren." Maria taps on the table. "With Dad not here, I worry, Ma. I'm so scared something bad is going to happen."

"I only have two girls now. And they're good girls."

"You mean like that one who takes off all the time? And that other one? With her mother? And that sister! God, what a family! I'm so glad she's going to live with her father. Imagine what he's like. But at least she's out of your hair."

"Cedar's a good girl. Nothing like her mother. Or her sister." I can tell Luzia is getting upset 'cause her accent is starting to come through.

"Oh Ma, it's only a matter of time . . ."

Luzia doesn't say anything. Maria snorts. Then they are quiet.

It's not like I expected Luzia to say more. Only wished she would.

I feel rage come over me like a wave. I am mad and sad, and want to run, want to take off for some reason. Go away. Not like I know where I would go.

I go to my room and pace back and forth, like that helps. I don't want to think about the bad stuff, but it won't stop coming. I want to go and be with Mama, find her, save her. I don't want to go live with my dad, another person I don't even know. Who took off before I could even remember him. I didn't even know his name. How messed is that? I know Mama. And Phoenix. But I'm not allowed to be with either of them.

The first time I heard Maria call us down was when I first moved in. She was going on and on about my mama being a low-life. I wasn't even thirteen and still a bit naive. I knew Mama had her problems, but still. The next time Phoenix called, that was the first thing I asked.

"Is Mama like, really bad or something?" I said each word slow.

Phoenix sighed. "Where'd you hear that?"

I only shook my head, even though she couldn't see me.

Phoenix sighed again and swore under her breath. "Elsie has her problems, hey? You know that." Phoenix has always called Mama by her first name. Phoenix has always been old like that, even when she was small. "And sometimes she's bad, and sometimes she's better." She was quiet for a long time. "I think she's just bad right now."

"But she said she'd take me home soon," I remember whining, not meaning to, but whining. Thinking of Mama at the funeral, driving there past her house. Hope.

"Cedar-Sage, you haven't lived with her for more than six years." Now it was seven, since I was six almost seven. Sparrow wasn't even three. Like almost half my life. More than half of Sparrow's.

"I know" was all I could say.

"I know you love her and I know you want to go home, but Elsie hasn't been able to take care of you for a long time. She was messed up even before Sparrow passed, and that shit messed her up for good."

That did it. I started crying and couldn't stop. "I wanna go home." I was such a little kid.

"I know. I know. Me too." Phoenix's voice was sad, but I knew she wasn't crying. Phoenix never cried.

We didn't say anything after that, but sat on the phone for a while longer, quiet. Sometimes we did that, when we didn't have anything to say but didn't want to say goodbye. She would sigh and I would listen to her breathe for as long as I could. Until someone told us it was time to get off.

Truth was I didn't even have a home anymore. The house in Lego Land was long gone, and Mama probably didn't even live in the grey house anymore. Phoenix didn't have a real home either, but she had plans.

"Cedar-Sage," she told me a few times. "When I turn eighteen, I am going to get a big apartment and then you can come live with me. You will go to school and I'll get a good job. If you get good grades and stay out of trouble, you can get on independent living and then you can come live with me. We just have to wait until I'm eighteen."

I used to count down the years. Now it doesn't matter. Now that she is really in jail, she's not going to be free when she's eighteen. She'll still be locked up. For real now.

"You are the best of us, you know?" she'd always say before she said goodbye. "You just got to hold tight and you'll do good. You are the best of us." She was never blubbery or clinging like Mama. Phoenix was nothing like Mama. "I love you, my sister."

That night, I sit with Nevaeh in the living room and watch TV. We do that sometimes, after Luzia goes to bed. She's okay with it, but only because she doesn't have any of the good cable channels.

I'm still raging and sad in waves. I know Nevaeh hates her too, so I say, "Maria was calling my family down again. Fucking hate that."

"Maria's a stuck-up old bitch," Nevaeh says right away, then lets the air out from between her teeth. Nevaeh is usually pretty cool. She turns to me and looks at me hard. Serious. "They're still your family, Freak. No matter what."

She turns back to the TV and keeps flipping the channels all lazy. I'm surprised. I thought she was going to laugh at me.

Nevaeh falls asleep shortly after that. She cuddles into the blanket. She likes to sleep with the TV on.

But I am wide awake and restless, and can't stop thinking. The TV is stuck on an old episode of *Cops*. I watch it but I'm really not paying attention.

I get up and open the heavy curtains a little so I can look out the big window. The quiet curved street. The full trees glowing green in the streetlights. I lean forward to press my face against the glass. Everything's so cool from the central air and feels nice. Every house is dark on this street. Nothing is moving except some of the leaves in the light wind.

I go over everything about today. Phoenix and her baby. Seeing Mama and going to my dad's. Shawn. I didn't even know that much. Just another person. Could be anyone. I know I should be happy but it only feels like another move, another place I have to go and get used to, all over again.

People I have to get to know. All over again.

If I was brave, I'd run away. If I was brave, I'd take off and go to that grey house, find Mama and stay with her. Just like that.

But I'm not brave. I'm not all that anything. Just a little foster kid scared of everything. Not hard enough. Not anything enough.

I keep my cheek pressed against the window for a long time. Until two streams of car lights flash over and I get embarrassed that someone will see me. I close the curtains quick, but not before seeing the imprint of the side of my face. I know I should probably Windex it off, but you can barely see it. And it's the only proof I've been here, really.

3

ELSIE

It's that stinking kind of hot. The kind that makes downtown smell like piss and armpits. Downtown mostly smells like piss and armpits, especially in summer, or after a hockey game, but it's really strong this afternoon. Probably over thirty degrees. Elsie breathes it in, tries to calm her nerves. She's sweating after a block and feels like shit all over. Bone, muscles, even her skin feels like it's trying to run away from her.

It's been forty-four days. Forty-four since she last had a hit. Almost twenty since she weaned herself off the last of her percs. Not so much weaned as ran out. Since she got herself to the walk-in clinic and finally got some methadone. Again. Not so much got as begged for. Not that it lasted long enough anyway. But it's been almost twenty days. The worst was over.

Twenty days since Jimmy kicked her out. Not so much kicked out as she left. But she knew he wanted her to go. He was sick of her. And he was always the one who hooked her up and without him she'd have to go get on her own. She could have but the only place she knew to get pills was down Portage and that was too close to jib. Which was cheaper. And she wanted to stay clean. She could have tried her buddy Mercy but she was trying to be good. Not so much trying but proud. Whatever works. Forty-four days. Nineteen days. It's the longest she's been clear-headed in a long time. Her body aches. Her knees throb with every step and her hips feel like they're going to break but she's still somehow fucking sober. It's the longest she's gone since she can remember.

Not true. She can remember. It's been since her baby. Her poor sweet Sparrow. Almost two years now.

She also got a high dose of good SSRIs too but waiting for those to kick in is agony. That's all she's got. That and hope. Weeks of hope for a good visit with her Cedar. Now that that's done she has nothing. No one. Just Uncle Toby. For now. Until he gets sick of her too.

Desperate for another smoke, she mooches off some office ladies hanging down the low end of their building's parking lot. Most are giving her the stink eye but one gives her a smoke already lit. She doesn't look Elsie in the eye but waves away the quarter she tries to give for it. Elsie thanks her, of course. She is nothing if not polite. But the rest of them are still giving her dirty looks. They're the kind of ladies who bitch about Indians on their Facebook pages and then get all weepy if someone calls them racist. They will think of this, she knows, this tired old brownish lady bumming a smoke off of them, the next time that happens. They will describe her and say, "See, see, we know what we're talking about. We've seen it."

Elsie walks away with a fresh wave of shame. There are many. Waves. Shame. She adds this one to the rest.

She gets off Ellice and heads through Central Park. She wants to avoid Portage like the plague. There's ten dollars in her pocket. A five and a bunch of coins and she doesn't want to go try and find something. Well, no, she wants to more than anything right now. Today. The need for it tenses her arm muscles and clenches her jaw. But she won't. Forty-four days. Nineteen days. So much longer than she's gone since she's gotten so bad. And she won't give that up. Not today. Not even today.

She finds a bench under the trees and finishes her smoke. She works to rest her palm on her knee to keep from smoking it too fast. Wants to make it last. Wants to inhale the nicotine and hold it inside. She thinks of her money again. It's enough for a drink. Maybe two if she goes to the Nor'wester where drinks are cheap. Or enough for a five-dollar pack from the corner store down the way and then one drink. She doesn't have enough for a real pack.

Or she can walk back to Portage and get fixed up real quick. It would take five minutes to walk. Even with her slow hips. Maybe another two to get set up. And then, nothing at all.

Last time she took too much was after all that shit with Phoenix. She got cleaned up to go visit her. Called that social worker every day for a week so she could go visit her. But her poor baby. Her poor little baby was gone. Phoenix was a monster now. So mean. So evil. It was her fault, Elsie knew. She failed. Went hard after that. For a month. More? Doesn't even know. Until she woke up cold. In the back lane of some office building. Her hair in a puddle of piss. It was the grossest. Lowest. She has ever felt. Been. It was the worst and she won't let it happen again.

No, it wasn't. Not the worst. But it still won't happen again.

She takes a last half drag at the filter and nearly burns her fingertips. There's nothing there but it was worth a shot. Pulls her knees up to her chest and makes herself sit there a minute. Sit with the pain of the day. Pain of the life. Her life. Elsie tries to breathe through it. She remembers how from a group she went to at some point. Back when she was trying. Breathe and relax. Breathe through it. She remembers. To breathe. And be here. In the moment, they called it. Breathe. Be here. The trees are bright with summer. Birds are singing in the sun. Kids are playing in the water park. And she thinks, I am a worthless piece of shit who has deserved all the shit I have gotten in this life. Every bit.

And there's been a lot.

She doesn't want to cry here. Doesn't want those families and these people to see her weeping on a park bench in the too-hot day. She is otherwise pretty fucking presentable. Wearing her best clothes to visit her girl and everything is clean. Her hair was brushed and pulled back before she went over there. Before the humidity made it all crazy and wild again. She even had some mascara on. Clean. Normal. Not like a woman who ever woke up with someone else's piss in her hair at all.

Breathe. Breathe. She thinks of the words they told her. I am worthy. I am loved. I am . . . what the fuck did they say to say? All these chants and good things. Mantras. That's what they're called. They told her she was filled with negative self-talk. That was her real problem. Addictions always come from somewhere, they said, and she should be talking positively to herself. Tell herself she is worthy of love or some shit. That's it. Should be. Really. Elsie remembers trying. For a while. But mostly when she tries, it just feels like something else she is doing wrong. And she feels nothing different by saying different words to herself. Only lies anyway. How is she worthy? Her kids have been in care for years. She has no hope of ever getting them back. Sparrow died. Her baby is dead. Her other baby just had a baby that she will probably never see. Another Sparrow Elsie has failed as soon as it's born. Another Sparrow for the world to break. And Cedar is going to live with her dad. Shawn. Shawn. Gorgeous nice guy Shawn who promised to always be around but took off to Alberta right after he got out of jail. Never heard from him again. Never got a dime. Now he's getting Cedar. Because he can and Elsie cannot. She is not worthy. She is not much of anything. She is only forty-four days from meth. Nineteen from pills. She is barely clean. She is pain. She is nothing. She is,

A guy in a suit storms by puffing on a cigarette.

"Hey!" Elsie says way too loud. He jumps a bit. "Got an extra smoke?"

"Naw, pack only came with twenty-five."

"Har har," she says flatly. Like she hasn't heard that one before.

He stops mid-stride. Turns to her. "I'll give you one for a blow job."

"Fuck off!" She sits all the way up and glares at him.

"Whatever," he says and adds "fucking skank" for good measure before storming off again.

Elsie shakes her head and sinks back into the bench. Hugs her knees in close again. She doesn't want to cry. She doesn't want to cry.

"Here." A smoke floats in front of her face.

She looks up to this young girl with pale skin that stands out in the heat. She's wearing big wide glasses, like the kind Elsie's Mamere used to have.

"That guy was an asshole."

"Yeh," Elsie takes it greedily. "Thanks."

"Don't mention it." The girl looks a little too long. "Take care."

She walks off before Elsie can offer her the quarter. Or anything. Then puffs too fast. Trying to block the thoughts. The words in her head. Without much success. She is,

Sparrow, Elsie thinks to the trees. Sparrow. The clouds blur in the perfect blue sky. What's that shade of blue called? The perfect summer day blue. Sparrow. Sparrow. Elsie can feel her daughter in her whole body. Her chest heaves with the loss. The loss of all of them. Her arms ache from the hug she gave Cedar when they said goodbye. That blessed hug. She hadn't really hugged anyone in years. Not like that. Felt like she hadn't been touched in weeks. Probably hadn't. Sparrow, my love. Elsie wipes the tears. Looks around but no one notices. No one is paying any attention to the strung-out woman on a park bench. She should know that by now. Know how invisible she is. She is,

She breathes and makes her drags longer. Breathe. She inhales them down as far as they will go. Breathe. Breathe.

She starts walking. Trying to get as far from Portage as she can. Walks past this bar she used to go to sometimes. The patio near-empty but she recognizes this guy she used to know under an umbrella. An empty glass and the thin newspaper in front of him. She's about to cross the street to avoid him when he calls,

"Elsie!" Like he's happy to see her. "How you been? Haven't seen you in a while?"

She clears her throat. "I'm okay."

"Come, sit."

"I can't, I don't," she starts.

"I'll buy you a drink. You hungry? You look hungry."

"Oh, okay." She walks around the little fence that keeps the patio in. She's trying to remember his name. Where she knows him from. What he wants from her. He calls the waitress over and asks after her uncle.

He offers up a pack of smokes as she sits. He seems nice. "Your uncle still living at the place down Main?"

That's right, he knows Toby somehow. Toby used to haunt places like this, back when he could walk properly. "Yeh, he'll never leave." She inhales the very harsh Export A. Nearly coughs. "It's subsidized."

"That's good. Good for him." He inhales like it's nothing. His face has that big smoker look. Grey and wrinkled but smiling. He sweats a bit in the sun. "And how are you? You look like you've had a day."

Elsie sinks a little lower in her plastic chair. Imagining how rough she must look. Mascara running by now. Hair messy. Clothes sweaty. "I had a visit today, with my daughter."

"Which one? Phoenix?"

Elsie forgets sometimes what people know. What she's told people. What she's probably told this guy while drunk or high or both. What he must think. This strung-out halfbreed. Past it and past passed over. Kids in care. Waste of fucking space.

"No, Cedar. She's my second youngest. Well, youngest." The words choke out of her throat. She doesn't want to talk about the rest of it. Shawn.

The waitress comes up and he gives her a peace sign. Sign for two. Elsie starts to cry again. She doesn't mean to but she does. He doesn't say anything. Just pushes the ashtray closer. Looks off to the park to give her an inch of privacy. Nice guy.

"You wanna talk about it?"

She shakes her head and reaches for another smoke.

"Need anything? Got a place to stay?"

"Yeh, been staying with my uncle. Trying to stay clean. He's good to me."

"He's a good old guy, Toby." And after a minute, "Glad he's helping you out." And then another. "Seen your aunty lately? Genie?"

Elsie thinks a minute. Remembers this guy knows the whole family somehow. Probably Sasha and Alex and everything too. That's why he's so nice to her. Thinks she's all connected and everything. Doesn't know they all don't give two shits about her. That she's the most useless one of all.

She shakes her head again.

"You should go see her. She's your aunty. Never met a nicer lady."

The sadness washes back over her. Another shame. "Haven't seen her in years. She's busy with her real family, I guess. Jerome and his kids and all."

He nods and their drinks come.

"Have you seen Phoenix? Since all that trouble?"

"In the spring. When she was in Remand." Elsie chokes it back too fast. She makes a noise with the straw and gets afraid he'll think it's a hint. Afraid he won't take the hint. "She, uh, she just had a baby."

"What!" He leans back in his chair. "I heard something about her being knocked up but I had no idea she was that far gone. Elsie! Shit! You're a Grandma!"

Elsie shakes her head shyly. Butts out her smoke and hesitates before reaching for another.

"Fuck! This is great. We have to celebrate. Kate! Kate, get us two more doubles. We have to toast this. What did she have?"

"A, a boy."

"A boy! Oh boy! This is great. Grandma Elsie. It suits you. Mazel tov."

She smiles in spite of herself. Doesn't tell him the rest. How she'll never see him. How he's named after the other child she neglected to death. All that. She pushes it out of her mind and licks her lips. Anxious for that double.

She leaves him around dinnertime. Happy hour. When the place fills up and he seems to know everyone. When she reaches for another smoke and he looks at her side-eyed. When she's drunk and should probably go and sleep it off. This much alcohol and the hot sun, she feels dizzy. She gets up and thanks him. He waves it off like it's no big deal. Not like that office lady did though.

He tells her to tell her uncle he says hi.

If only she remembered his name.

—

Feeling better, she walks down Princess. To Higgins. Then Main. She keeps to the shade 'cause the sun seems to make her feel drunker. She hates that. Tries not to stumble. Tries not to act drunk. Hates that. When the people driving by see her like that. She knows what they must think of her.

She's about to turn down Toby's street when she remembers the cash in her pocket. Remembers the Nor'wester. She could have one more. Or more. That time her friend Val became a Grandma. The celebration. The free drinks.

She tries to smile big when she walks in. The place is pretty empty. Val is in the booth in the back. But Elsie knows she'll be with Jimmy. She doesn't want to see Jimmy. Not yet. She sways to the other side of the room. Goes up to the bar. Pushes her crumpled five across the counter and orders a Club. This old guy she knows sits on a stool. She remembers his name too.

"Hey, Donnie, how you been?"

"Good, good, Elsie. You?"

"Can't complain. Can't complain. You know what? I'm a Grandma!" She tries to smile wider.

"No shit. Had no idea. No shit!" Donnie slurs a bit. He's a good guy is Donnie. "I'd buy you one but I am broker than a joker. Gare? Gare? Elsie's a Grandma!"

"Congratulations!" the bartender says and pounds her beer down on the counter. Takes her five.

"You should get her a drink," Donnie says. "Put it on my tab."

"You don't have a tab."

"What? Why? I should have a tab. The amount of business I give you."

"I would never trust you with a tab." Gary laughs. He's not a bad guy. Just a tight-ass.

"Aw come on, Gare. I'm a Grandma. I've never been a Grandma before."

"That you know of."

"Boom!" Donnie says like it's some big, funny joke or something.

Elsie laughs. It almost doesn't feel forced. She takes her beer and looks around. Can feel Val eyeing her up. But Elsie doesn't want to fight so hangs back. There's no one else here really. A couple old guys playing pool. A working girl taking a break at the table by the window.

The beer is nice and cold. She sips as small as she can. She could go home and tell Toby. He would be excited. He might even have enough cash to buy a case or something.

"Hey, Elsie, congrats congrats!" Mercy comes up behind her. He's a good guy but not quite right in the head. He got beaten up and near froze to death on a starlight tour years ago. Hasn't been right since. He's not stupid but just jittery most of the time. Sometimes repeats things like that kid in that storybook.

"Thanks, Merce. How are you?"

"Good good. What you drinking drinking?"

"Aw thanks, man, I'll have a rye. Double, if you can."

"Sure sure. So so is it a boy or or a girl?"

Elsie makes her smile wider. Donnie and Mercy lean in as she talks about her grandkid like she'd seen him. Talks about his little fingers and toes. A head of black hair. When she stops she realizes she's actually describing the first Sparrow. When she was born. She swallows hard. Then downs her whole double rye in one clean shot. Asks the guys if anyone has a smoke.

"Jimmy Gwetch's over there." Mercy points as he and Elsie go out for a smoke. Donnie limps on his cane behind them. Elsie helps him over the step at the door and takes an extra smoke out of his pack for later. He won't mind.

"Yeh, I saw him. I saw him." Elsie doesn't want to talk about her ex and her ex best friend Val but Mercy seems to. So she lets him.

"You should go say hi, go say. Be friends again."

She makes a groaning sound. An "I don't know" sound. But she's smiling with the rye. If there was ever a time to do it. She was feeling that smooth part of the drunk. When everything is fine. She wants everything to be fine.

When they go back inside, Mercy and Elsie head to the back booth.

"It's Elsie. Elsie is here." Mercy waves and sits down across from the couple. The now couple. For almost twenty days. Probably longer.

She looks down at them. Feels herself swaying. Tries to stop. Jimmy had his arm around Val but puts it down. Looks away. Val looks up though. Her face hard and ready for anything.

Val talks first. "I hear you're a Grandma."

"Yeh."

"That's good. Congratulations. Did you get to see them?"

Elsie nods even though it's a lie. Even though Val would know it's a lie.

"Let me buy you a drink, to say congrats." She moves slow out of the booth, and to the bar.

Val's good like that. Always has money to spare. Always offers another drink. That's also probably why Jimmy is with her now and not Elsie. Elsie doesn't really blame him.

"That's real great, Else, real great to hear." Jimmy's voice across the table. He's smiling his shy smile. The one that could always get her to do anything. No matter what. Jimmy's still cute in his way. He still looks like a young kid in a way. His face looks sunk in like he needs to eat. But Jimmy is still Jimmy. James, Jimmy Gwetch, it's all just Jimmy. Elsie's known him since they were kids. Knows more about him than anyone else on this earth. And him, her. They'd been on and off for about five years now. Since before Sparrow. He was there for all the Sparrow stuff. Val being the latest to get between them. But they always got back together. It's been almost a month now. Elsie was starting to give up hope. But he was looking at her like that.

Val brings a round. Then another. After the third, they're all great friends again. Val was one of the best friends Elsie has ever had. Her only real friend for a long time. Until. But Val can tell a great story. Mostly only the same five stories over and over again. But they're still funny so everyone always laughs. They laugh for a long time.

They go outside to smoke again and night has finally come. It's all the way dark and the cars push headlights over them as they puff. Elsie feels drunk and happy. She thinks of Shawn, when they were young and thought they were in love. He was so good to her. Good to Phoenix. She never thought he would leave her like that. Not him. But him.

Val says they should all go back to her place. Mercy laughs because he is so happy to have them all back together again. Val gives Elsie this big hug. Elsie loves this hug. Then Elsie goes to hug Jimmy and he lets her. As she pulls away she kisses him without knowing she was going to. Like it's just a thing they do when their bodies are that close together. For a moment, it's good. Perfect. The way it always is supposed to be.

Then something pulls the back of her hair and throws her down. She looks up and Val is yelling down at her. She swears and spit drips off her lips. Behind her Jimmy slouches down and disappears. Then Val stomps off, grabs Jimmy, and they go back inside. Mercy helps Elsie up and says, "Maybe you should go go."

Elsie nods. Feeling the urge to cry again. But fights it. Toby's is only a couple blocks from here anyway. She was going to go there anyway.

She crosses the street, trying not to stumble. Doesn't want the people in cars to see her stumble.

The weight of the day waves back over her. Cedar, Shawn, Sparrow,

Jimmy. All the people who were supposed to love her. Are supposed to. But no one does. She doesn't blame them. The dark trees blur overhead. There are no more birds singing.

Toby's apartment always smells like stale cigarettes and meat. It reminds her of their old house. The old brown one. Every time she walks in here she thinks of it for one nice minute.

It's dark inside. Uncle asleep in his chair. The TV glowing over him. Elsie stumbles to the kitchen and gets a big glass of cold water. Didn't realize she was so thirsty. Drinks another. Then starts rummaging for a smoke. Toby has one of those old rolling machines and none made, so she sits down and gets to work. It takes too long but she manages one. So full of holes it burns down to half right away.

"Hey, hey, Elsie." Toby at the doorway clutching his walker.

"Hey, Uncle, sorry to wake you."

He shakes his head and sits down to make himself a smoke too. Doesn't turn on the light. He actually makes two and passes one so she can light with the butt end of her bad one.

Elsie can feel it, here in the dark. It comes back. It always comes back. Like waves again. Like spins in the alcohol spins. It all comes up with all the rest. Shame. Sorrow. Sparrow.

"Phoenix had her baby."

"Oh yeh." Cigarette hanging off his lip and looking cool like in those old movies. "What she have?"

"A boy." Elsie exhales cigarette smoke and pain. "She named him Sparrow. Another Sparrow Stranger."

Uncle nods like he's proud. "It's a good name." Then asks, from far away, "You all right?"

It's Elsie's turn to nod even though she's crying. He only makes more smokes. And sits there with her.

After a while he says, "I got to go to bed, Else. You too. Sleep it off."

If only it was that easy. But she listens. Follows him to the couch and he hands her the blanket. Every morning she folds it up and puts it on the back of his chair like he likes it. Like Mamere, his mom, used to do. And every night he puts it back on the couch for her to use.

"Night," he says simply and makes the slow walker-walk to his room. Tomorrow he will make eggs and extra-greasy bacon. Weak coffee in his old perk. Won't ask any questions.

She won't sleep it off though. It all goes with her. All the time. She thinks of the ten bucks in her pocket. Then remembers it's gone. She thinks of where Mercy was staying last. She could go ask him to set her up. Or she could walk to Portage. Uncle must have some money here somewhere. She knows he hides it. Never found where yet.

No, she can't do that. Not to her old uncle. The last person who's always good to her. His couch, the only place she has left. It's old and musty. Smells like mould in the cushions. Only a wooden frame with cushions on top. Like the one at the centre Cedar sat on. Sweet Cedar. So much bigger than last time. Her face changing into a woman's face. A woman Elsie doesn't know. A grandchild she will never be able to pick out in a lineup. Or would she? Maybe he does look like her Grandpa like she said. Or like the first Sparrow looked. Like she thought he would when she imagined him out loud. Maybe.

Maybe.

Almost forty-five days. Almost twenty-one days.

She leans back and starts to spin but leans into them too. Lets them take her into sleep. She'll be up in a few hours to smoke or be sick. But this moment, in this moment she can rest a spell. She can rest even as she takes it all with her.

Her sorrow. Her worthlessness. Her children.

Her love.

Always.

Always with her.

4

MARGARET

On the day Phoenix was born, Margaret was working on a new puzzle.

The phone rang in the late morning. Margaret picked up the receiver and pulled the long cord to the table so she could keep working on it. It was her brother Toby, who told her the baby was born. Margaret knew it was coming, but didn't think it would be quite like this.

"It's here? Already? Was it quick?" Before she caught herself, suddenly anxious.

"Don't think so. Mom went to the hospital yesterday. She told me to call you."

"Oh," Margaret replied, understanding. They never thought to call her before it was all over and done.

"You're a Grandma!" Toby said stupidly, then coughed out his too-long inhale of a cigarette.

"Oh," Margaret said again, quieter this time. Then shook the feelings out of her head and lit her own long menthol slim. She exhaled before she went to speak again, then thought better of it and took another drag instead.

"You should go see her," Toby choked. "You should, go, Margogo. She'd love to see you."

"I doubt that," she said, not sure who he meant, but either way it was the right answer. She ignored the horrible nickname, too. No sense getting into that this morning.

She looked down at the puzzle. It was a five-thousand-piecer of puppies in a basket. Golden retrievers in a straw basket with a big golden sun in the background, so every shade of yellow you could think of. It'd taken her all morning just to do one edge.

"I'm gonna go down there in a bit. You should come," her brother tried again, like it was something to celebrate. Like a girl that young could ever be a good mother, or be ready to be a good mother. "Bring Joey and Alex. Uncle Joey and Uncle Alex!" Toby let out another rusty laugh, followed by a throaty cough.

"The boys are in school." Margaret butted out her smoke and thought about lighting another one but stopped herself. She hated chain-smoking. "And I'm busy today. I gotta start cooking dinner for Sasha in a bit." She heard Toby's disappointment in his phlegmy sigh. "I'll go tomorrow. I will," she said quick, to avert any more of his stupid guilt trip.

"Okay. Okay, that's good, Margogo. That's good." Toby gave one of his soft, annoying chuckles. "Can you believe she's a mom? Seems like only yesterday I was pushing her around on the swing in the backyard. Remember how she loved the swing?"

Margaret scoffed. Toby had been getting like this awhile now. Sentimental. They said it happened when you started to lose it. Toby had been losing it for years, if he ever had it to begin with. "Of course I remember, Toby. It's a wonder it's still up. Dad put that thing up in the fifties. You could have killed the child with those old chains."

"Naw, Dad knew what he was doing. That thing is still solid to this day. They can put the baby on it." Toby was nothing if not hopeful, and dim-witted. Hopeful and dim-witted were usually one and the same.

"Well, I don't know about that." Margaret picked out another smoke. Thankful for the slight change of subject.

"The porch too, still straight as an arrow, isn't it? Isn't that's something, hey? Remember when Dad and us built that thing. That was, was such a, a hot summer."

"Mmm" was all Margaret replied, all she had to reply. She knew

Toby didn't need her to say anything. He only wanted someone to listen. No one ever listened to Toby. Except their mother, who was obviously too busy today to listen, with the new baby and all.

He seemed to be getting even slower with age, and liked to talk more and more. Or had less and less friends. Lately he called Margaret nearly every day just to chat. It was so irritating as she always had something to do. Between him and Sasha and the boys always on her about something, and always wanting to talk her ear off, Margaret never got a moment's peace.

"Dad sure knew how to build things to last, hey?"

Margaret made another dismissive sound. She wasn't in the mood for Toby's precious rewrites of their childhood. "Listen, Tobe, I gotta get to my ironing." It wasn't a complete lie.

"Okay, okay, little sis, just thought you'd want to know, you know, Grandma!" She could hear him smiling over the phone. It was so grating. She heard him light another cigarette and cough in her ear before sputtering a "talk to you later."

"Uh-huh, yeh, bye." She rammed the phone down before he could say anything else, then focused back on all the shades of yellow.

The damn swing had squeaked for as long as she could remember. A good gust of wind and the thing squeaked around, so loud you could hear it in the house. Whenever someone got on it, it practically screeched. By the time Margaret came along, her brothers had already wrecked it. The seat was splintered, the paint chipped away. Jumped on so much it hung low, like the branch it was attached to would snap at any moment. She hated it. The chains were always cold, no matter what the weather. She'd grip them as best she could, pump her little legs to try and make it go. It never went much. It was a swing for little kids, babies, and by the time she was five, she felt she had already outgrown it.

Everything was like that in her family, messed and tired by the time she got it.

—

She was nearly done another side when Sasha came home. The man didn't do anything in halves, including simple things like walking in the back door. He swung the old screen door so far it almost got off its hinges and then hit the inside one against the wall. Then he stomped his boots against the rug and pushed them off, then stomped some more, even in his socks the man stomped, up the two stairs to the kitchen where he fell into the chair on the other side of the table from her. He literally fell into a seated position. Never sat like a normal person, never used the tiniest bit of stomach muscles to hold himself back, or up, but pounded his expanding girth down gracelessly. They had been married over a decade now, and had gone through three couches, two bedframes, and countless kitchen chairs, all because the man couldn't be bothered to use an abdominal muscle.

"What's for lunch?" Never a hello, how are you, nothing. Just straight to what he wanted.

Margaret didn't look up from her puzzle. "Don't know. Best have a look in the fridge."

"I thought you were going to make something. You said something about cold cuts this morning."

"I said we were out."

"What?"

"I SAID WE WERE OUT. OF COLD CUTS." The only thing worse than an aging man-child was a deaf aging man-child. Not even fifty but his hearing was nearly gone, and the man was already slowing down. Thought he was so hopelessly old. Invalid. So, of course that meant Margaret had to do even more things for him, things he couldn't possibly manage for himself, like cooking, cleaning, everything. Including entertaining him around the clock, it seemed.

For a while, after he first got out a few years back, Sasha drove long-distance truck, again. Like he did when they were first married. She loved that. She could count on three sometimes even four nights a week of him away. It was almost as good as when he was in prison. Came with decent money too. It didn't last long though. Nothing ever did with Sasha. He could only ever work nominal hard for a few months, a year at most, before he had to go and slack off again. It was so hard, of course. And he was getting so old, you know. So he gave up driving and got the bright idea to get this place. An old house with a long, treed, fenced lot and an industrial shop in the back. Easiest to hide in plain sight, he mused to her, and dreamt of making his millions cleaning cars for lazy gangsters. Margaret thought it was the stupidest idea in a lifetime of stupid ideas, but Sasha never listened to anything she had to say. Her husband, like her brother, like everyone it seemed, never heard a damn thing she had to say. She was stuck here, in another falling-down house with a man who was always a-fucking-round. Always here, wanting her to listen or cook or always something. It was enough to drive her to drink. Or smoke too much, which is what it was doing these days.

"Well I didn't know that." He started to drum his permanently paint-stained fingers atop the table, because he really needed to get more aggravating. "If I'd known that, I would have gone out to lunch, or to the store. I'm hungry now."

She didn't say anything. Didn't have to, of course. Instead she cocked an eyebrow up to look at him. Slumped in his weakened chair, back curled like he'd never sat up straight in his life, belly distended from beer and whiskey stretching out his threadbare, paint-splattered T-shirt. He furrowed his brow, looking too old for his years, and pouting like all the fight had been knocked out of him. His skin grey. He must have been smoking too much in the garage, or stuck himself in the booth painting cars all morning. It was almost summer and he should have been looking halfway dark by now, should have been getting out in the yard and working in the driveway or something, but no, he was holed up in there, working on whatever car that was dropped off for him to do. Too many cars. Too many half-painted, half-clean stolen cars littered the yard, asking for trouble. She agreed it was good money, for now, but knew it was never going to last.

Sasha sighed loud. Margaret started working on a yellow puppy face—two eyes and a tiny snout floated in the middle of the table. He sighed again. But she was not biting.

"Well, I think I'll go down to Sal's and see if anyone is in. Have meself a nip. K, Margey?"

"Hmmm," was all she said. Annoyed that everyone still called her by stupid nicknames. It didn't seem to matter that she always, consistently, introduced herself as Margaret, always that, her full name, Margaret. Her family still called her whatever they wanted. Never mind what she wanted.

It was her dad that started the nickname thing. Mac loved a good shortened name, never called anyone by their proper name. Her mom was never Annie before her husband, or so she's said anyway. Before Mac she didn't even speak that much English, and always went by her full name, Angélique, but after Mac started calling her Annie, she became Annie. Margaret doesn't remember anyone ever calling her mom anything else, except Tante Marguerite, who still called her Angélique, and who was the one who told Margaret how her mother had changed like that.

Margaret got it the worst though. Her dad teased her mercilessly. Had a nickname for every mood. The first one she remembers was Poopy Peggy. Her brothers called her that well into adulthood. Then Margogo when she was a busy little kid, Maggie Muggins when she "had a face on," Miserable Meg when she was in a particularly bad mood, and he always seemed to think she was in a mood. She hated them all. She hated the laugh he would give after calling her them. The laugh they all would give, even her mother. Her mother who always went by Annie ever after just because Mac said so.

Sasha did his whole noisy entrance again, only in reverse, the screen door slamming in finality. Didn't even latch the thing, Margaret thought with a sneer, knowing a good gust of wind would start the thing slamming. Her annoyance made her hands shake so she lit up another long menthol slim.

Grandmother, my ass, she thought. She wouldn't bother telling Sasha until she couldn't help it anymore. Sasha never reacted well with anything concerning her daughter, so it was best to avoid talking about Elsie altogether. He blew a gasket when the girl got knocked up. They didn't find out until she was almost six months along. The girl was either too scared to get rid of it or too clueless, and by then, too far gone to do anything about it. She still refused to tell anyone who the father was. Sasha wouldn't stand for it. It was him who insisted on putting her into that home.

"Best place for her, Margey. Better to go out and learn about how to be a mom, or better yet, get them to convince her to give it up. What's that girl know about having a baby, anyway?"

Margaret knew adoption would never happen, not with Annie at Elsie's ear, but agreed it was for the best for the girl to go to the shameful home for shameless unwed mothers, even though Margaret hated the idea. The embarrassment of it. But nothing else had made much sense. Her mother was too damn old, and it's not like the girl could move back in with Margaret and them. Lord knows, Margaret had enough to do as it was.

Oh the girl whined when Margaret told her. Of course it was Margaret who had to tell her the news.

"Why can't I just stay here with Mamere? She said I could."

"Your Grandmother is too old to look after you as it is, never mind pregnant. You wanna be grown up so bad? Well grown-ups live on their own."

"I wanna stay here. I'll do everything, I swear." She cried, she moaned, but Margaret held her ground. Until her mother came in to save the day, of course.

"It's just until the baby is born, my girl. Then you can come back home. By then you would have learned everything you have to do and you will be ready to do this." Her mother's voice was sweet as candy when she wanted it to be.

Margaret threw her hands up in defeat. Let them muddle through then, she thought, but also knew it meant she would be doing all the work. Maggie Muggins, indeed.

She felt for the girl, really. For the baby, especially. Neither one of them stood a chance. Sixteen was way too young to be a mom. Or be good at it.

Margaret didn't really become a mom until she was near thirty, had lived a bit of life, was educated, at least. Sure it was a shit show from start to finish, but at least she wasn't a child at the time.

Annie, on the other hand, was too old to be a mom by the time Margaret came around. She started late and had three boys first. Margaret, even as a child, was never more that an afterthought to her mother.

Annie was also a very sad woman. Too sad. She carried sorrow around like mothers were supposed to carry babies. She nurtured it, cared for it, more than she did Margaret anyway. Sure, dear Mamere Annie seemed super good at the baby stuff. She loved babies, and was great with all her grandchildren, but she wasn't ever like that for Margaret. When Margaret was a child, the woman couldn't be bothered to pay much attention to her only daughter. It was like once Margaret could walk and talk, her mother thought her job was done. Margaret spent her childhood running around, being ignored, never being enough. Unless Annie needed her, of course. Then her mom was all sugar.

By the time Margaret was old enough to notice, her brothers were up to no good, causing grief with their bad choices and worse decisions. John, the oldest, was always all the way no good. He started going to juvie as soon as they could put him there. B and Es mostly, but the odd car, too. The best thing you could say about John was at least he didn't do anything violent, as if that was saying anything good at all. Joseph, the middle one, was everyone's favourite. Could charm the pants off anyone. Truly. As a kid, he never got into a lot of trouble but always seemed to know a little too much to be wholly innocent. Even as an adult, he managed to keep it where they couldn't see it for a long time. Toby, the youngest, was also the dumbest. He followed the other two around like a mangy mutt, getting kicked and caught more times than she could count. Even as kids, her brothers were notorious in their neighbourhood, and they just got worse as the years went on.

As a kid, Margaret wasn't much better, really. She was scrappy, mouthy, always got into fights, at school and around their sleepy, elm-shaded neighbourhood. Always managed to get pushed into a corner she had to punch herself out of. She was smart enough, school was easy, but teachers still seemed to hate her. Still called her *That Stranger Girl*, the same way they called her brothers *Those Stranger Boys*, like it was something to be ashamed of. Margaret never was the type to back down, so true to her imposed reputation, she ended up being exactly like they all thought she would be, for a time.

Her mother endured it all in pathetic silence. Annie simply went about her days, going from washing to ironing to cooking to cleaning, back when she could do such things, all while Margaret sat in front of their old black-and-white TV, watching shows children had no business watching and playing with dolls whose affection was much less sullen. Not that anyone really paid attention to their children in those days. Margaret doesn't remember missing any one particular thing from her mother, but only had an overall feeling of lack.

When her brother Joseph brought home Genie, Margaret was nearly ten, but it was the first time she'd ever met a talkative, affectionate person. A happy person. Not one to write home about, Genie, none too pretty and a bit on the slow side, really, but she hugged Margaret. Real hugs. From that first day, Genie would hug Margaret nearly every time she came over, and as a girl, Margaret let her. It was a strange feeling to her, to have one's body touched so thoroughly, to press another body into it. It seemed like the most generous thing in the world.

Annie wasn't a bad mother, only one who struggled. Like her nurtured sorrow, Annie also had her stories, ones that followed around at her heels as she made her way about the house. Sometimes she sat at the kitchen table, lit a cigarette, and shared them. She would never complain, not about Margaret's brothers, or her father, even though no one would blame her if she did. No, Annie would only go back to a time before them all and want to talk about her childhood, her siblings, her parents who she never really knew. They were half stories really, bits of her life she only shared with her only daughter. She rarely expanded beyond the basic descriptors, and Margaret never thought to pry for more. Just let them sit on the Formica table in between them, the olden images dancing somewhere in the silver confetti trapped there. Dead people, dead long before Margaret, but still she knew them better than the cousins and neighbours, it seemed.

Annie, back when she was a kid, back when she was Angélique, had lived in a shantytown. A two-room lean-to with four kids, their dad, her mother too until she died soon after Annie was born.

"I remember that house. Every bit of it. The walls were only wood. I could look through. See the road outside! We'd slap mud all over the crack, to keep the cold out. Hope it'd freeze there."

Her mother died first. "I don't remember her, of course, but they always said she was beautiful. Marguerite said her hair was light-light like almost red in the summer. She was sick for a long time. Always coughing, they said. I only remember her hands. Strong, long hands. They looked old to me. I was nothing more than a baby."

Then her oldest brother. "Baptiste was a big boy, a strong one, the first son. He was tall, oh he was tall. Must have been over six feet. I thought he was a giant. He was thick, too. Tootie was tall too, but Baptiste was thick and strong. Tootie was only tall."

Her favourite sister. "Josephte was so beautiful. She was the most beautiful. Everyone loved her. Such curly hair. Like yours, my girl. Wild and full like yours. She was nothing like Marguerite and me. She was kind and dear."

Her dad and her other brother, Tootie, died too but she didn't talk about them as much. By the time Margaret came around, there was only Tante Marguerite and she was a very old woman. Probably not that old, really, but seemed so very old. She was a frown and two beady eyes, her mouth a mass of lines that never turned up. A collar to her throat, a skirt to the ground, she gave the impression of a nun. Margaret was always afraid of her. Toby told her she was a witch and if Margaret wasn't careful, she'd get cursed, so Margaret never moved around her, never so much as shifted her hands from her lap. Marguerite died when Margaret was seven and the girl felt only relief.

Margaret's father, Mac, was happier than her mother, but still never paid much attention to his daughter, aside from teasing she hated and stories she loved. She remembers her father in a room full of people, never hers alone. The boys worshipped him. When he wasn't with them, he was working. Mac worked on the roads for years, until he got too old for it. He was gone all summer, home all winter. Colder weather meant the return of her father and his noisy ways. Sometimes she looked forward to it. Sometimes she missed him all summer. Other years, she dreaded it. He was always laughing, or telling a story overenthusiastically. He always had something to say, often a jibe to point at her.

"Come over here, Miserable Meg. What do I have to do to put a smile on your face?" he'd ask with a cigarette dangling from his lips and a laugh that sounded like it came from a deep, deep place. "Did I ever tell you the one about the horse that walked into the bar?"

He had about half a dozen jokes he liked to tell over and over, as if they would be new to her. As if she would have forgotten them all the time he'd been away.

And he'd always talk about being a Stranger like it was a good thing, like it was the opposite of what the world seemed to think it was.

"Never forget who you are, Margogo, and who you come from. We are warriors, us. We are Métis. We have fought and won our freedom. We've never lived by their rules. Aren't meant to. We have to be free."

Or he'd make some joke about it, like he did with everything. "We're halfbreeds, all right. Half Indian, half White, and completely full of shit! That's why our eyes are brown. Full up with shit." Even when he was serious, he'd try to be funny. He was funny.

Margaret has no memory of ever hugging him though, of ever feeling that he loved her. Of course that's what parents were like in those days. It was his way. She knew that.

Or it was his way with her. He was different with Elsie. By all accounts he and Elsie were close in the end. The girl cried her eyes out at his funeral. Margaret hadn't seen the girl or her parents in months. That was years ago, when Sasha was inside and it was all Margaret could do to keep it all together. The boys were so small and always busy doing something and breaking something else. She lived in a little house on Bannerman that was as squalid as they come. It had mice and bedbugs and a leaking roof. It was all she could do to keep it together. Didn't have time to visit her family. Didn't want them to visit either. Didn't have time for her mother's opinions about Margaret's life. Elsie had shot up that year. She was all legs that Margaret could see, but still stuck to Annie's skirt like she was still five. Or maybe five again. Some children do that, they revert when someone dies. The thing that surprised Margaret the most was the way her mother cooed over the girl. The way she wrapped her arms around her and cuddled her like she loved her. Margaret has no memory of her mother ever being like that with her either.

In the afternoon, Margaret pulled the ironing board into the middle of the living room, in front of the TV, and dragged the heavy laundry basket beside it. She had put this off far too long and the pile was up to her knees. Her hands were getting weaker, her grip not as strong as it used to be, so she put off things that used to come easy, like ironing and the like. She didn't even try mending anymore. Easier to buy things really. Things weren't made to last these days.

The sun streaked through a crack in the drapes, made a glare on the screen, made it even harder to see. She fussed with them until the crack disappeared, but even with them firmly shut, and the air conditioning, it felt hot. Not even June and already too hot. Summer was always the worst season. Everyone always complained about winter but winter was simple, you just didn't go outside. Summer always tried to sneak in where it was not wanted, like a quiet afternoon when Sasha was thankfully still gone and she had a month's worth of ironing to do and some stupid shows to watch.

Margaret liked the loud talk shows with the moaning studio audiences. They had the worst people on those programs, literally the scum of the earth, who wanted to get attention and have their fifteen minutes of fame. What a fame to have, to only be known for being a worthless addict or having slept with so many men you don't know who the father of your baby is. Margaret scoffed and sneered through all of them, three hours' worth, all while she smoothed out Sasha's wrinkled clothes as best she could. She really didn't know why she bothered. She could set them to the hot cycle in the clothes dryer and fold them fine enough. But Sasha liked it this way. Dried on a line in the basement and ironed within an inch of their lives. His mother had always done it this way so she had to too. Even his old T-shirts with the holes in the armpits and colour so worn out they could all be brown. He let her use the dryer on them in the winter but still wanted them ironed. So every month now, used to be every week but she just bought him more clothes so he wouldn't notice, she pulled out the ironing board and ironed out the old T-shirts, made perfect pleats in his old jeans, and took especially precious care with the white dress shirts he liked to wear to the club every Friday.

One time when they were first married and she didn't know a hard press from a steam spray, she'd made a burned crease down the front of his favourite dress shirt. It was black with red trim and an embroidered eagle on the right pocket. He loved that shirt, and she didn't even know she wrecked it until he put it on one Friday evening and came blazing down the stairs, shirt half open, undershirt showing, white dust smeared across his upper lip, and both fists clenched like he was going to do something with them. She got really good at shirts after that.

Well, if she were being honest, she'd also tell the other part of that story. That he stood there huffing about his shirt, his fists like that. But Margaret Stranger wasn't one to back down, or even look scared, so she just stood straighter. Taller. So tall she looked him right in the eye, and tightened her grip on the hot iron in her right hand. She didn't do anything, but he saw it. She knew he saw it. She would have used it too. But she hesitated. Not because she didn't want to hit him. She did. She really did. She would have, hard, could have probably killed him with that thing. But the iron was still plugged in and she knew it wouldn't reach long enough for a decent impact. Instead, she moved to put it down, like she'd changed her mind, and he went back up the stairs. His useless hands no longer fists, just flapping at his sides.

Margaret was running around by fourteen. It started with a few hours here and there and then got longer and longer. She'd walk to Main Street and hitchhike to downtown. Back then they had dance halls and jazz clubs and sometimes she'd pass enough to get in—pass for older, pass for whiter. The odd time she got turned away, pointed to the more friendly Indian bars, but she had no interest in those. She wanted to dress up and see the pretty people. Those who had a bit of money and owned everything she didn't. She got really good at talking right, at looking right. She even dyed her hair a reddish auburn and put rollers in her unwieldy curls every night so they looked wavy like they were supposed to. It all cost her a fortune and her mother didn't approve. But Margaret didn't care. She even got a job so she could keep at it, filling her roots in all the time so strangers would think it was natural.

Her first boyfriend was a twenty-six-year-old guitarist. He was from the west side and tall and pale and perfect. In hindsight, she was little more than a groupie, but she was young and thought she was in love. It was one of his friends that got her the job at Eaton's and that was really when her life started to take off. She got a discount off nice clothes and could get her hair done in a real salon, not just Genie in the kitchen. She really felt she was on her way then.

She also got really good at school, much to the surprise of everyone, family, brothers, even herself sometimes, but once in high school, she excelled. None of her teachers there knew her brothers because they never made it that far, so she felt free. She liked school. It was something tangible to commit to. She'd never get home before six, would always pore over her studies at the library after classes ended. She knew they had to be as perfect as she herself was. She loved the library. It was an old brick building with dark hardwood tables and chairs. She felt more at home there than at home. She had dreams of going out east to one of those old universities, the ones with stone buildings with green roofs and ivy inching up the walls. Her teachers kept telling her to go for a teaching certificate, a teaching certificate for a halfbreed was incredible enough, but Margaret had no interest in teaching. She wanted a job where she had to wear the most expensive suits from Eaton's. She wanted to buy them without even needing a discount, to get her hair done once a week and walk in high heels every day.

The college out east didn't work out. That was the first blow. She managed to get a scholarship to the university at the south end of the city, but only if she went into Home Ec. She had no interest in cooking or sewing, so she transferred to Pre-Law after only one semester. She had to go part-time to be able to afford any of it, and still worked full-time at Eaton's, but it was her dream.

The Pre-Law classes were all in large auditoriums like Greek theatres, and she'd stare down at the professors performing down below. The only other girl there was Becky. She was blonde, blue-eyed, and far from perfect but willing to try. Becky knew how to do everything already, seemed to fit right in, as much as girls could in those classes. Margaret was shocked to learn that the girl was Ukrainian and lived across the bridge from her house. Poor like her, if not all like her. Margaret nearly begged her to be her friend. They were a perfect match. They were both going to be important. And perfect.

Margaret was finishing cleaning up and getting ready to sit down for her evening shows when the phone rang. She let it ring three times as she finished wiping the counter and looked out back. The evening was still bright. It was almost seven but the sun was still nowhere near setting. She watched the light from the garage door yawn open and a car drive up. Sasha, smoking and gut sticking out, waved it inside.

"Hello, Margaret. How are you doing this evening?" She knew she'd hear from her mother sooner or later, with all that was going on, but still she was surprised that she was almost glad to hear from her. Then angry that she was happy to hear from her mother like a stupid little kid.

She pulled the phone over so she could grab her oversized puzzle tray from its safe home on the dryer and put it back on the kitchen table. Once she felt it was safe and steady, she sat back and lit a smoke. "I'm okay, Mamere. How are you?"

"I'm good. Good. Tired but good. It's been an exciting few days."

"Mmm-hmm." Margaret tried not to talk too much. Clearly, her mother had some things to say.

"You heard? Toby called you? Elsie had her baby." Margaret heard her mother shuffling, in her own kitchen no doubt.

"Yes. I heard." Margaret took a long drag. "He called this morning."

"And? Are you going to go see her? Are you going to go see your daughter while she's in the hospital?" Margaret's shoulders went tense. Elsie was always her daughter when her mother needed something from her. Or when Elsie was lacking. The girl used to be a good student, with good grades, and even played a couple piano recitals, and when that happened, she was all "Mamere's Girl." But as a teenaged mom with a bastard child, she was clearly Margaret's daughter now.

"Why is she still in the hospital? Didn't everything go well?"

"It did. But they wanted her for . . . observation. Social workers came around and asked her all these questions. Asked me too. Since she is going to live with me after they let her go from the home. Asking me all these . . . shameful things."

Ah, that was the thick of it, Margaret thought. Her mother needed her to help them look good for the scary professional people. "What did they say? After all the questions."

"Just that they'd be in touch. They want to do a, what did they call it, home visit. So I've been cleaning all day. My hands hurt so bad, my girl. I am too old to be doing this all by myself."

"I'm sure Toby can pitch in some."

"Oh you know that boy could never clean to save his life. I never taught him like I taught you."

Margaret always thought her mother was the expert of guilt. Annie knew how to sneak it in there, how to hide it amongst pleasantries. Make it sound like it was a compliment. But Margaret could always find it. She also knew Annie wasn't wrong. The woman was pushing ninety. "I told you you're too old for all this, Mamere, you should move to a home. Let other people take care of you."

Margaret knew she said it too clumsily, too quick, and her mother bit back in an instant. "There's nothing wrong with me! I'm not an invalid. I can clean my own house! I just need help. I asked you to move in years ago. Any other daughter would. A big house like this."

"Mamere!"

"Margaret!" Their usual standoff.

Until Annie sighed, a deep wind over the phone wires. "I just need a little help is all. I don't need to be pushed out of my home. Especially now. Elsie needs me. She needs all of us." She was such a strong, proud woman. Too proud, Margaret would say. Her mother always prided herself on hard work, strong body, and wasn't about to change now. Especially not for Margaret. Annie never did anything for Margaret's sake.

"When are they going to let her out of the hospital?"

"Tomorrow. Hopefully." Margaret could hear her mother calculating her words carefully. "Can I give them your name? Can they call you and you can say you're a support to your daughter and will help us all get along here? Of course it'd be better if you lived here too, but at the very least . . ."

Annie let the sentence dangle, as she did whenever she mentioned Margaret moving in. Margaret thought the baby might be better off in care, or getting adopted to someone old enough to drink at least, but she knew better than to suggest such things. Her mother had strong opinions about adoption, about strangers raising their kids, as Margaret well knew. Now it was her turn to sigh. "I'll come by in the morning. Help you clean and talk to them when they come."

"Oh maarsii, ma fii. Maarsii." Her mother only ever lapsed into affectionate Michif when she was satisfied. Margaret hated that she liked it so much.

The next day, Margaret went over and cleaned everything left, which was most things. Toby watched while smoking uselessly in his chair. He had all but moved back in when Elsie went into that home. "To help out," he had said. But as far as Margaret could tell, she was still doing all the helping. When the middle-aged social worker got there, Margaret made nice. She seemed a fine enough person, only doing her job. Margaret used her big educated words and didn't smoke once. After that, she took her mother to get Elsie from the hospital.

The babe was small for full term, skinny like an old man and squalling. Elsie seemed broken all the way through and barely looked up at her mother, never mind the baby. Margaret kept expecting a scared, pimply faced teenage father to appear, but one never did show up. She didn't bother asking. Another thing she knew from experience.

When they pulled up in front of the shameful home for unwed mothers, Margaret immediately felt nauseous. She didn't want to go in, didn't want to walk those long hallways eerie with the stained glass at the end, like she had when they first toured the place. Didn't want to make stupid small talk with the workers. She helped her mom out of the car, then the girl and the baby. She gathered all the many bags and held the door open.

A sweet round lady with white, white hair came up to gush over the baby, and Elsie, and offer tea, in that order. Margaret was led to Elsie's room to drop off the bags then back to the big main room to drink weak tea and pretend she was enjoying herself. Her mother truly was. Annie had gotten ahold of the baby and held her close, peered at it intently through her cloudy eyes, smiled and sang all the old French songs they all knew by heart. Elsie, for her part, went to take a long shower and seemed to take her time getting dressed after.

Margaret did make half-hearted small talk and looked, every so often, at the tiny, wrinkly thing in her mother's arms. She was trying to be fine with it all, but she really wanted to run away. Run back to her ugly, rundown house that fronted a chop shop and her annoying husband and boys who were getting more mouthy by the day, but she made no move to leave, only watched her mother with the babe. Her mother was so good at this part. The baby part. Margaret knew that between these social workers and the old lady, Elsie would learn everything she needed to know about being a mother, and there really wasn't any room for her, for Margaret, to know this new person. This Phoenix Anne, even named after her mother, like Elsie was Elsie Anne. None of them needed Margaret for much, only cleaning, and talking good, that's it. That was all she was good for. All they wanted her for.

She was left out, again. Her mother and Elsie always left her out.

On the car ride home, her mother dozed. Spent from the day, Annie looked all of her almost eighty years. Margaret's mother had become an old woman.

"When is Elsie and the baby coming home for good?" Margaret asked, though she knew the answer.

"They have a few months there. Should be home by the end of summer."

"Are you sure you can handle all that, Mamere?"

She huffed, though still didn't open her eyes. "I'm not an invalid, me." Her accent more pronounced when she was tired. "Besides, I have Toby to help me."

Margaret's lips made a thin line thinking of Toby's helping. "Maybe I should move in now, Mamere. Maybe it's time."

That made Annie all the way awake. "What? You? What about Sasha? The boys?"

"Let me worry about that. I can figure it out. I think it's time I moved in." She paused, unsure for a moment more. "You're always bugging me to. Don't you want me to?"

"Of course. You just, you never wanted before. You always said no. Said the house is too much work."

"Well, it is. But this is different, I think." As she said it, she was unsure again. "I think," she repeated, as if to drive home that particular point. Pretty sure, right then, that she'd regret it completely.

She never regretted it, exactly, moving in with her aging mother, teenaged mom of a daughter, and her bastard child. Regret wasn't the right word. But Margaret never thought of it as one of her best decisions either. Not that she had many of those. It was only a decision. Didn't make anything all that better, and in some ways, it made things far, far worse.

YEAR TWO

5

PHOENIX

The long wall in her room, that's really a cell but they call it a room, is seven and two half blocks long and eighteen blocks high. It's those large bricks like blocks, cinder blocks she thinks they are called. She used to live in a house with a wall like that, with a block wall also painted shiny white like this one, so it all feels sort of homey, familiar. But the house's wall was only one in a big room with other normal walls. This is a small room—cell—and it is every wall. All around her.

Each block is bigger than her foot, twice as long as they are high, and there are like, eight long then eighteen high so that's 144 each wall, but every second row up is two halfs, so it's only really 135 full blocks and nine half blocks.

Phoenix took a while to figure out the math and then counted to make double sure.

Two walls at 144, or 135 and nine halfs, plus the shorter walls that are six and one half long each, but it's still eighteen high so that's 117. It's actually less blocks because she has to minus the door. And the window. But the walls are the same size.

Roughly, if every block is a foot long, it'd be 117 by 144 square walls. That's just a guess 'cause it's not like she's ever fucking measured. And it's not like she knows the imperial system that good, but basically the place is like eight by six around and about nine feet high.

Pretty fucking small.

Definitely a cell.

But at least she's alone. Outside, in other units, you have to share. Two bunks per room, four people. Either that or you have to live in the cottages. Those bitches have a kitchen and have to cook and clean everything, but still have to share with at least one other person. Solitary, or the Special Needs Unit as they actually call it, sucks in a lot of ways, but being alone isn't one of them.

The white shiny paint on the bricks has been chipped here and there, picked off, and she can make out jagged words and names under the layers of white. *Molly. Destiny. Brandi loves Lyssa. Fuck this shit. ACAB.* And other things she can't make out. Painted over, over and over. She runs her fingers along the bumps and craters, so many right around the bed, but mostly she runs her fingers along the creases. They're long and smooth and fit her fingers perfect. She runs each finger, one after the other, every morning when she wakes up, every night when she goes to bed, every morning when she comes right back after breakfast, every afternoon when they keep telling her she should go out on the grounds for a bit.

The house in Lego Land's wall was long and along the stairs and front door. Theirs was the last house on the row, that's why. The wall on the other side was thin and they could hear the neighbours' too-loud TV. Sometimes she and Cedar'd push their ears up and listen until they got bored. She listened to a whole *Fast and Furious* movie that way. She doesn't know which one, just remembers the screeching tires, explosions, and the Rock's big laugh.

She's in the special unit permanently now, or at least as permanent as it gets, but she likes it that way. They all know she likes it better that way but they keep trying to fix it, like it's a problem. It's quiet, for the most part. Unless the blue-haired girl has one of her psychotic attacks and ends up next door. The psycho screams and cries and tries to get Phoenix to talk to her. But it doesn't last long. She doesn't last long. The girl tires herself out, or gets pilled up and goes back out. Crazy blue hair likes being out. Phoenix thinks her name is Kai. Or Kaia. Or who the fuck cares.

After that first time, Phoenix was out after a couple days, but she didn't feel like being around all those bitches. It was like the place had gotten more fucking noisy and fucking annoying with time. Dez had got out, like Phoenix knew she would. Suspended sentence. That was it. Phoenix was the only one stuck in this place for probably the whole five years now. That Dakota who Dez had been hanging out with before proved to be a scrappy little bitch for all their wounded mouse-looking shit, and Phoenix didn't want to fucking deal with it. This one time Phoenix pushed them down, just a push over 'cause they were in her way, but the fucking bitch came back up swinging. Almost gave Phoenix a black eye, the crazy fuck. Of course, Phoenix was the fucking one who got into trouble.

After that she couldn't even be near the little cunt or shit would get started.

This one time they tried to put her into one of the cottages, with five other assholes, all them were older than her. She fucking hated that more than dealing with psycho Dakota. They were supposed to clean their bathrooms and kitchen but none of those slobs ever managed that. It was fucking disgusting. After about a week, she started a fire in the microwave with a big spoon stolen from the kitchen. It was pretty easy. But when guard Chris told her she couldn't make trouble just to go back to the special unit, she bit his hand until she broke the skin.

That's when they started talking about the psych ward.

That was new to her so she was fine to check it out. But it was even worse than anything in youth detention. It was in the old hospital downtown and was all separated by curtains so you could hear fucking everything. Everyone moaning or screaming or crying, and none of the doctors gave even the smallest of fucks. Phoenix didn't blame them. She'd fucking lose it too if she had to be there all the time. They gave her some Diazepam and she slept for a few days. Some shrink thought she might have postpartum depression and she almost laughed, but she liked the Diazepam so pretended to cry instead. They left her in there a while.

When she got back they let her go straight to special unit/solitary, so she got to relax a bit. She was also fucking dosed all the time so she wouldn't be much use anywhere else.

This old guy keeps coming to visit her. She thought for a while he was maybe a bored guard, didn't really notice much beyond her haze, but he keeps coming. Ben is his name. He keeps saying anyway. He pulls up a chair and sits outside her room with the door open. She's always on her bed, always running her finger along the wall, half out of it, these days. Barely there. He asks if she wants to come out into the hall where there's a sitting area by a big window. A couch and a couple chairs. But she doesn't. She's happy where she is, legs stretched out on her bed, head leaning against the nice cool wall, finger safe in the seam.

She thought it was a dream for a while. This old guy. Felt like a dream when he was gone. But Ben keeps coming, every couple days or weeks, who knows. She never really talks to him, only nods sometimes. It's not like she's even fucking mad or anything, just high. She wants to sit, hates the idea of getting up, and is fine to listen to him drone on and on.

He's all stories. That's all he ever seems to do is tell her stories. She doesn't always listen, not all the way, so she only gets parts, things about growing up on his dad's rez, moving to the city when he was a teenager, got in a bad crowd. Phoenix tried to listen when he started talking about the Nor'wester. It was a bar she knew her mom went to. She was so drugged out she wanted to know if he knew her mom. But she forgot to ask and then he was talking about something else.

They had started talking about lowering her dose, but fucking Chris didn't want that to happen. "It's so fucking peaceful around here," she heard him laugh out in the hall.

But one day her pill was different and she knew it was the beginning of the end. She felt the hot rage burn up inside of her, not as strong as it used to be but still there. All the things she had forgotten about were flooding back and she thought about the baby, her life, where she was. Everything got her mad all over again. And it didn't seem as bad but was also somehow fucking worse, too. Now none of her usual things helped her, not her uncle's songs or the old brown house or her Grandmère. Now it was like she was mad all the time and couldn't control it. Couldn't keep it down and use it where it counted, like she used to. She felt like a little kid. She was scared she'd start crying one day, like she used to when she was a little kid.

Ben comes to the door with a dining hall plate in his hand. "Aaniin, Phoenix. They told me you didn't get breakfast so I brought you some toast. They don't usually allow that but I'm a pretty big deal around here."

Phoenix is hungry. She didn't want to get ready in time for breakfast so missed it again. She is so fucking hungry once she sees the two limp pieces of cold toast. Can't remember the last time she ate. She snatches the plastic plate quick. Then feels ashamed about it. Mad at herself for being weak.

"Maarsii," she mutters. It was the first time she remembers saying anything to him. She regrets it immediately.

"Maarsii, hey? Well, tawnshi kiya, moon amie. I didn't know you knew Michif. I should have been talking to you in Michif all this time." He smiles big. She looks him over as she chews. He's a big guy, like tall and wide with a fuzzy white beard and skinny braids, like a neechie Santa Claus, she thinks. And almost laughs.

"That's all, that's all I know really." Her voice is raw again, her throat dry, but feels better choking down the toast. She doesn't remember the last she talked either.

"Well, that's the best thing to know. Saying thank you." He grins and she doesn't look away. Reminds her of her old boyfriend Clayton's grins. Clayton could out-grin anybody. He was like, why they said grin and not just smile, 'cause it was more than a fucking smile.

She nods and finishes her toast.

"You were hungry. Don't they feed you around here?" He looks around for show. "Oh yeh, I guess you have to go to the hall on the regular. I get that, I get that. You looked better today, Phoenix. More clear. They reduced your meds, hey?"

She doesn't answer. Doesn't really need to 'cause he keeps talking.

"I'm glad they did that. That shit was messing with your head. No one needs to sleep that much. You're a young lady. You should be out partying, and having fun, not in there sleeping your youth away. I says to them, I says, she's going to wake up and find herself an old lady, white-haired and fat like me, and then she'll really be traumatized. That's what I told them. And I guess it worked 'cause here you are, awake. Well, I should have known, I'm a really big deal around here, as I've said." He laughs all big. Phoenix doesn't. It isn't funny like she has to laugh.

He isn't really all that old, now that she looks at him. Old like sixty maybe but not old like going to die soon old. Her Grandmère was that old. She was ninety-three when she died. Phoenix was super young but remembers that. She also remembers how old her Grandmère looked. Like her skin was see-through in places and her eyes were all the way grey with cataracts. This guy was not that old.

"So you feeling better, then?"

Phoenix glares at him. She doesn't want to fucking get shrinked. She looks down and starts picking at her blanket.

"A lady of few words. Bless your heart. My wife, she never stops talking. She talks to everyone but especially me and I just, I love her to bits but you know, I got other stuff to do. But I'm all like 'yes, dear, no, dear' because that's what you gotta do, right? Happy wife, happy life, that's what they say. But you, no, you're not like that, you, you're the one that wants to listen, right? You like stories, Phoenix?"

Phoenix shrugs. She's feeling tired again. Feels that crazy mad come up inside of her, but doesn't have the energy to do anything about it.

"Okay, I'll tell you a story, but you gotta bear with me, Phoenix, you gotta bear with me because this is a story about the olden days. Like the real olden days back when I was a kid, and you're not going to believe this, because you know I look so young and fit hey, but when I was a young kid it was a crazy time in the world, called the seventies. It was way back in the seventies! Now that was way before you were born, that was probably before your mother was born even, and maybe even your mother's mother. No, just kidding, she was probably around, but it was way back when and there were no cell phones or computers in houses or even phones in some houses. I didn't have a phone in my house 'til I moved to the city and I was about your age then. But when I was a kid, way back in the seventies, we lived on the rez right, and it was like all rezes are, all dirt roads and old people and troublemakers. Me and my friends, we were the biggest troublemakers of them all. We had one bike between like four of us. It was my friend Binesi's but he was just a little guy so he let us borrow it all the time. Not that he had much choice, right? We took turns, hey, doubling each other, one guy doubling another guy and then the rest of us just running along beside them. Behind them mostly. Sometimes we'd go with one guy on the bars and another on the back of the seat and then there'd just be poor little Binesi running in the back. Poor kid just givin' 'er trying to keep up. But if you were pedalling with two guys, hey, you couldn't go very fast, which was a good thing for Binesi 'cause there'd usually just be two on the bike, so always someone running with him, hey? And so, we'd go all running all around the rez and getting up to all sorts. This one time . . ."

Phoenix settles in and listens for a while. He isn't as fucking funny as he thinks he is, but he isn't all that annoying either. Right now anyway. It's a good story. Almost as good as the good drugs. She almost forgets everything again. For a while anyway.

A few days later, Phoenix finally goes out one morning after breakfast. Fucking Chris was harping on and on about it, so she puts the fucking windbreaker on and goes out into the yard. It's empty. Most of the kids go out later, if they go out at all, so she has the yard all to herself, and Chris. It was fucking cold and bright. She didn't think it'd be so fucking cold. Snow already on the ground. Only a thin layer but the not-melting-away kind. The skinny just-planted trees are bare all the way. They'd even put the lights up already, a straight line of blue bulbs all around the yard. Far up so no one could grab them and they were kept on even now, in the morning. It was a snowy day too so the fog was thick and the trees white with the frost. Phoenix always loves that, when the trees got white and the world looked like a Christmas card. But she didn't think it would be so cold already.

But then she fucking realizes what she doesn't even fucking know. "What's the—what day is it?"

"It's Friday." Chris shivers into his coat, the good winter kind. He has mitts on and everything.

"No, I mean what—date?" She touches the little planted tree in the yard, surrounded by a little chain-link fence so no one would mess with it. The frost melts under her thumb, showing the brown bark.

"The tenth? Yeah, it's the tenth."

She looks at him. Her eyes open all the way. Feel like they haven't been open in a while. He is shorter than she'd thought. She blinks again, tries to remember the last date she knew. The last time she'd been outside.

He seems to know what she's thinking. "It's December, Phoenix. Almost Christmas."

She had thought it must be at least November, but even that felt like a stretch.

She counts back in her head. Walking around the yard, aimless, really, her legs feel tired already. Eight months since April. A year and eight months since last April. She tries to picture it. Sparrow, a year and eight months. The other Sparrow, the first one, was walking and talking baby talk by then. She had a few real words, like "mama" and "dada," and "cat" because she loved cats. That would have been when they were living on Arlington. First Sparrow'd run around that whole apartment, loved it when Phoenix and Cedar played tag with her or hide-and-go-seek. She couldn't run fast but squealed the whole time no matter what. And if she was trying to hide, she giggled and they always found her right away.

Phoenix wondered if the new Sparrow is like the first one, like his aunty. If he squeals and runs around, if he is as happy as she had been. Then. The other Sparrow would have been ten now. Phoenix can't imagine that, but then again, she can't imagine her son being more than a year and a half either.

She feels like she has forgotten about him. She has forgotten about him for how long now?

One time, on Arlington, she had to go downstairs to do the laundry and left Sparrow and Cedar upstairs by themselves. Cedar was watching an old DVD and not watching the baby. When Phoenix went back upstairs, Sparrow had gotten on top of the counter and had the laundry soap cupped in one hand and the toonie for the dryer in the other. Phoenix screamed and the baby almost fell off. Sparrow started howling, scared. Laundry powder went everywhere. Phoenix yelled at Cedar, who also started crying. And really, Phoenix probably also started crying because she was only like eight and didn't know any better.

"Okay, Phoenix, time to go inside." Chris fucking red-faced. How long have they been out here?

She tries to find the words but can't, only feels the panic of forgetting. "No!"

"Don't start, Phoenix. It's cold."

"No, I can't, I—"

He doesn't even try and talk to her, just buzzes for help. "Come on, Phoenix. Don't start."

"No, I gotta, he might be—" Everything gets blurry, everything gets cold again. She doesn't know where she even is anymore.

"Phoenix. You got to calm down."

She sees the two other guards, both in their winter coats. One says, "It's okay, Phoenix." Like she's a fucking little kid who doesn't want to come in after recess.

"No, he, I have to talk to—" She can't remember what she is supposed to do, only that Sparrow's in trouble. Which one, she isn't able to say.

"What is she talking about?"

"I don't fucking know. They got her jacked up."

"I gotta, I," she hears herself yelling. She can't feel the sound coming out of her throat but she hears it. It hurts her ears.

"We're just going inside now, Phoenix."

"Get the nurse here." They're inside the hall now, one of the chairs on top of her. She is lying on the ground. A guard holds her arms down. "Everything's okay, Phoenix," he says but he is too close, too close to her. Pinning her down. She can feel his breath on her and starts to scream. She tries to bite at his face but he puts his hand on her face.

"Hold her still. As still as you can."

"No, I, don't." Her voice yelling so loud she feels it.

And then she feels nothing.

She wakes up in the nurse's room, lying on the narrow bed with the soft restraints on each wrist. She doesn't remember much of anything. Her body fuzzy. Her arms and legs still asleep. She feels like the snowy screen on an old TV with no cable, like dark blue light in the morning before the sun comes up. She thinks of that crazy bitch, what's her name? Kaia? Kai? She thinks she can hear her crying. Or is that a baby?

She's back in her solitary room/cell, half-asleep with her finger on the seam between the bricks. There are seven and two halfs along this line, eight full ones on the next line down. There are eighteen rows, but today she can't remember how to put the numbers together. The paint is thick with many layers, all shiny white. Smooth under her fingers, even under her thumb. She thinks of the tree that day, how the frost melted under her thumb, the brown bark underneath. In the spring that tree will have long, skinny leaves a light green, like mint. But it wasn't called a mint tree. Phoenix didn't know what the tree was called, or what any tree was called. She sort of knows what a pine tree is. The ones that never lose their leaves but have the needle things. She knows there's a kind of tree called an elm and an oak but doesn't know which those are either.

"Tawnshi kiya, Phoenix. Merry Christmas. Do you celebrate Christmas? Can I say that?" White beard and braids at the door. "I brought you a Nanaimo bar. Figured it was the best choice. Everybody likes Nanaimo bars, right?"

He puts the plate on her hand, heavy and cold, and then walks back to his chair at the doorway.

"Maarsii," she says to no one.

"Maarsii. That's good. Michif is a good language to speak. We should all be speaking it all the time. To keep it alive. Do you know any other words?"

Phoenix shakes her head. She thinks she remembers something, but then forgets again. "I know more, I know some Nishnab. More than Michif."

"Yeh? I know some of that. Way more than Michif 'cause more people speak it. I'm Métis on my mom's side and she talked Michif to me so it's special to me. La langue de la coeur, she used to tell me. Do you know what that means?"

"Heart. Language of the heart." She picks at the chocolate layer on top of the bar. Picks off the bottom and breaks off a little piece. The only good part anyway.

"Yeh, that's right. I thought you'd know French. Stranger is a good

Métis name. An old Métis name. My mom was a Boyer. We're probably cousins, down the line! But I grew up with my dad's family, mostly, and they were Nishnaabe, Harpers from way over there. Lotta people to speak that language with you, especially where I grew up, well, more than Michif anyway. And my Kookum, Dad's mom, was a storyteller so she taught me only in the language so I got pretty good at it. Speaking of which, it's winter now, you know, and that's the best time for stories. I know you love my stories."

Phoenix kind of smirks before she can stop herself. She must be real fucking high.

"Wow, that was almost a laugh. High praise. I'm encouraged. Well I want to tell you a story. A good one. You can tell the best stories in winter because winter is the only time you can tell wiindigoo stories. You know what a wiindigoo is, hey?"

"Like a, it's a monster, or something," Phoenix says with another bite of the best-part bottom.

"Ho yah, it's a monster, all right. It's a cannibal, actually. It's a human turned into a monster that eats other humans. Cool, hey? They're said to only come out at winter, or get real bad in winter anyway, and they hunt people, and if you get bit by one you go crazy and have to start eating other people." He pauses, like he's waiting for her to say something.

"Like zombies," she says, quiet.

"Yeh, sort of. That's what they're like. Or more like, zombies are like wiindigoo 'cause wiindigoo are very old. Very old stories about very old creatures. They said if you got bit by a passing wiindigoo and turned wiindigoo yourself, then your insides turned to ice. When wiindigoo are killed you have to dig out their heart and let it melt 'cause it was ice. Cool, hey? It was even— I'm going to teach you a real old-timer word, this was a word we used way back in the olden days, the crazy days called the eighties, we said gnarly. That's what wiindigoo are, they're gnarly!"

Again Phoenix smiles, only a little bit but enough. Enough that she feels it, enough that he sees it, and it makes him smile wider. His wide bearded face looks so happy. She doesn't really fucking mind. She ignores it, really, and stares at the wall to listen to the story.

"So here's a gnarly wiindigoo story. This one is a really old story, an old man told this to me. He was from way up north, a magical place they write songs about. A place just like Santa's workshop! This place is called Thompson. And this old guy from magical Thompson told me this story from when he was a kid and they went on his dad's trapline . . ."

Phoenix eats her Nanaimo bar bottom slowly, wanting to make it last. It's so good she even eats all the chocolate top and the middle. They're not as good but she eats them anyway. It's something to do while listening to the story. It's a good story. And after that one, he tells another one. Ben. His name is Ben. He has a lot of wiindigoo stories. He tells them until it's dark outside. Until she has to get up to go get supper and he has to go because he's off now, but he's going to come back in a couple days, he says.

Phoenix nods and shuffles to the dining hall. It's turkey and mashed potatoes and a soupy gravy. She eats her whole plate, sitting alone, no one bugging her, no one even looking at her, with the wiindigoo stories playing back in her drugged-up mind.

6

CEDAR

The house intimidated the shit out of me. Felt fancy. And rich. I had never lived in a house like this before. It has three bedrooms, a living room, all on one floor. It's sort of like Luzia's house but bigger, and newer. I was intimidated by everything at first.

The kitchen has a dishwasher, and there are three bathrooms, one that's basically mine by myself. I have my own room, and the entire basement is another living room they call the rec room where my dad, Shawn, sits in his recliner, drinks beer, and watches sports. There's a bar down there too, with all different kinds of alcohol and glasses, another bathroom, another bedroom, a big storage room with matching boxes filled with Xmas decorations, an on-the-side fridge they call a deep freeze that's always filled to the top with meat and ice cream bars and pizza pops. Luzia's house had one of those too, but it wasn't even half as full and everything was outdated and unused, things like stewing meat or old berries from picking. My foster place before that, the one in the country, had one of those too, but I wasn't even allowed to go in that room, so didn't know what it was or what was in it. Here, I can go into the deep freeze whenever I like. I can eat whatever I want, whenever I want to. Upstairs also has a pantry full of food. They buy full-sized chocolate bars and huge boxes of cereal from a store called Costco.

I've never really seen a place like this before. Never knew people could live like this, except on TV.

The neighbourhood, too, is super intimidating. I still need to keep a map in my head just to get to the store, or find my school. It took a couple weeks of getting lost every day to figure it out. I think it's confusing on purpose, like they don't want people to find their way in. Or out. Their house, my dad's house, is on a cul-de-sac that's off a bay that's off a street that still isn't straight. I have to cross all that and still go four short blocks or make four different turns to get to the big road with the school, but each name and direction has to be just so. One wrong move and I'll be on a different bay or cove or cul-de-sac and will have to turn around 'cause there is never another way out.

For weeks I left early, just in case.

They seemed nice enough at the start.

They're still nice, just different.

I met them at the social work office downtown a few weeks after my mom told me what was happening. It was still summer, still too hot, and I still had the same respite worker. I thought Mama would be at the meeting too, but she wasn't. And no one mentioned it so I didn't ask. They just took me to the big room with the TV and the couch. It somehow looked really rundown from the last time I was there, like the furniture needed a wash. I felt embarrassed by it all.

They were in there waiting for me. A young-looking, dark-haired put-together man, only the grey on the side of his face made me think he was older, and a nice-looking blonde lady with shiny gold rings, earrings, necklace. Shawn and Nikki. Nikki stuck out her hand when she was introduced, then pulled it back and blushed, like girls do in the movies.

The social worker did most of the talking at first. "Cedar is going into grade nine, high school. Isn't that right, Cedar?"

I only nodded. Didn't look up much. My dad, Shawn, smiled whenever I did and it made me shy.

"And your daughter is about a year older?"

The lady, Nikki, piped in. "Almost exactly. She's going to be fifteen.

Her birthday's just a few weeks after hers. Yours." She turned to me. "You can celebrate together if you want."

She had deep blue eyes, almost grey, and when she smiled, the lines around them twisted. Her makeup glittered under the yellow lights. She even wore lipstick. I could see the line around her lips and it didn't smudge at all.

"And they have a room for you in their house," the social worker continued as if she was trying to convince me of something. Like I had a say.

"It's just a bed, dresser, desk right now," Nikki said. "I figured you'd want to decorate it however you like, and bring your own stuff, type thing. We can go shopping when we get school supplies and stuff. You can get whatever you'd like, really." Nikki took a breath and looked at my dad, at Shawn, and said, quiet, "I'm so nervous."

"It's okay to be nervous, Nikki," the social worker said. "I think that's to be expected. I bet Cedar is nervous too." She smiled over to me. She was nicer than she usually was, more polite. I could tell Nikki and Shawn were not like the other parents in here, or even like the foster parents. They looked richer. Something in the way they sat there, the way Nikki looked uncomfortable, made everything around them look more poor. I didn't know if they were rich or anything, really. It was only a feeling. A too-good-to-be-true kind of feeling. A too-good-to-be-trusted.

Nikki said, "We've got everything ready that we can. And Faith, my daughter, is so excited to meet you. She would have come too, really wanted to, but we didn't want to, you know, overwhelm you with all of us on the same day." She took my dad, Shawn's, hand in hers. "We wanted to have more, have a little brother or sister for you, but God decided that wasn't to be. But we've, I've, always wanted to meet you, Cedar. As soon as I heard, as soon as we heard, about everything, we just knew we had to get you somehow. Knew we were your real family." Her eyes filled with tears. I was afraid for her mascara. That her eyes would run dark and be ruined.

Nikki kept talking, stopping only to awkwardly laugh. "My daughter is also Native, well, mixed, too, Métis, I guess. Like you. Her dad is from Alberta. He's not, um, around, but she, she is the spitting image of his mom. Thank God she doesn't look a thing like me. So I know, I know what it's like. And, well, I married your dad, didn't I? We're a pretty . . . we're open and diverse, you know. We don't see colour in our house."

The social worker leaned back. Looked like her job was done and she could relax now. Shawn, too, my dad, seemed like he usually let Nikki do the talking. I wanted to tell her that's not what Métis means. That it's not mixed, not like that. But I only looked at my dad, at Shawn, but tried not to look like I was looking. Did he look like me?

Or would it be, did I look like him?

High school was just as horrible as junior high. I have no idea what all the fuss was about. After all that talk last year about having to be more mature and responsible now that we were going to be in high school, nothing seemed to have changed. Not at this suburb's school anyway. As far as I can tell all my new classmates are just as stupid, disrespectful, and more annoying as the old ones, only now they're all richer. And whiter.

It's a huge school. I thought that would make it more intimidating but really it's less so. There are so many kids I can literally disappear in the crowd and no one notices that I'm new or a freak or whatever.

I don't mind, not really. Though at first I had a bit of hope that I would find some friends, or at least one. Even tried smiling at some girl in my math class but it didn't really go anywhere. I thought about joining a club, to have people to sit with at lunch, but when I looked in, they all seemed to have their groups already. It seemed like I was somehow too late. Nothing I wasn't used to. I never was much for fitting in.

Faith has already been there a year so had friends and doesn't pay much attention to me at school. She doesn't pay much attention to me at home either, but at least there, I have a door to close.

Nikki was right—Faith does look real Indigenous. Not that she would care or I would say anything to her. Faith doesn't seem all that interested in that sort of thing. She has beautiful straight black hair that falls down her back almost to her waist. Her eyes are the perfect brown and her skin the perfect tan. She looks like she could be a model, like all she needs is a turquoise necklace and a traditional dress, instead of the yoga pants and crop top she always wears. But Faith doesn't pay much attention to all that. Doesn't pay attention to much, from what I can tell. Except for her boyfriend, friends, getting high at lunch, talking back to her mom, and asking for money. I stayed pretty clear when I first got here, and Faith made it really easy. And since then we've just kept doing that.

I didn't meet her until I came over here for a visit. They said it was only an overnight but those basically meant that I was moving in. I brought my backpack with a change of clothes, and that was really all I wanted to take anyway. We pulled the car into the big garage and Nikki took my backpack out of the trunk and said, "I'm just going to give these things a quick wash, okay?"

Not that it was question. She held the bag with an extended arm and disappeared down the basement stairs.

When she came up she got me to change into an old pair of sweats of hers and checked my head for lice. I wanted to tell her I hadn't had lice in years but didn't think it would stop her.

That's how I met Faith, with Nikki frowning over my messed hair like I was some ghetto kid. I tried a half smile at this older girl with a full face of highlighter but knew from the way Faith sneered that she wasn't ever going to like me.

Later we all sat down at the table for dinner and Nikki talked the whole time. No one seemed to mind. The other two seemed used to letting her fill up the space with words and sighs and laughs that never felt real. I kind of liked it, at least at first, because it meant I didn't have to say anything. And I learned a lot. All about Faith's dad and how he was no good and Nikki never knew much about his family, had only met his mom a couple times but she heard a lot of stories and they weren't very healthy "or whatever." And how my dad was nothing like Faith's dad because he was good and kept a job and only drank beer when he was watching sports, "so you don't have to worry about that, if you were worried." And they were all happy to move here because the houses were cheaper than in Alberta and it wasn't only because Shawn had lost his job, because most guys had lost their jobs during the oil bust, "damn Liberals and commies and environmentalists or whoever," but now he's got a good job with Hydro he likes much better anyway, "don't you, honey?"

But it was another question without a real answer because Shawn ignored it and looked right at me and said, "I heard you're really smart, get good grades and all that."

I swallowed. Wanted to say the exact right thing but in the end I only nodded.

"What's your favourite subject?" he continued.

"Umm." I swallowed again. "History, I think, or maybe Indigenous studies."

"Oh, you'll have to teach us all about that," Nikki cut in. "Poor Faith doesn't even know what tribe she's from, do you, honey?"

Faith shrugged.

"Well." I talked slow. "Alberta has a few nations. Nehiyaw, Dene, T'suut'ina."

"I don't know any of those."

"Cree?"

"Oh I know that one! Maybe that's it. I was never very good at all that. And what does it matter anyway, hey? Gosh, you look a lot like your daddy, did you know that? Did your mom ever tell you that?"

I wanted to shake my head but it felt harsh. "Not that I, remember," I managed.

"Well you do, you really do. Must be all that Native blood. It's like it's, stronger than white blood, hey?"

I thought of saying something about recessive genes, but it didn't matter anyway because Nikki just started talking about something else.

Until Faith pushed her chair out with a hard scrape on the floor, leaving her plate full of food.

"We're going to watch a movie, you should join us," Nikki called after her.

"I'm going out," is all Faith said and went down to her room in the basement.

Nikki rolled her eyes. "Don't mind her, she's just fifteen going on three! And doesn't mean to be so rude!" she yelled after her daughter who wasn't even there. "She's a good girl, really. Just nervous, I think. She always wanted a sibling. She used to tell us all the time. And we really thought we were going to have another baby, one together. Didn't we, honey? I really didn't want her to be a spoiled only child like this. But I guess God had other plans." She looked up to the ceiling, as if God was right there.

"Don't worry." My dad, Shawn, leaned over to me. "We're not churchy at all. Nikki just talks like that sometimes."

"Oh you! You really are going to go to hell," she said, but smiling, and tossed her napkin at him, but only in play.

Nikki talked all night. She talked as we cleared the table and filled the dishwasher. "Just give that to me, honey. You have to do it a certain way to get them all clean." She talked as she wiped the counter and table, twice. She talked while we made popcorn, with a real popcorn maker and everything. "I try to eat as little processed food as I can. It's not just 'cause it's healthy, but it tastes better." She even talked through the movie, when Faith came home and went right to her room, and all the way to when she offered to walk me upstairs and "tuck you in."

My room was pretty empty but it was all there, a skinny bed, dresser, desk. Well, not empty, but kind of blank. The only real things were my newly washed clothes folded and placed neatly atop the dresser.

"You can organize however you like. And put whatever you want in here, like posters or whatever. We can go out and buy things next week, if you want. What sort of things are you into? Faith likes all that rap stuff, Tupac or whatever. I don't condone it at all, but as long as she keeps it down."

Before I could answer, Nikki turned down the hall. "Shawn, come say good night. Say good night to your daughter, honey."

He appeared from around the corner with an awkward, "Night, C. Sleep tight."

"Oh come on now, you gotta do better than that! You didn't lock the back door, did you?" Nikki nudged him, again only playfully and went down toward the kitchen. "Or turn off any of the lights!"

Shawn looked after his wife. "She means well. Talks a lot when she's nervous. Good thing we're the quiet kind, hey?" He winked. Tilted his head with a smirk and winked right at me. I am pretty tall but he was still a bit taller. Up close I could see his hair actually had a lot of grey in it and his eyes wrinkled all around too, but no one would ever call him old.

It was a good wink.

"Have a good sleep, C." He reached out and patted my shoulder. It was quick but warm. Then he went into their room across the hall.

I stood there another second, but then closed the door quick when I heard Nikki coming back. I had had enough. All her talking had tired me out.

I could still hear them talking through the doors. Nikki mostly, but every now and then my dad would answer. Shawn would answer. Faith's room was below but I could hear the thumping bass. It wasn't loud, just there. Everything else seemed really quiet, the neighbourhood, the neighbours. I didn't even hear a car pass.

I fell asleep trying to make out the words to Faith's music, thinking C was a great nickname. Trying not to think of my real family. My real real family, I mean.

By October, I had given up on trying to make a friend. A real one anyway. It's amazing how the place is so big no one notices me. No one is the least bit interested in me at all. I got a little hopeful when Nikki gave me an old phone of Faith's—"I can't believe you've never had a phone! I mean, the safety issues alone!"—that I could connect with people on socials, which is sometimes so much easier than talking to people in real life. But I don't even know what to do on there. I hardly ever post anything, it gives me way too much anxiety, and I hardly ever get any likes at all anyway. Mostly I only look around, creep on the kids at my school, search my mom and Phoenix's names over and over. Neither of them is on anything that I can tell. I even tried nicknames and middle names like some people have, but nothing. I rooted through all the Strangers, hoping to find someone Mama had mentioned. I started following a Lyn who was an artist, a really neat artist too, and a June who was a professor and posted about Indigenous issues and stuff so she seemed cool. No idea if I'm related to them but I follow their work and pretend that I might be.

I do follow a few kids at school, kids from other schools I went to, and a few even follow back. I found Nevaeh who is in a group home now but seems happy. She posts funny videos on my wall so I don't look like a total loser. Nevaeh's good like that.

School might be a letdown but at least libraries are the same everywhere. In high school they let students eat lunch there so once I found that out I was all set. I pretend I'm working on a paper or writing a story, and I can read any book I want. They even have a few good ones, compared to my junior high library. I finish every assignment pretty much as soon as I get it and even work on some extra credit for English and social studies. I made the honour roll that first semester, and Nikki and Shawn made a big deal of it.

"We'll have to go out and celebrate. What's your favourite restaurant?"

I told her I didn't care but really, I don't know any restaurants. Couldn't remember ever going to one that wasn't fast food, never mind having a favourite.

All in all, everything got pretty normal pretty quick. Or I got used to it, the waves of it. Shawn is away during the week. He does a four-day shift at one of the dams but is home most of the weekend. He's sometimes talking, sometimes quiet, mostly depends on whether or not Nikki's around. Nikki manages a call centre so has to work a lot of evenings, which she likes because she gets to sleep in. Nikki doesn't like mornings. Faith is out most of the time, too, and when she is at home she ignores me. Faith ignores everyone, really, except for a big freakout every week or so. Nikki always blames PMS or says she's on her period or something lame like that, but whatever. I ignore it like Faith ignores me. I've lived with a lot of high-maintenance assholes, she's nothing new to me. Her freakouts never last long. She screams and slams doors. Shawn, if he's home, says nothing. Nikki runs around, sometimes helping, sometimes yelling, depending on her mood. She usually ends up giving Faith whatever she wants pretty quick, whether it's staying out later or getting more money. "She can't help it," she told me once. I didn't even want to know what she meant.

When Shawn's home he likes to hang out in the rec room, drink a beer or two and watch hockey. I started doing my homework down there, writing papers by hand in my notebook before I had to type them up on the computer at school. Never watched hockey before, didn't even know one team from another, but if Nikki wasn't around it was great. Shawn would even start talking. By Thanksgiving, I knew all the best teams and players and who to root for. It helps to have a home team, I learned.

"Once you have a home team you know where your loyalty lies. For years we didn't have a team, and then, who knows. Some of my friends still root for Detroit or Chicago, and when I was in Alberta it was all about the Oilers, for sure. But now we got the Jets back so that's all we need as far as I'm concerned."

Seems logical enough to me. I even looked up buying him a T-shirt for Christmas, even with his favourite player's name and number at the back. It was a lot more expensive than I thought, so I'll have to save up somehow.

Just before supper on a Friday, Faith appeared at my door. Shawn had ordered pizza and we were going to watch the game. It was the first time Faith'd ever been to my room.

"I'm supposed to take you to this party I'm going to. Be ready in five minutes." She walked down the hall without another word.

I was surprised but did what I was told. Pulled my messy hair in a ponytail and put on my old hoodie. When the pizza came, I wasn't even hungry anymore.

I figured it was some present or something, maybe for getting good grades. Obviously Nikki forced Faith to, but I went anyway, and was actually kind of mad that I was so hopeful about it. Not that Faith gave me any reason to.

She met me at the back door, said "Come *on*," and practically raced down the street. Her long, skinny legs moved fast, like they were trying to lose me. I managed to keep up but had no idea where we were or where we were going. By the time we got to a house loud with music, I was out of breath and sweating. But Faith still looked perfect.

"Don't embarrass me" was all she said before going inside, barely holding the door open for me to slip through.

There were so many kids, on the couch, standing around a huge fish tank, all over the kitchen. I recognized some of them from school, but I didn't know their names. There was this one guy who I am sure is Indigenous but I've never had the nerve to ask him. There was also an Asian girl and a few Black kids but nobody seemed to feel out of place here. Only me. I felt completely out of place here.

Faith ran over to her boyfriend with a bounce and silly giggle. I had seen it at school, knew Faith's hair-twirling and his indifferent stoner grin as he looked us both up and down, approving Faith, disapproving me.

I leaned against a wall and kept looking around. Not wanting to stare or anything, I ended up looking at the floor. I thought I looked shabby in my old hoodie, and I pulled the ratty cuffs over my hands and tried to look like I wasn't super uncomfortable. Faith's friends came up and nodded at me, like acknowledging me because they had to but not really saying hi. Some guy came up and stood next to me awhile but only looked at his phone for a few minutes before walking away again.

"You should mingle," Faith said too loud and handed me an open beer.

I had no idea how to mingle, or roam around the room like others were doing. Everyone seemed to know everyone else.

"I don't know anyone."

"Well just, like, talk to someone." Faith rolled her eyes.

I held the beer awhile but didn't move. I looked at my phone, pretending there was something there worth looking at, but only scrolled some websites I knew, and quickly put it away when someone brushed against me. Mortified someone would see what I was doing, or know how lame I was.

My beer got warm, and Faith and them went out to smoke a joint for the billionth time, so I left.

It was easy enough to go. As soon as I was outside, I wished I had gone earlier. No one even noticed, I was there or I was gone. Invisible as always.

But I had no idea where I was, either, so I roamed the winding, dark streets. Didn't mind much. It wasn't that cold yet. The leaves were starting to fall and stuck to the wet ground. It was raining a bit, like a mist, with almost a fog, so the streetlights looked blurry and the world soft.

I finally found where I was and my house, Shawn and Nikki's house. The back door opened to the sound of sports news and the smell of pizza. I was suddenly very hungry. I went down to the basement, pulled my hands out of my sleeves, and sat on the couch across from Shawn, who was nursing a beer.

He smiles. "That fun, hey?"

I only shrug and lift a slice of cold pizza out of the open box in front of me.

"I'm not one for parties either. Nikki likes them though."

"She's still, at work?" I ask the obvious questions between mouthfuls.

He nods. His eyes blurry like the night, tired maybe. After a bit he says, "I guess you never met your Uncle Joey, hey? Well, Joe he likes to be called now."

I shake my head, remembering my mom's middle brother's name. The one that moved away and never came back.

"He's a good guy. Haven't talked to him in a long time. We were best friends, hey? That's how I met your mom."

I nod now. Not 'cause I remember though.

"When I met 'im, they were all living in the brown house—him, his parents, his little brother Alex. He was just a little snot-nosed kid when I knew him but he's some big-time important dude now.

"Your old Grandmère lived there too, it was her house, and your mom and Phoenix, of course. All those people in that place. I mean it was pretty big but not that big. All the other family used to always be around too—your old Uncle Toby, well, Great-Uncle, he's your Grandma Margaret's brother, and Aunty Genie, or Great-Aunt too, I guess. She was such a nice lady. She and your Grandma Margaret didn't get along but Genie still visited your Grandmère. Real respectful, that Genie."

I don't move. Don't want to spook the story.

"That's how I met your mom, hey? Through Joe. Joe's a bit of a different sort of guy, hey? He grew up, well, not rough at all, but his dad's, Sasha, that's your mom's stepdad, right? Well, Sasha's what you call connected. Meaning he's into some not-so-legal stuff. That's what your other uncle, Alex, does now too, or so I've heard anyway. But not Joe. He never really had the stomach for all that. Not the real bad stuff anyway. I mean we used to get into trouble, hey? We were stupid young guys who thought we were all tough, but when push came to shove, Joe didn't want all that. Neither of us did. He was, is, he's just a weird person, goes to the beat of his own drum sort of thing." He looks right at me, so I nod, not knowing what else to do.

"The first night I met him, we were at this party, hey? Back when I liked parties, I guess. Well nothing much was happening so Joe, he gets like, bored. So he pulls this six-pack out of the fridge, not his beer at all, but he takes it anyway, and a bottle of Jack and just says 'Come on' to me. First thing he ever says to me. We hadn't ever talked or nothing, never saw him before in my life, just a 'come on!'"

He laughs, takes another swallow. Keeps going. "And I go because I was what, eighteen and stupid, like I said, and he looked like he knew what he was doing. He's not— You don't ask questions with Joey. He was never much for talking, just doing.

"So we walk some and he gets me to hold the booze. Well, we were drinking the Jack but I was carrying the six. Then he goes by Sev and steals one of those bags of wood. Like doesn't even think about it or look or anything, just takes it, and the two of us wander down Main Street dragging this big-ass bag of wood."

He laughs again, harder this time. "I didn't know where the fu— heck we were going, but I follow him and he takes me to this old warehouse on Alfred, this big, tall building but all empty, and leads me around back. So now I'm thinking, this guy is going to kill me. This is where he takes people to kill them. But still, I hold his beer and follow him. He goes to the back door and pries it open. It was only nailed shut with plywood, like it kept having to be nailed shut and not well, so it was easy to get in.

"We get inside and it's all dust and garbage and a bunch of leftovers from squats where people used to sleep, but Joe, he leads me up these dark stairs, dragging the wood behind him. And now I'm sure he's going to kill me but I'm thinking I'm so tough like I can take him if it comes to it. And I'm curious so I go anyway. He leads me all the way up to the roof, then drags the wood to this busted-up old barrel that's clearly been used for fires before."

Shawn pauses again, this time mostly for effect, and smiles. "So he throws the wood in and starts fu—starts making a fire! He even had an axe up there so he can split the wood to light it! So I watch the guy, your uncle, make this fire. When it gets going he leans back on an old broken crate, cracks a beer, and says, 'Beautiful, ain't it?'

"That's when I finally look around and the city is all lit up in the night, and it was summer so the trees are all full and dark everywhere. It was, it was really pretty. I had never seen anything like it. I was just a little 'hood boy, hey? And there's not many tall buildings in the neighbourhood. That was the one tall building and it was only what, four storeys high.

"Anyway, that's how I met your Uncle Joe." He laughs, takes another, longer pull to finish his beer.

I want to say something but don't know what. Then I remember something my mom told me. "Is that—? You went to jail with him, right?" But regret it as soon as it's out.

"Well, yeh," he laughs again, but nervously, maybe. "He was real good at breaking into places." He thinks a bit and starts again more serious. "Not that that's right or anything. But we were just kids. We came from nothing, or not much anyway. And like I said, we never got into the really bad stuff. Never hurt anybody, ever."

"Where is he now?"

"Still in Alberta. He was up there before me. That's why I went over there. 'Cause he said he could get me a job."

I let the words hang there. No idea what to say. Or maybe, too many questions I want to ask, about where he was, and why he didn't come back.

But I don't say anything, only put down my half-eaten slice of pizza and get out my phone to search for Joseph Stranger, but then think that's probably not his last name, if his dad was different than my mom's. I don't even know. And don't even know what his last name would be. I was going to ask but my dad, Shawn, looks like he's off somewhere far away, thinking about something far way. It seems okay, not like when Mama does that, but it also feels like I shouldn't bug him with any more question. So I get quiet too and pretend to watch sports news for a long time.

I never go out with Faith again. Never go to another party. Faith doesn't ask and I don't want to anyway. I spend weekend nights watching hockey when it's on, highlights when it isn't, and listening to Shawn tell stories, listening to him fill in all the blanks I have. Sometimes he even talks about me.

"When you were born, you screamed. A lot!" he says one night. "No one could hold you, not me or your mom, only your Grandmère. She was almost blind by then but still would sit there and hold you for hours. You were quiet then. When she would rock you. I had missed you being born, always felt bad for that. You came too fast. Too much in a hurry, your Grandmère said, you did everything in a hurry when you were a baby, you got teeth right away, were walking early. Or so they told me. I never knew when babies did what. Still don't. But they said you were fast at everything. Born smart like that."

Sometimes he mentions Phoenix, too. She was super young when he met her and he really seemed to like her, even before he started dating my mom. When they were only friends and he'd come around with her brother, my Uncle Joe. He called my mom Else.

He never talks about any of it when Nikki is around. When Nikki is around, he's quiet, about everything.

Nikki gets off around midnight usually, and I make sure to go to bed before then. Shawn too, I can hear through the door, goes to bed before Nikki comes home. Faith gets in after, when the house is all dark and quiet. The neighbourhood too.

They all sleep in. Every weekend, no one is ever up before eleven. Except me. I like getting up early so I can make toast or cereal and read and wait.

Nikki wakes up talking and I like to listen sometimes. With all the shifts, I don't see her much during the week. She sends me long texts though, complaining about her co-workers or Faith or telling me what chores to do. I never mind. The cleaning is way less than I ever did at any foster places and now I get an allowance. I never really had one before. Except that one foster lady in the country who'd give me fifty cents to do things that took hours. I was there almost a year and didn't even make twenty bucks. Here, I get twenty bucks every week. Less than Faith manages to get even though she never does anything, but I don't mind, really.

On weekday evenings, when everyone's out of the house, I get to watch whatever I want on the big TV downstairs, can eat pizza pops every supper, and sometimes even play the radio loud on Nikki's stereo in the upstairs living room. I get to know all the Top 40 music well enough I can sing along, even dance, if the curtains are closed and I'm sure no one would be home for a long, long time.

It's a good life, better than I ever thought I'd have. It would all have been perfect, if I had just felt different.

7

ELSIE

It's been thirteen days. Thirteen days since she stumbled back to Uncle Toby's place with an empty zip-lock bag that used to be filled with percs. She even licked the plastic clean. All the good it did. But then it was done. Away Elsie went on another long detox.

The shakes are the worst. Once they're finally gone she feels better. Doesn't much mind the throwing up and fever. She can roll through that. But the shits and the shakes. Those are the worst. Toby had some old T3s and back pain meds that got her through the first few days. She never liked T3s because she can't ever sleep and they turn her guts to rocks, but they can help when you're trying not to shit your pants.

Today Elsie feels clearer. Her knees are aching, so she barely gets up. But it's the first sign of getting by.

She had got by. And it got easier. Slowly. She felt like she was finally on her way. For good. For real.

Until she saw Mercy on the street. She'd been doing so good. The SSRIs had finally got right and she made it to see her worker and everything. Got a job at a grocery store, even. Packing up groceries for lazy customers to pick up. It was the best job. Elsie never liked most jobs where she had to talk to people. Be nice to people. But that one, she only had to wander the store and organize the groceries in the bins. Barely had to talk to anyone. It was nice.

But then she saw Mercy on the street and it was like no time had passed at all. It was like all those months she spent building herself up again were for nothing. The first thing she asked him was if he had anything and if he wanted to hang out.

She thinks she was lonely.

They went back to his sorry bachelor suite. He was living in supported housing like her uncle but for younger special needs people. It's a crazy place with screaming and stink and lots going on down the halls. But Mercy's kind of crazy himself so fits right in. They ground some percs up and Elsie was flying before she even sat down. She stayed there for days, weeks. Who knows. Talking and watching TV. Ordering food when he had money. Catching up on people she hadn't seen in a while. It was good for a while.

She knows she was lonely.

She didn't want to leave. He asked her to leave. Said he couldn't have anyone else living there with him or else he'd get kicked out. Elsie knows it was just an excuse. She had even made the crazy guy sick of her.

So she stumbled back to Toby's with her empty bag. Feeling every inch of it.

"You should come with me," Toby calls from the bathroom. He's getting ready to go see Aunty Genie. Put on his good pants and everything.

"I don't know, Uncle," she says from the kitchen, rolling her umpteenth smoke of the morning.

Thirteen days and she hasn't left the apartment. So afraid of what's down there. Who she will see. Who she will be.

"Come on. She'll love to see you." She can hear his walker on the lino, moving slowly over to her. She starts another rollie for him.

"I don't know about that," she says, lighting up.

"I just hate taking the bus by myself."

She knows he's full of shit about that. He takes the bus by himself all the time. But he knows. Knows the right guilt will make her give in.

"Fine." She smiles and sighs. Her shaky hand butts out her smoke and she gets up. Her whole lower half aches and she swallows too many Tylenol just in case. Just in case she reveals something of her sad addict state to her old aunty she hasn't seen in years. Not since her mom's funeral probably. Or Sparrow's. Elsie doesn't remember anyone from Sparrow's funeral. Only Jimmy, holding her up because she wouldn't let him go, and all the Oxy he would grind down for her so she could snort it quick in the bathroom.

Apparently, Aunty moved to a condo on the far side of town, so it's a long wait and a long bus. Toby inches his way over the ramp to get on board, just to reinforce Elsie's role as helper, but he makes it to the front seat on his own.

They both stare out the window the whole way. They're like that, him and her, all of them, she thinks. Quiet. Grandpa Mac used to say all Métis were quiet like them. Thoughtful, he called it. Elsie doesn't know about that, but all them Strangers have always been quiet people. The kind who stare out windows and never have to fill up space with silly small talk. Jimmy used to hate it. He's the high-strung type who always likes to talk and always thought something was always wrong with her. Come to think of it, Sparrow's dad was like that too. Always trying to get her to talk. Not in the right way though. There wasn't much right about Sparrow's dad.

The condo place is nice, clean. Parking lot filled with cars. Elsie helps Toby across the street and he makes some comment about getting old. Makes her think he might not be acting after all. She feels guilty about taking the last of his Tylenol. Finished up his back meds the other day too. Only over-the-counter stuff but not free. She'll have to try and get another job or something. Go back to Welfare. Again. She has to finally fix her broken self and stop fucking up all the time. But for now she will walk beside him. Help him over the curbs.

"Oh you're here! Oh Elsie!" Aunty Genie practically screams. "How are you both? Oh it's so good to see you!"

Aunty Genie is only a Stranger by marriage so is the kind who is always talking. "Come in, come in. Toby, take the couch, don't go too far. Did you two take the bus? That's such a long ride. You should have told me. I'd have gotten you a cab."

Toby shakes his head. Shrugs this off in a gruff way. Toby never willingly accepts anything from anyone. Not even Alex who is always trying to give him stuff. Rides. Money. He brought over a big flat-screen TV a few months ago. Set it all up and handed Toby the remote. Toby said he was mad but had to take it at that point. If only 'cause he couldn't figure out how to take it down.

Elsie helps him sit as Genie flutters around getting drinks and putting a tray of crackers and cheese on the coffee table. She's healthy, is Genie. She moves smooth and quick for someone as old as she is. She talks about how she replaced a hip a few years ago and goes to morning yoga and has been up since five. "I have never been much of a sleeper but now it's getting worse, eh?"

Toby nods like he knows what she's talking about. He gets up early, too. But not by choice. The coughing usually wakes him up early. He also finds a way to take about three naps every day. Mostly in his recliner that goes almost all the way back. Also a present from Alex.

Elsie asks to use the washroom and Aunty points down the one little hallway and keeps talking. The walls are lined with framed photos, all neat in a straight line. Most Elsie's seen before. But not for a long while. One of Mamere and Grandpa Mac in front at the old brown house in Elmwood. Elsie's old brown house. It's an old photo from when they first moved in, so like the fifties. She remembers the photo well. Mamere used to keep it on her bedside table. In it, Mamere was pregnant with her mom, Margaret, but it didn't show yet. As a little kid, Elsie would stare at it for a long time. Trying to see the baby under the dress. Another is from Genie's wedding to her Uncle Joseph, the one her brother was named after. The one who died before she was born. It's in the sixties, so everyone's eyeglasses are black and pointed. Everything slightly blurred. Mamere and Grandpa Mac stand straight and tall behind the bride and groom. They look proud. And annoyed. And unsmiling. As they did in photos. Aunty Genie all young and smiles. Perfect in white. She was only eighteen, already pregnant, of course. But Elsie could never tell in that one either. Uncle Joseph was their only son who got married. Toby never did, never wanted to, he says. And Uncle John was too busy going in and out of jail. Elsie's mom must have had a wedding. But later and to Sasha. No one liked Sasha. Elsie was pretty sure they eloped or something because she's never seen a picture of that. And Mamere had pictures of everything.

The other photos are Genie's grandkids. School photos of June and Lyn, her cousins. Who were younger but so much more perfect than she ever was. Jerome was Genie's only kid. He was almost a teenager when Elsie was born. Then had kids super young, with Renee. A short, curly-headed girl who they all thought was white. They had the two girls. The ones that were always so perfect. Still are. Elsie's mom had her two boys right after. Mamere used to pose her younger grandkids and great-grandkids all in a row. One after the other. Elsie, June, Lyn, Joey and Alex. Mamere loved those photos. Elsie hated it. Hated being the oldest. The odd one out. She always thought she looked sad in them. All those kids had each other. But she never had anyone.

There's some new photos too. One of Jerome and his second wife, Kelly. Looks like a wedding. They're on a beach, wearing summer clothes. There's others of some young kids too. She'd heard he had more kids. Much younger than her cousins who are like her age. Or maybe one of them had a kid. There are three of them. Three of them she doesn't even know.

She lingers in the bathroom a little longer than she should. She can hear Aunty droning on about something in a quiet, serious voice. Doesn't want to sit there awkwardly yet. It's like she doesn't remember how to be normal. She opens the medicine cabinet as quiet as she can. Aunty has a pretty high dose of Oxy. Explains why she's so spry. Elsie counts the pills. Seventeen. So takes six that won't likely be missed. Aunty also has sleeping pills. Small pink things. Elsie takes a few of those. She swallows the Oxy without even thinking about it. Without even water. She dances them in her palm and swallows as easily as she breathes. It's a shame. Another wave of something she is so deeply ashamed of. Doesn't even fully know all of it. Or pay attention to it. All the pain and sadness there. She fills the little pink plastic cup with water and drinks it long and slow. The cup matches the toothbrush holder and soap dish and lotion dispenser. This is the kind of lady Aunty Genie is.

Back in the hall Elsie can hear the old people's voices rise as they obviously change the subject when she opens the bathroom door.

"You doing all right, Elsie dear?" Aunty calls.

Elsie nods. Sits in the chair by the window. It's too close to a large plant but it feels warm and nice. She could almost sleep, so she takes the coffee Aunty keeps offering.

Genie's saying, "She's teaching art or painting now. Says it's going really well. All this Native Studies, she calls it. I mean, we always knew she was very interested in the Native stuff but now she says she found out her Great-Grandfather was a Métis shaman, have you ever heard of such a thing? A Métis shaman! So now our little Renee is a real true halfbreed, I suppose. News to me. I've known the girl most of her life, but now, now she's more Indian than all of us, or so she says."

Elsie has heard this before, this is Renee, Genie's ex-daughter-in-law, mom of Lyn and June, who she loves but also loves to talk about.

"Used to be the blondest girl you've ever seen! Her mother too, blonde blonde. Mennonite, she was. Don't know why Renee has to get into all this Métis stuff, I mean, she's a white girl. White as white can be. She should just be a white girl. Goes by some made-up name she thinks sounds Native. Raven something." Aunty snorts.

"It's like that nowadays. Everyone wants to be Indian now." Toby softly chuckles, but it causes him to hack.

"Pssh, not like the good old days when everybody tried to hide it. In those days, someone like Renee would thank her lucky stars she could pass. I always wished I could pass. Always tried." Genie looks off out the window. "Margaret was like that, so beautiful. Your mom, too. She had the most beautiful hair when she was younger. Light, light skin and dark brown curly, curly hair. Looked all the way French, almost."

"Hmm, born-again brown, Dad used to call them." Toby chuckles again, this time with less hacking.

"Born-again stupid, if you ask me. Don't know why they're jumping on the bandwagon now, not after their families probably tried to breed it out for generations."

"Different generation, Genie. Think they can get something now. With all these court cases and settlements." Now it's Toby's turn to look disapproving.

"Never got me anything but trouble." Aunty Genie makes a face but smiles quick after. "Elsie dear, eat, eat! You're skin and bones over there."

Elsie leans forward obediently and makes a couple cracker and cheese sandwiches. Takes a napkin. As she leans back the plant brushes against her face again. It's one of those tall tropical-looking ones from the eighties with dusty broad leaves. Aunty Genie has probably had it that long too.

Her Elders sit in silence for a spell before they get on old stories. It never takes that long with these two. Never has with anyone in Elsie's family, really. Nothing breaks an awkward silence like a good "remember when . . ." She wonders if that's a Métis thing too. To always talk about the good old days. Not that they were good. Only old. And shared.

"Remember when your dad and you guys put that front porch on the house? Oh but that was funny, you younger guys didn't know what the heck you were doing."

"Joseph kept sneaking away to swig from this flask he had. That old one with the engraving, remember? Oh he got drunk that day. Dad was so mad at him."

They laugh, remembering it all. Elsie can see, even though it was before she was born. She knows the story. Has heard it over and over. Can see Grandpa Mac's face as Toby scrunches his up in imitation. Can imagine Mamere in the doorway with her hands on her hips, scolding her sons as they laughed their way through their big afternoon chore. Joseph put in a whole row crooked. Toby almost broke his thumb from accidentally hammering it. Grandpa Mac was so mad at the time but in most of his retellings of the story, he'd always end up laughing, too. They had to fix it all the next day. Hungover but Grandpa made them work until it was right. Until he died he could point out the nail holes from the row Joseph had put in wrong. He'd mention it whenever he sat out there. Which was nearly every evening.

"That was just before you, Elsie dear." Aunty turns to her. Trying to pull her into the conversation.

Elsie smiles. Feeling light and warm in the sun. Clean long enough those few Oxy make her actually feel something. Just a bit. Just good.

"That was the summer before you were born," Toby adds. "Margogo was just getting a tummy. Boy, she was grumpy then."

They laugh gently. Aunty sighs. They're getting close to the hard time. That winter was the winter Uncle Joseph died. Right before Elsie was born. Aunty lost her too-young husband and was never the same. None of them were, really.

"I was going to adopt you. Did you know that?" Aunty's face is long but loving.

Elsie nods. "Mamere told me." She had. A few times. When she was trying to explain away why Elsie's mom didn't love her. Elsie's mom, too, had mentioned it. Mostly screamed it. As a wish that should have come true.

"I always wanted a little girl. And you were such a perfect little girl with your blue blue eyes and big hair. You were born with a full head of hair. All curls. Oh I wanted you." Her smile fades. "But after all that, I couldn't. Just couldn't."

The air changes then. When she says something out loud. When the things they were all thinking become a little more real. They sit with it. Used to it. Toby and Elsie used to it from years of Mamere sitting with it. When it was almost like it had its own seat at the kitchen table. The loss of her son. The uncle Elsie never knew but knew more about than most alive people.

Aunty Genie doesn't want to sit with it too long though. She waves her hands in the air and says, "Oh but my, it's getting late. I should get supper on." And grabs the nearly empty plate of crackers and cheese. "Do you want to stay for supper, you two? I can pull out an extra pork chop. I only ever thaw the one these days."

Uncle Toby gives Elsie a look as he calls to her back. "Naw. We should head out. I'd like to get home before dark."

"Oh yes, the days are getting shorter now, aren't they," she says. It makes no sense other than making conversation.

Elsie can tell Toby wants a smoke. Then maybe a beer. And to fall asleep in front of his big TV. She doesn't really want to move. So comfortable with the sun still warming her chair even though it's too damn close to that big plant.

Aunty packs up the rest of the crackers and cheese for them. Elsie feels overly emotional about this tiny, kind thing. Then Aunty gives them both real hugs as she leans her good hip against the open door.

"Now don't be strangers, you two." A loaded statement in their family. "Come and see me again soon."

Toby pulls a smoke out in the elevator and lights it as soon as he is outside. It hangs off his lip as he pushes his walker out in front of him and says with a shake of his head, "I do love Genie, but man, that woman can talk."

Elsie laughs. Lights her own and walks beside him. Helping him over every curb.

It's been three days since she stole that Oxy from Aunty. Three days since she took those sleeping pills. It was a great sleep. But still she woke up jittering and wanting. Wishing she had kept a few back. Had a couple more great sleeps.

She got Uncle some new back meds and painkillers. Easy enough to pocket. Went to Welfare with her tail between her legs.

"What happened with the grocery store job?" the social worker says gruffly.

Elsie shrugs. But it's not like the worker doesn't know. Or thinks the worst of her. Elsie knows what's on her file. The list of all her fuck-ups and fall-downs and relapses. The worker has this running list of dates for it all. Elsie doesn't know all the dates but still knows it all. Can feel it. Every time.

"Your family worker left a message. You missed your last appointment."

Elsie nods even though she didn't know 'til just now. The waves start. The pure sadness. Dark waves that make her want to drown her whole worthless self under them. If only they were real water and she could.

"I'm giving you a food card. I can't give you cash anymore."

Elsie takes it greedily. Excited. Almost happy she didn't get cash.

The thing Elsie likes best about pills is they do everything for you. If you want to sleep, you can. If you want to party, you can get in the mood. There's no work. There's no risk. If you get sad, you can change it. That's the best part. The good part. Staying that way is the thing. You can't. It's like two beers and you're happy, five beers and you're loving everybody. But you can't stay like that. You either get more drunk or less drunk. You never stay perfect drunk. Same with pills. They wear off. Or you take too many. Or you can't seem to take enough.

After Sparrow she took too many for a long time. Needed to. Any doctor would have given her tranquilizers and sleeping pills anyway. She was only doing the work herself. It was necessary. For a long time. She couldn't live with that pain. She couldn't look herself in the mirror. She thinks she was oblivious for a year. Or more.

That took a lot. That was Jimmy. Always keeping her high. He was good like that. Took care of her like that.

Thing is, the pain was still waiting for her when she cleaned up. They say time heals all wounds but she knows that's bullshit. That year felt like no time had passed at all. And really it didn't. The world moved on but she didn't. She doesn't.

But a food card means she doesn't even have to think about it. She can't get high and there's no use trying. She makes her way to the store to stock up on chips. And fruit. For some reason she really wants to eat fruit. She even gets a couple nice-looking steaks and potatoes. A new pouch of tobacco too. She's almost giddy going home to Toby's with her two yellow plastic bags on either side. She even walks all the way, she was that energetic. Two days but that was such a small relapse. She barely has any shakes or anything. If she keeps going she should be good. Might even be able to start that job search her worker was saying she had to.

The light's starting to fade when she gets to his building. Thinking of the medium-rares and baked potatoes she'd make. The silly reality TV show he'd make her watch. She's looking forward to it. Doing something good for Uncle.

She should have known better.

Should have known the back of his head before he even turned. Jimmy. Sitting on the bench in front of the building. Smoking fast like he'd been there awhile. Jimmy. Slumped like he was high. He looks up and smiles his smile. The one she knows better than almost anything. The one she could never say no to.

"Else," he says like a breath and a dream. The side of his face is red like from a fall. Or a good punch.

Jimmy.

And Elsie knows everything before he even says anything more.

She knows.

Everything that must have happened.

Everything that's going to.

8

MARGARET

On the day Cedar-Sage was born, Margaret was raging. Silently, only in her head, of course, while she went about doing every fucking thing for every fucking body, but it was a keen, bright rage.

Sasha was generally the target of her hate. She thought marriage must be good for some people, men mostly, but she's never seemed suited to it. She spent years trying to make it work for her, to find something enjoyable in seeing the same face every day, having the same conversations over and over, but, like many things people seemed to like so much, the joy of it eluded her. She was perpetually annoyed. Sasha always thought she was annoyed at him because he was the one who was there, the safe one, he called it, as if he knew what that meant, but he was wrong. He was the least safe person in her whole life. Maybe that's what was so annoying.

Sasha could be loving, kind, generous. He could also turn on a dime, make best friends worst enemies. She once saw him beat a man to near death all because he was high and thought the guy had cheated him on a car sale. The guy lived, thankfully, had two black eyes and an arm broke in two places and, it turns out, was perfectly justified in his low-end negotiations as the car in question was actually a big fat lemon. But Sasha was never the least bit apologetic or even acknowledged his mistake. The guy continued to be in the periphery of their lives for years, never took one step out of line like Margaret in those first years, never a step out of line. Back then, she kept herself and everything else together, as the boys were born and young, as she grew big with them and then grew small again. As

Sasha seemed to get a handle on his addiction only to lose control of it, again and again. As he risked his freedom and her safety with stupid scheme after stupid scheme until he was finally inside for a good stretch. Through all of it, she kept herself together. But resentment is something that grows, first a sprinkle, then another, until it's a storm. Nowadays, Margaret was all storms.

She knew what Sasha really wanted from people, and over the years, she got good at giving it to him. He didn't want challenge or criticism or even conversation, just agreement. He wanted to be reassured he was smart, respected, funny, sexy, whatever he wanted to be at the time. It was Margaret who was challenged. Challenged with trying to come up with new ways, it seemed, to compliment him, to not beat him with the spatula or throw the frying pan at him. Or walk away and never come back.

Margaret was exhausted. She had been, she thinks, since birth. Because before Sasha, before she had to take care of him all the time, and while she still had to take care of him all the time, she also took care of her mother. Her sad, sad, mother was also a subject for Margaret's near constant internal raging. Annie always needed something too. She needed to tell stories, needed to share her opinion, needed help with something, needed a hand to hold, and only Maggie Muggins over here could do it. Annie was a different kind of high maintenance to be highly maintained. Especially after Margaret's dad died, the woman was always so needy.

Now in old age she was the neediest she'd ever been. Annie always wanted to talk, always begged Margaret to sit with her, watch TV with her, be there with her. She didn't seem to realize Margaret had shit to do. Always had shit to do. She had to clean the house, over and over, because no one else did anything. She had to care for her mother, Sasha, two ungrateful teenage boys, a low-life teen mom of a daughter and her messy toddler and another one on the way. But no, through it all, every day, Annie wanted to talk and be listened to, and then Sasha would want to talk and be listened to. Margaret swore she was going to die from all the listening she was forced to do. Margaret dreamt of silence and aloneness, and times spent without a thing to do or clean or cook.

Any day now, Elsie was going to pop another baby. Another girl. She had gotten the scan and found out because that's what they did nowadays, and of course it was another girl. This one at least had a father. A low-life, go-nowhere boy barely out of his teens. Shawn was his name. Little spoiled halfbreed mutt who lived on Selkirk of all places, never worked a day in his life from what Margaret could tell. Elsie says he's going to help but Margaret had yet to see it and will believe it when she does. Fucking Elsie. The girl never took after her, not in anything. Never listened either. Margaret knew she shouldn't have let her go running around bars, getting up to all sorts. She had told her, when Elsie turned eighteen and wanted to go, but the girl never listened. And now, another human coming, any day now. Another thing for Margaret to do.

This is what Margaret thought of as she did the dishes, vacuumed at least once a day because no one could ever be bothered to watch the crap they dragged in, did laundry. The washer was constantly running, the line outside the brown house constantly hung with clothes. This is what she did day in day out, clean, and watch little Phoenix, keep her constantly corralled into a safe space, away from all the stairs because the poor thing kept falling down them. This fucking house was full of stairs. And what wasn't falling apart needed to be repainted, but of course Sasha never got to it and the boys were more useless than their father because he never bothered to teach them anything. It was all left to Margaret. Maggie Muggins for sure.

They had moved in on a rainy Saturday not long after Phoenix was born, and it took forever even though they left most of their stuff behind. No need for most of the broken furniture or to rent a truck, Sasha and the boys hauled their crap in the back of an old K-car that worked at the time. Garage stuff had to go in the basement and the rest had to fit in the attic. Toby went back to wherever he was staying before, but had left a bunch of his stuff behind up there. The boys had to dig through piles of it and use the bunk beds that were older than their mother. They loved it, they said, but Margaret couldn't even go up there for all the mess. She left it to them, to root through like rats. At least they seemed happy enough up there and didn't bother her all the time.

To her credit, Margaret's mother offered to change rooms and give Margaret and Sasha the master. It only made sense for the old lady to move to the downstairs bedroom anyway. That way she only had to go up the stairs to bathe, which she did, like clockwork, after supper when her knees didn't hurt as much as they did in the mornings.

That was what the house had become, clockwork. It was all a routine, and it was monotonous but never still. Still would be sitting down and having nothing to do, and that never happened. That's what marriage felt like to Margaret, too. Monotony. Boredom. Boredom accented with bouts of rage. But again, maybe it was just her.

Sasha, too, had become a creature of habit, painfully so. For a while it was refreshing. She got her hopes up. Old man Sasha on a routine seemed better than unpredictable younger Sasha on coke. But then it got annoying. Up at seven, he'd yell at the boys to get up as he went in the shower. He wanted breakfast ready thereafter, two over-easy eggs, not overcooked, and toast buttered all the way to the crust. Then he'd go out and pretend to work at something. Without a shop at home, he'd go to his buddy Steve's set-up in St. Boniface and together they would smoke and drink and every now and then paint a car. He did all his work through there, though. Nothing came to the house. No one so much as called. That was the deal when they moved here. None of his bullshit anywhere near the house. Just give her the money, she told him, like a regular working man.

"I want no heat, not a whiff, anywhere near my mother," she had insisted as she packed their clothes into black garbage bags.

"I won't, I won't. Don't be afraid for your mom. She'll be fine."

"I'm not afraid for her. I just don't want to hear her . . . opinions."

Her mother had always had an opinion about Sasha, and Margaret didn't want to give her any excuse to go off again. Not that the old lady could or should say anything after they all moved in and supported her and fucking Elsie and her baby. Babies. But that sort of thing never stopped her mother before, so Margaret wasn't taking any chances.

As tiresome as it all was, nothing major had happened in the two and a half years since they all lived together. Four generations of Stranger women, and her useless men. Toby was also around whenever he could be, whenever he needed a free meal or ran out of smokes. And Genie visited all too often. Margaret hadn't been alone in months.

There had been a lot of people living in the old brown house when she was growing up, too. When there were all her brothers, Genie and Jerome for a long while, the odd cousin on her dad's side, as they moved to the city, one by one, her Tante Marguerite for a long and memorable winter, then Jerome and Renee when they had their first baby, eventually Elsie too. It seemed normal for it to be so full. Back then her mother, as needy as she was, at least could always be counted on for a day's work, but Annie was getting older, and now Margaret only had herself. Elsie couldn't be trusted to do anything other than what she was told. Except getting knocked up, of course. That, she took initiative all on her own.

"Did you finish washing all the baby clothes?" Margaret asked her daughter as she came down the stairs that morning, and not for the first time. "You got to have it all ready. Any day now." Margaret was washing up all the breakfast dishes and half turned from the sink to have a look at the girl.

"I know, I know." Elsie woke up late and was getting Phoenix a cup of juice instead of a proper breakfast. Her belly stretched out in front of her shamelessly. She wore one of that Shawn's T-shirts instead of proper clothes. Little Phoenix ran up and hugged the back of

Margaret's legs. She was a decently behaved child, still not potty trained, but that was her mother's fault.

"You should fold it too. Properly. So it all fits in those little drawers."

"Mamere was going to do that this morning, while I'm taking Phoenix." As if taking the toddler to daycare she didn't even pay for was such a chore.

Margaret took a deep breath. "You can't just get her to do things for you, Elsie. She's too old."

"She offered!" Elsie snapped, and closed the toddler's backpack. Had to get her all brand-new things, this one. Name-brand things. Too much damn money. A waste, Margaret told her at the time. "She can't just sit in a chair all day, you know. She wants to do stuff."

"Well, isn't that convenient for you." Margaret turned back to her pan and scrubbed harder than necessary.

The girl took her own deep breath and turned to Phoenix. "Say goodbye to Grandma. We gotta go."

"Be-bye," the little one said.

"Bye, darling." Margaret smiled quick before returning to her usual frown. To Elsie's credit, Phoenix was at least clean, hair pulled up off her forehead and in a matching outfit every day. It was the least she could do, of course.

Elsie hadn't wanted her to go to daycare but Margaret insisted. The girl got subsidy after all, so it wasn't that much, and Margaret got roped into paying what there was anyway. The child needed proper social interaction, not just an old lady and a young girl and the TV all day. The bloody thing was always on these days. Always too loud with both old Annie and Sasha being so deaf. There was always a laugh track or some annoying theme music or commercials that were somehow louder going on in the background of Margaret's life. At least in her old house, when she used to have some time to herself during the day, she could turn it off sometimes.

Margaret relaxed her face when the girl shut the door, properly at least. Not like the slams the boys left behind. Her skin seemed to pucker every morning as she made her ungrateful sons and husband their eggs and toast, and finally in the nearly quiet, with everyone but her mother on their way, she could work out her wrinkles. She relaxed her mouth from its intense line and drooped her eyes so her forehead could flatten out. She dried her hands, then gently touched her face, massaged her forehead smooth and pulled her cheeks up and out to her ears. She had read somewhere that this helped, this pushing back of her face, as if that could stop time and all the pain that rested there.

She found her mother in her big chair, a basket of laundry propped on her side table. "You know she should do that herself."

"I don't mind. I like being useful."

"She's never going to learn if you keep helping her so much."

"She's young. She's always learning."

"You've always spoiled her."

"Kids should be spoiled."

Margaret made something of a hmm sound, something that could be construed as agreement, or maybe just a grunt. She didn't say what she was really thinking, that she never got spoiled, not in the slightest. Instead she looked around at the house, somehow messy again. She needed to dust and vacuum this room. Sasha wanted roast for supper. He liked beef roast on Tuesdays. Another one of those things his mother used to do that Margaret had to do too.

"You should rest, while you can. Baby is going to come soon." Her mother's voice was low. The TV played some talk news show, loud, annoying American voices.

"She's still got a week to go."

"Phoenix was early. This one might be too."

"Really?" They had rarely talked about the little one's birth, about the time Margaret wasn't there, hadn't spoken to her daughter since she found out Elsie was pregnant and put her into that stupid home. She had been left out of everything, including the birth, until they needed something from her. It still made her livid. She swallowed, hard. "I was always right on the due date. With all of them."

"I know. I was all over the place. You were early, your brothers were late." Annie smiled down at a little pink sweater. Margaret knew it was one of hers. Her mother must have made it for Phoenix, back when she could crochet for hours. "Well, Toby was just a day late, but John and Joseph were nearly two weeks late each. Slow ones, those two."

Her mother rarely mentioned Margaret's two older brothers anymore. She must have been feeling sentimental, with the baby coming. Margaret made another gentle hmmm sound, knowing her mother wanted to talk. Knowing to just let her talk.

But she didn't.

"Go rest. I know you were up 'til all hours last night." Her mother reached over the sleepers folded in her lap and placed her old hand on Margaret's. "Nap. While you can."

Margaret was exhausted. But she was always exhausted. She hadn't even remembered that she couldn't sleep last night, until her mother said something. She was so used to pacing and smoking in the kitchen most of the night. Of course her mother noticed, being in the next room.

It was a usual fight. Margaret, tired of letting slight after slight go, went off on some small thing, seemingly small thing. Sasha called her crazy like he always did and told her to calm down. Two things that never quite worked the way he wanted them to, unless his goal was to make her feel even more crazy and feel even further away from calming down. Which it very well could have been.

They had been at the bowling alley. Monday nights they bowled in a league with other couples. Mostly they smoked and drank beer, but bowling did happen intermittently.

They'd all been talking about Chrétien, the prime minister, and Paul Martin, the once finance minister now in a party takeover.

"Martin's going to get it," Margaret had said enthusiastically, and laughed. "He's going to win. It's a total coup." Relishing the talk of politics like she did.

But Sasha gave her this look. It was only a look, small, but it said settle down, and it said it firmly. Anyone else would think he was only smiling, smiling with a slight tilt of his head, but she knew. She knew it was a message, one that told her she was just a little girl and didn't know what she was talking about and should stop making a fool of herself.

It didn't matter that she did know what she was talking about. That she was really good at talking and arguing and knew politics and law. And loved it. It only mattered that she was being too smart for her own good. It only mattered that he wanted her to stop.

It was a second. Only a second. And it looked like a smile. No one could have seen it, or known what it meant. But she did. She sat back in her chair, recoiled from the conversation. Sasha smiled at his stupid friends and swooped into the silence, talked about Chrétien and all the things he pretended to know. The things he heard on the news, or that Margaret had told him herself. Ideas he now passed off as his own.

Margaret let him. She didn't say anything, only puffed hard. Raged in her head, like she did.

She was still fuming when they got home. When Sasha threw his clothes on the floor and flopped into bed, all his weight getting there first.

She picked up his sweaty shirt and jeans and sneered, quietly. "You're such a slob."

"Why are you being such a bitch? Calm down." They had grown used to fighting quietly. Their whispers somehow more sinister than screams.

"Don't fucking tell me to calm down. You calm down. And stop being such a slob."

"Fuck you," was all he said and rolled over to go to sleep.

She knew not to push it anymore. She knew not to try to articulate her anger, what she was really angry about. There was no point, he wouldn't get it, wouldn't even try to. He would only call her a child, tell her to calm down, say she was overreacting, being too sensitive. She knew he hated it when she got all high and mighty, as he called it. When she tried to act too smart for her own good. Or more like, "just want to make me look stupid." Because he thought it was all about him. Everything was all about him. He didn't like it when she talked politics or argued or talked too loud and excited about things, like she did sometimes when she had a beer or two. She knew she overdid it but she had been so happy to talk about it when someone brought it up. She had been reading about Martin and his attempts to take over the party leadership, loved the excitement of it, the drama. The way it was all so behind the scenes like a steamy soap opera but played out in the fucking House of Commons. She loved that stuff. Always had. Never got much chance to talk about it. Besides with Sasha, who she always felt she was teaching about everything, not debating.

She knew she went too far. She knew if she pushed him now, as he pretended to sleep, it would only get bad. So instead she gathered his clothes, and then the basket to make a load, and went downstairs.

She worked on her puzzle while the washer went. Made tea and smoked cigarette after cigarette. Her lips made their line thin and her forehead wrinkled and she breathed a little better every time a piece found its place and soon she didn't want to go to the basement to find a hammer and go upstairs and beat him with it.

That's what she always got wrong about being a wife, she thought. Wives were supposed to be simpering, quiet things. They could be sad and unhappy but only in a refined, resolved sort of way, and they had to be quiet, definitely be quiet.

She could never be that way. She was too fucking angry.

"I can't sleep now," she said finally, and moved her hand from under her mother's. "Too much to do."

Annie wasn't offended. "There's nothing to do. Go rest. When did you go to bed?"

"Around two," she said but knew it was later. She had finished her puzzle. Had been going through them quicker and quicker. She needed a new hobby. A new game to smooth her mind.

It was Annie's turn to make made an agreeing grunting sound. She knew Margaret was lying.

Margaret thoughts jumped around the house, the boys' messy attic, Elsie's bedroom—her double bed pushed against the wall with an awaiting bassinet beside it, and the crib crammed in beside the dresser on the opposite wall.

"The girl should move out. Get a place of her own," Margaret said, thinking of housing she knew, applications to be filled out.

Her mother went back to her folding. "She's better off with her family around her."

"But those babies all in that room. Phoenix should be in a big bed by now. There's not enough space!"

"Elsie's not complaining."

"She'd have a lot of nerve if she did."

"It's like the old days. All of us here. I like it. The old way."

"Crazy way is more like."

Annie smiled at her. "You like it too."

"Well, Joey's nearly eighteen. Maybe he'll stop running around with that Shawn and get a job, move out." Lord knows her eldest always talked about it. Even as a little kid he wanted to be out on his own. Always talked about getting as far away from all of them as possible. He had always been the independent one, the only one like her at all.

"Maybe. But for now, we're fine. Go nap."

Margaret did feel tired, liked the sound of a nap. A nap in the bed without Sasha in it. A space all to herself. "Maybe."

But as she got up, all the thoughts rushed in again, and she turned to her mom. "Did she ever tell you who Phoenix's father is? He should be involved, or at least pay something finally. He'd likely be as useless as this Shawn boy but the girl should have a father."

The old lady looked up. "She doesn't need a father. She's like her mother."

Margaret frowned, not really knowing which "she" her mother was talking about, Elsie or Phoenix, but realizing it worked for both of them.

Elsie's father's name was Jacob Penner. Still is, likely. He was not the sort to die young so he's probably still around somewhere. Margaret was in her second year of law school when she met him. He was a year ahead and was an absolute know-it-all about everything. He was their constitutional law tutor. Margaret was lost in constitutional law, and wandered closer to family and criminal law, things that she could relate to, situations she was familiar with. She liked to be able to see it. The constitutional stuff was abstract and far above anything that someone like her would ever know. So he impressed her. He had all the answers. That's what she remembers first when she thinks of Jacob Penner, though she's tried not to think of him that often: that he knew it all.

He was also tall, and blond, had these bright blue eyes, just like Elsie's but even lighter. Jacob's eyes were light like clear water, like the sky when it's nearly white, like no colour at all. And she thought he liked her. She remembers that second of all. He liked to talk to her, flirt with her. He didn't treat her like the know-nothing halfbreed she was, or even an easy date, like every other boy from school. Jacob seemed to even respect her. They talked, got to know each other—or mostly he talked and she got to know him. But he smiled a lot and told her she was great. He took her on real dates, to dinners and movies. He had his own apartment in a high-rise downtown and a new, clean car. He was a country boy not used to the city, so nervous about living downtown that he kept a baseball bat behind his front door. She found it so endearing.

"To catch the odd foul ball," he told her with a laugh. And she laughed even though she doubted he'd really be able to use it.

He had so much of everything she had never known before. He had a foreign coffee maker and a VCR before anyone had one of those, and he liked her. It felt like her life was really coming together.

"So what's his apartment like? A real bachelor pad or what?" her friend Becky had asked over paper coffee cups and cigarettes in the food hall.

"Not what you would think. He's really clean, organized." Margaret mulled over his walls, couch, table as she dabbed her smoke on the side of the ashtray nice and neat. "Really plain, actually. Nothing on the walls. It's like he's waiting for a woman to come in and fill it up for him."

"Oh yeah, I bet you got those paint swatch things just ready to go, hey?" Becky laughed, but Margaret could see her jealousy. Becky hadn't had a date all semester and her mom had been threatening to set her up with sons of her friends from the Ukrainian Club. They both felt it, the weighted need to do something important, to be important, and marry someone worthy. Their families were counting on them, had paid hard-earned savings for them to sit here, smoke too much, and talk about boys.

In university, Margaret was as lucky as she was smart. She was fair-skinned enough and always wore nice clothes. Catholic-raised, well-mannered so even though her brothers were all troublemakers and her family dirt poor, no one openly suspected she didn't deserve to be there. She still worked at Eaton's on weekends so got all the latest clothes and knew how to use accessories to make her few suits look different every day. She kept every part of herself in pristine condition, gave herself a manicure every weekend and a decent permanent whenever she could save enough. She lived too far away for anyone to ever need to visit, and would meet dates downtown or at school so no one ever had to come by. She thought she was managing her college career rather well, if she did say so herself.

"Oh that's nonsense, Becky. We've only been on four dates, really. And I haven't even met his parents yet," Margaret said as if she was like the girls in the movies who counted dates and met parents.

"Wouldn't it be great, though? You could have a June wedding. You could be Mrs. Jacob Penner!" Becky sighed and took a long, unladylike gulp of her coffee.

Margaret sometimes wished Becky would have been a little more graceful, or stuck to a diet for a change.

Margaret stubbed out her smoke with a perfectly manicured finger and continued to act as if it was all no big deal. "Not everyone is looking for a wedding, Becky. Some of us are committed to being professional women."

Becky giggled. "Okay there, Margie. So are we still going to the Pal this Friday or are you in a far too serious relationship for that?"

"Of course. Jacob isn't the type of man to hold me down," Margaret said, even though they had never discussed it and she didn't have any idea what type of man Jacob was.

That whole year, they continued to go to the Palomino Club every Friday for ladies' night, and Margaret would accept drinks but never give out her phone number. Becky loved that because then she could get all the attention, and boy, did she need it. She even lost a few pounds, and Margaret lent her some of her more revealing clothes as she herself started to dress a little more modestly when they went out. And all year, she and Jacob had their standing Wednesday night date when they would go out to dinner or a movie or a drive, then back to his plain, clean apartment. They never went anyplace else, or out on any other evening. He mostly went home on the weekends or was busy with school, third year was so much more intense than second, plus he was in constitutional law so it was that much more complex.

The odd time she would ever get up the courage to ask for more, he would only have to smile to reassure her. "Law school is tough, baby, even for me," he'd say. "I have to put my pedal to the metal if I'm going to land a good placement in the spring. Soon it'll all be worth it."

At Christmas she expected an invitation to his hometown, but it never came. He went out after his last exam and she didn't hear from him again until after New Year's. She thought for sure it was the end then, and was fine with that, ready to move on, she told herself. But then, first day of classes he met her at her locker with that smile and a small present. It was a woollen scarf, homemade by one of his aunties, and just like that she was a goner again. Until spring, until the world came crashing down that spring.

Margaret had had a diaphragm since she was first in university so it's not like she didn't know better. She had this old friend who knew all about that stuff and set her up with a discreet doctor. All she had to do was go for a quick exam, to make sure she wasn't pregnant already, even though she knew she couldn't be, and he would sign her over a prescription no questions asked. She borrowed a ring off Genie when she went to fill the prescription, just in case. And signed her name Mrs. Margaret Stranger, as if that made any difference. The pharmacist still seemed to look at her sideways and above his round wire glasses, but he couldn't do anything, she had the prescription, and that was the hardest part.

And it's not that she stopped using her diaphragm. She just forgot it one night and then got out of the habit. It was months before anything happened. She was beginning to think she was barren, but then she was late, and almost immediately started getting sick in morning classes.

Becky, of course, noticed right away. "You're knocked up, aren't you," she said as Margaret left the toilet stall one morning.

"Don't be silly!" Margaret clapped back with a hoarse whisper and looked around to see if they were alone.

"You are!" Becky was truly naive, and stood there with her mouth wide open, hugging a couple textbooks to her chest. "What are you going to do!"

"What people have always done," Margaret said cool as a cucumber and drank water from her cupped palm. "Get married, of course."

Becky laughed and freed an arm to hug her friend. "Oh I'm so happy for you. We can have a June wedding after all!"

Margaret smiled along, but if she was being honest, she felt a fear growing along with the baby, even then.

Margaret woke up around lunchtime. Her mother was still in her chair, and Elsie was now sitting on the floor in front of her, both cooing over the small clothes, piled in neat piles, still not put away.

She was hungry but lit a cigarette instead, pulled her puzzle board off the dryer and set it on the table. It was finished. The New York City skyline at night, all the lighted windows, dark skyscraper outlines, and shadows all there, all complete. This was her favourite part, she thought as she put her cigarette in its place on the edge of the ashtray, then pulled the sides of the puzzle together. She loved taking it all apart, breaking up what she'd painstakingly put together and rubbing the pieces together until they separated. She took handfuls of the pieces, put them back in the box, and fit the lid on neatly. Then she stacked it low on the shelf under all the other completed puzzles. Some people liked to keep them together, some people glued them and framed them or took a picture to remember their accomplishment. Margaret never cared. She let them sit finished for a day or an hour, until she wanted to start another, and when she did she tore the last one apart. She never did a puzzle twice, only piled the boxes together until the next time she went to the thrift shop, where she traded them in for a new pile.

She pulled a new one out. A creepy clown doll with red-yarn hair sat on a wooden table against a patterned wall. It'll do, she thought. They all do.

Of course it didn't work out with Jacob. After it was all said and done, she was left to her stupid family porch while summer stretched out and her mother gardened and her father went off to work. She doesn't remember thinking much, not after everything. She mostly only sat there, feeling cold. Beaten. She felt beaten and defeated. Had nothing left. No fight. Just sadness. She cried that summer, cried like she never had before or since. It was pathetic. She got knocked up, then kicked out of school. She was alone. Useless. No better than all the other girls who got themselves in trouble and wrecked their lives.

It was Becky who tried to come to her rescue when she finally visited.

"What are you going to do?" Becky whispered. "You know, about the, you know?"

Margaret shrugged. It was all she could think to do.

"I know this woman. She's down on Redwood. Cheap, I think. My cousin went there. Clean enough, she said." Becky whispered in careful steps, the way you talk about such things.

Margaret nodded. "How much?"

Becky waved her hands as if swatting mosquitoes.

"I can't let you do that." Margaret looked at her friend. Becky's sweet round face. "I already owe you . . ."

"And you'll pay it all back," Becky said decisively, like it was settled. "I have no doubt."

Margaret pulled the blanket around her, so cold even in the summer breeze, and felt the tears coming again.

"Oh, love, don't do that," Becky had said. "It'll be all right. It's all going to be all right."

Margaret only nodded, as she did.

Becky lit two cigarettes and passed one over. They smoked in silence for a minute or two before she spoke again. "I just can't. I can't believe he . . ." She looked hard at Margaret. "He's a fool, Margie. Don't let it break you. Don't let that fucker win."

Margaret was pretty sure he'd already won. She had nothing left, never had and looked like she never would. Not even any fight left, it seemed.

Becky made all the arrangements. Margaret had an appointment on a Saturday. She would even pick her up. If she had snapped out of it all earlier, it's what she would have wanted. If she was thinking clearly, she had thought many times in the years that followed, that's what she would have wanted for herself. What she should have done. Would have. But for her mother.

The all-knowing, opinionated Annie had other plans, and Margaret was clueless as always until she walked down the stairs the next morning. Her mother and Genie sat at the kitchen table. They got quiet as she walked in. She should have turned around, but her mother motioned for her to sit.

Cup of tea poured in front of her, like a lamb being fattened for slaughter. Her mother spoke first.

"I know you're in trouble, ma fii. Your *friend*"—Annie spat out the word—"I heard your friend."

Margaret slunk back in her chair, knowing what her very Catholic mother was likely going to say. But she didn't say it. Instead, Annie turned to Genie and with a chin told her to go.

"I always wanted more children." Genie never was particularly graceful. She blurted out all her feelings right there at once, like she did. "I wanted lots and lots of babies. But God decided I could only carry Jerome."

Margaret cocked an eyebrow at Genie's sobs. If anyone could snap her out of her sadness, it would be annoying Genie.

"I didn't know I couldn't have more children. I didn't know. They didn't tell me," Genie started, not even she knew what she was talking about. "I thought I was just getting my appendix out."

Margaret looked at her, confused. Her mother didn't say anything.

"You remember when Jerome was little and we were living here awhile? When Joseph went to Stony?"

Talking like Stony was a place to visit and not a penitentiary. Margaret wanted to scoff but only nodded.

"Well, at first I went to stay with my cousin 'cause they weren't so far from there, so we could go visit. Joseph wanted that, to see his boy. And, well, my stomach, it got sick. It hurt so bad and I went to the nursing station and they said it would burst if they didn't operate." She stuffed a tissue to her nose but kept going. "They rushed me back to the city. Oh I was so scared. And I was going to call your mom but there wasn't time, and I hurt so bad. I signed something. I know I signed something but they didn't tell me. They didn't tell me that."

At this she just cried. Cried out at everyone and no one, and couldn't talk anymore. Even Margaret felt sympathy for her, however briefly.

After a moment Genie started again. "I still didn't know. Not until my monthlies didn't come. My stomach had stretched out and was hard, and my time didn't come. I would have thought I was expecting again, if your brother hadn't been inside. But it wasn't that. I went back to the nurse's station and they told me like I must have known, known that I had done that, like I would do that. 'But you signed it,' they said. 'You signed.' I don't remember reading it. I was screaming in pain and didn't even see clear and I thought I was signing, oh I don't know what I was signing. But no more babies. That's what it meant. No more. They took my guts out and didn't even tell me. I felt . . . I don't know what I felt. They had taken part of my body, my womb. They took it. And I couldn't have more babies. That's all I thought about. No more precious babies. Oh, we were going to have ten! But now I was barren. Useless and barren like an old lady at twenty-one!"

All cried out, she sat slouched and stared off, hands around her cold cup of tea. The three of them did that, just sat.

Then Margaret realized where this was going. She didn't have an opinion about it, not at first. At first she had only thought of what Genie had said. She'd heard of stuff like that happening. Crazy stories her brothers and cousins had told her. Things she didn't want to believe. People, from smaller places, up north mostly, not knowing what they were signing, or not even getting to sign. No paper needed for people who weren't treated like people. She never wanted to believe it, but like most things she heard about what they did to Indians, she should have.

But now, she knew what they were going to ask her, or what they wanted her to offer. She hadn't thought much about what happened next. She wanted to have a baby with Jacob, sure, but didn't think twice of getting rid of it when all that went to pot. She sort of knew what the procedure would be like, had read Dr. Morgentaler's book when it came out the year before. It was controversial, of course, but they had debated his case in class. Most students thought he was an immoral killer, but Margaret could see his point. What's more humane? Women had a right to decide what to do with their own bodies. He was supposed to start a clinic here in Winnipeg but it had been delayed a bunch of times. She couldn't wait. She'd have to go to some back-alley woman she knew nothing about. That was "sort of" clean. But still, when it came down to it, it was a relief when Becky suggested it. Margaret wasn't ready to be a mother, not like this, not alone.

But no one was asking her to.

"Um, so," she started, but didn't know where she was going to go.

Thankfully her mother continued for her. "It all fits, Margaret. You don't want to do . . . that. You will never be able to live with that. This is the old way. Good way. You can still see him grow up, and be his aunt."

Margaret couldn't see that either. Couldn't see anything. It all blurred somewhere in the future.

"Please." Genie's voice so low Margaret barely heard it. "Please let me, I would love to."

Margaret didn't really decide. She only did what she had been doing, what in her cold shock and pathetic sadness of that summer was all she could manage, what seemed the easiest. She nodded.

It was a very creepy clown. Margaret felt uncomfortable as she put the pieces around the dark eyes, white cheeks, a grin that could easily be seen as sinister. Late at night, her house all dark, mother snoring in the next room. She leaned back and lit a smoke, trying not to look at the eyes, the droopy mouth. She thought of that silly old urban legend about the girl doing a puzzle at night.

"Mom?" Elsie in the doorway and Margaret nearly knocked out of her skin. "Sorry, sorry. Didn't mean to scare you."

"No, no. It's, stupid puzzle." She looked long at her daughter standing there with her curly hair messy with sleep. She looked like she did when she was a chubby little kid. Blue eyes lined but awake. Her beautiful blue eyes. No one else in the family had blue eyes.

But then Margaret saw the pain in them. "Are you getting contractions?"

The girl nodded, like the child she still was, and started to cry as she bared down to a squat, holding on to the door frame. Margaret moved quick, butting out her smoke as she moved to the girl.

Elsie cried, "It hurts. It hurts, Mom!"

"Okay then, let's go get you checked out."

"Shouldn't we wake Mamere? And call Shawn!"

"No, no, let her sleep. I'll leave her a note. Phoenix is sleeping?"

Elsie nodded but started to sob again. "Where's Shawn?"

"I don't know. At his place, I think?"

The girl bared down again, already.

"We'll call him when we get there. We should go." Margaret grabbed her purse from the counter, her car keys.

Elsie stood still, and cried loud.

"No, no, none of that. Not like you haven't done this before." Margaret pushed her, almost gently, toward the door.

"But, I—"

Margaret knew Elsie wanted Annie, her comfort. The one she always wanted.

"Let her sleep," Margaret said again, trying to be soft. "She can explain to Phoenix in the morning. Phoenix is too young to know what's going on."

That seemed to do it. The girl nodded again, like someone who couldn't do anything else, and let herself be led out into the chill night.

Margaret was always proud of that. That she got to be there when Cedar-Sage was born. It was a quick labour. The baby came before the sun rose and Margaret got to be the first one to hold her. She was the one the doctor gave the wrapped baby to. Oh, Margaret relished that moment. That new, fresh baby face, wrinkled and soft. The baby didn't cry then, only looked. New eyes wide and her Grandmother's face was the very first one she saw. Margaret whispered to her then, breathed her breath on the baby like Grandmothers were supposed to, and hers was the first breath Cedar-Sage ever breathed.

YEAR THREE

9

PHOENIX

Tuesday is library day. Phoenix had to have a job so they gave her that. She doesn't mind. It's quiet. She gets to take her time and read the book spines and backs. She's good at reading, a bit slow but doesn't mind it. Not like some. She likes the stories, the real-life ones mostly. Like the crime and murder and crazy shit that happened in real life, that was probably her favourite stuff. She's read about the Manson family, Jonestown, a bunch of those satanic murders from the eighties. Chris told her she should be careful, he might have to report her, but she's pretty sure he was joking. They're not that fucking stupid. She just likes it. How people knew the psychos were crazy when they were kids by how they tortured cats and shit, how they themselves rationalized what they did, how they were all batshit but in different ways. It got her thinking about psychology, so she started reading this old Introduction to Psychology textbook. It was like from the nineties, but that didn't seem to matter for a lot of the stuff. She was surprised psychology wasn't all about psychos, that it's about how people think and learn and what brains did. It was still interesting but in a different way.

Chris seems pleased with her and her reading. She does her library job, cleaning the library room and reorganizing the books, well enough. She gets to stay in the solitary cell/room as long as she behaves and keeps it clean. Phoenix never minds the cleaning, and the behaving is easy after she got drugged properly.

They got her off the Diazepam 'cause it made her fuzzy and forgetful, but put her on a high-dose SSRI. At first she thought it was fucking stupid 'cause she was never really all that depressed, but it did level her off pretty good. Now it's like she gets mad but not that mad, and sad but not that sad. She never gets really happy either, but that isn't new. It helps her, as Ben calls it, live in the moment. Ben's big on the moment and the present and not going too far in the past or future. He also harps on and on about meditating, but Phoenix isn't fucking all that Zen just fucking yet.

She also gets to stay in the solitary wing because the Centre's overcrowded, or at least that's what Chris told her, but really, Phoenix thinks they got wise and put all the psychos in one place to keep an eye on them better. Kai is in here too, on one side of Phoenix. She's bipolar with psychotic episodes and has borderline personality disorder and anxiety, or at least that's what she will tell anyone who will listen. Her blue hair faded to a grey and grew out so her light brown roots are almost down to her ears. She also talks about that all the fucking time, how the first thing she's going to do when she gets out is go to a real nice salon and fix her hair. Her mom is going to take her. Her mom is a big lady who visits every week or so, always bringing her stuff and telling her she is the best and all that. Kai comes back with new sweats and pictures of her cousins, all of whom idolize her. Or so she says.

Kai also threatens to commit suicide at least once a week, and does weird shit like cram a bunch of clothes in her toilet to flood her cell/room. She steals Phoenix's shit too, if Phoenix gives her the opportunity. First time she did that, Phoenix ran in there ready to pound on the bitch, but Kai curled up into a ball on her bed and started crying and howling, saying she didn't mean it, she didn't mean it. Thing is, Phoenix actually, like, felt sorry for her. She didn't feel all that mad. She lowered her arm and took back her fucking towel and went back to her room/cell. Phoenix didn't know who was more surprised, Kai, who sat up and stopped crying, Chris, who stood down the hall with his arms out, ready to go, or Phoenix, who sat on her bed for a long time after, staring up at the window where she could only see the sky, and even forgot she was angry, like it was no big deal or whatever.

That's when she realized she really was on pills, maybe was really depressed and thankfully not all that psycho. Which she knew by comparing herself to Kai but also to Dene. Dene's on the other side, bigger even than Phoenix and always blubbering like an idiot. At first Phoenix thought she was delayed, like mentally and shit, but Dene is worse off than that. She likes to pretend, or really thinks, that she's a little kid. She talks in a baby voice, and has a doll they let her keep for some fucking reason. Phoenix thinks it is pretty fucking stupid but hey, if it makes the crazy bitch happy. She also does shit like wet the bed and herself and always smells like piss. She's mostly quiet though, and'll sit out in the hall, on the floor by the window, holding her doll and staring out the windows for hours. Phoenix thinks she must not be all that psycho or else she'd be in the fucking psych ward, but what does she know.

Ben comes on Mondays for sure and other days if he has some time. He never comes on weekends. He always comes in the morning, sometimes with a go mug full of coffee or brings a couple donuts. He sometimes brings some for Dene or Kai too but he only ever talks with Phoenix. The others go off to their programs or jobs and Phoenix has the wing for just them. They started sitting on the couches in the hall after Ben complained the plastic chair hurt his back, and Phoenix was okay with that 'cause no one else was around. Not that she ever says much but in case she ever does.

He tells his stories, talks about his wife and grandkids. He has two daughters and three grandkids. Phoenix knows them all by heart. Francine is his wife, Fancy he calls her, they have been together for almost ten years but she isn't the mom to his kids. She has a son who has a son, and that's Ben's first grandkid, Oliver. Oliver is eight and plays hockey. Ben spends a lot of time driving Oliver around to hockey games and shit. His proper kids are Mel and Jazz and they are in their thirties. Their moms are different, one good, one bad news, but that doesn't matter anymore 'cause he isn't with them anymore. Jazz doesn't have any kids, but Mel has two, a girl and a boy, and they live near him and he drives them around places too. They all seem to have a lot of programs like dance or sports or some shit. That's what Ben says his life is like, driving people around. He has a van and doesn't seem to mind. He never thought he'd have a life like that so he really enjoys it. He thought he'd be dead or in prison by now, he says that a lot. Most likely dead, he always adds.

Ben also does a lot of ceremony. Weekends he does ceremonies. He has a lodge out of town, a place he shares with a few other people. A nice place in the bush by the river, he says. He does naming ceremonies, blessing ceremonies, and a whole bunch of things Phoenix has never even heard of, but he tells her about them, about how he was taught by an Elder he met when he was in prison and went on to follow his dreams into the healing life. That's what he says, follow his dreams, but it isn't like how people usually say it. For him it's actually following his real actual dreams. He dreams things and then does them. That's how he became a pipe carrier, and that's how he found he had the gift of naming. That's also why he started working in youth corrections because a dream had told him to.

It sounded stupid at first to Phoenix, but then she got used to him. And when you got used to Ben, you got used to him talking crazy shit about his dreams all the time. They're like another kind of his stories, and he is always telling stories, about his life, his old life, his dreams, but the old, old stories are her favourite. Wiindigoo stories, especially.

"Hey there, my friend, how are you this morning?"

"Okay."

"You still reading that textbook? Man, that thing is big. What are you learning about today?"

"Memory." Phoenix pauses. She wants to say it right. "How we put what we know that are, like, the same into groups and only remember things as, like, groups."

"Sounds like stereotypes."

She thinks about this for a while.

"It's a nice day out today. Feels like spring. Never used to melt this much when I was a kid. When I was a kid we had snow up to our armpits and froze all the way through all winter. Not like you kids, always warm and inside. You guys got it easy."

Phoenix scoffs at this, but only a bit.

"Oliver had a hockey tournament this weekend so we went up to Sagkeeng and was in that arena all weekend. Was colder in there than outside. Good thing they have a Tim's out there. I never asked you, are you a tea girl, Phoenix, or coffee? Which do you like better?"

Phoenix always takes a while to answer his questions but he always waits. "Never drank coffee, but I like tea. With milk and sugar. It's okay."

"You're like me. I like tea and lots of sugar. Can't have sugar anymore, not since the diabetes, but I like it. That fake stuff is no good, no good at all. Rots your insides worse than sugar, if you ask me, so now I suffer through without anything at all, just milk and tea. It's no fun getting old. But Fancy, no, she like coffee best. She drinks it black, like just black, nothing in at all, and dark, she says the darker the better. Stuff's like pitch-black that stuff she drinks, can't see through it at all. No wonder she has so much energy, that woman, I tell you. She's never tired."

Phoenix kind of half smiles. She knows all about Fancy but has never met her or anything. Fancy is a nurse and ten years younger than Ben. And he's never loved anyone like he loves her. Phoenix always remembers that, that time he got a faraway look in his eye, and it wasn't fucking pervy or anything, just faraway, and Phoenix knew he was thinking of his woman, Fancy, and that he loved her. Phoenix likes that. It sounds nice.

"So how you feeling today, my friend? How was your weekend?"

"All right. I played cards with Kai mostly."

"Did I ever tell you about the time I almost lost my cousin's car playing poker?"

Phoenix shakes her head, even though he had told her before, but this way he tells it again. He always tells it a little bit different anyway. She likes when he tells his stories. She doesn't have to talk, only listen.

The story ends with him and his cousin racing off in the almost-taken car. That was the winter he spent in Alberta. When he's done he says, "You know, winter is almost over, so if you want a wiindigoo story, today might be the last day I can do it. Can't tell them once it's spring."

"Yeh, maybe." She's pretty sure she knows all his old wiindigoo stories, he's been telling them to her all last winter and this one. They're like the movies Cedar used to watch over and over when they were kids. They only had two DVDs, really, Pocahontas and Finding Nemo, and they must have watched those two a thousand times each, but somehow each time Phoenix saw something different or remembered something differently. Sometimes she just liked to hear them playing in the background while she did something else. They were comforting or some shit.

"I know you like these monster cannibals and all, but did you know some people think they weren't real at all?"

She nods, but he really doesn't check her for an answer.

"Some people think they were just stories warning people about starvation, because some winters people got so hungry they actually thought about eating each other. This was many years ago, when everyone followed the buffalo, or if they were further north, the deer, and when they couldn't find them, which was most of the winter, if they didn't have enough food, they'd starve. Then later, when the game was all overhunted and gone and people were stuck on reserves because they weren't allowed off, they were starving again. This time they would be waiting for rations, but a lot of the time rations didn't come, or if they did, there wasn't enough or it was all rotten, so they were starving again. Starving and beaten down. I think about that a lot, how my Great-Grandfather or Great-Great-Grandfather must have felt starving and stuck all those winters. That must have felt pretty hopeless. I remember thinking that when I was in prison and feeling pretty stuck. And cold! It's so cold up in Stony. That old building is so old and not well heated, or at least it wasn't when I was there. My whole time there, it was always cold, those three years. I told you about that, hey? When I went to jail that time?"

Phoenix nods 'cause she knows he'll be looking this time. But she also leans back into the couch. The sun shining bright. One of those super-clear kind of days that happens in the winter, makes it feel like winter isn't so bad.

"It was for stealing. I was only nineteen. Even eighteen maybe. This was before my kids were born, before I had a decent thought in my head. I was running around with these guys and up to all sorts. The stealing wasn't the worst of it but it was what I got caught for and I don't remember thinking a thing about it. I mean not just the consequences, but I didn't think I'd get caught or could get caught, thought I was just so smart and clever. But it was more than that. I didn't think I was doing anything wrong. I mean, not really. I was a poor kid, not poor like some, but we never had much. After we moved to the city, my sisters and parents and I all shared a two-bedroom apartment, the upstairs of this duplex. It was so small you could whisper from one side and hear it on the other. My sisters, there were three of them, all needed their space so they shared a double bed in one room, my parents the other, and I got the couch. I was on that couch for five years. And I was fine with it because I never had much more than that, hey? So when I started stealing, I started stealing from people who had more than me, which was everybody. But they didn't do anything better than me, I thought. What did they do to deserve all those things, those cars and houses and nice furniture? I didn't think that was fair. I remember this one house we broke into, the one we got caught for, it was a real nice house. It had like four bedrooms, all perfect. And the lady had all this jewellery, and the basement had one of those rec rooms with a bar and a freezer full of food. I remember thinking this is what I want with my life—a nice rec room with one of those chairs where you pull a lever and they go back. That's all I wanted. I thought it was so neat. And you know what, I got one of those now! Yeh, I got one in our new house we bought a few years ago. They're called recliners. Didn't know that back then, didn't know that 'til the salesman told me that's what they were called. And I have one now. I love it. I love my recliner. Thing is, back then I didn't know how to get it, didn't think I could get it, so I tried the only way I knew how. I tried to steal it. Well, not the recliner, I didn't take that, but I took other stuff. I took it because that was the only way I could think to get it. That night, the guys I was with took a bunch of booze and we took the jewellery and stuff, but I also took a bunch of steaks. I grabbed like five of those steak packages from the deep freeze and took them home and cooked my family a big meal. Told my mom I had gone to that Moffat's Men temporary work place and got a job for the day. She knew I couldn't get a real one, but she never thought I was doing all the trouble I was doing. That was the worst part about getting caught—my mom going to court and crying when I got time. My dad wasn't sad, he said he knew I was trouble and was ashamed of me and hard like that, but my mom was all heart. Wore her heart on her sleeve, that woman, was always so kind, and was so hurt I would do something bad. That's when I vowed to get better. To not do criminal things anymore, anyway. Seeing my mom upset like that when I went down, I knew I couldn't do anything like that again."

Ben's stories always go like that. All winding and seeming to not make sense. But after he leaves, Phoenix ends up thinking about them, thinking about all the things he said and'll nod to herself. She can relate to him being a messed-up kid. To people having more than her and thinking they didn't deserve it. Wondering why they had something that she didn't. Why the world ended up like that. She can't relate to the sad mom thing though. Whenever Elsie cried, Phoenix just wanted to get the fuck out of there or she'd smash something. Not her face though, so maybe that meant she actually cared, or something.

"Oh but you wanted to hear a wiindigoo story, hey? Before the ground melts. We should stop talking about them until the snow falls again. Ever wonder why you like wiindigoo stories? I always wonder that, why I like what I like and stuff, hey? Like I really like, have always liked, roogaaroo stories. I love them roogaaroo stories. You know, like those werewolves. Of course you know, they're Métis, roogaaroos are. Just like you. I always ask storytellers their roogaaroo stories. I am greedy for them. I think I like them because I use to be like that, or feel like that. I used to think I would change like that and couldn't help it, not at the full moon but when I was, say, drinking or something, I would change and not be myself. I would become like the roogaaroo, like a monster. I did that with my woman back in the day, with Mel's mom. She was so good and so patient with me, like my ma, she had her heart right there for the world to see, but I was mean, and I was still drinking then and I would yell and sometimes I would push her. I remember not feeling bad for her either, like I would feel bad about what I did, but I was jealous of her. She came from a good family, they were Métis like my ma, but they were lucky and had a house they owned and everything, and my woman Mel's mom was really fair-skinned and had light hair so everyone thought she was white, hey? So I thought, I thought that meant she had an easy life. She didn't. She had her own struggles, like we all do, but I thought she had it easy, so even though I was mean to her, even though I said mean things to her and pushed her and stuff, I thought she could handle it, I thought she didn't have all the stuff in her life like I had had stuff in my life so she could handle one bad thing happening to her. Isn't that awful? I was wrong, of course. I was really wrong to do that, and she left me, finally, like she should have all along, and she took my baby girl, Mel, who deserved better than me. When her parents came to get her things, it was her dad, who was old by that time already, and her mom who was quiet like her, and they packed up her things, all quiet like. I remember the dad telling me, 'Billy'—that was her brother—'Billy,' he told me, 'he wanted to come but I didn't trust him not to beat you up, and I don't want my son getting into trouble for what you started. The only reason we're not calling the cops is because you have a daughter now, so go work and make money for her so she can have a good life. We'll pray for you, but if you ever hurt my daughter again, I will kill you.' I remember being scared actually because this was not the kind of man who just threatened people and I figured if he said it, he could actually do it. But I was also really ashamed at myself and how I acted. That made me mad for a long time, and then I would do stupid things when I was mad and get ashamed about that too, over and over, until I stopped. So, what was I saying?"

Sometimes Phoenix was sure Ben did get off track and didn't know what the fuck he was talking about, but other times, more times now, she's pretty sure he's faking it, to see if she's listening, or to see if she can tell what he's talking about, if she can relate and think about her own life and shit. All Ben's stories seem to be the same as Phoenix's life. When she first thought about it, she thought he might be trying to trick her. But then she thought he might just be like her. Or her like him. And if that was it, if he could have a good life after all the trouble he caused, the hurt he caused . . .

Phoenix never finishes that thought though. Never.

"The roogaaroo. You were talking about the roogaaroo."

"Oh yeh, the roogaaroo . . ." He leans forward and rubs his hands together like he does sometimes and has a confused look on his face. "Why was I talking about the roogaaroo?"

"You like, you like roogaaroo stories. I like wiindigoo stories."

"Oh yeh, yeh, you do. You know, some people think wiindigoo stories aren't about the wiindigoo at all but they're about mental illness. Like if the roogaaroo is our rage then the wiindigoo are about things that go wrong in our heads. They used to have wiindigoo hunters in villages. Like for real. Wiindigoo hunters. Those were the people that had to go fix the wiindigoo, either through ceremony or if they didn't get better, by killing them. They would do these crazy ceremonies because the wiindigoo were all frozen, right, so you know what cured them?"

Phoenix shakes her head.

"Fire. Fire and sweat. So they would take these people who were called wiindigoo and put them in the lodge and they would sweat out the wiindigoo and that would make them better, or not. Some people couldn't be helped but I think most were. I think most were probably just needing some love and that's what ceremony does. But we all, we like a good story, hey? We're all just gossips, so we only ever remember all the bad ones, hey?

"They had trials too. They made committees of hunters and they would decide what to do with these wiindigoo. I bet they all hoped they could cure them but couldn't cure everybody. You know who they think was a wiindigoo? I love this story. Did I tell you this one? You remember Thomas Scott? Of course you do, good Métis girl like you. Thomas Scott is the guy everyone thinks was killed by Louis Riel but he wasn't. He was sentenced to die by tribunal, and that tribunal, they think, was to determine if he was a wiindigoo. Can you believe it? So cool! Unfortunately they didn't think he could be cured so he was killed by firing squad and then they hid the body. No one knows where they put him 'cept the two guys who took 'im, and they went to their graves never telling anybody. That's what you do with a wiindigoo, you bury them where no one knows, so they can't go lure someone else to their grave and make them wiindigoo too. Those two guys never told anyone. Lived to be old men but never told a soul. Can you imagine? That blew my mind when I heard that. There are other stories like that, about wiindigoo hunters and tribunals. Quite a few people went to jail for doing wiindigoo trials and stuff, sentenced by the Canada court because they, the Canadians, didn't think communities should be killing people or curing them for being wiindigoo or anything like that. But can you imagine? Wiindigoo hunters. Cool, hey?"

Phoenix only nods. Her mind spinning with things. That's another thing about Ben's stories, there's so much of them. She has to wait until he's done to think about them. To unwind them. She'll sometimes be, like, doing something else days later and think about one of his stories but in a completely new way. That's how she knows Ben isn't only an old guy who talks a lot, his stories have real medicine, they stay with her and make her feel better even when he is away.

"So never mind me talking so much, must have had too much tea this morning. You want a wiindigoo, so here's one, here's an end-of-winter story I heard once from this old woman I met when I was staying in Alberta. Man, that was some beautiful country. Beautiful people, beautiful stories too. This old woman must have been about ninety back then so she's long passed into the spirit world, but what a lady. You could tell she was really pretty when she was younger, and when she was younger, this one winter night . . ."

Phoenix leans back into the couch a bit more. She's so warm in the sun on the couch. She's fallen asleep to Ben's stories before, some days when she's so tired. He doesn't seem to mind, must have seen her close her eyes and then come to a bit later. He told her it doesn't matter. Stories work their magic even when you're sleeping so she wasn't missing any of their medicine at all.

She first thinks of it one night when she's playing cards with Kai. Kai is really good at this Filipino game called pusoy dos. She was the worst explainer ever but once Phoenix got the hang of it, that's all they play. It's better with more people but Dene is crying in the corner, quietly pissing herself and rocking her doll, and Chris doesn't join in anymore. He used to but Kai didn't put up with him much and usually would just start doing some of her crazy shit like talking about all the guys she used to fuck until Chris ended up having to tell her off. So he sits around and reads the paper instead. It's still light out. After all those months of dark so early, it's nice to have the light still out.

Every now and then, when she isn't a total ass, Kai's good shit, so Phoenix thought she'd be one to ask. "Ever do, like, ceremony?"

"Yeh. Course. My Grandpa was a powerful Elder. He did the Shaking Tent ceremony. That's why I'm so nuts. I'm not, not really, just full of spirits now."

Good shit maybe, but also fucking full of it. Phoenix doesn't say anymore, just deals the cards.

"We used to do ceremony all the time, when we lived back home. Not so much once we moved to the city, after my Grandpa died."

"Do you got your, like, Indian name?" Phoenix says, setting up her cards in pairs and suits.

"Yeh. Course. I got that when I was born. I even had a walking out ceremony."

"What's that?"

"That's when you're one and you, like, walk on grass for the first time. It's a really big deal. My Grandpa was so powerful, so my ceremonies like that were a big deal. Everyone came out to them."

Phoenix never heard about that one but she knows about people getting their names, sometimes when they were babies, sometimes when they were older. Ben had said he got his when he got out of prison, so he was already an adult.

"You don't have your name?" Kai laughs a bit, 'cause she's being a bitch like that. "You gotta have your name, else you can't hear it when your ancestors call you home."

Phoenix doesn't say anything, but she remembers this forever, likes the sound of it. Pictures a bunch of old people in the clouds, singing like angels with their arms out, waiting for her. Calling her name.

"How do I—? What if I wanted to get my name?" she asks Ben the next time he comes around.

"Well, first you have to ask for it, traditional like, with tobacco. And then I have to start filling in forms. They check how you've been and if you're okay to have a ceremony in here."

"It would be in here?"

"Could do. Just need to bring my bundle and spread it out. I've done it before. They like to have more guards around when I do it, because I'm so powerful, hey? Naw, I'm just jossing you. I just bring a lot of stuff they don't usually let in."

"Do you think I . . . could?"

He leans back and sighs, like he's really thinking of it. Like he would. "Well, you've stayed out of trouble, if that's what you mean.

But it's a big responsibility to get your name. You can't just do it to do it. There're responsibilities."

Phoenix nods like she knows. But all she really knows is that she likes the sound of it. A name. A way for her ancestors to call her.

"You know, if it gets approved, you can invite family to come. Maybe your mom?"

Phoenix shakes her head right away. "I, I don't even know where she is."

"We can see if we can track her down?" Ben is never pushy, but even he can't hide being happy. Phoenix has been seeing it, in these adults around her. Every time she does something right, everyone gets so fucking happy. It's embarrassing.

Phoenix shakes her head again. "But my sister, Cedar, she can come. She's in care. I think."

"Yeh, she'd be easy to find. We can ask. We might not get it but we can ask."

Phoenix nods. She can't help but feel a little happy too. A little.

"You have to be sure, you know. And you have to ask me properly. Now, we don't have any tobacco but maybe we could do a handshake for now."

Phoenix nods again, and feels shy all over.

"Well, go on, ask me." The old man leans forward in his chair now. Sticks his big hand out.

"Will you?" she stumbles. "Can I . . . get my name?"

"Sure." He smiles. And takes her outstretched hand. His is warm, smooth, and wraps all the way over hers.

She pulls her hand back quick and shoves it back in her hoodie pocket.

It's the first time she has touched anyone, besides a fight or getting restrained or some shit, in fucking years.

10

CEDAR

"I want to try and see my sister." It comes out more of a blurt than words. "And my mom. If I can." As quick as I can before I lose my nerve.

I know by how my dad puts his fork down and clears his throat, his hand in a fist in front of his face, how Nikki looks at him as if, for once, she doesn't know what to say, but I know exactly what they are going to say. I know I shouldn't have said anything. Even Faith gives her mom this side eye that makes me think she knows more than I ever thought. Faith, with her usual indifference, always making me feel both ignored and annoying.

It takes a while before anyone says anything. No one eats. Only Faith pretends and pushes her mashed potatoes around her otherwise empty plate. When he finally does talk, my dad's calm seems practised.

"What brought this on?"

I shrug but don't look down, not yet.

I get that it must seem like it's out of nowhere. No one has ever said anything about my mom and Phoenix, least of all me. Holidays and their birthdays have passed without any mention of them. Only I know them, think of them, talk to them in my head. Imagine calling them up and saying hi. For all her talking, Nikki never talks about the one thing I really want to talk to her about. Or at least what I always think about. I don't know if I want to talk about it anymore. But now that I've said it, I can't un-say it.

"I dunno," I say. I feel defeated. I poke my fork into the butter melting a swirl on the potatoes. "It's just been so long since I've heard from them."

"They might not be doing that well," Nikki says like she knows what that means, and takes a gulp of her wine.

"I know your mom would see you, if she could." My dad, the only one who actually looks at me.

I catch the annoyed look Nikki gives him. That gets me mad enough to keep going. "I know we can, like, leave a message for her with the social worker. That's what I did before."

Faith starts eating again, her dainty little half bites, but her eyes dart around, watching the show.

"But that was when you were in care," Nikki says. "She knows you're not in care anymore. Doesn't she?" She looks to Shawn, who nods slightly. "So what good would it do?"

I sigh, if only to build up more courage. "She's gotta be somewhere. And you're right, she would see me if she could."

Nikki leans back in her chair, pushing her plate away.

"And, well, we know where Phoenix is. Or at least, who to talk to, right?" I've always known this process, of workers talking to workers who set things up. It's an easy but endless system of messages and "we'll see" and waiting. I have done this forever. More years than I've done other things. Don't see how it would be any different now.

"I don't know if I'm comfortable with that," Nikki snorts and takes another gulp of wine.

I look at her, a little longer than I should. Don't have to ask, she'll tell me anyway.

"I mean, she's a dangerous criminal, Cedar. I don't think she'd be a very good influence on you."

I take a breath and put my fork down.

"I know she was," Nikki sighs. "I know you lived with her when you were little but you haven't seen her in years, Cedar. Years. You have no idea what she's like now. If she'd even want to talk to you."

"She's my sister," I manage.

"Faith's your sister now. And we're your family. You should be thanking your lucky stars you have a roof over your head and food on the table but no, you want to dredge up old things and make everyone upset. Ruin dinner." Her eyes fill with tears and she gets up to go refill her glass. She pauses at the sink for a moment, to stare out the window and "get herself together." She does this when she's upset.

I take another deep breath and look over at my dad, who shakes his head in that way he does when we should leave her be.

So I do. I clear the table, carefully start to load the dishwasher exactly how I was taught to. I walk around Nikki's shaking back at the sink and don't even flinch when she snaps, "Oh just leave it!" I go to my room and turn on some tunes and review my bio homework.

After they go to bed, I can hear Nikki yelling at my dad in their room. I can't make out more than a few words, but I'm not surprised at the ones that slink through their door and across the hall. I've heard them before. "Fucking monster," "freak," "junkie loser," "nowhere near me and my daughter," "my house!"

Downstairs, Faith turns her music up, and when I finally fall asleep it's to my dad's calm drone and Faith Evans singing "I'll Be Missing You."

I didn't say another thing about it, but didn't forget it either. I never get how people forget things. People who are so happy and never seem to think about anything but what's right in front of them. Looking around my school, all the girls who are obviously so insecure and hungry, the guys who are so hard up and angry, but everyone still laughing like life's a fricking party. Looking at them, I can understand the meaning of the phrase "ignorance is bliss." Other than that, I am pretty sure I live on an alien planet. Or maybe I am the alien. Either way, no one around me is anything like me.

Grade eleven now and I still don't have any friends. Not real friends. There's a few kids I talk to in class, who ask me for notes if they missed, who might even crack a joke with me about a teacher or something else in our mutual school world. Or we like each other's posts on whatever. But it never goes more than that. I took driver's ed last semester and my driving partner was the girl who was always late so didn't have a choice who her partner was. She was still always late, so I mostly had to practise with the instructor on my own. He was nice enough, but I didn't really want to be in the car alone with him after school, especially once it got dark.

Faith broke up with her stoner boyfriend, only to start going out with a jock. Her friends are pretty much the same, only some are now cheerleaders. I know one of them from an English class, Sydney, and she's pretty nice. The others are something like Hailey, Bailey, maybe another Sydney, and super bitchy. It is all so cliché it's laughable. Most days I feel like I'm watching an updated John Hughes movie unfold in real time. I can predict where it all goes. They all end the same. Only I am forever Duckie, without an Andie or any real purpose at all.

Nikki and my dad are barely around during the week, so they don't even notice this. Nikki keeps making passing comments about "your friends" and "your pals," never notices when Faith snickers. I know I am that friendless freak of the school. I don't really care much. Not really.

On weekends I like to hang out with my dad. We watch hockey and sports news mostly. Sometimes football. Sometimes movies. I still don't know that much about all the sports, but enough to keep up in conversation. I might even like it. Though I think he can tell I'm into the movies more. Action, only action. Maybe a few in the suspense category, maybe a comedy. I can't do horror, and drama is always too boring. We've watched all the *John Wicks*, *Fast and Furiouses*, anything Jason Statham or the Rock is in. I make the best popcorn in the air popper, so that's my job, and we always order pizza or burgers or chicken. It's truly great.

If we're still up when Nikki gets home, then it all becomes about

Nikki. She'll have to talk about her day, talk about her co-workers, talk about herself. Even if we're in the middle of a movie, we have to stop it or else miss everything because she'll talk either way. I can't fricking stand it and try to be in bed well before. Took me years before I realized Nikki never actually asks about anyone else's day. Once I noticed, though, I couldn't un-notice.

But I keep going, always doing my chores. Even doing Faith's most of the time. Not that she seems to care, or notice. I still do all my homework right away, and watch the things my dad wouldn't like during the week. I even got into makeup tutorials, and got really good at contouring and kind of good at eyebrows. It's all completely fine with me. Better than any foster place. Better than that place in the country because no one yells at me. Better than Luzia's because at least I'm not so sad like I was. It's not better than Tannis's though, because even if we never got enough food and it was all horrible, at least then Sparrow was around. Definitely not better than when I was small and lived in the red house in Lego Land because even though my mom wasn't always well and Phoenix was always mad at me and Sparrow's stupid dad was there, we were all together. My dad is awesome, Nikki is fine, Faith is whatever. But they are not my family. Not like that, anyway.

I've always been sad, in a way. It's kind of like a hardened sad, like how pudding gets a crust over top if you leave it too long. I have a crust on me. I can feel it. Pretty sure everyone can see it, too. That's why things are the way they are. That's why everyone always stays away.

The first time I thought about dying was right after Sparrow died. It seemed to make sense. My sister died. I had no one. I could die and be with her. But I didn't know, really, what that meant or how to even do it.

By the time I got to Luzia's, I think I had it all figured out. I thought I just had to take a bunch of Tylenol and I would keep sleeping. I wanted that more than anything. Wanted my brain to stop thinking of all the things it kept thinking. That I didn't want it to be thinking. I wanted to simply stop. Not be sad or be anything, really. I wanted to just stop.

But I couldn't get anywhere near pills at Luzia's so I had to buy my own. I only had, like, less than twenty dollars so I took that and snuck off from school one lunch hour. That alone took me months to be brave enough to do. Not that it was all that hard. Kids left the school grounds at lunch all the time. But I thought someone would see me if I did, so it took me a while.

When I got to the convenience store, they only had those travel bottles, so I got one of those and a Slurpee and a hot dog. I thought that'd be enough. Walked back to school with it bouncing in my pocket, so sure the teachers could hear it and know what I was up to.

I hadn't yet learned how invisible I am. Always am.

No one asked. No one found out. And a few nights later, I swallowed all of them. It took a long time because I was awful at swallowing pills. Had to chew most of them and they tasted so gross. But I got through and then lay down like it was any other night, only I didn't think I'd get up.

I did though. Luzia knocked on my door in the morning like she always did in the mornings and I was groggy but most definitely alive. I told her I was sick and stayed in bed all day. Slept 'til I heard Nevaeh get home from school. My head was kind of sore. Kind of cloudy. But not dead. Definitely not dead.

I took it as a learning opportunity and thought I only needed a little more next time.

"Okay, your dad and I have talked and thought about this a long time," Nikki starts with her hands folded in front of her, nodding to my dad across the glass dining table. I sit and wait, knowing what's coming. "I know you're missing your mom, your biological mother, and your first sister, Phoenix, and that's hard, I know. But sometimes, just because you miss someone doesn't mean you have to see them, you know?" She doesn't wait for an answer, or even a nod. "But she's your mom, biological mother, I get that. It's important to have your closure or whatever you want to call it. So I did call that social worker. I did try. And she said she only has an old number that's disconnected now and one for some guy named Toby that no one ever answers and there's no voicemail. So there's nothing else she can do. She said that the only way she can get ahold of your mom is if your mom checks in. And she hasn't. That's all she can do. You can't help someone who doesn't help themselves." Nikki stops with a quick intake of breath, and then exhales loud, like she's stopping herself from saying more.

"I remember she used to live at this grey house. She pointed it out to me one time. Could someone, like, go there?" I try but I know the answer even before I'm done saying it.

"That social worker has so many cases. It took her a week to get back to me as it is. I really don't think she has the time for this."

"But you, we, I could point it out."

"Cedar, I am not going up to the fu—to the North End and knocking on random doors. Do you know how dangerous that is? Do you know what kind of people live there?"

Shawn finally says something. "Now, now, it's not that bad, Nik. It *is* a pretty wild plan, though, C. Like a needle in a haystack kind of plan."

"But," I start, but I don't know what I want to say, not really.

My dad smiles. It feels like a sad smile. "I did get ahold of your Uncle Joe, who called your other uncle, Alex, who lives here. He says he sees her the odd time, but she doesn't have a phone. He said he'd let Alex know, though, next time he sees her. It's not hopeless. She is somewhere."

"As long as no one is going up into bad neighbourhoods," Nikki continues.

"No one is going anywhere." My dad puts his hand up like he is literally stopping her right there.

I think about this. I could look on Facebook again. All those maybe cousins and family my mom would always mention. I've looked through the list of Strangers so many times, trying to remember the names my mom used to mention, but the only ones I'm really sure of are Grandma, whose name was Margaret, and Mom's brothers Joe and Alex, and they weren't even Strangers.

"As for Phoenix, though— Cedar, you need to look at me." Nikki's makeup is smeared a bit around her eyes, like she had been rubbing them. That's how I know she was stressed. "I really don't think you should see her, hon." The last word, half word, clung like an afterthought. Like it didn't ring true. "She's just . . . it's just that we don't know what she's like, and you don't either. She has done horrible, unthinkable things, and I don't think you should be spending time with someone like that. Even if you do share some DNA. I mean, what if, what if she did something to hurt you too? I would never, ever forgive myself if something happened to you." She didn't add a "hon" this time, only tears. Big sloppy crying-in-front-of-me tears that meant she must be really upset.

I didn't say anything. Just let her cry. Like this was happening to Nikki more than it was happening to me, and in a lot of ways it was.

"You're in such a good place right now. You're doing so good! And I—we don't want anything to jeopardize that, not for anything. You should concentrate on being a kid, hanging out with your friends and getting through high school. You shouldn't be worrying about things you have no control over, you know? You should just let what's in the past stay there. You're better than that. Better than them."

I can feel the speech's end, and them looking at me, so I nod. But if they asked me what I was nodding at, I wouldn't've been able to say.

"Okay, then. I hope that can be the end of that," Nikki says and gets up.

I don't think she meant it to sound so much like a threat.

Or maybe she did.

The second time was my first winter here. Nikki always had plenty of painkillers and even a bunch of prescriptions. I didn't know what Diazepam would do so I stuck to the Costco-size Tylenol. I took a few more than last time and still woke up. Slept through my alarm but woke up breathing. I took more then but only slept 'til it was dark. And I was starving so I decided to do more research and try again later.

—

The Friday after the no-seeing-Phoenix talk, there wasn't a game on, so my dad and I rewatch the first John Wick and get an extra-large pep and mushroom. Love that movie, except for the puppy part.

"We should get a puppy," I say to avoid the scene.

"I wish." My dad takes a bite of pizza that takes off half the slice. "Nikki thinks she's allergic." His mouth is full as he talks. It's endearing. Like he's more relaxed with me than with anyone. He'd never do anything like that in front of Nikki. She'd say something about it and he'd get embarrassed.

"She *thinks* she's allergic?"

"I think she's just allergic to the possible mess."

I laugh but think on this awhile. My dad has a way of saying things inside of other things. We've watched John Wick so much we can talk through it. We stop to watch the big action sequences but know it so well, it's easy for us to jump in and out. It's different than when Nikki does it.

"Did you ever have a dog?" I ask him.

"Naw. Had a cat once. His name was Gilbert. He was cool."

"What happened to him?"

"He ran off. He liked to go out and roam the neighbourhood. Was a free man, was Gilbert."

I love how my dad gets when it's only us talking. It makes me brave.

"Did you hear back from anyone? From my Uncle Joe?"

"I talked to your uncle again. He said his brother called him but nothing new. Alex has a lot going on." He looks over to me, like checking. "I got the impression he doesn't think your mom is doing too well."

I nod and choke back something. "She hasn't been doing well for a while. Not since Sparrow."

My dad gives me this half smile for comfort. "That would mess me up. I think that would mess anyone up for good." He pushes at my knee with his knee like he does sometimes. His version of a hug.

"Sparrow's dad, too, wasn't a good person." I never talk about the past past, the part where my dad was supposed to be around. Don't want to make him feel guilty. I've never mentioned Sparrow's dad. Never wanted to.

"Yeh, your mom, when I knew her anyway, she was always kind of sad. She had this . . . sadness I guess that made you want to take care of her. I can see how she could get in with the wrong people. I mean . . . I should have been there, for her, for all you guys, of course. But two years is a long time and she was young and alone with two kids. Well, she had her family, but she was alone."

I take another slice and drink of my Coke. I don't want to say what I'm thinking. About when he got out of jail and still didn't come around.

"How is—how's Joe doing?" I ask him. My uncle. My mom's brother. Even though it feels like he's more of my dad's friend than my relative.

"Joe's doing good. Working in Banff, he said. That's a beautiful place, holy sh—smokes. You'd love it there."

"He doesn't ever, like, come visit?"

"Him? No. I don't think he's ever been back here. He doesn't talk to anyone, really. His dad, Sasha, and his brother once in a while but . . . Joe didn't really get along with most of his family. His dad too, he said. After his mom died, his dad washed his hands of all the Strangers, he said."

This is what I think is so sad, all these people who don't talk to anyone else. No one seems to talk to my mom. I always thought if I knew everybody in my family, I would always want to talk to them. That we'd be like Nikki and her sister who talk on the phone all the time, even though they live two provinces away. Or her mom who is in Arizona but still FaceTimes on Sundays. That's what family should be. I wonder what happened to make it not like that for the Strangers. Can't think of anything that would make me want to stop talking to anyone. Even after Phoenix did what she did, and all the warning against it, I still would give anything to see my sister again. Anything.

My dad nudges me gently. "What is it? Where'd you go? You look like you got real sad there."

He's right. And feeling seen by him makes me even more sad.

He leans over awkwardly, to put his arm around me. It's a warm arm. "Hey, it's all right, it's all right, C."

"I just, I love it here and thank you for everything, and I know I shouldn't but I just, I miss them." I don't want to cry.

But my dad keeps holding me there. I can't help it. And he doesn't let go. Not until I breathe out and wipe my face with my sleeve.

John Wick's gun is empty so he throws it at the guy he's fighting. I want to say something funny, because we always say something funny at this part, but my dad beats me to it.

"Signature John Wick move! I really hope they patented that."

There's lots of ways to kill yourself but most of them hurt. Traditionally, males have used "aggressive" ways, the kind that really hurt, and females use "passive" ones, like pills. You can OD on Tylenol for sure and it can kill you, but if they catch it early enough, you have to go to the hospital to get your stomach pumped. Or they make you drink charcoal so you throw up whatever you've taken.

If you look up "how to kill yourself" online, you don't get what you're searching for but instead get suicide prevention websites that give you tons of stories about people who have recovered, got help, got better.

Some of them even sound a bit like me, but never all the way. But it did get me thinking about something Phoenix told me once. When she was in the Centre and getting her traditional teachings.

"You know Indigenous kids commit suicide more than any other group in the whole wide world. That's how sad it gets, I guess. Elders teach that we are sacred, that every person and thing and animal is sacred, and we should honour our ancestors by trying to live a good life. And the reason we're all so sad is not our fault. It's because of all the shit that's gone on around us, been done to us. It's because we live in a world that doesn't value us or show us that we're loved. But we are. By our ancestors."

I was pretty young when she told me that. Didn't even know what an ancestor was. I couldn't even think that far back, just thought of my mom, maybe my Grandma Margaret. Grandmère Annie, maybe. That's what I thought ancestor were, just your older family. Not that I was wrong but I could never even think of all those who came before them. Still don't even know them. Only imagine who they might be.

I bought another bottle but never used it. Not yet. I keep it though, with the empty travel one and the other empty one, in the box with all my special stuff. Not really special, just not thrown out. In there's that old burner Nevaeh gave me, the one and only letter from Phoenix, a feather Sparrow once found on the sidewalk. Things I keep because I don't want to let them go, but it's not like I like to look at them all the time or anything.

Weeks later my dad knocks on my door. He has been mowing the lawn. It's Saturday afternoon, Nikki was at work and Faith was still sleeping off her Friday night. I was doing a short story for English. It was a slipstream, a girl who could travel through history and met a bunch of strangers who turned out to be her ancestors. Her family.

The knock startled me. I was super into the story and had just given up trying to explain the scientific process of time travel and decided to go with magic instead.

"Come in." No one ever knocks on my door except maybe Nikki, and that's only ever to talk about chores.

My dad looks all white as he walks in. Well, not white but pale. His phone cradled in his palm. "I didn't want to say anything because I didn't want to get your hopes up." He hands me the phone. The screen blinks "blocked number."

I take it. Not knowing what else to do.

"Don't tell Nikki," he says with one of his winks, and a bit of colour comes back to his cheeks.

I can hear the background noises through the phone, a clang, a yell, before I even put my ear to it.

"H-hello?"

"Cedar-Sage!" Her voice too loud, but then it goes quieter, more gruff. "How the hell are you?"

"Good, good," I stumble.

"You sound, your voice is . . . different."

"You—yours does too." I swallow the big lump in my throat. The one that got in there, like, instantly. I want to feel happy, but I'm so scared all of a sudden.

"Yeh, I guess," Phoenix says as if to no one. "How . . . how are you . . . my sister?" She says again. Her every word an addition, but not an afterthought. These are her heavy, loaded-with-thoughts words.

"I'm okay," I say, hearing my voice crack. "You?"

"Ah, you know. Same old." My sister pauses for a long time, swallowing her throat lumps, too. Voice cracking, too. "It's good to hear you, Cedar-Sage. My sister."

That second one did it. It broke everything. With it, the fear went away. It was Phoenix. Just Phoenix. Who she was more important than what she did, what anyone said. To me. Maybe only to me.

"You too, Phoenix." I smile, and even though she can't see it, she can still hear it. "So, how's jail?"

Phoenix laughs one of her big, big laughs and starts to tell me a story.

11

ELSIE

Jimmy. Fucking Jimmy Gwetch, with his worn out freckles and soft brown eyes. He has a way of smiling at Elsie. Like he looks at her and then has to look away. Has to look down or something, like he just can't contain his joy. Joy for her. For seeing her. But he doesn't want to show it.

That's what gets her. Every. Time.

Took her years to realize he did that with everyone.

He sits there, in front of her uncle's building, had clearly showered and washed his clothes. When he saw her, he stood up. Stood in front of her and smoothed the side of his hair. Like he wanted to be presentable. And then with that fucking smile. Elsie thought she was lost again. Before he even took the grocery bags from her. To carry, to help.

Then she knew she was lost. Again.

She tried to be good. She went up to Uncle's place like she'd planned. Made them all the steaks. Shared hers with Jimmy. He passed her a handful of T3s as she cooked. So nice. So generous of him. He never had much of anything. But what he had he shared with her.

She only swallowed half. Only a slow, normal kind of buzz.

When she walked him back to his place. She wasn't going to stay. But then he went to get smokes from his brother and left her there in his basement room. It was his brother's house. Jimmy had the basement. It has a separate entrance so he could come and go as he pleased. But the upstairs door was often locked so Jimmy had to knock. Make sure his brother's wife wanted to let him in.

The basement was the same as the last time Elsie was there. Months before. Cold cement walls carved with people's initials, pictures. *A J ❤ E* right above the bed. A mattress and an old comforter that needed to be washed but smelled like Jimmy all over. She wanted to lean in and breathe it. But then remembered. Val. He left her for Val. Well, he didn't want her anymore. So she left.

She'd been staying with Val. Jimmy wasn't doing well and she needed to be away from him for a spell. He was using too much and was bad into meth. Elsie fucking hates meth. Hates needles. Her stepdad used to inject coke when she was young and he was fucking crazy. And meth is even crazier than coke. She had to get away. But then, of course, Jimmy got clean. Like he always does. Up and down and on and off is Jimmy. His brother even put him up in a rehab centre out of town for a while. But too soon he was back. Appeared in the Nor'wester with a clean shirt and clear eyes. That's when Val stopped bashing him and started eyeing him. Started dropping hints about Elsie staying too long on her couch.

She's never been one for competition. So she just slunk away. She couldn't compete with Val. Val had a place in the development and always had her kids. She had it together. Was on disability for a bad hip so her cheques always came. All Elsie had was another couch at Uncle Toby's. A dead kid and two live ones she didn't even really know. Taken away from her too young. All of them. Too young. She only remembered them like dreams. Nightmares she would wake up from. Always that she was forgetting her kids somewhere. Forgetting they were gone for so long. That was the worst of all. When she forgot how they all were gone.

She'd been with Jimmy for years. On and off. Since right after the girls got taken away. Sparrow's dad hung around for a while after they were taken. They lost their place. 'Cause you can't have housing without kids. So they moved to a rooming house. It was only supposed to be temporary. But you can't get your kids back without proper housing. So she lost her first appeal to get them home. Then her cheques stopped. 'Cause you don't get money to pay for your kids if you don't have your kids. So then Sparrow's dad went away. He just left one day and never came back.

You can tell a lot from a person by how they leave you. Some go quiet. Some loud. The ones that don't say anything are the worst of all.

She went around looking for him for a while. Thinking something happened. Until she saw one of his buddies who said something about him going home. Then she knew he'd left her. Like she knew he would. Then she was stuck. Alone. In a dirty old building. And her door didn't lock properly so some sniffer stole all her stuff. Clothes. iPod. Everything. That's when she slunk over to Toby's for the first time.

She met Jimmy a week or so later.

She didn't love him at first. She thought he was just a guy at the bar. Trying it on. She didn't need another bad-idea boyfriend. He knew Mercy. Everyone knows Mercy. And Mercy said he was a good guy. Jimmy seemed normal enough. Pills do that. Make you look kind of normal. As long as you have them. If you don't you twitch. You get sick. Elsie didn't see him get sick for weeks. And by that time, she was already trying to love him.

This basement is pain. Jimmy argues with his brother upstairs as Elsie looks around. Concrete walls and an old reinforced steel door. Bars on the windows because it's just off Main Street. There's nothing here but one old mattress. Comforter. Old bathroom with a sink and toilet. When she used to stay here, she didn't want to ask his brother's wife to take a shower, so she cleaned herself in the sink. Dried herself off with a T-shirt or whatever was handy and not gross. There were never any towels. Rarely any toilet paper. She'd swipe napkins from a coffee shop or the McDonald's just so she had something to wipe her ass.

They used to panhandle. Different corners, of course. Him with a sign that said "Out of Work, Anything Helps." Elsie had made one that said "God Bless." Spelled out the words, each letter careful and clear. Like Mamere taught her. And said God because that's what her Grandmother taught her too.

It was Jimmy who taught her how to steal. How to walk in a store hunched over and keep your hands in your pockets so they can't tell when something is in them or not. It was Jimmy who taught her how to try car doors and go through to get change. Old CDs. Anything they could pawn. They went into houses a few times too. She thought it was amazing how many people don't lock their back doors during the day. So easy to slip in and out. Quick and smooth. Just like Jimmy. She remembers standing in this one kitchen. It was a big kitchen. The kind with matching cupboards and an island thing in the middle. She stood there. Too strung out to do what she was doing. And ran her hands over the black countertops. The high chair in the corner. All the things she would never, ever have. No matter what she did. She stood there until Jimmy ran in with an armful of laptops and yelled at her that they had to get going.

She thinks she loved him. Wanted to anyway. Because love is such a good excuse to do bad things. If she loved him. She was doing it for him. Wasn't just a bad person.

This basement is pain.

Jimmy rushes down the stairs with two smokes in his hand. "Fucking guy being all cheap." He hands her one. "I wish he would just leave that bitch, you know. If it wasn't for her." He starts on a familiar rant.

Elsie lights her smoke. Sits on the bed.

"It's our parents' house. Mine and his. More mine than *hers*."

She can only look at him. Half smile like she's agreeing.

He sighs. "I'm glad you're here, Elsie."

"Why'd you do it? Why'd you go off with Val?" She surprises herself by saying it. Surprises him more.

"That's all over with. Val could never be you, Elsie. You're my Elsie."

She did always want to be somebody's. This almost makes her cry. She looks away. Puffs on her smoke to fix herself.

"I like, love you, Elsie. You know that. Val was just, nothing, something. I don't even know." He reaches out to take her hand. "She doesn't matter."

He lets go too fast. Smokes too fast. He always smokes too fast. Elsie knows he always regrets it.

"You have any—you have any money left on your card? We can go get smokes." His eyes the sweetest they can go.

She nods. Butts her smoke out in the can by the mattress.

He reaches over again, both arms this time. He looks shy, awkward almost, and closes his arms around her. Falls into him. Can't remember the last time she hugged someone like that.

He kisses her softly. His lips chapped and dry.

Is it love or just habit?

Habit or addiction?

Addiction is nothing if not comforting. Safe. In its way, addiction is so safe. It's something to do. A task or calling. It's knowing what will happen. Hope it'll be better this time. But you also know everything that will happen. And you're fine with it. You give in to it. Like they say you're supposed to give in to love. Maybe it is love. Here, with Jimmy, Elsie feels loved. And safe. Almost safe. Almost cared for.

Cared for or controlled?

Controlled by him or by what he gives her?

She was good at first. At first she went back to Uncle's after a few days. Even made her welfare appointment.

"Your family worker left another message. She wants you to call her back."

"Whenever I do, she doesn't answer. I don't have a phone, you know."

"You'll have to find a way, Elsie. No one is going to do it for you. It's about your kids."

"Did she say how they were?"

The lady looks at Elsie a long time. Shakes her head.

Elsie leaves another message before she leaves the office: "Hi, this is Elsie Stranger. I don't have a phone. Please tell my kids I love them."

It was the same every time.

She wants to add: I'm sorry, I'm sorry for everything. I didn't mean to, but sometimes I just can't remember things like that. I take appointment cards and then lose them. Sometimes I get so sad I can't get up. Barely have the energy to roll a smoke. Sometimes it feels like days go by, weeks, months, and I haven't done a thing . . .

But she was trying to be good. So good she even went back to the walk-in. Got some Xanax to try and stay clean.

She tried to feel a little better. Tried to taper. But that's hard with Jimmy Gwetch around. He always has something. That and they started hanging out with Mercy again. He looked like the meth went right through him. Had a sore on his cheek that never seemed to heal. Between the two of them guys, they always had something. But she tried to be good.

She got set up with this program for casual workers. A warehouse where she only had to go in the mornings. Sign in and she can work for the day. Organizing orders for shipping. Just checks out after. If she misses a day, they don't seem to care. No one seems to care there. They only want her to put a bunch of things in a box and seal it. Then go fill another. It's simple, mindless, and okay. Most of the other workers are harder up than her. Meth heads. Retards—sorry, mentally slow people. Some schizos. So she looks pretty good at it.

She did that for a while. Until she got paid. Until they gave her a paper cheque even though they weren't supposed to. She was going to give it to her worker to put on a card. But Jimmy found it and took it to Money Mart. She did owe him. And they did get enough percs and Oxy for a while.

After that she was back on the cycle. Back hooked. Back bad. Days were only different because they were a little lighter coloured than nighttime. She remembers being at the Nor'wester one night most of all. Val was there. Giving her the stink eye. They got kicked out so Val followed them outside. Screaming at Elsie.

"You know he still comes to me, don't you? Whenever you go off somewhere. You're so full of yourself, you think you're so much better than everyone, but you're nothing. Nothing." Spit was flying out of her mouth. It looked like slow motion.

The cops showed up. Dark blue blurs in the night. "What's going on here, ladies?" Old, fat cop.

"It's all good, Officer," Jimmy stammered, "all under control. Just a little, a little man problem." Jimmy stammered. Smiling so wide you could see his crooked teeth he usually tried to hide. "It's me, remember me, your old pal Jimmy Gwetch. You know me, hey, Christie?"

"Hey, Jimmy Gwetch, I thought you were keeping out of trouble these days."

"I am. I am. Just having a drink is all."

"Well Gary called me, said you were causing trouble. Messing with his till, he said."

"Naw, naw, just a, a misunderstanding." Jimmy's smile fades but he still tries to hang on.

"Stay here." Officer Christie, the fat cop, goes inside while the young cop stands watching us. Val is fuming. Staring at Elsie like she wants to fight but doesn't say anything with the cops there. Jimmy tries talking to the other guy but he looks down at them. Makes them all sit on the curb while the other takes his time inside.

Elsie rights herself up. Or at least can see clearer. The night is otherwise quiet. It's not late. But fall time so already dark. Not cold. But she starts to shiver anyway.

She looks at Jimmy. Sees his face change to something unfamiliar.

"Jake. Jakey, son." Jimmy gets up. The cop bars his way. But he tries to go past. "That's my kid. Jake. Jake. It's me." His voice sounds uneven.

A young guy comes over on the other side of the cop. He looks nice. Put-together, wearing dark pants and a light jacket. He looks like Jimmy. But is taller. Thicker in his face. Healthy.

"Jakey. Man, you're all grown up. Man. I'd know you anywhere, Jakey. You walk like my dad." Jimmy laughs nervously. Uncertain.

The officer leans over to the young man. "You know this man?"

The young man backs away. "Naw," he says with his chin all the way up. His face so angry. "Naw, I don't know that guy at all."

The young man turns. Goes back to another young guy he was walking with. He doesn't look back.

"Jakey. Jake. Come on, man." Jimmy almost whines. "Don't be like that. I'm your old man. Your dad. You know me."

"Come on, Jimmy. Jimmy, right? Sit down," the cop tells him.

He does what he's told. Sits next to Elsie, but he's changed. Gone pale. He starts to cry. Cries right there on the street. She puts an arm around him. But he doesn't stop. He never said much about his kid. Other than he had a good mom and was fine. Elsie knew his mom. Like she knew Jimmy. From back in the day. Lou was her name. Louisa. She was a social worker now. She had all the luck. Not like Elsie. Not like Jimmy. Jimmy bent over. Crying into his knees.

She looks over. Even Val's face's softened for him. Your kids not knowing you. Not helping you. Sick of you. That was the nightmare. The only one worse was you not knowing them. But you'd always help them. If you could.

It was after that, Christie finally came out. "Okay, Jimmy Gwetch, it's your lucky day. Gary isn't going to press charges but he says you're barred. So no coming back here, you hear?"

Jimmy stops sobbing long enough to nod.

"All right, you all can go. Go home and don't get into any more trouble."

Jimmy gets up. Shakes Elsie's arm off him. She follows after but he says, "No!" It's under his breath so no one hears but her. He makes it sound mean. And it works. 'Cause she stops.

The cops get back into their car. Jimmy walks off. Val gives Elsie one last dirty look and goes off down her street.

Elsie stands there a minute. Not really knowing what to do. Trying not to sway with booze. Trying to remember herself.

Trying not to cry. But the street blurs anyway.

"You have to leave now, Elsie," the cop calls from his passenger seat. "You have somewhere to go?"

She doesn't remember how he knows her name. But nods and takes a step. They pull into traffic.

Uncle is still up when she gets there. He turns from his chair and grunts a greeting. She goes to the table to roll some. Her hands are shaking. The smokes are full of holes. Burn too fast. But she gets through about four before she feels better.

When Elsie first went to live with Mamere and Grandpa Mac, she was always amazed at how nice they were to each other. She lived there a lot, off and on since she was born. But when she was nine, she went there for good. She knew they were nice and kind but figured that would fall away. That if she was there all the time, she would see who they really are.

But it never happened. They were grumpy. Strict. Super strict, felt like. And could get annoyed at her. Mamere often got sad. She would have really quiet days when she would look out the window too long or take a long nap that no one would wake her up from, even after it was suppertime. But they were never mean. Their yells were loud and fierce. But they never called each other any names. Or Elsie. Or Uncle Toby who still lived there too.

Her mom and Sasha weren't like that at all. They would fight like they were fighting for their lives. Big screaming matches where they'd hit and slap at each other. Break things. Throw things. Wake them all up. Storm out of the house. Elsie would take her brothers up to their room. Read them stories. Or play as loud as she could so they wouldn't hear. When they were small they were scared. By the time she left,

Joey was almost seven and it just seemed to annoy him. Alex was still a baby at five. Still a bit whiny and clingy. But Joey would take care of him. Tell him to toughen up and be a man. Or tell Elsie not to baby him so much. When that happened. Which was often.

Anyway, Joey would have to take care of him. 'Cause Elsie went to live with Mamere and Grandpa Mac. Wasn't given a choice. She was acting up. Getting on her mom's "last nerve." Sasha never paid much attention to Elsie so it's not like he cared. He was away working most of the time anyway. But when he was home, they would fight. Stay up all night and fight.

Mamere and Grandpa Mac weren't like that. Not ever. Not from summer all the way to Christmas. Which to her nine-year-old self was so long to be there. She loved it there. She didn't worry about her brothers. Not like she thought she would. Sasha had gone to prison soon after. They didn't see much of her mom and brothers for a while. But she wasn't worried. Joey was older and strong. Alex was perfect to her mom. They'd be fine.

Grandpa Mac was gruff and tough and a no-nonsense kind of guy. He'd never complimented Elsie or anyone. Never said "good job" even when she brought home good grades. Or won a soccer trophy in grade four. But if she caught him looking—he'd be looking at her super soft—but if she caught him he'd stop. He looked at Mamere even worse. His eyes blurred, like for a minute he lost all thoughts except how much he loved her. Elsie loved that. Always wanted someone to look at her like that. But no one ever did. Not 'til Jimmy. Not 'til one day she caught Jimmy looking at her too long. And when she turned her head, he looked down all quick. Made that shy smile. That's when she loved him. That's when she knew she would love him. No matter what.

The worst was when she caught him looking at Val like that. Must have just been a thing he can do. Can turn on. Can turn off.

He turned it off that night at the Nor'wester. She didn't hear from him for a long time after. She went to his place the next day. Tried to see if he was there. No one answered her knocks, and she couldn't see through the bedsheet-covered window. A few days later she went again. Even went to the front door to ask his brother. But no answer again.

He knew where she was. She told herself.

He always knew where she was. If he wanted her.

—

"I want to help you, but you're not making it very easy for me," her worker tells her. "They said you're a good worker and they like having you there. But you gotta show up, Elsie. That's the thing. You gotta show up."

"I will, I will." She nods and looks down. She's almost crying. Again. Always fucking crying. Relieved that she can have another chance at a crappy job.

"Now go call your family worker. She keeps calling me. You need to get a phone."

It's been fifteen days. Fifteen days since Jimmy walked away and she went back to Toby's. The shakes have stopped. The nausea has slowed down. She feels better now. It feels different this time. It feels like the last time.

But she's said that before.

She walks over to the scratched-up table and public phone. Some old lady is glaring at her but she doesn't look up. You never know if someone is just staring or wrong in the head.

She hunches over the phone and dials. Expecting to leave her usual message.

"Clara speaking."

"Oh hi, uh, it's Elsie. Elsie Stranger."

"Elsie, hi, I've been looking for you."

"I know, I, I'm sorry."

"I hear you're working."

"Yeh. Sorta. I guess."

"That's good. They tell me they're starting parole proceedings for Phoenix soon. Her sentence is up in a few months and they're looking at options for her transfer."

"Like to a halfway house?"

"Likely. But let's meet and I'll tell you all about it."

"Okay," Else whispers. Crying again. It must be the sober. But at least it's not a bad cry today.

"As for Cedar, I got a call from her stepmom. She wants to see you, Elsie. Or wanted to, that was months ago. I would think you would want to see her too, yes?"

She couldn't say anything. Only look up at the carved-out letters on the yellow board in front of her. Rita + Dan, one read. For a good time call . . . another said.

"Do you want that, Elsie?"

"Yes," she almost shouts. Then lowers her voice to the receiver. "More than anything. How, how is she?"

"She's doing good. In school, getting good grades. She said, the stepmom said Cedar was thinking about university. That's great, isn't it?"

"Yes." Her voice cracks. "Yes, it's great."

"Okay, well keep working. Keep doing good. How about you come see me on Friday? Do you work Friday?"

"I think." Her voice cracks open again. "I think I'm supposed to go there every day."

"Oh, okay. Let them know you're coming to see me Friday. They'll let you come. Sound good?"

"Yes!" she says again, wiping her eyes with the back of her sleeve.

"Okay, see you then." She hangs up quick.

Elsie keeps the phone to her ear until the dial tone comes back on.

She almost bounces as she walks through the doors. Elated. That's the word. She thinks of all the things the social worker said. Hopes it is all true. Phoenix probably doesn't want to see her. But Cedar. Her dear Cedar-Sage. She was always the kindest kid. So considerate of everyone. Even as a little kid she was taking care of Elsie. Always wanted to get a cold cloth for her head when she was sick. Or tuck her in when she was sleeping on the couch. Cedar.

She veers away from Portage Avenue. Not feeling its pull today. Turns to go out the park way. It's cloudy but still warm enough. A few kids play on the slide. Dressed good in mitts already. Laughing and throwing leaves at one another. For once, watching kids play doesn't break her heart. Her full mama heart. Her legs still hurt. Still need to be stretched out. She's tired all over. But she barely feels it that whole walk home. Back to Uncle Toby. His couch that is the only home she's really had since her kids got taken away almost nine years ago. Nine years. Nine years since they put them in a car. And she watched it back out of her usually empty parking spot in the old townhouses. It didn't seem real when they went. They were gone and all the places they were supposed to be were empty. Their toys everywhere. Sparrow had even made a mess that afternoon. After they left, Elsie cleaned it up. Put all the blocks back in the toy box so Sparrow could play with them again. When she came home. But she didn't. They didn't. None of them came back. Elsie convinced herself for months and months that it would just be another month or two but it had been a lifetime of months. Nine years of months.

Longer than some lifetimes.

Her Sparrow. Poor Sparrow.

She tells Uncle she's going to make him supper. But all that's in the fridge is eggs and bread so that'll have to do. She puts the pan on the heat. Feels her body still sore. She thinks of the back meds in the bathroom and thinks, just one, maybe two.

She shouldn't be so achy anymore. She thinks of the Xanax. Wonders if she'll have enough.

It's when she cracks the eggs that she is first suspicious. And when the smell of them cooking hits her, she knows. She is nauseous. Feels nauseous.

It was the same with Sparrow.

And Cedar.

Was especially bad with Phoenix.

Same every time she was first pregnant.

No one could cook eggs anywhere near her.

12

MARGARET

When Margaret lost her eldest son, she thought back to when she lost her brother, the one she named him after.

"Once I'm eighteen I am outta here! I'm getting as far away from you as possible!" Joey had yelled this at Margaret since he was a little kid. Oh he was a terrible teenager. Terrible child since birth really, but as a teenager, he was impossible. One time, when he was twelve or so, not long before they moved into the brown house, he had been bike riding along the riverbank with his little brother and being stupid. He had run into his brother on purpose, rammed into him like he didn't care, broke the poor kid's collarbone and an arm in two places. At least he had the decency to run home across the bridge to get his dad, who of course was doing nothing and not working so went over to get Alex with the car. Sure Joey was crying and making a big show of it, knowing he was in trouble now, knowing how fucking stupid he had been. Margaret had left him in the hall, snivelling and hiccupping like a baby. She couldn't even look at him, couldn't get away from him fast enough, so left him in the house alone, to wait, to think about what he'd done. Poor Alex's bone was pressing out under his skin. She had to hold it lightly as Sasha managed to hit every fucking pothole on the way to the hospital.

Later that night, Alex, with a cast and sling, smiled at his brother when he came in. Like the boy hadn't tried to deliberately hurt him. Alex never knew any better. He always loved his brother as if Joey was a good brother. But Margaret, still mad, didn't talk to her eldest son. He tried to get on her good side, even did the dishes, cleaned up after supper, but she wasn't having it.

Finally, after Alex had gone to bed and Sasha had gone out smoking, Joey, being as useless as always, brought her tea just how she likes it, of course, and said, in his trying-to-be-small sheepish voice, "I am so sorry, Mama."

How Margaret glared at him, this gangly twelve-year-old with the look of his father. She saw it then, the same meanness, the same violence. He was like her in so many ways, but not like her at all in others.

"I know what you did, you little monster." She sneered. "You're a monster."

He backed away like he'd been stung. He kept trying his little feel-sorry-for-me sad face, but he said nothing.

The room rang with her anger, like a bell that kept a high tone. She wasn't going to let him be like his father.

When he got to the stairs, once he was far away and she couldn't grab him and throw him over her knee like she used to, he yelled, "When I get eighteen, I am outta here! I am never coming back to this crazy fucking family!"

He swore like a child who never swore before. Margaret almost laughed. Would have, if he'd been in the room and tried that. She would have laughed in his little manipulative face.

But when he turned eighteen, he hadn't even finished high school. Had dropped out, after flunking out no doubt. After being too busy running around and getting up to no good. Not that she thought he'd be likely to finish even if he had applied himself. He was as stupid as his father in that sense, couldn't string a sentence together to save his life. She gave up trying to get him to read when he was still in elementary school. He was lost to anything that didn't have pictures. The teachers had wanted him tested, offered to take him to shrinks and other snotty people who would only judge her parenting and try to put him on drugs. No, she wasn't having their bleeding-heart ways. She was his mother and knew what was best for him. She knew he only needed a kick up the backside. Sasha tried, until he got bored. He was too stupid himself, so the boy ran wild.

Last time she ever saw him was his eighteenth birthday. She was trying to be nice. In the midst of all she had to do with the babies, Phoenix who was such a busy child and running all over the place, and now this newborn too. Annie was barely doing anything for herself anymore, and Elsie was always complaining about aches and pains, like a twenty-year-old would know of such things. And, just like she thought, that Shawn never seemed to be around. But for Joey's birthday, Margaret was trying to be nice. She was even making a nice pot roast for him, had set the table with balloons tied to the back of his chair.

"I'm moving to Alberta," he announced to the kitchen.

"You're what?" She stood there holding her oven mitts, waiting to take the thing out of the oven.

"I'm moving to Alberta. They're hiring all sorts of people at the tar sands up there. I'm going to go next week."

Her only thought was that he'd meant it, what he'd said. What he'd always said. All to get back at her for trying to be firm with him.

"You're too young," she babbled. "It's too far."

Somewhere in the house the baby cried. She wanted to go check, knowing Elsie never did quick enough.

"It's only a day's drive away."

"And then what? Then what do you do, in the tar sands?"

"Whatever they need. They put me somewhere."

"How can you be so sure? You don't have any skills. You don't even have a diploma." Margaret collected herself and pulled the roast out of the too-hot oven. She felt relieved at the thought. Knowing he'd never go through with it. "What makes you think they'd even want you?"

She didn't see his pout but she heard it. "I think I can do something useful."

Margaret stood up and blew the air out from between her teeth, letting out a "psht" sound before she could help it.

The boy, because he was still just a little boy, stood there with his feel-sorry-for-me face on. It almost worked. For a second she felt bad for it. But then he seemed to fix his expression, reached over to the kitchen table, and took one of her cigarettes without even asking. The nerve of this boy.

He lit up and blew over, right in her face. Right over his mother's face as the heat from the roast wafted over her. She was literally sweating from the work she'd done for him. For what?

"Well it gets you out of here, that's one thing it's good for."

"Oh yeh?" the boy said stupidly, trying to challenge his own mother.

They stood there, locked in their standoff for a breath. Or what should have been a breath, but neither of them breathed, until Sasha came in. Smelly from being in the shop all day, he smacked Joey on the back affectionately.

"So we going down to the bowling alley later? Larry can finally serve ya—legally." The fat man chuckled, thinking it was hilarious that his friend had been serving the boys since they were far too young.

Margaret leaned against the counter and lit up. "You should hear this. Your son's new grand plan for the future."

"I got a call for an interview today, Dad," Joey said so gently. "I'm going up to Fort McMurray next week."

Margaret was almost swayed, until she realized. "You knew about this?"

"They're hiring for all sorts of jobs up there. It'll be good for the boy."

Margaret gulped at red wine all through dinner. She couldn't stomach the pot roast or even the potatoes. She watched her family praising and loving her son. Joey lapped it all up like he was starved for attention, as if he hadn't been given too much attention his whole life. Toby came in with a bottle of cheap rye. Alex beamed up at his older brother, ever wanting approval he never got properly. Even Annie stumbled out of her room, her weight leaned on her thin metal walker, and all but fell into a chair. Elsie mashed potatoes for her Grandmother like she was a child and they giggled together in their little intimate circle of two.

Margaret kept gulping, and when she felt like it, leaned back and lit up, even though people were still eating. Sasha glared at her. Who the fuck is he, she thought. As if she hadn't made all this food and this wasn't her fucking house.

Later she scrubbed out the roaster and Sasha came up behind her, tried to grab at her waist of all things. She flinched and he swore under his breath.

"We're going out." He stomped away, barrelling his way through as he does.

"Hmph," was all she said.

But then Joey, with all his nerve and eighteen-year-oldness, came in too, with a pile of dishes for the counter and a body full of rage.

"You know, I thought you'd be happy for me. You're always telling me to get it together, think of my future and whatnot."

"Future," she scoffed, refusing to turn from her work.

"Yeh, future. I got a future now."

"Future? You're just a little boy. And now you'll be a little boy playing with . . . whatever they give you. If they hire you at all."

"You're so fucking impossible!" he yelled. Yelled at the back of her head so hard she could feel the breath.

She turned now, dried her hands with the towel, and glared at her son, who, after yelling, looked spent, almost cowered.

"*I'm* impossible? To want the best for you? To want you to be what, more than a boy with a dead-end job? Playing at being an adult?"

"That's not what I'm doing . . . I am a man now, you know."

"Man? You're not a man. How the hell did you get to be a man so fast? You're just a little boy."

"No," he started, but she was going now. She even threw the towel to the floor.

"You're just trying to get back at me, for what?" she said. "I was always too mean or too something. And now you just want to get away from me so bad you'll do anything. *Anything*."

Joey took in a breath so big and so long his whole chest heaved with it. "You know, this might be shocking to you, but not everything is about you, Margaret."

It wasn't so much what he said. As years went on, Margaret couldn't've even accurately said what he'd actually said. It was more the way he said it, the way he cocked his head and took a breath and knew exactly how to get to her. That, and she knew he was going to leave and never be the son she always wanted him to be. He was always impossible and now he'd be impossible and gone. Gone gone, like she didn't even matter.

Margaret had hit her kids a few times, spanked them when they were young and she could still put them over her knee, slapped them with her wooden spoon when they were older and she had to chase them down to make them be respectful. But now, this little boy before her thought he was a man, so as the rage grew inside her, an incongruent response to his horrible words, she thought she'd hit him like a man. If he was such a man now, she'd punch him square in the face.

She was aiming for the nose, but never had great aim. And he moved at the last minute so her fist landed on his lip and chin.

It hurt, oh it hurt. A flash went up her arm and nearly blinded her. She must've hit his teeth with her knuckles. She blinked and when she opened her eyes again, she saw it. He could very well hit her back, and hurt her. Really hurt her.

She leaned into her feet, ready for the impact, but he didn't move. He only took a deep breath again, heaved his whole chest, let his split lip drip blood onto his white T-shirt.

She felt sorry for him then, this boy-man bleeding. She moved to touch his face, help his wound, but he pulled back and smacked her hand away. With hate. He hit her with such hate. She recoiled. He hung his head and walked out of the room without a word.

The front door slammed and Margaret looked up and around her kitchen. It was only then she saw little Phoenix standing in the doorway, standing there with her big eyes and messy hair.

"Come here, love. Come see Grandma." Margaret reached her arms out to the child.

But the stupid thing ran out and up the stairs instead.

And Margaret was left, all alone, to clean up everything, as always.

It had really always been like this, always bad. Joey was never right, not since birth. He wasn't born right. He came right on time but with such a rush of blood and hurt. There wasn't anything she could do to stop it. His placenta had detached, and by the time she got to the hospital it was too late. She didn't feel a thing until she was bleeding down her legs. The baby had probably been losing oxygen for hours.

She didn't even get to hold him. They pulled him out and rushed him off with tubes and an incubator, kept him in there for days. She didn't hold her son for days.

The nurses were worse than useless, had brought in social workers who asked her if she had done anything. If she had drank while she was pregnant, as if she was some sort of moron. They all thought she was just a stupid Indian. Thought she did something wrong. But she didn't. She did everything right. Took vitamins even. She hadn't done that with Elsie, couldn't afford them then, but for Joey she splurged. All the good it did.

In the end, they didn't have anything on her, or Sasha, and let her take him home, but that's when the trouble really started. That's when she saw that her son wasn't right.

He would barely stop crying, the odd moment to eat and then go right back to crying. She couldn't figure it out. She tried everything. Elsie, for all her faults, was at least a good baby. Margaret had had her mother to help her then, too. But with Joey, she was on her own. Sasha was completely useless, of course, and her mother never came over to help her. Annie was still too busy caring for useless Genie and poor

Jerome. Margaret never felt so alone. She took to taking him out in the car every night, all night, so Sasha could get some peace and quiet. He had to, he had said. Couldn't work otherwise, he had said. Like he did anything anyway. And Joey cried. Nurses came and visited. She finally got her mother to take Elsie for a bit but Annie acted like she didn't want to. Margaret was at her wits' end by then. After a few months, she just let him cry. She left him in his crib, changing him, feeding him, but mostly leaving him be. Eventually, eventually, he stopped.

But he never got much better than that. He hated his little brother, would glare at baby Alex, hover over his crib, and Margaret was worried he'd do something. Alex was a great baby, so easy to love, slept through the night at ten weeks. So good. Joey was always so jealous of his brother. He could never get enough attention, or love, always lashing out trying to get back at his mother. Even at eighteen, he was still at it. Still trying to get back at her for something that was never her fault.

Joey was nothing like the man he was named after. Joseph, her brother was enigmatic. A big word she had to look up once and immediately thought of her charismatic, charming, funny, loving brother. Joseph could get away with everything. Joseph could sell ice to Inuit, or get a baby to give him candy, any of those clichés. Enigmatic. And he loved Margaret. He was always kind, decent. Sure, he teased her like her other brothers and dad did, but Joseph always did it with this grin that told her it was okay. That told her everything was going to be okay.

Joseph could also charm the pants off anyone, had strings and strings of girlfriends, even as early as elementary school. Everyone was so surprised when he brought home the homely Genie. There was nothing very special about Genie, but Joseph seemed to love everything about her. Until the day he died he was devoted to her.

Of course Genie was pregnant right way, likely on purpose to trap him. Things worked out pretty good for silly little Genie. Until they didn't, of course.

Margaret never really knew what her brothers got up to, never asked. Growing up, their lives were largely mysterious and shadowed to her. She knew they were up to no good, would hear the stories her mother would tell about their charges, knew the cops knew their house number by heart. But to Margaret, her brothers were jokers who laughed through dinner, and teased her relentlessly about being the good one, until she wasn't, and then they teased her about that.

When she was pregnant with Elsie, they were relentless. "You don't even look pregnant, you just look like you put on a few, you know," John told her in her seventh month. He said it with a shrug like it wasn't even funny, then cracked up and imitated her waddling up the stairs, complete with a sigh. Toby laughed so hard he spit coffee all over the couch.

Even after they were out on their own, John and Joseph often came over for breakfast, after obviously being up all night. Annie would cook them eggs, just as they liked them—John scrambled, Joseph, over easy—as if their lives were normal. Never talking about the haze of booze around them or the fresh scrapes on their knuckles. Margaret sort of had an idea that they did all sorts, beat people up, stole things, kept things, were into drugs for a while, but as a kid and later as a law student even, she was more oblivious than their mother.

One time in first year, she went and observed criminal court downtown and the prof in charged asked her if she was related to Joseph Stranger. She didn't trust his smirk so she just said,

"There's a lot of Strangers." Then added, with an air of authority, "And every Métis family has at least one Joseph."

He had continued to smirk.

When Genie moved in she told Margaret a story about going to a barbecue at the Hells Angels clubhouse. It was on Scotia by the park, right on the river, and everyone was wearing their leathers and most of the women even had tattoos and they were all beautiful. Genie relayed the story all in a hushed voice full of danger and excitement. That the booze was free and there was even a caterer. Genie was always as clueless as a mouse in the wall, so what the hell would she think. Margaret should have put it all together long before it all went to shit, if only to what, warn her parents? Protect her mother from the recklessness of her favourite sons?

John was the worst of them. He was always into something or other. She couldn't count the number of times the cops came to their house, or her dad had to bail him out. Her brother had been in Headingley, Stony, Remand, seemingly in rotation. John was the bad one, everyone said so.

Joseph, on the other hand, had only been in once. A three-year stretch in Stony Mountain Penitentiary for a B and E, but then he cleaned up his act because he loved Genie so much. Or that was Genie's story anyway. This was after the Hells Angels party, of course. Joseph got caught when Genie was pregnant, so actually missed the birth and only saw his son through prison visits until Jerome was almost three. That's enough to cure a man, or so Genie said. They had married before he went away, of course, so there was notably less shame than there could have been.

They never had any more children, of course. Margaret never knew about the forced sterilization, only that they wanted more kids but didn't have them. Everyone knew that. Once he was out they moved back to the city, got jobs, got a place, all seemed well for a long time.

Toby only ever did minor stuff but still managed to get caught over and over. He had finished a few small runs in Remand and Headingley, mostly for drug dealing or possession. Annie thought that he was only trying to be like his brothers, and that was stupid to begin with, but Toby really took it to the next level. Mac always said Toby ought to smarten up, but he wasn't all that smart to begin with. He was always sort of delayed in one way or another.

As far as Margaret knew, for years Joseph was living the clean life, working in construction most of the time. They had a little house down on St. John's that Genie kept pristine, and Jerome was the spoiled only child. Margaret remembered him as a fat and whiny little boy. Greedy. And he didn't change much as an adult.

Joseph was a smart one, that's what everyone said. Joseph was too smart to be up to no good. Ready to adopt a new baby, they said once that was happening. Annie couldn't've been more proud of him. Their little family moved to a bigger house on College that Genie was cleaning up as if it were a palace. Hadn't been in trouble in years, our Joseph. Really turned his life around. An example to his brothers.

So that morning, when the police came to the house, Margaret didn't think it could be as bad as it was, and never, ever thought it'd involve Joseph. She opened the door, her belly swelled out in front of her, and the sky clearing and bright behind them. When they said it was her brothers, she only sighed and called for her mother. Then thought, brothers, plural, and thought maybe John had gotten Toby to do something.

It was when they asked to come in and sit down, that was the bad part. They never did that unless something really bad had happened.

"Mrs. Stranger, is your husband at home?" one said as they sat on the couch, side by side.

"No, he's at work. What is this about?"

Annie stayed standing in the kitchen doorway.

"Can you call him, please?" one looked at Margaret and said. She thought he looked familiar, but they all kind of looked the same.

Margaret, however, didn't move. The baby kicked inside of her. "What is this about?"

They turned back to her mother, hesitant. "Your sons have been involved in a robbery. A bank robbery."

"What? Toby?" Annie rubbed her hands on her apron and then stood with her arms limp to her sides.

The officers looked at each other. "No. Not Toby."

"Who? John. Oh, that John!" Annie reached for Margaret, who

obediently took her hand and led her to her chair. The caring mother in front of the police. Then, once she settled, all matter-of-fact, "What's he done now? Robbed a bank?"

The officers both leaned uncomfortably forward. One rubbed his hands lengthwise, over and over. "Ma'am, I do think you should call your husband."

Annie nudged at Margaret's hand. "Call Joseph. He can get that lawyer. For John."

"Ma'am . . ."

Then, Margaret thought of it.

Brothers.

"Where's Joseph?" she blurted.

Her mother instantly frazzled by her tone. "Joseph? Was Joseph involved? No . . ." She paused and everyone gave her the silence. "Not Joseph. Not my Joseph, he's good. He's expecting a baby." She pointed to Margaret and then wanting to drive the point home with a firm nod. "Adopting this one. That's how good he is."

"Ma'am."

Their faces weren't right. Margaret tried again. "What happened?"

But they didn't look at her. They looked at each other, and then at Annie. When they finally spoke, it was in pieces. "Your son. Joseph. Was shot. Fleeing the scene. He was fleeing. The scene."

Something like a shadow passed over her mother's face, and Margaret thought that's the worst of it. She sighed.

Annie rattled and looked so old suddenly. Her whole face changed then. "You shot him? But he's, he's such a good boy. Where is he?" She patted Margaret's hand that lingered close. "We have to go. Is he at the Health Science?"

"Ma'am," they started again.

And Margaret knew. Knew.

no

"Mom," she started, not knowing what she was even going to say.

"Ma'am, Joseph didn't—" The officer stopped like he too didn't know what to say.

no

The moment was so long.

"—survive his injuries."

no

The moment, for that's what it was, only a moment, didn't make sense. Wasn't real. They were all so still. Margaret stood by her mother in the chair. Officers on the couch.

no

"What?" Annie said in the smallest voice, so small Margaret was probably the only one who heard. She couldn't respond. Only hovered her hand by her mothers and thought,

no

Just no.

Later she heard from Genie that it wasn't the first time for John. He had already done a few banks. This was back when you could do that sort of thing. When there were banks all over. Small neighbourhood banks on street corners with little more than an old security guard and maybe a security camera at the most. The thing was, John had gotten quite good at it. He didn't have a gun, of course, no one did in those days. But he took an old pop bottle and filled it halfway with water that he tinged with the slightest bit of pop so it was just off of clear. Then he put a long strip of cloth in, letting it hang out a bit, and held the bottle in one hand with his thumb over the top. He'd go in and wave it around, high enough so people could see but careful enough so the water didn't slosh around too much. He had read about it in a book or something, apparently it was supposed to look like a bomb. Molotov cocktail, Margaret learned later. Anyway, it worked and he had made his way through three different north side banks over that long summer and fall when Margaret was growing a baby in their childhood home. He got so much money and was so confident about it that Joseph wanted to get in on it. Just the one time, of course, Genie had explained. To get some extra money for the baby and everything. Joseph had really kept his nose clean, really was working construction and doing good, she said, but John talked him into it. Margaret didn't ever find out if it was Joseph who wanted in or John who talked him in, but regardless, it was both of them at the Bank of Montreal on Mountain that day in early December, and both of them ran out the door before they realized they were surrounded by cops. John dropped his bag and put his hands up, but Joseph, too stunned to think that quick, didn't drop the screwdriver in his hand. The lone screwdriver that, along with the pop bottle half-full of stained water, were their only weapons. The police officer who shot him reported that he couldn't see what was in his hand, given that it was blowing snow and Joseph was wearing a thick coat. The officer could be forgiven for thinking it was a gun. He did, however, see well enough to shoot her brother four times through the chest. Though he had missed the first couple shots. Those were lodged in the concrete side of the building. Probably still are.

They all sat there that evening, radio going quietly in the background for no reason. Genie made a big show of it, young Jerome sat stunned and pale and blubbered into his big belly. Mac paced. Annie fretted in her chair. At one point, Toby went to get food, burgers and fries from the drive-in that only went cold on the kitchen table.

At about eight, her mother finally spoke. "I want to see him."

Margaret said, "They won't let us see him, Mom. He's still . . . under investigation." The baby kept kicking at her. It was like it knew, too.

"What more can they do to him? He's dead!" Annie whined.

And Genie moaned.

"They have to . . . investigate." Margaret tried not to picture it. Her brother's body on a metal table. Cut open and prodded.

No.

"Then I want to see it. Go there."

Margaret looked to her dad, then her brother. No one seemed to know what she was talking about.

"Go where, Mom?"

"To the bank. Where they . . ." She couldn't finish.

Genie moaned.

"I want to go there."

"No, Mom," Margaret started.

"Annie, you're not thinking straight," Mac tried.

"Take me there!" Annie rarely yelled, so when she did, it meant something.

Genie couldn't, so stayed behind. Holding her pale, fat son on the couch. They would be right back, Mac said.

Margaret didn't want to go but did.

Toby drove, and when he pulled up to the yellow-taped corner, Annie climbed out of the back before the car was even stopped. Toby and Mac caught up to her on the other side of the snowbank.

Margaret didn't get out. Didn't want to climb out and over the snowbank in her condition, didn't want to see it either. Could see enough. In the streetlights. Something dark spattered on snow. Took her a minute to realize what it was.

Her mother realized. Fell to her knees, her son and husband on either side of her, holding her arms so she didn't fall all the way. But she tried. To fall all the way. It looked like she was melting closer, closer to the ground. To the beaten-down snow and blood.

It was all soundless to Margaret in the car. She knew her mother wasn't screaming, wasn't making a show of herself, wasn't making a sound. Was just crumbling, toward what was left of Joseph. The first Joseph. The good one.

Neither one of them made any noise, but inside, Annie and Margaret were screaming, were wailing, were dying.

After that, things sped up again. In a heartbeat, Margaret went from three brothers to one. They had a modest funeral at Cropo and too many gangsters showed up to leave them with any doubt as to Joseph's real job. John pleaded down to a fifteen-year sentence with no possibility of parole for ten, and Genie was left a widow with a young son, and never stopped crying.

No one said it but Margaret knew there was no way the silly woman would be adopting her kid now.

By Christmas, Margaret was sure she was just going to pop with no idea what to do with this baby once it got here. Annie insisted Genie move into the brown house so she could look after her and Jerome properly. No one gave Margaret or the baby a second thought, really.

It was Margaret who brought it up one morning over coffee.

"No, Mom, I can give the baby up. They have lots of good homes that really want babies. It's easy."

"No. No. You cannot give that baby up. She is family. She has to stay with us. She is ours." Margaret remembered her mother always referred to the baby as a girl, even before it turned out she was. "You can't do that, my girl. You can't. You'll never forgive yourself."

Margaret didn't have the strength to argue. She had only just woken up and was tired already. Going down the stairs had nearly done her in. Her mother was so bereft, Genie was a goner, even old Mac was too quiet and sad. Only Toby really seemed normal those first few weeks, and that's only because Toby was always so out to lunch to begin with.

So the baby came. Margaret went to the hospital in the middle of the night. Her dad drove her and Annie there without a word, and drove away once they were out of the car. It hurt like crazy, so Margaret got all the drugs. When she came to, her mother gave her a little pale squalling thing wrapped in a pink woollen blanket. The baby was smaller than Margaret thought she would be, uglier, but also whiter. She had dark little hairs on her head but looked just like Jacob Penner.

Margaret realized she hadn't thought of him in months, not since before Joseph. In her still-drugged-out state, and because she hadn't really thought about it before, she named the baby Elsie, after one of the few things she really knew about Jacob. He had a Grandma named Elsie who always cooked all of Jacob's favourite things. Margaret couldn't remember the names of the things, the foods she had never heard of, but remembered the name Elsie. It seemed to suit the little thing, and Annie was in no mind to question or oppose, so it stuck.

Annie was great with the baby. Took her immediately, rarely let her go. Margaret let her, welcomed it at first. It was a long time before she started feeling left out. Left out of their Annie/Elsie twosome, always together, always wanting each other. At first, Margaret welcomed the sleep, knew that her mother needed something to love, something to do. And she did everything. And Elsie loved her, more than she ever loved Margaret. Far more.

These days, Annie was just old. No other way to describe her. No other way to put it. Old.

She barely moved, and always stunk. They put a porta-potty in her room so she didn't have to make the trip across the house at night, and had hired a health care aide to come in and bathe her twice a week. It was just a sponge bath so she only smelt a bit less like BO and more like baby powder, but at least it was something.

Margaret was the muggins who got to clean out the porta-potty and change her aging mother from nightgown to nightgown every morning. She thought of putting her in a home each time she did it, but never did. The expense, for one, was so much. The legal stuff too. Everything was still in Annie's name. She still had her wits about her, or so she said, so she refused to sign over power of attorney. The house wasn't even theirs yet. There were so many things to do. It was enough to drive Margaret to drink.

Of course it couldn't last long. They had to get her to do it sooner than later, but to Margaret it felt like a final insult. You can clean up my shit but can't have my house, not yet.

That or Annie really didn't have much of her wits about her after all. Which wouldn't be surprising. She never much had any wits to begin with.

"Margaret? Margaret?" she called from her bed. "Help me up, dear."

Margaret came in from the living room, duster in hand. "What are you doing? Why are you getting up, Mom?"

"It's December. Time to get started on baking, don't you think?" She leaned heavily on Margaret's arm before leaning on the walker. "I know you want some of my pain croosh."

Margaret groaned and thought of the mess the frybread would make, most of the work down to her, no doubt.

"You don't have to make pain croosh, Mamere." Margaret walked slowly behind her.

"I want to," Annie grunted, her walker banging the doorways as she went. "It's Joseph's favourite. When is he coming home?"

At first Margaret wasn't sure which Joseph she meant, if her mother was finally going senile and thinking of her dead brother. But then remembered it was also her son's favourite, Joey's favourite. Margaret hadn't thought of it. Had blocked it somehow, and now she was ashamed to say she didn't know when or if her son was ever coming home. She hadn't talked to him since he'd left. Sasha had, but he never said much about it, and Margaret didn't dare give him the satisfaction of asking.

"He's got to be coming home soon. There's only days left." Her mother strained into the kitchen chair, no doubt now parked there for Margaret to do all the running around. Of course Elsie wasn't even home to help. Up to no good somewhere, no doubt, never around when she needed her.

Annie didn't have to tell her there were only days to go. Between the shopping and the cooking and the decorating, the nattering children going on about what they wanted, and oh the incessant music on everything, Margaret knew exactly what day it was, and everything she had no time to do.

Like make pain croosh, apparently.

"Now, if you get me the ingredients I will mix it and braid it. We can put it in the oven if you don't have enough beef drippings."

Annie hated making it in the oven so she must be really trying to milk it now.

"Mamere, I—" she started, thinking of how best to say it.

"Margaret, dear, do I have to say it?" Then she whispered. "This might be my last time."

That was the real deal, big-time guilt there. Margaret sighed again, but stood still.

"Oh, don't worry," Annie said, waving her hand dismissively. "He'll come home. Don't worry."

It wasn't even what Margaret was thinking, but it was really what she needed to hear.

She got the flour, a bowl, a cup of water for her mother. Then phoned Sasha to bring home a pint of beef drippings from Cantor's.

Margaret never saw her son again. That day, his birthday, when she busted his lip, that was the last moment she would ever see him.

Joey never did get to Alberta. Well, at least not that next week. Instead, him and Shawn got picked up that weekend for a string of B and Es they had been doing, to fund travels and childcare no doubt. The fools pled guilty right away, on the advice of some cheap lawyer Sasha had called, and got shipped out of town in record time. Oh how Elsie cried her eyes out. Swearing up and down that she'd wait for her man, like she knew what that meant. Shawn had priors so got two years plus and went to Stony. Joey, for all his trouble, had miraculously gotten to eighteen without a criminal record but still had to do a few months in Headingley. He never came home after that though. Never called her. Apparently he stayed at a halfway house before he took off, breached bail and went out west after all.

He called Sasha finally and told him he'd got some menial work in construction somewhere in Alberta. Decent money, he said. Or Sasha said, thinking that meant anything. Margaret knew Joey didn't care about money, only about getting back at her. Didn't even call her himself, such a coward. Avoided the trouble of having to crawl back to her, hat in hand. She figured he'd do it eventually. When the heat wore off and he missed home. She knew he'd have to come back at some point.

She was wrong.

But, Annie wasn't. It was Annie's last time ever making both Josephs' favourite frybread. She never got a chance to make it again. Margaret only made it one more time, but that was after Elsie and the girls had gone. Margaret was the only one who knew how, and she had never bothered to teach Elsie. Annie hadn't either. The girl was never interested in cooking anyway. So Annie's frybread, her pain croosh became one of those things, one of those many things, that are lost.

YEAR FOUR

13

PHOENIX

SSRIs always work until they don't. And then they really don't. Phoenix felt it. It was like taking off a sweater: she was suddenly cold. After a while of that, they seemed to work again, for a bit, and then, nothing. It was like she had nothing at all. Nothing between her and the world but her skin, and it had grown soft. She had become something different, something weaker. She sat there in her fucking solitary cell reading shit and talking shit with an old man. She was fat and soft, had no fight in her. She hated going to the dining hall, being around anybody. Kai started to really grate on her, like she was standing too close even a few feet away. It felt like something rubbing against her, trying to bruise her.

Fucking Chris said she was just fucking depressed. That's what he told her when she wouldn't get out of bed. Didn't want to go do her job or even take a shower.

The worst of it was, she was fucking crying. Not just the odd tear but she wanted to bawl. She wanted to howl out like Dene did and cry and blubber like an idiot kid. She didn't though, not howl anyway, but she was still fucking crying and couldn't stop. She didn't want anyone to see her like this so she stayed in bed, under the blanket, facing the wall. She couldn't fucking take a shower, what if someone was in there, what the fuck could she do with her useless fat, blubbery arms and face. She felt sick.

Ben didn't make her get out of bed. He got her to sit up but then moved the plastic chair back in the doorway and talked from there. "You are sick. That's what mental illness is, it's an illness. Depression is no different than having like, cancer. You're sick, and you have to take care of yourself."

She stared out through her watery eyes and rubbed her finger along the seam of the blocks. The only thing that didn't hurt.

"They say depression is the same as rage but turned inward. I think you exhausted yourself getting mad at the world and now you're turning all that energy onto yourself." He was talking slow today. Or she was hearing slow. "I remember this one time, when I was still in prison . . ."

She didn't want to hear his stories today. She blocked out his voice, thought of any other thing. She thought of talking to her sister. They talked a few times a week and sometimes about nothing. One time Cedar read her this letter Phoenix wrote her years ago. Shit, it was funny. She was pumped, at first, to talk to her sister. Told her all sorts of stories. Mostly bullshit she thought was funny and would make her laugh. Couldn't much lately though. Now she only wanted Cedar to talk about her life so Phoenix could listen. And she did. Cedar's good at shit like that. She'd eat a pizza pop and bitch about her stepmom and stepsister between mouthfuls. Not real family, she said more than once, but Phoenix thought she was more trying to convince herself.

Cedar hadn't visited though. They hadn't seen each other since the funeral and that day was a blur of Elsie being a fucking joke and Cedar crying. Phoenix was at the Centre then so had to go with guards. She didn't have to be handcuffed the whole time, but that was the only good thing of a horrible day she doesn't like to think about. Before that they had had visits, a few times, like three, before Phoenix started getting in trouble. All of them went downtown and Elsie even showed up on time back then. Phoenix was maybe twelve so Cedar would have been nine or so. Her and Sparrow were with that lady, Tannis, and Phoenix could tell Cedar fucking hated her. But she was getting by and doing a good job taking care of Sparrow. Phoenix doesn't remember much about her littlest sister back then, only that she was quiet and wouldn't let go of Cedar. Cedar didn't stop talking though. She told all these stories she made up, to Phoenix and Elsie, and everyone tried to seem happy. But it was over too soon. And then the visits stopped, and they didn't see each other again 'til the funeral.

Cedar didn't come to the naming ceremony. They asked her. Whoever they were. Ben was the one who told her, the day before.

"They asked her stepmom but she didn't think it was a good idea. Sorry, Phoenix." He looked sad, like he was really disappointing her, but she wasn't surprised.

Since they'd started talking on the phone, Phoenix had heard all about this new stepmom person. Cedar talked about her all the time. The lady was white, wore too much makeup, and seemed to be afraid of everything. Cedar couldn't go downtown. Couldn't even leave the suburb they lived in. Nikki didn't even know they were talking. It was Shawn who made it happen. Phoenix remembers him, a bit. She remembers a guy with black hair and an apartment they would go to. She remembers Elsie laughing. Her mom's curly hair falling in her face. Cedar, a chubby baby waddling under her hands. Shawn bought Phoenix fast food. Shawn let her watch anything she wanted on TV. He held her hand when they walked over to his place from the brown house. Over the bridge and down Selkirk. Sometimes he carried her, if it was really cold. Even though she was already three or four even and was supposed to walk. She wanted to go in the stroller but Cedar was in it and there was only room for one. But Shawn helped.

Then Shawn was gone.

Sparrow's dad started hanging around, but he never gave Phoenix a second glance.

Until he did.

The day of her ceremony seemed like any other day but more. She ate and showered and felt a fluttering at the pit of her belly like something amazing was going to happen. But she didn't let herself smile.

When Ben came, he pulled an old grey suitcase behind him, and his daughter Mel was with him. She was like forty with long hair and a wide smile, and quiet. She introduced herself and shook Phoenix's hand, soft and warm. Then they set up by the couch in the hall, spread out a large star blanket overtop the ratty old one in front of the chairs. Ben moved to the floor with a grunt, and his daughter, his skaabe, his helper, sat beside him, her legs pulled together and tucked beneath her long skirt. Then she took things out of the suitcase, one by one.

Phoenix watched from the couch, trying to remember them. The turtle rattle, the abalone shell, the long sprig of sage. She knew the tobacco, the smudge stuff, but not others, and now tried to learn them all.

"Ah miigwetch, miigwetch ndaanis," Ben said each time his daughter passed these things to him, and he placed them in front of him, making a curve of them, and touched them gently, with respect.

Chris stood along the wall with his hands folded in front, his head bowed, for once not smirking or making some wise-ass comment. They had brought in a couple other guards too, like she heard they would. They also emptied the unit. Dene and Kai were off at their jobs or whatever, so she didn't even have them. Only herself. And Ben, and his daughter who didn't look at Phoenix again, and all these things she should know but didn't.

After a song, Ben put down his drum and talked a long time. He talked about his life, his story, things Phoenix knew already so she wasn't really sure why he was telling her again or if he was telling the guards or if he was just saying. But she listened, and as he talked she saw his life, his time in prison, his time out west, down south, the things he was proud of, the things he wished he could change. It was when he stopped his usual stories and sighed that he said something new.

"That's why I am here. That's why I do this work. Because these kids, this kid here, is no different from me. We are the same. We are, all of us, all the same. That's why when this young girl passed me her wishes, I knew I could find her name. I could learn what her ancestors call her, what they will call her when she is an old lady and it is her time to go on to them."

He talked about his gift, how he got names, how he found them. Phoenix thought the ceremony'd be like magic, but it was only like Ben.

Then finally he asked her to stand, and he told her her name.

"G'wichikwaanakwaadok," he said to her, then in each direction, then to the Sky, then the Earth.

"G'wichikwaanakwaadok," he repeated until she heard it in her head. Then in her heart.

"G'wichikwaanakwaadok," he said one last time. "Out of the clouds, it means in my language. You'll have to find a better Michif speaker to tell you how to say it in that language, but it will mean the same thing. Out of the clouds, or like, appearing from behind the clouds. That is you."

He smiled then, and Phoenix was suddenly conscious of holding his hand and walking with him in this circle. Of hearing her name for the first time. And of somehow knowing what it meant before he told her.

When the ceremony was done, after Ben shook her hand again, after he and Mel started putting all his things back into the suitcase, Phoenix went to her room and sat to write Cedar a letter. She hadn't written her a letter since they were little kids, but she wanted to tell Cedar all about it, while it was still fresh. But the pen sort of wouldn't move. She couldn't find the right words or the right way to say it. So she pulled out the little paper Ben had given her, where he had written it down, and she copied it out, careful,

G'wichikwaanakwaadook

G'wichikwaanakwaadook

G'wichikwaanakwaadook

until the whole paper was full.

Then she sat there, staring up out the window at the dark. Not that she could see anything out it even when it was light.

She thought getting a name was supposed to make her all happy, supposed to give her purpose and responsibility. But she really felt fucking worse after. Like there was nothing left to look forward to. Like she remembered there was a world outside, and all the people in it she never got to see. She thought of her ancestors and only really knew her Grandmère, Grandpa Mac but only in pictures, Grandma Margaret but she wasn't likely to welcome her into the afterlife. She thought of her uncle who she didn't even have a number for anymore, and he would've moved on since she'd been in. Made himself untraceable to her. She even thought of Elsie and wondered where she could be now. She could guess. Cedar had wanted to see their mom, but Phoenix never gave it a second thought, or hadn't. Elsie, on the long list, of things she didn't want to think about.

Until today, when she couldn't stop thinking of any of them.

All of them.

After the ceremony the fucking guards kept treating her like she was fixed. Chris was talking about her going back to the cottages, and told her she should get her GED. Like I could do that, she thought.

"It'll look great when you come up for review next year. With all this ceremony stuff, too, it'll look like you really turned things around."

Like that's why she was doing it.

She didn't like to think about getting reviewed. For so long it felt like it was so far away but now it felt too soon. She didn't think anyone would let her out anyway, and didn't want all the fucking bother. She didn't want to try and please them all, or try and get her GED or any fucking thing. She couldn't even finish a fucking Psych textbook, only read like four chapters and couldn't remember anything about it.

She felt nothing, or didn't want to. She really liked the idea of not feeling a thing ever fucking again.

She was about a week overdue for a shower when a new bitch guard started working. She talked real loud and kept telling Phoenix she needed to get out of bed, all chipper like she was fucking special. It was fucking annoying. Kai fucking loved it, she loved fresh-meat guards like this and started talking this bitch's ear off about her fucking magical Grandpa and all her millions of mental problems and all the other things Kai talked about over and over again.

They started playing cards out in the hall, right in front of Phoenix's door, like they were trying to lure her out or something. Even Dene was playing and in a good fucking mood. She was still talking her baby talk but laughing and even winning by the sounds of it. Phoenix was even more fucked up than that fat fuck, fucking great.

"So what's her problem?" the new bitch guard said loud, obviously wanting Phoenix to hear. Phoenix thought she sounded familiar but didn't know where she would know her. All the guards/mentors started looking the same years ago.

"She needs to readjust her meds," Kai whispered, but Phoenix could still fucking hear her. "She's depressed."

Dene giggled. "She's swad, poor widdle Phoenix is all swad."

If only she could fucking move she would beat that psycho's ass so fucking hard.

But she must've been depressed because she just fucking lay there.

"Okay, Phoenix, time to take a shower." New bitch guard came in with another bitch guard from another ward and both grabbed an arm.

"I don't wanna fucking take a shower!" Phoenix tried to pull her arms back. "Fuck you!" She wanted to yell louder but her voice cracked.

"You stink. Your room stinks and you are going to take a shower." Yeh, that bitch guard looked familiar, staring down at Phoenix and trying to yank her up. Phoenix kicked and tried to get her arms free but didn't yell. She didn't want anyone to come out and see. It was nighttime so there might not be many girls in there, so she finally gave up and let them drag her. They turned the water on and shoved her into the stall with all her clothes on, held her down so she wouldn't hurt them or herself.

"Now are you going to do it yourself?" The guard looked at her square in the face. She wasn't angry or mean about it, but she didn't smile or nothing either.

Phoenix wiped the wet hair out of her face and nodded.

"Okay, good," the bitch guard said and shut the stall door.

Phoenix peeled off her wet clothes. She could hear the guards talking about something funny and laughing, probably at her.

The soap and water felt hard on her skin. She made the water cooler, then hotter, but it still hurt. She shampooed her hair as quick as she could. By the time she turned it off, she felt like she'd been holding her breath. The guard passed a towel over the door, then some clothes.

"There. Feel better?" the guard said, smiling now.

That's when Phoenix recognized her. She suddenly felt mad all over, wanted to rage and beat the shit out of this fucking half-ass fucking useless, but all she could do was cry. The bawling kind, so she had to lean in and bend into this stranger, like she did that night three years ago.

"Hey, hey, it's okay, Phoenix. Everything is going to be okay," the guard told her, like she had told her that night three years ago.

No one was in the shower room, and Phoenix thanked fucking god no one came in. Not for the entire time she hunched over and cried as Henrietta knelt beside her and rubbed her back, no one came in. And it was a long fucking time.

She thought of her kid every day. She thought of the feel of him in her arms when they wrapped him in a blanket and gave him to her. She remembers thinking it was weird he had clothes on, a little yellow sleeper with a zipper and a diaper. It didn't seem he should have clothes on yet, so newly born.

Then he was gone. There was nothing else to remember.

She didn't know anything else of him.

She lay in her bed long after morning came again, long after her hair dried in knots behind her. She couldn't move anymore. The shower made her so tired but she couldn't sleep, only stare at the wall. That fucking wall. She closed her eyes and could only see white cement blocks. She opened them and there it was again, with glossy paint that reflected the light behind her and if she tilted her head one way it was blinding.

In her head she told her own story, like Ben told his. She walked herself through all that she'd been, all that she did. Like the last night she was out, when she walked to the brown house she used to live in, just to see it again. Only this time, in her imagination, she got to go inside and sat on Grandmère's lap while she told her own stories, stories Phoenix knew better than her own, even the ones she didn't remember. Phoenix sat there with her, smelling the Noxzema smell of her, the scotch mints on her breath, her hot breath against the back of Phoenix's head.

In her mind, she stayed there when Grandmère died, when Grandma Margaret yelled at her 'cause she got syrup all over her pyjama top. When Uncle Toby put his hands over his ears like he was a little kid because everybody was yelling, and Sparrow's dad was swearing in Elsie's bedroom but Elsie just cried and cried and wouldn't get out of bed.

Then she went with Elsie and Cedar and Sparrow's dad and they never saw anyone else again. She didn't remember that first apartment, or the next, only the one on Arlington where she had to pull the stroller up three storeys, four flights of stairs, two breaks. Sometimes Sparrow laughed at the bumps, but sometimes they made her cry.

Sometimes Cedar carried the groceries so the stroller wouldn't be so heavy.

Then the Lego Land house. Its long white wall on the main floor, not as shiny as this one, but not as marked up either.

She remembered the basement. She never thought of the basement. It was on her list. But now it was like she couldn't help it. She pulled the blanket over her head and couldn't stop thinking about it. The basement with its dark grey cement walls. Unpainted, unmarked. The only thing that decorated that place was the beer bottles on the windowsill, the broken ones on the floor, spilt ones on the blanket, the mattress where Sparrow's dad slept. He said he liked to sleep there because Elsie always wanted to sleep with Sparrow and Sparrow always woke up at night. He said he wanted peace and quiet. He told her to be quiet.

She didn't know she was screaming. She knew she was hitting her head but didn't think it was that hard 'til Chris peeled the blanket off her. The pale blanket wet with red. She tasted it in her open mouth. That's when she knew her mouth was open. She heard it. But it didn't sound like her. It must have been some other voice. Some little-kid voice. A little kid trapped in a basement full of beer bottles.

After that, she got to see the doctor and got something new that made her a little more lively. That was Chris's word, "lively." Within a week, she was patched up with six stitches and a headband of gauze but felt like she could do stuff and got that hazy, not-all-the-way-angry feeling.

"Xanax," the doc had told her, not looking at her. "That should do it."

He had really long nose hair and jowls that hung off his cheekbones. Phoenix was doubtful but high on t3s and sleep deprived because they were all paranoid about a concussion and kept waking her up.

Then she was floating. It was a good float.

She went out into the hall and sat with Kai and Dene, actually wanted to go out there. Dene smelt like piss but Phoenix didn't even say anything, just let the idiot snuggle her doll and rock back and forth like it was a real baby. Phoenix even might have laughed.

"You guys wanna play pusoy?"

Kai dealt the cards but Phoenix couldn't keep it straight. Was it poker hands, and what were poker hands? Her own hands were asleep in places and swollen to soft. She kept wanting to touch them. She slapped down a flush but it was clubs and spades mixed together, and when Kai pointed it out, Phoenix only laughed.

"Wow, you're so hwigh." Dene's eyes like black circles and the sun nearly blinding.

"Yeh, isn't it great!"

She dreamed thick dreams of babies and birds and the white wall bricks turning soft like clouds that she could go through, come through, get out of. She didn't care if she was going crazy, as long as her head was soft.

But she must've looked like she was having too much fun because she had to go back, pluck out the threads in her forehead and readjust her dose. She knew it was the end.

The scar stretched like a wave, uneven but stretched across her forehead where the bone is hard. Puckered and red like it was angry, it reached from end to end.

She knew it was impossible but was hopeful something had slipped out.

"You're looking better. Band-Aids off, gots colour in your cheeks again. How you feeling?"

Ben looked tired, came in with a go mug and sat down on the hallway couch with more than a little noise. "Man, I swear this thing gets lower to the ground every Monday."

Phoenix was reading her Psych textbook again, same chapter all week, but put it down on her bed and went out. But didn't say anything.

They had ground her out and reduced her dose. She could concentrate a bit but still slept a lot.

"What are you reading about today?"

"Attachment."

"Oh yeh?"

"Like how they let baby monkeys alone for so long they started cuddling up to robots."

"Some old medicine in that. Babies need their mothers."

Phoenix nodded and looked out the window.

"How old is your boy now?"

Phoenix knew he knew everything. Everything she'd ever done or had happened to her was written in a file somewhere. Every adult that had ever talked to her had read it. Phoenix never knew what it was like to have secrets. Not those kind.

"Three. Three last week."

"Ah." Ben sighed and wiped something invisible off of his knee. "That's hard." He said it like it was undoubtable. And it was.

Phoenix only nodded again. She had been thinking about when Sparrow was that age. They were in the big house in Lego Land by then and Phoenix was ten, Cedar was seven. They had a big party that year. Sparrow's dad invited a bunch of people, including his family from far away, and the house filled with people Phoenix and Cedar didn't know. It's not that they weren't nice, just weren't theirs. The whole bunch of them swallowed up Sparrow, made her something different, more different than Phoenix and Cedar anyway, who had no family there that day. They went up to their room after Sparrow opened all her presents, more presents than they had ever seen all at once. Sparrow was so happy, so there was that.

Phoenix and Cedar played quiet for a bit before Sparrow came up the stairs with her new doll and stroller, and then they all played together while the family and their mom got louder and louder downstairs.

That Sparrow, the first one, belonged to Phoenix. Phoenix and Cedar. This new one though, she didn't even know what he looked like.

"Have you ever been in contact with your son? Or his Grandmother?" Phoenix thought it was one of his questions, the ones he knew the answer to but just said to start a conversation.

She shook her head.

"Ever think about it?"

"He's, he's in a good place."

"Yeh, I'm sure he is, but that's not the question."

Phoenix looked out the window for a while, before nodding.

Ben said, "What would you say?"

She shrugged, felt uncomfortable all of sudden, felt the anger rise up from her throat like it still did, all the time, even though it was just under a lot of stuff now. Even though it didn't do anything when it got to her face but made her cheeks hot and she worried that she would cry again.

The old man sighed, again. "You know, I didn't know my little girl when she was that age." He talked slower now. "I wasn't— I didn't feel ready to be a dad, or a husband. I tried, but I didn't feel good at it. I know now I just didn't feel good enough, so I did things to, you know, sabotage it. I was really good at sabotaging my life for a long time. Whenever something good happened to me, I would find a way to mess things up. I really messed things up with Mel's mom, I don't blame her at all for kicking my sorry arse out, but at the time I just thought I was mad at her, mad at myself. So when she kicked me out I took off, went away for a while."

"Was that when you went out west?" He was pausing in his stories more, and sometimes she had to prompt him.

"West? Naw, that was years before. Naw, after that one I went down to Arizona. If you ever get a chance to go to Arizona, go. It's so beautiful there, all desert and sun and weird rocks and brown people. The Navajo are down there and they really got their stuff together, they really know how to live. We could learn a lot from them up here. I went down there and found another woman, a beautiful girl, her name was Tanya. She was something. Her people were ceremony people so I learned about their ceremonies. Her dad was a really blessed medicine man, her mom too. Why they let me hang around I will never know, but they seemed to like me, for a time, and I learned a lot. But then I went and screwed that up and two years later I was back up here and wanted to see my kid, right? Course, I never stopped thinking about her. I would call her mom sometimes and sometimes I would talk to her on the phone. One year I was making good money and shipped her up a bike. She told me later on the phone it was too big, but it's the thought that counts, right? So I never stopped wanting to be her dad, but that doesn't mean I was doing the work of being her dad or anything. I was just half-arsed trying, I guess. But then I was back up here and wanted to be in her life all the time again, but her mom, god bless that woman she was tough as old boots but better looking, she didn't let me get my way at all. She told me to get my act together, get a job, a place, and wanted me to prove to her I could be a good dad. So of course I was all mad again, thinking she was breaking my heart, kicking me out all over again. But I knew she was right, so I did what she said and got the job, the place, started living the life I should have been living all along, and finally, slowly, I started seeing Mel again on the regular. That took time, 'cause you know, I had to rebuild her trust and my kid had to get to know me again, but we did, in time, with a lot of patience on all our parts, we got it together. We weren't super close until she was a teenager, really, but we grew on each other and by then she was living with me, but that was mostly because she wanted to be by her baby sister, and that's, well, a whole other story, but you know what I am saying?"

Phoenix never really looked at him when he was telling his stories. It always felt so personal, so she felt she should look away. Out the window or down at her lap, but now she looked up at him as he finished and took a drink of his coffee. He looked older than when she had met him, thinner too. His eyes were still shiny but the white of his beard looked more white, his face more droopy. She hadn't noticed until today. She wanted to ask how old he was but was too shy. He smiled at her, like he did all the time, but still looked tired. She smiled back but just a bit, and finally, nodded.

She said really quiet, "I wouldn't expect much, like, at all from them."

"Do you want to try and write a letter to him, maybe?"

She shook her head right away. "Shouldn't I ask first?"

"I could see about asking the social worker, or seeing if they're willing or something. I could do that." He paused and looked out the window too. "I don't want you to get your hopes up though. You can write him a letter anytime and that's as good for you as it would be for him. But they might not want to hear from you, or be open to it, just yet, you know? You might have to wait a few tries, you might have to prove it to them. You'll have to be patient."

She didn't think she could write a letter. Wouldn't even know where to start, but she could think about it awhile. Maybe ask Cedar. Maybe wait. She could do that real well.

She was good at being patient. She had been patient her whole fucking life.

14

CEDAR

Grade twelve is the exact same as the rest of high school. Don't see what all the fucking fuss is about.

I wanted to start the year off right. Join a club or two. Get into the graduating experience. Really participate. But once again I'm late to the party. Everyone is closed off even more than before. It's all circles and cliques as usual, only now they excitedly make plans and seriously discuss new, undefined things, like grad dinners and university applications. They buzz around me like they've always done, and it's more annoying than ever. I live with my earbuds in these days.

Sometimes I don't even play anything. Sometimes I have them in, look down at my binder or whatever, and only pretend I'm listening to something. Then I can hear them, going on about their small, selfish lives, oblivious that I can hear it all.

"My mom wants to take me grad dress shopping, like now. She says everything decent will be taken by Christmas!"

"I don't even know if I want to take a date to grad. Might be more fun just to hang out with you guys."

"But then you'd be all alone! What are you going to do when slow dances come on?"

"Do they even have slow dances anymore?"

"At grads they do. For sure they do."

"Oh my god, what if he doesn't ask me! If he doesn't ask me by the break, I'm going to start DMing Kyle!"

"Of course he's going to ask you! He'd be crazy not to. You're gorgeous. You're so fucking hot I can't stand it."

"Do you think I should get strapless or sleeveless?"

"Oh my god, maybe I should start messaging Kyle now! Just in case!"

It's more entertaining than anything on The CW. Same thing, really. Same overmakeuped and sucking-in-their-guts females. If they spent half the energy they spent on their looks on literally anything else, they could like solve climate change or something. I don't get it.

Don't get me wrong, I like makeup, hair, and sometimes I feel like a blob and want to look different, but that shit gets boring after a while. I can feel my brain melting and I've gotta go read something on Vice or something just to remember I can think.

By now, all I care about at school is grades. I'm managing a ninety-two average and am not going to slow down for anything. I managed to join school council, if only for something else to put on my university application. It's really a waste of a lunch hour. All they ever do is gossip or fight, but I get to be the secretary and take notes, which I like. It also means I don't have to contribute, I can just listen. The kids on council are slightly more tolerable than the rest. They're more like me and getting ready for the next part of their lives, instead of acting like this was the most important part. I mean really getting ready. I am not just thinking about it or dreaming about it anymore. I am planning it. I applied to both universities and I am going to get my name down for a dorm before Christmas break. I am not taking any chances. I've even started researching scholarships. This has to work.

I go see the guidance counsellor.

"Since you're Indigenous, you're eligible for all sorts of bursaries," she tells me. "I wouldn't worry about being able to pay tuition. I mean, you're not lucky enough to get Band funding, that's the best kind, but even as a Métis you can get an entrance scholarship, and maybe even something for books. You guys are very lucky."

I can't roll my eyes at her, but I smirk at her ignorance.

I don't want the funding anyone can get. I want scholarships only the good students, the best students, can get. The ones with the long forms and big payouts. I also want to stay in the dorm even if I have to pay for it.

"You have good grades but you'll have to write an essay. A good one. Are you sure you're up for that? It might take some time. And that's on top of all your regular school work."

I give this lady a long look. Try to think of how Phoenix used to look at people when she was being tough. She always had the best tough look. That's how I want to be. I really don't though. My face is more of a resting sad face than a bitchy one, but I try.

This guidance counsellor looks young, even to me who thinks every adult is ancient. But this one, Grace, still has round cheeks, rosy they would be called, and soft eyes. She smiles a lot. Too much to be completely trusted. She doesn't know me at all. Only knows what she thinks I am and she's wrong. It's okay. I am used to proving people wrong. Teachers and counsellors always start out this way.

So I try not to scoff. "I think I can manage. And I'm going to try for the dorm. If I keep working I can have the deposit by the deadline."

"Okay, but I just don't want you to get your hopes up."

I don't answer her. I know I don't have to. I just have to do it and then the look on her stupid face will be better than any comeback I could ever think up.

On Saturdays and Sundays I work at the Dollar Store. From first thing in the morning 'til mid-afternoon I unpack boxes in the back and price out the merch. I like it. It's quiet. And easy enough I can think. I've planned whole stories there, novels I will write someday and every essay for every scholarship I can find. I only make minimum wage but if I stick around, I can be a cashier in a few months. They get fifty cents more an hour. So far I'm only filling in during the Christmas rush, but if I keep at it I can get permanent.

"You only have to prove you can do it, and then they'll keep you on," Nikki had said when she drove me over that first day.

Nikki didn't seem to realize I do that every day.

—

"How's school going?" Dad asks at the dinner table.

Nikki glares at him. She doesn't like to talk about how well I am doing at school because Faith is most definitely not. She had flunked out and was now taking classes at the adult ed centre. Or I should say skipping classes at the adult ed centre and still can't find a job. Though I don't think she's really trying.

"Fine," I say. I appreciate the subtle ways Dad tries to rebel.

"Faith is doing pretty good in her geography class, aren't you, hon?" Faith's "hons" are always given more depth than mine.

She only grunts. I see her squirm in her chair. I used to think Faith was the coolest kid, but lately I can see she's always been super insecure like the rest of us. Couldn't un-see it once I saw it.

Dad tries again. "Grey Cup this weekend. What you think, C?"

"I think we should go to Kevin and Stacey's party this year, don't you, hon? It's been years and I finally have it off."

"Sure, sure. That could work. But C and I have been watching all season. We got some money on the game, don't we?" He turns to me. "You should come."

"I don't know. I have a lot of homework." I arch an eyebrow at him 'cause going to their party is the last thing I'd ever want to do. I also know Nikki wouldn't want me to go. "You can pay me when you get home."

"Whoa, tough words from someone who doesn't know a touchdown from a field goal."

I smile wide but feel Nikki's glare.

For some brave reason, I think it's a good time to try this again. "Did you— Have you heard from that social worker yet?"

"Me?" Nikki says all innocent. "No. I bet she's really busy."

Dad grins his famous get-anything grin from across the table. "You can try again, can't you, Nik? It's just a phone call."

But Nikki's not impressed by any of this. "Okay, well, I can call again, but she wasn't all that optimistic last time. I don't want to, you know, get your hopes up." She waves her wine glass in my direction. Nikki, too, used to seem so happy, but these days all I see is her bitterness.

And why the hell do adults think getting my hopes up is like, the worst possible thing?

"I think I got a job," Faith cuts in. Then straightens from her slouch and glares at me. "I mean, it's no Dollar Store dream job but I'll get tips."

Nikki doesn't even bother to call her on her shade. "Oh, that's great. Where is it, honey?"

"Piper's Pub. Downtown."

"Isn't that the place where they all wear super-short skirts?" Dad asks with his mouth full.

"Yeah, but it's fine by me." Faith looks at him challengingly. "You get more tips that way."

It's Nikki who keeps asking. "Oh honey, you're certainly pretty enough to pull that off. But will it be safe? Maybe if you get your licence we can get you a car?"

"Brody can drive me and pick me up." She starts stirring her spaghetti with her fork, looking smug and satisfied. "But if I get too many hours, I might not have time for school."

"Faith, honey, you should finish school. You only have two more credits after this semester."

"I'm not finishing this semester, so that's five and I won't have time." Faith's voice has a way of sounding low-key but still holding this "about to blow" feeling in it.

Nikki fumes into her wine glass. She looks to Dad to say something, but he only shrugs. He never knows what Nikki wants, especially with Faith, so he does nothing, to be safe.

Nikki takes a long gulp and puts the glass down with a small tink on the table. "You have to finish school."

"I don't have to finish anything. I'm eighteen now. I can do whatever I want."

Nikki talks in her measured, angry tone. "While you are living under my roof—"

"Maybe I won't live under your roof, then. Maybe I'll go live with Brody."

"You are not living with a boy. You're eighteen!"

"You're just jealous because you're an old hag who wants to wear my jeans and pretend you don't need plastic surgery."

I almost laugh out loud at that one but don't have time because Faith swings her chair out, ramming it into the wall behind her.

"You little ungrateful—" Nikki starts, getting up too, but Faith storms downstairs before she can finish.

Nikki stands there a minute, then drains her wine before storming after her.

Downstairs a door slams followed by another and then there's yelling. I can't make out the words, only that they yell over each other and seem to repeat everything over and over. I roll the spaghetti around my fork and take a long time chewing it.

"More garlic bread?" Dad asks, handing over the basket.

As it happens, I do have my hopes up and don't see why they can't stay there. Dad and I have had no luck finding my mom on Facebook. No one seems to talk to her or know her number or anything. And that social worker never bothers to answer her phone. Not since she talked to Nikki that one time. That was spring and now it's fall and I still haven't heard anything. But my hopes are still staying high.

Phoenix told me she thought Mom was staying with Uncle Toby, but neither of us knows if that's true. I vaguely remember him. We visited once when Sparrow was a baby. We took the bus, and I held on to the side of the stroller like I was supposed to. He had an old stinky apartment on Main Street. I used to drive past the building before I moved down here. I remember him smiling down at me and his face grey with too many cigarettes. The whole place smelt like too many cigarettes. Not in the way that our house did after Sparrow's dad had people over but like that smell that was in everything and made it all grey. Even smelled grey.

I don't know if that's even true, or if it was just a dream or something someone told me. That's how I remember everything about my family, like it might not be my own real memory at all. Only something I thought about something my mom or Phoenix or my dad said to me. The brown house, Grandma Margaret, Grandmère Annie. I know the stories really well. I can see them as clearly as if they happened to me. I put them all together like puzzle pieces. The old squeaky swing in the backyard, the sunny porch in the front, the bikes stored in the back shed. So even if they're not mine, it's almost as good that they belong to someone I know. Someone I love. Green, green grass free of dandelions because that was really important to Grandpa Mac, a white fence he repainted every summer, cooked meat and potatoes with everything. They could be my memories. I was there for some of them. TV and pancakes in the mornings, Grandma Margaret's stern face, Grandmère Annie's warm smile and cloudy eyes. It's almost enough.

I thought of going to that old building on Main and seeing if that old uncle still lived there. Might have moved into a different place. Might not even be around anymore. Like the Grandmothers, like everything else, I am probably already too late.

Phoenix calls me on my phone on weeknights, when she can. I don't think anyone has noticed. Dad's a great secret keeper, and Nikki seemed happy I stopped asking about my sister, at least.

"Hey Cedar-Sage, how you doin'?" Phoenix always talks a little too loud, as if she's yelling from space and not the youth centre on the other side of the city.

"All right." I put the phone on speaker and click through channels on the big TV.

"Starting to get cold out there, hey? I think it'll snow soon." She sounds a bit more tired these days, different from when we first started talking and she was full of energy. Now she seems kind of tired, and calls less and less. Sometimes it makes me awkward. We don't always have much in common, except maybe old music. Phoenix told me all these bands to listen to, old-school stuff that she said our uncle liked. Alex. I've never found him anywhere but she says that's the kind of music he likes, and that's been my playlists these days. Aerosmith and AC/DC and stuff.

When she's quiet I have to fill up the space and I never know what to say. My life is so small and boring. Sometimes I try and tell her a story, but I get all awkward about it and think I'm boring her. She says I'm not but she's obviously biased.

Mostly I only want to listen to her talk. I love her stories. Not only the family ones, but she has all sorts of stories. Some are funny shit that's happened to her and others are old, traditional stories she's heard from Elders. Some I am pretty sure she made up just to make me laugh. I love them all. Phoenix is a great storyteller. Better than I could ever hope to be.

"I had this dream about Grandmère," she tells me. "We were back in the brown house. 'Member her old chair? She was sitting in it like she did. Rocking back and forth. That's all I think she did ever, in the end. All she could do. She used to pull us up on her lap and rock us and tell us stories of the old days when there was still lots of bush along the river and they would fish in it for their supper. Her and her brother Tootie would go fishing there when they were small, and that's what they'd eat for dinner. Isn't that awesome? I think it'd be cool to fish in the river. Can't no more though. Too polluted."

I make a noise like an agreement and keep clicking channels.

There's never anything on cable. Phoenix has the best voice. It's like an old song I play over and over and never get sick of.

"I'm going to try and see my son, Cedar-Sage. I'm going to try and see Sparrow Junior."

"What!" I stop on a news station. Phoenix has never mentioned her baby. Not that he'd be a baby anymore. That was three, four years ago. But she's never mentioned him so I've never asked.

"He's living with his Grandma and Great-Grandma—just like we used to, hey? Never thought of that 'til now. That's neat. But when I get out, I want to see him."

"Are they going to let you?"

"Dunno. Hope so." She seems to sigh but I can't fully hear with the noise behind her. "Gotta try, right?"

"Guess so."

She really sighs this time. Changes the subject. "Did you hear from Elsie yet?"

"No, not yet." I start clicking again and pause at a home reno show.

"You will. She loves you, Cedar-Sage. She's all fucked up but she loves you."

"She loves you too, you know." I wish I could see her face. Sometimes I don't think I remember what she used to look like, never mind what she looks like now.

"Yeh, I know. But I got so much on here. I'm just not ready to see her. Even if she is clean, which I doubt."

"I know." On TV beautiful people walk through beautiful rooms and out to a deck that looks out to the ocean. I don't know which one it is. It's so big and blue.

"And you know, I've been thinking about a lot of things in here, all the time. And, well, the things that happened to us, they weren't our fault, right? But they weren't really Elsie's fault either. She didn't mean to let us down. I know she tried her best. I'm just not ready yet. To see her. But I hope she's doing okay."

"Yeh." You gotta have hope, I think, and tell her, "I'm really glad you named your son Sparrow. I hope I can meet him one day."

Phoenix sighs again. "Me too. Both things. Me too."

The other Sparrow wasn't supposed to die. No one thought she was going to. It was the furthest thing that could have happened, ever.

But it still happened.

She was only eight. I was almost eleven, and school had just started again. I remember feeling annoyed when Sparrow got sick because she would miss school and it had barely started. It was still as hot as summer. Never felt right going back to school then, when it stayed hot in September. Sometimes even felt hotter than the summer. It was really hot then, when Sparrow got sick.

We were living with Tannis. Had for a few years. There were a lot of kids at Tannis's. Her two kids, who were older and each had their own room in the basement, and then the foster kids, four of us, including me and Sparrow, had the rooms on the main floor, two of us in each. Ours was small and had nothing but two beds and a dresser. A few toys in a box under Sparrow's bed. And it was super clean. Everything had to be very tidy at Tannis's house. That was her favourite word, "tidy."

Everything was also on a schedule. Every morning, we got called once and then had to get out of bed and get dressed. We had to be at the table to eat by seven thirty and making our lunches by eight. The foster kids had our own lunch stuff and couldn't take from Tannis's kids' stuff. They had the good stuff they made commercials about, but the foster kids' lunch stuff was usually only cheese and bread, no-name granola bars, and maybe some fruit if we were lucky. We weren't allowed to eat if it wasn't a mealtime. Weren't allowed to go in the cupboards unless Tannis was there watching us. I think I was always hungry when we were at Tannis's house.

I was very good though. I got really used to and good at cleaning.

Did most of Sparrow's stuff too because she was so little and was the kind of kid who was always in the moon. That's what my mom used to call it, "Oh sweet Sparrow, always off on the moon." Sparrow was the kind of kid who had to blow the dandelions when they got fuzzy, or stop and talk to dogs, if they were friendly. Sparrow didn't care for schedules or tidiness.

She was also strong, and kind, and was barely ever sick. Until she was really sick and never got better.

I took care of her. I always took care of her and when she got fevered at night, it was only a fever, so I got a cold, wet cloth to put on her forehead, tucked the blanket all snug around her little body, and lay there so I could pat her back when she coughed. I did all the things Phoenix and my mom used to. I mostly slept on her bed or her on my bed anyway, especially when we first came to Tannis's house, after they took us from our home and the people who loved us and told us that this was better. To be clear, it was never better. It was way fucking worse.

It felt like Sparrow was sick for a long time, but if I think about it, it was really only a few days. I was up most of the nights and still went to school so it felt like a long time. Tannis said it was nothing to worry about, and let her stay home and in bed. Tannis stayed home all day and watched TV and did laundry or made things tidy or whatever, so it's not like Sparrow was alone.

That last morning, I felt her head before I went to school. It was finally cool. I was relieved. I thought that meant she was better. She was sleeping, so I let her sleep. I went to school feeling better that she was better.

After lunch I got called to the office. My social worker, the one at the time, was there to get me. I don't remember the words she said in the car as she drove to the hospital. Not the words anyway, only the meaning, that Sparrow was very sick, that she could die. I thought she got us confused. Like she was talking about the wrong kid and she'd picked up the wrong sister. Sparrow was getting better.

But Tannis was at the hospital, crying so hard her mascara was running down her stupid face in thick black smears. Her husband Gary was there, too, looking dumb and not doing anything. The nurses were crowding around Tannis, comforting her, like she was the one who needed comforting. So I thought maybe it was one of the other kids who got sick, one of her own kids, 'cause those were the only ones I thought Tannis would cry about. I sat in a chair in the corner and kept quiet.

Then my mom came in wearing a brown uniform and I got excited for a second. But she didn't see me and didn't seem to even hear what the doctor was telling her. She just stared at Tannis. Then lunged at her. Hands out to grab her stupid throat. Tannis screamed pathetically and made a loud gagging sound like she was super hurt. I saw, though, my mom never touched her. It was all chaos then, yelling. Gary even stood up. Guards ran in and held my mom down. Took her by both arms and dragged her away. She hadn't even seen me, sitting in the corner, giving up hope that this was all a mistake.

When they finally let me go in and see her, a nurse told me to say goodbye. I still didn't believe her. Not all the way. I walked down that hall, looking down at those big square floor tiles, and knew she had to get better. Was getting better. Maybe they all just didn't know that. I thought once I saw her I could tell them. I would fix it.

Sparrow looked like she was sleeping. Tubes in her nose and a plastic thing on her finger. But she looked fine. I held my sister's hand and didn't say anything out loud. Sparrow knew that I didn't say much out loud when other people were around, especially back then, so she wouldn't've cared. She knew I was there. I don't know how I knew that but I did. I sat there for a long time, thinking she would wake up because she knew I was there. But she didn't. And finally they made me go and sit back in that chair for a while.

I didn't know where Phoenix was, or if she was coming too. I thought some social worker must be going to pick her up. But she never came. And my mom didn't come back. Tannis stayed on her phone, calling people, telling them, crying like she cared. Gary did nothing, again. And neither of them said anything to me.

After a while, another social worker came in and told us all she died. She did it like that. To all of us. Like it was more important to tell them than me. I was mad about that later but at the time I think I was still not believing they were talking about the right kid. Still thought they had made a mistake.

Tannis wailed like she really cared, and Gary held her, still looking dumb. I just kept sitting there, pulled my knees up to my chest and gave myself my own hug. Some nurse kept trying to talk to me, my social worker tried to give me a can of pop like that would make it better, but I just sat there 'til they moved me again. This time back to Tannis's.

I took me a long time to believe it all the way. I really didn't. Not when the other kids told me it was true and they were sorry for me. Not even driving to the funeral when my mom told me she was better and going to take me home soon, but when we got there she forgot about me and was really out of it and hanging off some strange rough-looking guy. Not even when Phoenix got there and held my hand the whole time, or when Tannis said we all had to move because she was too sad and couldn't foster anymore. Not all those months out in the country when the nights got so dark it scared me and I hated not being able to see around the bedroom when I went to sleep. For all that time, most days I woke up thinking it was all a dream.

I don't think I really believed it until I got to Luzia's place, until I sat on that newest-new bed with the red blanket, in a room all to myself for the first time, and I could be really truly alone.

I started to cry that first night. And did every night for a long time. As soon as I could close the door behind me and not have to worry about anyone seeing me. I wanted to be able to howl like Tannis had, but I was quiet. I cried like I did everything else, as quiet and as good as I could be.

I settle into the upstairs living room after school with a sandwich and spread my history homework out on the coffee table. I'm not supposed to eat in the upstairs living room but do it all the time when no one is home.

I'm halfway through the chapter on the "settling" of Vancouver when my phone vibrates. I never turn the ringer on because the vibration thing seems loud enough.

"Hello?" I clear my unused throat and try again. "Hello?"

"Hi, Cedar, how are you?" Nikki's singsong voice. There must be a co-worker or someone near her.

"Fine."

"Good news. Your mom finally got in touch and we can arrange a visit, I think."

"Oh," I say but then can't think anything else to add. "Oh."

"I thought you'd be happy. You've been harping on me for long enough. Do you not want to see her anymore?"

"No, no. I do."

"Okay." She pauses to make sure I know she's sighing. "The social worker and I agreed we should monitor things for a bit. Maybe we can try for something in a month or two? If all goes well?"

Something hot in my throat grows big. "Why?" I say slowly. "Why so long?"

"These things take time. You haven't seen your mom in, what, three years almost. We can't go rushing into these things."

My insides boil.

"Just be patient, Cedar. We'll figure it all out. I gotta go. Love you." Her singsong voice ends with a click.

I stare at the switched-off screen in my hand. Trying to figure out what I'm feeling. Glad that my mom got in touch. Mad that I have to keep waiting. I think of what Phoenix said, about it not being mom's fault. And if it wasn't, why were they still treating her like it was?

I lean back against the couch and stare out the window at the street. The quiet, tree-lined street with a thin blanket of snow just fallen. Just like Phoenix said it would.

15

ELSIE

It's cold at six a.m. The sky is a grey pink and the smoke from the fall fires lingers all the way downtown. It could snow again soon, she thinks, and pulls the sides of her windbreaker together. It could get warm yet. No way of knowing at six a.m.

Elsie inhales the day and her cigarette and huddles further into her thin jacket. Her stomach empty and her head a dull thud from lack of coffee. She only had a small sip of water after she dry-brushed her teeth. She did everything she was supposed to.

The city is quiet. Main Street, even. The odd car passes but she is alone mostly. She flicks away her cigarette and just breathes, puffs of cold air. She thinks of Jimmy, she thinks of her kids, her thoughts lingering around Sparrow, that pain, that love, but it all feels kind of lighter today. Lighter somehow, this early.

Last night she dreamt of her babies. Before they were taken away. Before she ever had that fear or knew that nightmare. It was when they were living on Arlington, a little apartment, just her and the three of them. Sparrow's dad was in Remand for a while and she didn't have a phone so they were free of him. That summer Sparrow wasn't even walking and there was a schoolyard close by they'd visit. Cedar and Phoenix would clomp all over the play structure and she'd sit with the baby in the grass. Her baby. They had nothing, sometimes not even milk, but they were all so happy.

She'd wake up feeling the sun on her face, feeling the grass under her bare thighs and smelling the top of her baby's head.

Sparrow.

The warmth stays with her even in this cold. She walks down Main, sighs into her strides, and turns after the underpass. She thought she'd feel different somehow, today.

The building is familiar. She has walked by a few times. It's an orange brick and kind of plain. She'd never have noticed it ever, if it weren't for the picketers there sometimes. Sometimes they would walk there, back and forth, with sad, stern faces and signs that read things like,

PRAY TO END ABORTION

JESUS SAVES

EMBRACE LIFE

Each with a small fetus and short umbilical cord in a bright blue kidney bean in the corner like a logo.

Thankfully there is no one here at six a.m.

She puffs out one more long, grey breath and pulls open the glass door.

The fluorescent lights are buzzing. Two clerks chirp behind a long white counter. The opening is scratched-up Plexiglas with small speaking holes. She can hear one older lady telling the other about the night. Shift change. Their tones friendly and to the point, but she can't really hear the words.

One turns to Elsie at the counter. "Yes?"

"My name is Elsie Stranger. I was told to be here for six thirty."

"Do you have a medical card or treaty card with you?" the clerk says with a tired sigh.

Elsie passes her worn old medical card through.

"Is the address the same?"

She shakes her head.

"Photo ID?"

She shakes her head again, this time looking down.

"Okay, you'll have to fill this out. Do you need help with the form?" the clerk says in a hurry.

Again Elsie shakes her head, but this time she looks up. She takes the clipboard and sits down, takes up the pen tied to the clip with a long piece of red yarn.

Address.

History of mental illness?

Prescription medications?

Viable, full term pregnancies? If so, how many?

She passes the clipboard back and the lady starts to tap at the keyboard, typing quickly.

Elsie picks at a nick in the countertop and waits.

The clerk stops and the printer starts to churn. She disappears and emerges with a small plastic strip.

"Left wrist, please," she says like a woman who has been up all night.

She pulls up Elsie's sleeve, her wrist small and pale. Her small homemade green along the inside. Phoenix. She got it not long after her first baby was born.

The clerk fastens the clasp. Then dictates directions efficiently. Go here. Turn there. Wait.

Up an elevator and through a set of doors, Elsie is in another cluster of upright chairs in a waiting room. She sits on the closest one. There's an end table and an old issue of Maclean's but she just crosses her legs and pulls her jacket around her. Her head still a dull thud. She wishes for a coffee, another cigarette, anything. She feels so heavy now. Here.

She can just see the sky through a window on the other side of the plastic divide. Stares as the clouds slowly break up and blue peeks out in between them.

She tried for a long time. Did what they said, and visited when she was allowed. The four of them in those smelly visiting rooms with the mouldy furniture and cheap Native art hung up to make them feel like they knew them. Most of the time Elsie could only cry, held Sparrow on her lap and felt how different, bigger, how many more words she knew, every time. She could only feel that she was missing it. Cedar would be happy and bright, talk nonstop and laugh and hug her over and over. Elsie pulled her close. Never wanted to let her go. Phoenix didn't talk to Elsie much. Phoenix mostly stuck out her chin and tried to be tough. She had always done that and it's always hurt Elsie, but she also understood. She saw that in her brothers, her uncles, her mom. No one messes with Strangers. Except for Elsie. She's never been tough. Has only cried her way through life. It never got her anything but she never learned how to stop.

"Elsie?" A short woman with frizzy black hair kind of appears beside her.

She nods but doesn't get up.

The woman extends her hand. "I'm Dr. Lee and I will be performing your procedure today."

Elsie takes the small hand and shakes delicately.

"Come with me." Dr. Lee waves her up, and Elsie follows her down the hall.

They turn two corners and then go into a large room divided by a maze of pale curtains, grey, green, and cream. Some have pale pastel flowers on them and all have that industrial hospital-soap smell to them. Through the fabric, Elsie can hear one woman softly crying, and another whispering short, gentle sentences. She can't hear the words though.

She follows the doctor into an open space with an upright cot covered in a paper strip. There's a dark monitor and a stool.

"Please." Dr. Lee motions. "Make yourself comfortable."

She sits on the cot, crinkling the paper underneath, and noisily adjusts herself and leans back on the paper-covered pillow.

"Now," the doctor says quietly, "I am just going to take a look to see that everything is as it should be." She sits on the stool and picks up the corded wand.

A thought breaks through Elsie's haze and all she can think is

This is real

This is real

This is really happening.

Tears well up but they don't fall.

The doctor places a warm blanket over her middle, then efficiently pulls her shirt up a couple inches and squeezes soft gel on her abdomen.

The tears slip hot across her temples. Into her ears.

She notices the doctor adjust the monitor so that it is turned away.

She remembers this. Her other pregnancies had ultrasounds too. Exciting events where she first got to see them, her babies. By the time she saw Phoenix, the baby was already almost born and squished inside of her, waiting to get out. With Cedar she got to see at around twenty weeks, and the baby was a fuzzy black-and-white head and hand. Elsie couldn't tell anything else.

Sparrow, though, she got to see her lots. There was some issue with the fluid in there so they kept calling her back to check. Every couple weeks, Sparrow's dad and she would leave the girls with his sister and take the bus over to the hospital where they'd huddle around the narrow cot she'd always almost fall off of 'cause she was so big, and wait for the baby to come on the screen, to hear the

whoosp,

whoosp,

whoosp

of her little unborn heart.

Sparrow.

On the way home, they'd pass the soft paper print-out back and forth until it was crinkled and worn.

He was a good guy then. She was a good mom then.

"Okay," the doctor says quietly and wipes the gel off Elsie's middle while the little printer starts. The doctor rips the paper off and turns it face down on her thigh. "I'll lead you back to where you can get changed." Her voice even and practised, and she pats Elsie's arm.

Elsie nods and lays there another moment. Feeling the tears cool in her ears.

They walk again.

The doctor passes her off to a clerk who leads her to a locker area and a stack of hospital gowns.

"You can wear another one over like a housecoat if you're cold." This one half smiles like it's a clever thing to do, and leaves Elsie with the silent close of the curtain behind her.

Elsie stands in the locker room for a long moment. The empty ones have keys on wristbands dangling.

She moves slow. The room is cold, and she feels even heavier all of a sudden. There is a weight on her, something pushing across her head, shoulders. She pulls on a blue gown and manages to tie the ties behind her neck, behind her waist. Then pulls a green gown over and ties it in front. The sleeves are short and she's still so cold, so she keeps her socks on. There's a hole in the toe and they need a wash, but she would be so cold otherwise.

Another waiting room. This one bigger, with reclining orange vinyl chairs and a handful of women in them, some upright, some reclined. A TV plays the movie *Dreamgirls*, just beginning. The young singers smile at each other and laugh in backwards wigs and bright dresses. Elsie settles into a corner and looks at the pretty girls around her.

A blonde girl who looks about twelve with her face in her phone.

An older lady with dyed black hair and blue vine tattoos twisted up both arms.

A doughy woman whose cheeks hang like jowls, coarse black hair sticking straight out of the pale flesh of her legs.

Nobody talks to each other. The older woman stares at the movie, so Elsie does too. Her headache easing in the comfy chair. Her tears drying stiff and salty to her skin. After a while the large woman looks her over. Elsie tenses, but then the woman smiles a quiet greeting.

They all sit there a long time before, one by one, they are called in.

Elsie is last.

She gave up completely when Sparrow died. She gave up everything and would have died had it not been for Jimmy caring for her, or at least keeping her high and numb.

She remembers she was working. She was saving up to get a new place, on the list for every good family housing in the city and working at a donut shop. She hated it. Jimmy hated her working there and wanted her to quit so they could be together more. But she wanted her kids and they wanted her to have a job.

She got the call when she was at work. Ran all the way to the hospital still in her uniform. She didn't understand when they told her Sparrow died. Elsie thought she was just sick. Sick, they said, but she had gone. Elsie didn't even hear what they were saying. But stared at the foster mom, her curly bleach-blonde hair messy, mascara running down her face, surrounded by nurses comforting her. Like she was the one who was supposed to be upset.

Elsie could have killed her.

She doesn't remember going at her, only holding her blonde hair in her hands and trying to punch at her face.

She was never a fighter, never like her brothers or uncles. She was always more like Mamere, who always said she never punched anyone in her life, only wanted to. Only wanted to.

Elsie couldn't punch Tannis, but not for lack of trying. All those people there pulled her off and someone was screaming,

"What did you do? What did you do?" she heard someone screaming over and over and it was a while before she realized it was her who was screaming.

They took her into a room and she felt a prick at her shoulder. Was asleep before she could think. And that was the first of her long oblivion.

She tried to stay straight at first. Was so woozy and confused she kept waking up, making herself wake up and say, "Why? Why? How?"

She got the story in pieces.

Thought it was just the flu.

Didn't wake up.

Pneumonia.

Too quick.

But Elsie knew the real reason. She wasn't there.

If she had been there, she could have taken care of her baby. If her baby hadn't been in a place with so many other babies. If her baby had been with her because she knew her better than anyone. Even though she had missed so much, she still knew her. Her baby. Sparrow.

Sparrow.

When Jennifer Hudson starts singing that emotional song, they finally call her. The voice hits the high note and Elsie shivers as she walks.

A nurse pokes an IV in the top of Elsie's hand. Elsie watches the metal spear through her cold skin and vein before she gets up and manoeuvres the tall IV pole into the next room. The small tires squeak. Through the swinging door, the tiny Dr. Lee greets her from behind a green surgical mask.

"Hi, Elsie." Her eyes smile and she gestures toward the bed.

Elsie leans against the pole and another nurse helps her onto the bed. She bends her knees and places her socked feet in the stirrups. Sighs quickly then, but only breathes shallow. She closes her eyes and feels instantly sleepy. Her skin sinks into the crinkles of the paper bed-cover, and the doctor and nurses whisper. A machine turns on. A low drone. Her knees slowly pushed apart. Soft hands. Gloved and powdered in latex.

The speculum and her tears open simultaneously. Every gentle prod brings a new wave of something. Like parts of her that haven't been touched for so long. Parts that haven't felt feel. Her body shakes, her stomach churns, and she can't think of anything. She tries to think of one thing, one good thing, but feels a hazy high. The world grows grey and fuzzy.

She feels it. When it happens, she can feel it. She squeezes her eyes shut. When she opens them again, there is a nurse at her shoulder. Her hand presses into Elsie's arm. Warm.

The drone sounds stops. Then metal on metal, a soft clink.

"There," the doctor says, close. "You are not pregnant anymore."

The nurse looks down at Elsie's face, looking for signs of what? Elsie can't meet her eye. The lights feel bright. The ceiling tile white and stained. Those tiles with dots in a square framed in flat white slats crossing the ceiling, all perfectly straight and uniform.

—

She doesn't remember much of the funeral. They had given her tranquilizers at the hospital and the small parts those didn't touch Jimmy filled in with percs and Oxy. She remembers the songs Phoenix picked. That Tannis lady stood up and talked with her mascara still smudged. She remembers hugging Cedar and not wanting to let go, not wanting to send her back there and terrified that she would die too. But Cedar smiled up at her, at that horrible moment she smiled at her. Sweet Cedar. Phoenix hugged her too but not as long.

She remembers a car ride. Remembers sleeping against the window. Then she doesn't remember much for a long time.

Jimmy's basement. Jimmy's mattress. Jimmy's sister-in-law yelling down the stairs. Jimmy.

Nothing else was real. Nothing else mattered.

Until one day she wanted to be clear. She wanted to sit out in the grass and feel the sun. It was spring then, months had passed. The grass was wet from just-melted frost but she sat there anyway. Her bare thighs cold on the ground. She was shocked that that hadn't killed her.

In the recovery room, she sits up half-asleep under a thin blanket thick with the smell of hospital laundry soap. Hospitals always smell the same. Industrial soap and faintly of blood.

She stays there a long time, in and out of sleep. The needle protruding from her right hand, she can feel it when she moves her fingers. It's a dull echo of a pain, like something inside of her that shouldn't be there.

She went to the clinic to get the test done. Couldn't afford the home one so just went there. When they told her it was positive they asked her what she wanted to do. She knew right there. Told them right there.

They sent her to a counsellor. A young girl with very red hair and those oversized glasses like Mamere used to wear. Her sweater was pink. She looked like she came out of a magazine. Her voice was kind.

Elsie told her about Sparrow and her kids getting taken away. Told her about Phoenix being in jail. Everything. Like she had been waiting to tell it all for forever.

"I can't go through that again."

"It might not happen like that again, Elsie."

"But so many kids get apprehended, like right at birth. I don't even have my own place."

"Well, they can help you with housing. They can help you. It doesn't have to be the same."

Elsie didn't trust this idea of help but didn't say anything.

"I'm not trying to say one way or the other. I'm just saying there are ways, if you want them."

Elsie shook her head. Shook it for a long time. Thinking. Knowing. "I can't do that again."

"What?"

"I don't want to." She looked up at the counsellor, the glare from the window blurring out her eyes. She was so pretty. "Any of it. I'm not healthy enough. Not ready."

The counsellor nodded. Smiled. Wrote down on her clipboard.

Elsie knew as soon as she found out, all the reasons,

I am not well enough

I could never live through that again

None of it

Cedar wants to see me, she thinks.

Cedar wants to see me

Cedar

"Do you have anyone who could pick you up? We're not supposed to let you go on your own."

Elsie doesn't want to get up, but feels suddenly so hungry. "My uncle would have but he's elderly. Has bad days."

"You need someone to pick you up. We can't let you go on your own."

She can think of one person but doesn't say anything.

"You're going to need a few days' recovery, Elsie. Do you have anyone to help you?"

She nods, hoping they're not going to ask for any names.

"You need to call someone. We can't release you without someone to take you home."

After she phones, she goes back to the recliner and pulls the thin blanket over her shoulders. The movie's switched to *Back to the Future*. Michael J. Fox skateboarding through the 1950s, and she dozes off again.

She dreams of nothing. Or wakes up thinking of nothing. And then gets up and does everything in reverse, all the getting in and getting here, backwards. Like it's coming undone.

When Elsie gets back to the front desk, she's standing there, waiting.

"You have to sign her out," the clerk behind the Plexiglas calls.

Val turns and signs her name on the paper without looking.

Outside is a full sun and warm afternoon. Elsie ties her jacket around her waist and her friend, former friend, hands her a smoke. She's surprised she doesn't feel that sore. The odd cramp and numbness in her stomach. Hungry. Tired. Not heavy though. Not heavy at all anymore. She just stands there. And thinks,

It's over

It's over

It's over

"So is that what I think it was?" Val asks between puffs.

Elsie nods, almost doesn't. And then after a breath, says in an almost whisper, "Do you hate me?"

"Hate you? For what? For that?" She lets the air out from between her teeth but doesn't look at Elsie. Just looks out, into the sky, as if she's searching for something. "That's the old way, you know. Well, not that, but in the old days we knew how to stop it, if we wanted, what medicines to use. No one looked down on it. It was always your choice." Val stops, thinks, finally turns to Elsie. "It's your choice, Elsie. Always."

Her tears are hot. Like a burning.

Val sort of laughs. "I wouldn't've had Jimmy's baby either."

Elsie sort of smiles.

Poor Jimmy.

A cab pulls up. Val flicks her smoke away and moves to the car. "Come on."

Elsie waves her hands and stammers, "Oh, you didn't have to. I can't pay for a cab."

"My treat," Val says and shimmies over in the back seat. "You've been through enough."

Elsie thinks of that as she slams the door, as downtown passes beyond the window, as the sun shines warm on her.

Enough

Enough

Enough

16

MARGARET

On the day she buried her mother, Margaret was so very tired.

As soon as they could, people started leaving. After all that work, everyone only came in for a drink and some food and then they were in a rush out the door. They all left their mess behind, of course. Saying goodbye and "I'm so sorry" and "Let me know if you need anything." Useless. Like Margaret would call any of them. What she needed them to do was bring their plates to the sink. There she was stuck being a waitress in her own house. This damn house. Elsie was no use, she had sulked up to her bedroom with her dumb-as-a-stump new boyfriend after she had mooched enough cigarettes off the relatives and had a few too many glasses of the wine Margaret had bought.

Genie lingered in the kitchen. Not that she was helping, only thought she was. Parked in Margaret's own chair, she wittered on about loneliness and silly clubs and hobbies she had found to pass her weary golden years. Genie wasn't much older than Margaret but you'd think she was at the end, the way she was going on.

"You'd be surprised how much comfort it can give you, counting stitches and seeing it come together. To finish something you can give to your grandchildren and make them warm. So lovely," Genie said with a faraway look as her tea went cold. She was always a simple kind of woman, always in the moon as Annie always said, used to say. "I just love the look on their faces when I can wrap a sweater or scarf around them. It's like I'm giving them real love."

Margaret leaned against the counter and lit a smoke, trying not to scoff. “Don’t think I’m taking up knitting, Genie. Besides, Elsie’s kids wouldn’t go for knitted stuff, I don’t think.” Rough little girls, they tore up their clothes faster than they grew out of them. No sense wasting work after kids not taught to appreciate it.

Genie’s daughter-in-law, Jerome’s too-young second wife, Kelly, came in from the living room, looking plumper after too many hors d’oeuvres and frumpy in an old sweater and cheap polyester skirt. At least it was a skirt. Better than Jerome, that useless layabout of a man, who was wearing a black fleece pullover and jeans. To his own Grandmother’s funeral! The shame of this family.

“How you feeling, Mom? Almost ready to go?” Kelly talked too loud to Genie, and with all the grace of a semi truck. Kelly never had much class but had really let herself go after having kids. Some women do, Margaret thought as she smoothed her waist, still flat under her freshly ironed shirt.

“Oh yes, I suppose we should.” Genie looked out the window at God knows what.

“It was such a lovely service,” Kelly said uselessly, shook her chubby face. Her hair pulled back nicely at least.

Margaret only nodded and puffed away. She knew she’d want to light another as soon as she put this one out.

Kelly was such a silly woman, but she was nothing next to Jerome’s first wife, the exceptionally silly Renee. That one had shown up to the service at the funeral home but had the decency not to come to the house. Not like she was family anymore. But still she had completely irritated Margaret for the full five minutes they had spent together. Renee had cornered her to “pay her respects.” Margaret didn’t understand that. If Renee had really wanted to be respectful, she should have left Margaret the hell alone.

“Oh she was a great woman, Margey. Such a powerful matriarch,” stupid Renee had sighed. Her silver earrings jingled around, making noise and catching the light. Probably meant to do that, to show how expensive they were. She was head to toe in her Pretendian costume today, was Renee. She wore a bright blue rayon dress and beaded jacket over top. Even her sandals had turquoise on them. She looked like she had one of those spray tans, was far too tan for it to be natural, and her hair that used to be curly and blonde was now dark and straight. Acting all high and mighty like she did whenever she saw Margaret. It was all Margaret could do not to laugh in her face.

Renee had gotten into all this Indian stuff a few years ago when she found out her Great-Great-Grandpa was a Métis shaman or something. Or so she said. Margaret thought it was all bullshit. Never had heard of a real Indian being called a shaman, never mind a Métis one. Jerome had even laughed about it but didn't call her on it, of course. Would never God forbid rock the boat with his crazy ex-wife. Still scared of stupid Renee. "No skin off my nose what she says she is," he said into his beer one visit. "Not my problem anymore."

Sasha didn't think it was funny. Not like Margaret did. "I don't understand those people," he said. "Thinking they're all neech just because someone in their family once kissed an Indian or something. Why does everyone wanna be Indian now? Wouldn't want to be if they had to grow up Indian like we did."

"Doesn't matter to us," Jerome said. Margaret could tell he wanted to change the subject.

"But it does matter," Sasha insisted. "When people pretend, it does matter." Sasha was real bent up about it, but as usual didn't quite know why.

Margaret scoffed. "Truth always wins out, I say. They'll find her out one day. Always do."

Jerome only asked for another beer.

It was soon after that the lady got a fancy job at the university and started going by some made-up name even though everyone still called her Renee. Margaret never had to do that. Never had to play at something she wasn't just to get to where she got. As far as she got.

"Going to that funeral home always makes me think of Joseph," Genie said, interrupting Margaret's fuming about annoying Renee to be annoying herself. "My poor young Joseph. Sorry, Margey, but we were all thinking it."

Like hell, Margaret thought, and took a deep breath and then another drag.

Kelly put a fat hand on Genie's shoulder. Everyone's always so soft with Genie. "I can't imagine what it was like losing him too young like that, Mom."

The damn fools couldn't even stay on the right dead person for a day. Couldn't even keep it about her mother for two minutes. Like the old lady lived too long to be worthy of their mourning.

She was almost sympathetic though. To Genie, at least. She did always think of her brother when she went to that funeral home, and she knows Genie hadn't been right in the head since Joseph died. Margaret almost felt for the old woman. For a minute.

Genie patted Kelly's hand and looked up with a stupid smile. "I have my Jerome, at least. All my blessed grandchildren."

Margaret wanted to laugh. Jerome was nothing like his father. Had none of his grace or charm. Didn't even look like him much. Margaret used to question how Jerome came out just looking like Genie and no one else. Annie told her to hush, but Margaret knew her mom had thought it too.

"I'll go find Jerome." Kelly stomped away to find her useless husband, like he was an invalid and not a grown man. She knew full well he was on the porch with all the other men, with Sasha, Toby, John, all of them smoking too much and drinking too many beers. All they needed was the excuse of the day to go at it. Though it wasn't like Sasha needed much excuse these days. Working less and less as far as Margaret could tell. Coming home with less and less anyway.

Her brother John had been out two months. After a simple parole breach, after a burglary charge, after the bank robbery all those years ago, after whoever could keep track, John had been in more than out his whole adult life, and he seemed to just appear again one day. After that, he was over at the house every day, eating everything and never shutting up. He'd become a muscly old man with more homemade tattoos and scars and no ambitions or goals of any kind. None that Margaret could see anyway. He made their mother happy though. Those last weeks, he sat with her every day, talked with her and made her tea. Margaret thought it was what Annie was waiting for, actually, to see John a free man again. Her mother went pretty quick after that, like a long breath held in too long.

He was holding her hand when she went. When her mother couldn't get out of bed anymore and refused to go to the hospital again. John brought her tea while Margaret did everything else, and Elsie skittered about pretending to look after her kids. John was the one who was holding her hand. Not Elsie, who screamed when she saw and made a big show of herself hugging and kissing a corpse, calling "Mamere, Mamere." Not Margaret, who stood at the doorway, unable to go in, could only watch her mother's skin turn to stone. She looked different right away. How quick. How strange.

John didn't let go. Sasha went to go get Toby. Margaret had to call 911 herself. Her voice was calm. She said her mother was dead. No, no need for an ambulance. Send a coroner. She didn't know if that was the right thing to do, the right procedure. Her father had died in the hospital. The nurses had taken over that part.

After Kelly left the room, Genie was off on the moon again. Margaret, saved from more useless small talk, butted out her smoke and got back to work. She was tired, bone-tired. Elsie, of course, was nowhere to be found. Margaret had been on her feet all day, had made the mini quiches first thing and dainty sandwiches too, the kind you had to get special bread for so you could roll them and cut them up into little circles. She had to special-order it days ago. She cleaned everything, and cooked a turkey, a ham, bought all the plastic dishes and cutlery. Sasha claimed to be working, and Elsie wouldn't stop crying, so as usual it was up to Maggie Muggins again.

"Time to go, Mom." Kelly had returned with Genie's jacket and helped her into it. "Jerome's starting the car."

Genie only smiled stupidly and let herself be helped into her own clothes.

Kelly turned to Margaret, barely a polite smile on her face, and reached out for a cold handshake. "Take care, Margaret. It was a lovely service," she said again. The stupid things people say at funerals.

Genie reached over to hug Margaret, and obligingly Margaret leaned over a bit. "Now you let me know if you need anything at all. Anything. Just call. She really loved you, my girl. She really depended on you."

Margaret nodded into Genie's bony shoulder and wondered, which was it—loved or depended on?

The two women wobbled away, Genie twittering about sad times and families coming together. Margaret scoffed, probably too loud. Family, my ass, she thought as she lit another. Jerome visited less and less, and Kelly never came with him. Genie could be forgiven, being older, but still barely managed a phone call a month, and had only ever really talked to Annie. As for Jerome's kids, the younger ones were kept away, which was fine, they were young, but the older ones didn't even bother to show up, and they were grown adults now so they should have. Lyn the artist was forever travelling apparently, was in Scotland, of fucking course. And the other, June, was still in school, somewhere in Ontario. Or so Renee had said when she cornered Margaret, just had to brag about her high-achieving daughters. For all their achievements, those two would have barely recognized their Great-Grandmother. They had rarely visited since they were small. At least Margaret had taught her children respect. Had done the best with what was handed to her. Not like Renee who got all the breaks.

"How you doing, Ma?" Alex stomped up with his heavy feet and pulled out a chair, roughly scraping it along the linoleum. Margaret scowled down at him, and in an instant he said, "Sorry."

He had been in the backyard with his "boys." Not good ones, as far as she could tell, but they'd kept quiet today at least.

"I'm fine," she said and turned to the sink, flipped on the faucet.

Behind her, her son sighed, then went to clear plates in the living room. He was a good boy. Nothing like his brother, Joey, who didn't even bother to call his mother, even after this. The coward.

"He'll call when there's a little less heat," Sasha had said matter-of-fact, like her son breaching parole and taking off across the country didn't matter. Like the "heat" was the most important part. "You can't expect him to come home now. That would be asking for trouble."

Her useless son finally had all the excuse he needed to never talk to her again.

When nearly all the visitors had gone, she heard the TV go on and knew it was those two girls going to stare at that thing again. Cedar was barely two and could already work the remote. Margaret could scarcely figure it out. But that was all they did all day sometimes, sat too close to the screen like the zombie children Elsie had spoiled them to be. Margaret pulled the dishes into the suds and started scrubbing.

Then Sasha came in reeking of beer and cigarettes, like he'd been incubating in them. She didn't bother to turn around.

"A few of us are going down to the Legion. Say a proper goodbye and that. Then I'll drive John back to the halfway house." He kissed the top of her head.

"He has to be there by eight. On the dot."

"I know, I know." He gave a wheezy sigh.

She didn't bother saying anything. Just kept working away. She heard the back door slam and her husband and brothers make their noisy way to the car and then away. An old muscle car on its last legs, and the thing was way too loud.

Alex brought in some plates and then said slowly, "I'm going to head out, too."

"Where are you going?"

"Just to a friend's."

"Mmm." Margaret knew "friend" meant a girl, otherwise he would have said some boy's name.

Alex knew how to move quietly, politely in the world, at least. When he wanted to. He closed the back door carefully, and with the last click an eerie quiet descended. Besides the TV moaning on some stupid kids' show in the living room. Margaret wiped down the counters and heard the refrigerator click on its too-loud hum. She went into the living room and straightened up around the little ones, who didn't even notice her. She fixed the folds and pillows everyone had messed around. She heard some kids yelling at each other down the street and wondered if it was Alex and his friends. It was still sunny, still warm, that early part of spring when everyone realized they could finally go outside and go crazy. That time of year when everyone was out and up to no good, yelling their trouble up and down the street without any consideration for anyone else. The last thing she had to do was close the curtains. She hated them open, thought the whole street could just look in and know her business. She had only opened them because people were coming over, coming to this old dump of a house to eat her food and talk about things like condolences and well wishes. Margaret always felt better when they were closed, like they would be now that the room was as empty as all those words. All gone because they meant nothing in the first place. Not even an echo was left. Margaret pulled the curtains closed so hard they almost tore off their small metal hooks. Phoenix looked up from her show, startled.

"Did you girls get enough to eat?" she asked them because chances were no one had asked them yet.

Phoenix nodded, and nudged Cedar-Sage, who moaned, "What?"

"Grandma is talking to you," the girl said in a voice older than her years.

Cedar-Sage fixed herself. "Yes, Mamma?"

"Did you get enough to eat? Are you hungry?"

"No, Mamma." She shook her little head too much and Margaret almost smiled down at her.

"Okay then, you girls finish this show and then go up to bed." It was still light out, but the day was long and these girls should get to bed at a decent hour for a change. Not that their mother would see to it. Elsie probably wouldn't come out of her room now. So far gone since the old lady went. Crying like she couldn't help it and moping like she couldn't handle it. Margaret couldn't understand it. It's not like it wasn't expected. The lady was in her nineties, after all.

When everything finally felt clean enough and she knew she wouldn't see anything from the men for hours, she pulled her own beer from the fridge and sat down for a smoke. Theme music played in the living room, and obediently Phoenix shut off the TV and told her little sister it was time for bed. Margaret didn't even have to remind her or help them. Phoenix took Cedar-Sage by the hand and up the stairs they went.

"Goodnight, Grandma."

"Night, Mamma."

"Night, girls," she said with an exhale. They could be such good girls sometimes. She listened to them brush their teeth and softly speak to Elsie, who seemed to only groan in response. Didn't even get up to tuck them in. Damn Elsie. Margaret would go up and check on them in a bit. That grown woman acting like a spoiled child. How did that girl manage to avoid growing up so thoroughly? Margaret thought she knew the answer but tried to think of something else.

She pulled out another beer and took a half bowl of chips with her to the couch. She didn't drink beer much. It left her bloaty and made her pee too often, but what the heck, she thought, and turned the TV back on. She flipped channels, went through each one because she could never figure out how to use that guide thing, until she found a stupid reality show about decorating, the kind where everyone spent too much money on unnecessary renovations. She liked these shows, if only to be mad at the stupid people with too much makeup on and more money than sense.

The girls were asleep by the time she checked on them. She looked over at Elsie, but she was facing the wall her bed was pressed up against. Thankfully her stupid boyfriend had left. He had barely said two words to anyone ever, never mind since all this had happened.

He only sat there beside Elsie like that was doing something. He didn't have a job, of course, but at least he seemed to stay out of trouble, for now. Not like that Shawn who was still in prison, the moron. Margaret hadn't heard anything about that one in a long time, and doubted she would.

When the beer was gone, she finished the rye. When the chips were gone, she ate the rest of the little rolled sandwiches that she had so carefully wrapped in plastic. She flipped channels to Judge Judy. Margaret loved that lady. The firmness, the certainty. Margaret always wanted to be that type of woman. Knew she could have been, if given half the chance. Always was, if only they hadn't taken away her one and only chance.

She was stupid when she found out she was pregnant. She was stupid and excited, and didn't think long enough before she told him. She went over to his place with a stupid, pathetic smile on her face. She had gotten ready, of course. She had a fresh permanent done at the salon, had manicured her nails a few days early. She even wore her best dress, his favourite, she thought. She was the best she could have been. It was their usual Wednesday night, and she went to meet him like she always did, let herself in and walked the length of the room, feeling him looking at her with desire. She sat down gracefully, on the nice chair by the window. She felt like she owned the place, and hoped that she almost did.

But,

"You're what? I thought you had a diaphragm or whatever!" Jacob sat on his plain couch with his hands over his face.

Margaret tried to play it off like it was nothing, and lit a cigarette, casual. "That old thing? It was nearly five years old, dear. They aren't, you know, a hundred percent or anything."

"This . . . this is appalling. You probably didn't use it right. You have to use them right, Margaret." She knew right away she should have played this differently. "I can't believe you could do this, Margaret."

She tried to salvage what she had. "It was a mistake. It happens, honey. We just have to, to fix it is all. If we move fast, no one need ever know a thing." She was still clueless at this point, was even still a bit excited. All that talk about June weddings from Becky. She would be a lovely bride.

Jacob looked up. "I can't believe you're so brazen about this. Has this— Have you done this before?"

"No! God no, what would make you think that? I'm just . . . girls are more mature than boys, they say. I guess I just feel ready, that's all. Truthfully, I've been ready for a while. School is a bore. I'm ready to do what I was meant to do." It was a bunch of things she had heard girls say before.

Jacob looked at her oddly, then stood up. Resolved, it seemed. "Okay then, how much? I can't imagine these things come cheap."

Margaret jumped up. "Oh Jacob! We don't have to have a big wedding. Just a dress and a suit will do fine."

"Wedding!" He looked her up and down. It was a moment but it somehow changed everything inside of her.

"What are you . . . ?" Margaret sat back down, knowing, finally, what he was talking about.

"I . . . " he only started. Then he too sat back down and put his hands back over his face.

Margaret looked out the window at the black night sky. Fourteen storeys up they were above the streetlights. If she got up and looked down she could see the whole city down there, bright and tiny like a scattering of Christmas lights. She wanted to, get up and go look, like she did sometimes when she was there. When she gathered her clothes and things to leave each night before ten, so she didn't miss the last bus home. She loved being up so high, loved the space of this apartment she pretended was her own, for a few precious hours each week anyway. But she didn't get up. She continued to sit there, hoping he would change his mind and say something wonderful. She didn't look at him and refused to cry, butted out her smoke, folded her hands together over her lap, and tried to look as worthy as possible.

"I can't marry you, Margaret," he began, even though he didn't have to. "Oh, you sweet dear. You are lovely, and I have really enjoyed our time together, but I can't marry you."

Something in his tone broke her. She struggled not to let the tears fall, be seen.

"I, of course, will help you in whatever you have to do. Do you know how . . . how much these things are?"

Margaret shook her head. She did know a thing or two. Had read about Dr. Morgentaler and all the controversy. She remembered thinking she could do that, if she had to. She had thought that when it was all only a hypothetical.

"Well, I'm sure you have a friend, or someone. Around where you live I imagine there are lots of girls . . ." He knew enough to stop talking. Or maybe he never cared enough to say more.

Somewhere there, Margaret sighed, felt something, growing. She wiped her face roughly. "Why can't you marry me?"

"Why? Oh, sweetie. I have always . . . well, been expected to, really, marry someone from my community. I know I may seem like a big-city lawyer to you but I'm really just a good old country boy at heart. I can't bring a . . . a *Catholic* girl home. I mean, it's for you, sweetie. I'd hate for anything . . . We're not . . . *they're* not as worldly as me. We come from very different worlds . . . sweetie."

She knew this, had heard versions of it before, from him, from others, many times. She had just never heard it so completely. So clearly. Or perhaps she had but this was the moment she chose to hear it all and know it, accept it. This was the moment she chose to know that no matter how many manicures, permanents, and good clothes she had, she still had never passed enough.

So she didn't pass, she thought, standing up. She wobbled as she straightened, chin up. Chin out. He continued his good-guy routine and again offered to pay for anything she needed, but she only stood there, not passing, and glared at him. Low track halfbreed it is then, she thought.

She walked, head high, to the door.

"Your purse, sweetie. You forgot your purse." He nearly laughed. He was so happy now that she was leaving.

But she wasn't.

She went to the corner where he kept his little protective baseball bat, the one he thought he'd use to beat up all the bad guys, and lifted the thing in one hand. She swung it easily into her palm, measuring the weight of it. She had swung a bat before. She had swung a bat many times before.

She took it in both hands and turned to him. His hands waved in front of his face just as he realized what was happening. He was saying something that she thought was neither important nor necessary. She swung right and felt it hit his side. A soft giving. She always had the worst aim. But he fell over to the couch. Already. She could have laughed. She probably did.

She swung up and knocked him again, this time a bit higher. He only cowered from it, no fight and no fun at all. So she just started swinging. She hit the wall, but that was unfulfilling, so she hit the television and that took a few hits to yield an almost satisfying crack. She hit at the side table and knocked over their two nearly full glasses and that felt better. She went over to the kitchen and swung into the coffeemaker, the toaster, things flew, some broke.

She turned when she heard her name. Jacob Penner was up, holding his side and yelling. She would have stopped if he wasn't yelling, if he wasn't calling her all sorts like he had any right to be mad. But he was acting all high and mighty and mad and how dare she and who did she think she was and she was going to pay for that and what did she think she was doing what right did she have crazy overreacting child enough crazy stupid squaw bitch enough calm down.

And that's when she started swinging for his head.

The cops came to the house as she was pulling off her jacket. She had walked home, all the way in her kitten heels, but she didn't feel her blisters as she stomped down Main Street and across the bridge. It was her hands that hurt, palms raw, biceps throbbing as if she was the one who'd sustained the impacts.

Her mother came from the kitchen scoffing the way she did whenever the cops came to their house.

"Evening, Officers. Mon Dieu, what did they do now?" Annie said, ready to tell them where John was staying or call for Toby upstairs. Annie was tough love all the way. Back then.

"Ma'am, we're here for a, Margaret Stranger."

"Margaret?" Annie's face dropped. "No, not Margaret." Her accent came out. "Must be wrong house. Our Margaret is in school. She is going to be lawyer."

"What's going on?" her dad called from the living room.

"They say they're here for Margaret!" Only then did her mother look at her. Margaret, standing there in the shadowy hall, pulled her jacket back on as her father walked up.

"Can't be our Margaret," he said. "She's never been in trouble. She's in school. She's going to be a lawyer."

"Dad," Margaret tried, but her voice was so light.

"What is this about, Maggie?" He turned to her, like he didn't know she was there until now. His face was all surprised, not the good kind.

"I . . ." she started but couldn't finish.

"Margaret," her mother's voice rose. "What you do? What did you do?!"

As Margaret approached the two cops still standing in the dark of the porch, she looked up at her brother standing on the stairs.

"Is she arrested?" her mother stumbled. "Is she? What did you do?"

"I— Don't worry, Mamere. It's going to be okay."

"Where are you going?" Her head turning back and forth between Margaret and the cops, as if she'd never experienced this before. "Where are you taking her?"

Her father pulled her mother close to him, and tried to calm her. Toby didn't move, only stared with his jaw slack. That's what she remembered, what she remembered most about that moment, as they closed the door and led her gently to the police cruiser, Toby's hangdog face. It was almost funny.

Joseph and John thought it was hilarious. Goody Two-Shoes Maggie all in trouble. They didn't know why when she came home the next morning. When they were sat at the kitchen table laughing their asses off at the sight of her, hair dishevelled, clothes wrinkled and stinking. Margaret didn't know if they were over for their usual breakfast or if Annie had called them. She didn't know which would have been worse.

She had called Becky to bail her out, promised to pay her back. Becky borrowed her dad's car, and to her credit, didn't say a damn thing the whole way home.

But then she was home. Margaret stood in the doorway, her shoes scuffed and all her toes blistering and swollen now, and let her brothers' jokes die out around her.

"So what's this? Did they charge you?" Her mother's hands on her hips, dish towel in hand.

Margaret nodded, looking to the floor. At least her dad had gone to work. She was thankful for that.

"What with? What'd you do, Poopy Peg?" John barely kept his laugh down.

"Assault," she said, and looked right at him.

Her brothers both howled again.

"Holy Christ!" John slapped the table. "Fuck!"

"Language!" their mother yelled. Her thirty-something-year-old toddlers at the table.

"Can take the girl out of the hood, hey, Maggie." Joseph smiled his get-away-with-everything smile.

Toby came in from the living room and handed her a lit cigarette. "You okay, Mags?"

She nodded, again. Puffed lightly but didn't look up. It was that, that little kindness, that made her cry.

She never did get to be a lawyer. Jacob showed up at the hearing with an arm in a sling and fading bruises on his face. Apparently he had a concussion and a couple of cracked ribs. But he was a forgiving man, you see, so he didn't want her to go to jail or anything. Felt sorry for the girl. Had a crush on him, you see. Got some silly ideas into her head. Not right in there. One of those, you see. Hard life.

They stayed the charge, conditional. But she would never get a licence to practise. And she could never go anywhere near him. Not that she would.

"Best thing you could have hoped for," her lawyer, her former professor who generously acted on her behalf, had told her.

She didn't say that it was so far away from what she had hoped for. So far away from the best of anything she had ever hoped for.

Margaret stumbled up to bed but couldn't sleep. She heard Alex come in after midnight. At least the boy tried to be quiet. Sasha stomped in after two, not bothering to be quiet at all. She pretended to be asleep then, as he grunted himself out of his clothes and literally fell onto the bed that squeaked loud in protest. She pretended to be asleep so she didn't have to talk to him, but regretted it once he started snoring like his life depended on it. At five she gave up and got up to make herself a fried egg sandwich and drink coffee. Went back to the couch and found a legal drama on cable, the kind where everybody was doing everybody else and betraying everybody else over and over. It was one of those marathons on the channel so she could've watched the damn thing all day, all the while getting interrupted by the same stupid commercials for old people—one about life insurance, one about selling gold, one with an irritating jingle about a cruise through the Caribbean, all with beautiful white-haired white people looking wide-eyed and smug.

The girls came slow down the stairs just before eight, sleepy-eyed in matching nightgowns she'd got them last Christmas. Cedar-Sage unselfconsciously climbed into her Mamma's lap and Margaret smelled that beautiful little-kid smell off the top of her head, still clean from yesterday's bath.

"You girls hungry?" she murmured into the girl's soft hair.

They both nodded.

So Margaret peeled herself off the couch, nudging the babe to the side, and grabbed her empty coffee cup as she went. "You girls watch your silly show and Mamma will make you some eggs."

Margaret moved across the house mindlessly, like she was wandering, like she didn't have to think about a thing. And she didn't. Not really. Sasha snored away upstairs and there wasn't so much as a peep from Elsie's room, or Alex up in the attic. Probably wouldn't be 'til near noon. Annie had always taken up so much space in her house, in her thoughts. Without her, it was like there was nothing there. Margaret didn't feel sad or lost. She felt nothing. A great big nothing all around her.

Sometime in the night, she had decided. She put in the toast, and the pan to heat, then pulled out a pork loin to defrost. When Sasha got up, she'd tell him to go get John and Toby and bring them for supper. They were going to have a family meeting.

She looked around the kitchen, this place, this room she had known all her life, and she really didn't have a feeling about it either. She knew what she had to do, what she wanted to do. Elsie wouldn't like it, but she was going to have to grow up sometime. Toby wouldn't like it, but that was him being sentimental, and she wasn't going to let her slow brother take this from her. John would think of the money and not much else. Sasha would be happy, and Margaret hated doing anything that made Sasha happy but this wasn't about him. It was about her. It was about their dad who paid off this house before he died, and a housing market that would get them ten times what he had paid for it. It was about Margaret finally getting something after all that work, all that hassle, all that being depended on. Annie would roll over in her grave, but Margaret wasn't going to think of that either. She had never got anything she wanted, anything that wasn't second-hand or that three brothers hadn't gone through and wrecked first, but with this money they could buy a condo. She could buy a car that wasn't ten years old and cleaned within an inch of its life. She could go on a trip. She'd been thinking of that, going on an airplane and going someplace warm in the winter. Just like those old people in those commercials. That's the only thing Margaret thought about then, that she was going to get something, have something of her own, finally.

She really didn't think of Elsie, but then, she never thought of Elsie. Elsie was never more than an afterthought to Margaret.

The roast was overdone and the potatoes were lumpy but Margaret could be forgiven for being a little off. She was anxious. Excited. She had called a realtor that afternoon and with a little information, the lady had given her this huge figure they could sell the house for. It was astronomical to Margaret. Margaret thought about investing. She had always wanted to invest money in something, have savings, watch it grow like they talk about on all those commercials. Sasha would hate this. He'd always burned through money as soon as he got it, so he'd take some convincing. But it really was exciting. In its way.

"Smells great, Margogo." Toby was the first one in with the ass kissing.

"Can you set the table?" she barked at him as she tossed the iceberg lettuce and tomatoes.

"Almost smells as good as Mom's," John added. An almost compliment.

"Sit down, sit down," she fretted, and called up the stairs. "Elsie! Alex! It's ready!" The girls were plopped in front of the TV with a familiar theme song going too loud. Margaret had fed them Kraft Dinner earlier and made sure that low-life who Elsie kept around had gone home, or wherever it is he went in between doing nothing and spending time with her daughter.

It was really Elsie she was most worried about. Poor spoiled Elsie was going to kick off. Margaret knew it.

The men grumbled on for a while, talking about business and cars and such. Sasha was in what he called semi-retirement. Not like he was collecting a real pension, he was just being lazy and working less. He said he was busy enough but he was bringing in less money when he was at an age when he should be getting in more. Margaret couldn't stand it, couldn't stand him complaining about his back, his knees, couldn't stand him in the house in the middle of the day. Her father was many things but he never sat down while the sun was out, never. He worked himself to death, really, was still doing odd jobs even long after he started collecting old age pension.

Margaret sat down, passed the potato bowl around, and said, "I want to sell the house." She passed Alex the gravy. "We'd all get our shares, split three ways. That, plus Mom's death benefit, should set us all up pretty good."

She let the words fall over the table and waited as the dishes slowed their circle.

John was the first to speak, as if he'd been around all along and his opinion was even all that important. "Great. Mom should have sold it years ago." He was practically rubbing his palms together.

"Oh!" Toby said slowly. "Why?"

"Why do you think? This house is old. And paid off. It's better to sell it now than five years down the line when everything's fallen apart." She could see Sasha nodding. It was something he had said to her more than a few times.

"No!" Elsie's voice rose unevenly. Margaret had been avoiding looking at her, but now her daughter's face was wrinkled up, ready for more tears. "How can you? This is Mamere's house."

"And she's gone, Elsie. It's ours now." Margaret swept her hands over the table but was really pointing at the adults. The real adults. Elsie was little more than a child.

"Well if it's mine too, then I say no." The girl was trying hard not to cry but it wasn't working. Never did.

"Not yours. Ours." Margaret pointed at her brothers, and her husband. "Inheritance goes generation by generation, girl."

"Well what do I get?" she whined.

"What? Nothing. Why would you get anything? You weren't her child. You are my child."

"But I always lived here. I almost always lived here. My whole life."

"And now you can live someplace else. It's not the end of the world, Elsie."

Toby reached over to pat Elsie's shoulder as the girl gave up and cried. She really made a show of it, huffing and puffing. Even Margaret almost felt for her. The room was completely filled with it.

"It'll be good for you to get out on your own, Elsie," Margaret said firmly. "Take those girls and start a real life for yourself. Stand on your own two feet."

John gave an awkward half smile. "I like this old house, too. Been here since I was a kid. But your mom's right. It's old. And hey, it's not like any of us has ever any sort of money like this. This is good."

"Why does it have to be about money?" Elsie sobbed into an old Kleenex she pulled out of her sleeve. An old-lady thing—Kleenex in the sleeve. Like Annie did, used to do.

Tired of this, Margaret took her plate and stood up. "The world is about money, girl. Sooner you realize that, the better off you'll be."

The men sat around and finished up but Margaret stayed in the kitchen. She smoked quick before she wiped the counter and scrubbed the roaster. Annoyed that her excitement was wrecked so thoroughly. Annoyed she was so annoyed. Elsie always had that way about her. She knew exactly how to push Margaret's buttons.

When she heard Sasha, Toby, and John go out to the porch to smoke, she went back to clear the table. Alex got up and helped, mouth still full with this third helping, but Elsie just sat there.

"Where am I supposed to go?"

"Elsie, you're a grown woman. It's time you started acting like one." Margaret didn't stop stacking the plates. Alex came up behind her and took them. Such a good boy.

"I . . . but where? How?"

Margaret stopped and sighed. "Go to Welfare. Get them to put you in one of those housing blocks. They have them all over the city."

"Those places." She leaned forward. Her arms stretched over the table where her plate used to be. "Those places are crap, Ma. They're, like, full of druggies."

Spoken like a truly sheltered child, Margaret thought. She cursed her mother under her breath. Her hapless mother who'd let this girl get so bad. "Then you work hard and get something else. That's what people do, Elsie."

Elsie rested her chin on her outstretched arm. Truly beaten by life and everything in it. Margaret grabbed the salad bowl. "Think of your kids. Don't you want to show them how to be a grown-up? I'm too old to keep looking after them."

"You're younger than Mamere was when she was looking after me."

Margaret looked down and the girl stared up at her for once. Trying to be strong. Trying to show her mother all her sass.

"Watch it," Margaret said finally. "That was completely different. You're more than capable to look after two children."

"Three," she said quietly.

"What's that?" Margaret stopped again and stood there, still with the salad bowl in hand.

"Three. Children." The girl sat straight up. "I am going to have three children. To look after."

Margaret could see Alex pause in the doorway behind her. Stilled by this standoff, he waited. Margaret tried to breathe, tried to calm down, but her mouth opened in an involuntary huff. "What?"

"I'm pregnant. Obviously," Elsie said, flippantly.

"Oh you stupid girl." She was sure it was exactly what she said last time. Only then it was Annie who calmed her. "You don't have your Grandmother to take care of this one, you know."

Elsie looked down at her lap, ready to fall apart again. Her voice was barely more than a whisper. "I know."

Margaret put the bowl down with a thump and stomped over to the girl. "Get rid of it. Do us all a favour and get rid of it. Now."

"I'm not, how can you say that?"

Margaret towered over her. "Who cares what I said, just go do it."

"No." The girl hunched, as if protecting it already.

"Why not? You stupid girl. Why the hell not?" She knew that she was yelling, but didn't care.

"It's a sin. Mamere said . . ."

"Fuck Mamere. Fuck sin. She's gone. And didn't know better when she was here." She stuck out a finger. "Do it. Or you'll regret it."

"Why? 'Cause you're going to make me regret it?" Elsie looked up again, and this time, she didn't look away.

Margaret stammered. "No. No, I'm not going to make you. I don't have to. You just will. You'll end up hating it. For having it."

"I'm not going to hate my kids, Mom. I'm not you."

If she was being honest, Margaret loved hitting things. She loved the way she felt when her fist, her hand impacted things. She loved to smash glasses, slam doors, ram pots back into the cupboards, slap smug grins off of stupid faces, but she never liked to hit her children. When she did, it was always because she felt she had to. Had to teach them. Had to let them know. But at that moment, for once, she hesitated. She watched Elsie's brave face fall into tears again, and Margaret hesitated. Not because she didn't want to, or didn't think she had to, or didn't know the girl should learn, but Margaret hesitated because she was afraid if she started, she wouldn't stop.

Margaret turned at a noise that sounded like a bird and saw the little girls peek from behind their uncle in the doorway. Little Phoenix with littler Cedar's hand in hers, both looking as scared as snared rabbits. Margaret forcefully took a breath. If she was honest she kind of admired the girl for once. Such a wimp and wisp of a thing who never stood up to anyone. Wouldn't say shit if her mouth was full of it like her dad used to say. And many times the girl did look like someone had shoved a pile of shit in her mouth. It was good she stood up, even if it was completely disrespectful to do so to her mother.

Margaret got herself together and smoothed her shirtfront, then calmly took the salad bowl to the kitchen. She put a warm, gentle hand on Phoenix's head as she passed, but the girl stiffened.

As soon as she was gone, they both ran to their mother like she was the one who needed care. Never mind who actually fed them and reminded them to take a bath, never mind who promised they could have pie if they were good and let the grown-ups talk.

Margaret lit another smoke and leaned against the counter. She heard the men's talk start up again in the porch. They had stopped, probably to listen, but didn't even have the guts to come inside and check on them. On her. Margaret. It's her who will end up raising this one, and the rest. If Elsie has her way anyway. Margaret will refuse. Right there decided. She would not let her daughter take advantage of her anymore. She was going to sell this house, take the money, and get something she wanted. No one was going to stop her, least of all Elsie and however many brats she wanted to bring into the world.

Yes, Margaret grew resolved there. She stood straight and smoked while Sasha laughed his stupid laugh in the porch, at something John said, no doubt, and Alex cleaned up quietly around her. Margaret's lips went thin and determined, and she had made up her mind. She wasn't ever going to raise any of Elsie's kids.

And she was right.

YEAR FIVE

17

PHOENIX

"Morning!" Henrietta calls brightly from Phoenix's open door. "Need anything?"

Phoenix shakes her head and continues combing out her hair. Trying to make it smooth, trying to make it presentable. She goes over it so many times, until it's almost dry. It's the only way to make it look halfway good. She doesn't use conditioner so this is what she has to do to get it under control. Some days she braids it but today she wants to look clean and smooth as much as possible.

Henrietta lingers in the doorway a bit. Phoenix can feel the guard's eyes piercing over her mask. She's looking her over. Not in that way. Henrietta looks for problems. She hovers, thinking she's helping, thinking she's checking, but eventually moves on. It's annoying but nothing Phoenix can't handle. The guard has added a new vibe to the place. She's different than the gruffness of Chris and the other guys. Phoenix doesn't mind that much, considering how else it's been over her time here. How boring it's been since lockdown. Considering how it could be. She doesn't like different all that much, but it all changes all the time. Dene got out. Before everything went to shit, bitch got to pack up her fake baby and go home. She straightened out her back and walked out like a normal person. Gave Phoenix a sly smile and wave like she'd been faking it the whole time. Phoenix wouldn't put it past her, wouldn't blame her either.

Then the world went to shit, and everybody started wearing masks and face shields, but really Phoenix's life wasn't all that different. She'd been social distancing her whole life.

They were trying to phase out the unit, or so they say. She'd been the only one left here, except for Kai, but they'd been transitioning her into a cottage for a while now so she was only really around to sleep. Then they needed the beds so the unit is full of little annoying fucks. Phoenix still has her own cell/room though, and is fine to get locked in for longer, while the other bitches moan like being bored's the worst thing. Phoenix can't wait 'til this shit's all over.

"It's the only constant, they say," Ben had said on one of their last visits. He'd gone back to sitting on an uncomfortable chair at her door.

Phoenix had looked at him funny so he gave a half smile and explained himself.

"Change. The only constant is change. That's what they say."

Phoenix didn't say anything at first. Then, when he didn't say anything more, Phoenix said, "I hate change."

"Yeh, I hear you," he sighed, and looked over his shoulder to the window, and some bitch walked by behind him. "But the only thing you have control over is yourself. You can be constant."

Phoenix made a sound like a grunt. She was the only thing she wanted to change. Everything about her, if she could. Her body, her brain, the thoughts that kept coming, the things she hated, the things she'd done.

Ben sighed again. Said something about the weather.

He'd been getting tired for a while now. Tired of her, she thought, mostly. But also old, probably. He hadn't been around for a couple months at first, then he was calling her for a while but that didn't last long 'cause she didn't want to stand there and say anything with that stupid mask on, out there down the hall. He finally came again in the summer but never took his mask off, even though he stayed so far away. Chris had said he heard his wife was sick, but Ben didn't tell Phoenix anything about that. She thought he was probably just sick of her. He'd been visiting her for years, really, and she didn't exactly change. What more could he do?

It was okay, really, made her sad but okay. Phoenix was used to people around her fading away.

"Big visit today, hey?" Henrietta's back at the door suddenly. Phoenix tried not to jump. Then feels embarrassed with all her combing and puts it down. "Got about an hour yet. I'll let you know."

Phoenix nods and thinks of what to do. She doesn't want to sit on her bed because she'll get all wrinkly. It's only her scrubby sweatsuit but still, she wants it to look good. She barely ate any breakfast because she was afraid of getting anything on it. So she sits upright at her desk, looks down at her front, and tries to suck in her gut. It's just an old fucking issued sweatsuit but it's her only option. She did the best she could. She even borrowed eyeliner off Kai and tried to make a nice line across the top of her eyelid. It didn't really work out but she smeared it off clean enough. Kai had told her smudged lines were in so she hoped she got it right. Just a little bit of makeup made her eyes look brighter. It was the best she could do.

But now she had a whole hour still. She looked around for options but only had the old beat-up Psych textbook and some blank paper. She doesn't want to write anything so she opens up the worn pages of the Abnormal Psychology chapter and starts reading. She knows it all by heart basically, but the words seem kind of comforting somehow, "the study of behaviour . . . to describe, predict, explain . . ."

She likes the idea of being able to put it all into boxes. To find a place and pill to make it all go away.

Henrietta beeps the door and lets Phoenix go on ahead. She looks around at the tables and different-coloured chairs, all in one big room, tall partitions of clear plastic looking brand new in between them all, and feels incredibly sad. Phoenix has never been in this room before. Nearly five years in here, but she's never had a real visitor. Her calls to her sister have been her only outside contact. She didn't want to talk to any of her friends. All those chicks she thought had her back had ratted her out, so fuck them. She never gave a shit about Elsie not coming around, and wouldn't know where to start with most of her family. She did try calling her uncle once, years ago, but the number was out of service. Some girls got special credits for good behaviour and got some computer time, but Phoenix never had good behaviour. So nothing. She didn't fucking care most of the time. Hadn't even thought about it much. She knew she had burned all her bridges. She knew what her family thought of her, probably said about her, and was happy to be away. Everyone knew where she was, that was the thing. If they wanted to, they could try and come see her, but no one ever did.

'Til now. But this one wasn't going to be a friendly time. This one was going to be fucking painful.

"Hi, Phoenix." She's the only one in here, the other tables empty. An older woman, put together, almost rich looking with cheekbones so high Phoenix can see them over the fancy floral beadwork mask. She looks perfect. Her eyes shine behind the glare of the plastic partition. She sits straight-backed on a blue chair and doesn't get up.

Phoenix sits and rubs her hands down her thighs, adjusts the elastics around her ears. She doesn't know what to say.

Luckily the older woman takes over. "Thank you for seeing me. I know you probably didn't want to."

Phoenix shakes her head a bit but doesn't get to the words.

The woman puts up her hand. "No, no, let me finish." Her words picked over carefully, almost slowly. Her voice as perfect as the rest of her. "I appreciate this is weird for you but I'm not here to be mean, and I want to do it right. It's, well, it is nice to meet you, to see you, in person. You can call me Lisa. I'm Clayton's Grandma."

Phoenix nods. She knew that. A long moment passes before Phoenix realizes she should probably say something. "I, I remember when he, when Sparrow was born. The social worker told me Clayton's mom lived with you."

"Yes. Jesse. We share a house on Polson, not far from the river.

Been there almost ten years now." She looks out at something for a minute. "I'm very proud of that, you know. I never thought I would own a house of my own. So when I got one, I got a big one. Enough to have my daughter and my grandson come live with me. That's what I always wanted."

She looks strong and sits with her shoulders back and never slouches at all. Phoenix has no idea how old she is but doesn't think she looks like a Grandma. A Great-Grandma. Her hair is black and barely grey, cut to her shoulders, and she's dressed in, like, office clothes. Phoenix can see her mask isn't really beadwork, only a fabric, but still. Formidable, Phoenix thinks. That's the word you would call someone like this.

"I grew up, well, not that different from you, you know. And now I've managed to make something of myself and take care of my family. I'm glad I could help, when Jesse was on her own with Clayton, and now with Sparrow."

"How is he?" Phoenix looks down as soon as she says it, adjusts her mask again. "Sparrow. And Clayton, but Sparrow." The words, names, seem wrong to say out loud, the ones she's said a million times in her head. Her ex, ex whatever, and her son.

"He's good. Sparrow is. He's smart. In nursery now, or was, had started this year. He liked it so much. He's . . ." She pauses for the first time, thinking. "Very loved."

Phoenix nods again. The woman, Lisa, blurs as Phoenix's eyes fill with tears she doesn't want to fall, so she looks down again, trying to will them away.

After a couple hard swallows, she says, "I'm, I'm glad. That he's doing good." She thinks of saying more but doesn't. She remembers that day. Her baby in her arms, Henrietta looking on, the women in the hallway who wanted to take him away but didn't want to come in.

"Clayton, on the other hand." Lisa's voice turns tense. "Well, he has his struggles. He does not live with us any longer. He isn't much in the picture. These days."

Phoenix swallows again. "That's, that's too bad." Again she thinks of more, wants to say more, about Clayton, about him being a good person. But she doesn't really know that.

"Sometimes young people take longer to grow up," Lisa says. "Clayton has, he's had a hard life. I like to think he's taking care of himself as best he can."

Phoenix thinks of him when she knew him. Young, they were so young, and the boy was always smiling. Not smiling, grinning. Clayton grinned so bright it was like being in the sunshine when it was pointed at you. Even then, Phoenix knew he was probably only being nice to her because he was dealing for her uncle and because of who her uncle was. She could feel it wasn't all real, when he would pull away all the time, but she didn't care. She liked him, loved him, so much. Enough to ignore it.

"I guess you know he's still involved with your uncle," Lisa says with an extra bite to her voice.

"I, I haven't talked to anyone, like, at all since I've been here. I don't know what anyone is doing." Phoenix itches her nose and suddenly wants some water. She wants to get up and go to the cooler but thinks that would look rude. Doesn't know if she can even have a drink with this thing on.

"Oh, well, that makes sense, I guess." Lisa looks over at nothing again. "I just wished the boy had more sense. Getting involved in all that nonsense."

Phoenix folds her hands and tries not to feel thirsty.

"And you? How are you getting on, in here?" She says "here" like it's the worst place in the world.

"Good. It's good. I've been, like, studying. So I can maybe get my GED sometime. And I'm up for review soon." They've been saying "soon" forever.

"I heard you had some trouble and got your sentence extended." Her eyes look harder now than they did when Phoenix came in.

Phoenix nods. A swell of anger rises in her throat but she can't get mad at this woman, no matter how hard she's trying to be. It's not an all-the-way mad anyway, only another thing she doesn't want to think about. "Been good, good awhile now. Got a job. At the library. Or had one, before. Should be out soon." Soon.

"I came here to tell you. I wanted to say, when we got your letter. We wanted to respond." Her talking different now, unsure. Angry. "Jesse was going to come too but it could only be one of us and I wanted it to be me." She stops like she's waiting for something, so Phoenix looks at her, tries to look at her a long time, tries to have nothing on her face but hopefulness.

"I wanted it to be me because Jesse is, well, Jesse has a soft heart and I didn't want to risk her changing her mind." She sticks her finger out. Smooth red polish on her nails. "But, Phoenix, know this. Know that I come here with the decency to say this to you in person and I mean it. We do not want you seeing Sparrow when you get out. Not now, and likely not ever."

It was like a bomb those words. All those words she said like they were practised. Probably were practised all the way here.

No, not a friendly visit at all.

Phoenix feels the anger bubbling up, but more than that she feels the sadness. The embarrassment of having to beg, in a letter, to see her son. And then this. Her eyes betray her again and fill up.

"He's my . . . he's my son" is all she can think to say.

"You signed him over. On the day he was born you signed over your rights. You did that."

She thinks of it, always thinks of it. That day. The last day she felt him squirming inside her. Then he was out.

"I, I wasn't thinking." It had all just happened, she thought.

"When you did that you forfeited all access."

"I didn't want to." Thought he'd be better off without me.

"Jesse can even formally adopt him, and she should. I told her she should but these things take so long. Even in normal times."

"I don't want to take him away." Only see him, only know him.

"I think even visiting would be so confusing to him. He doesn't know you. He calls Jesse mom. He knows she's his Grandma and that his mom did something bad. That's all he knows. That's all I want him to know."

She winces but tries not to let it show. She feels so much these days. She misses the days when she didn't feel anything.

"I wouldn't tell him anything." That's all I'd want him to know too.

"He's in a good place. And who knows when you'll get out anyway. A couple of months, years, and what if you go back in again?"

"I'm not going back in again, not after this." Never.

"Phoenix, you've been in and out of centres your whole life. What makes you think that's going to change now?"

Something about her tone, the way her stupid fucking head tilts at the question. The way she has no fucking idea. And the way she is in front of Phoenix, between her and her boy, blocking her way to him, and Phoenix can't do a fucking thing about it.

"He's my son," she says more firmly. "I can get a lawyer."

"And what's a lawyer going to do? With your record? After what you did? You're on the sex offenders list, for Christ's sake. You can't even walk him to school."

Phoenix doesn't think about it. That day, that night. The worst thing she could ever do. No need to think about it. She knew she did it. She doesn't know why she did it, doesn't remember. Doesn't remember a lot of things that she did, only that she's done them. But this bitch doesn't know that. She doesn't know what Phoenix has been through, what Phoenix has felt all this time, did all this time, waiting. If she did, she wouldn't be like this. Like fuck, she came from the same place.

"I just want to, see him," she says through her clenched teeth. Trying to stop everything that's going on inside of her.

Lisa digs into her pocket, pulls out a wallet-sized photo, and pushes it against the plastic so Phoenix can see.

She's afraid to look and takes a breath first.

In it, a young boy smiles. Grins, really. His eyes bright and happy. His long hair pulled back, into a single braid or bun she can't see. He's wearing a white button-up shirt and red bow tie. Behind him, the blue-painted background of school photos.

"He insisted on the tie. He likes to dress up." Lisa smiles.

Phoenix smiles too, and her tears fall. "He's, gorgeous." He looks like the first Sparrow, and Clayton. So much like Clayton.

"He takes after his father. Gets away with murder just like that one does." Lisa looks up, like she's said something wrong. "But he's not spoiled. He's well taken care of."

Phoenix can only nod. Her throat burns with words and grief she can't stop.

"His Grandma spoils him a little, I think." Lisa makes a small huffing noise like she disapproves.

"He looks like my sister." She doesn't mean to say it and doesn't explain. "What's he, what's he like?"

"Oh all the usual boy things, trucks and dinosaurs, and his dad got him into that wrestling nonsense. I think he watches it because it reminds him of his dad."

Phoenix meant what's he like as a person, but it doesn't matter. She wants to hear everything that Lisa tells her. About Sparrow. About her son.

About her son she cannot see.

Lisa reads her mind. "Can I offer you some advice, Phoenix? I'm going to anyway, so I'm sorry, but I say let it go. Don't disrupt this boy's life. This beautiful boy." She points a hard, red nail at the picture. "Know that he's doing good and get on with your own life. You are not going to have an easy time once you're out. I've watched people go through it and it's never easy, but for you, it's going to be ten times harder. You have no idea the damage you've done, the hurt you've caused."

Yes I do, she thought.

"You will not have an easy time and you don't need to bring a child into that. Let it go. Let him go and live his life in peace. You owe him at least that."

I owe him everything. And more. She knows.

"Are you hearing me?"

Phoenix nods, still not looking up from the picture. From that perfect, sunny grin. She wants to curl her fingers around the photo, cradle it in her palm, hold it. Him. She looks to the guard with them in the visiting room. It's Chris. "Can I get this?"

He nods and moves to take it, check it, makes sure it's okay. Makes sure she can touch it.

"Phoenix?" Lisa repeats.

"I hear you." Phoenix looks up. Hard. "Heard you."

The old lady leans back, looking a little older for a minute. Her eyes squint like she's really looking. "Okay, then. I hope so. I hope that is the end of this."

Phoenix takes a big breath in. She knows, has heard, all this woman has said. It's nothing she hasn't thought to herself a million times. To hear some other bitch say it though. This bitch who doesn't know her at all. Doesn't know anything.

"I do wish you luck, Phoenix. I hope you can do some good in the world. Somehow." Lisa clutches her hands together like a prayer, like she's making a show of it.

Phoenix lets the air out from between her teeth and gets up, kicking the chair behind her, letting it fall with an uncomfortable clatter.

She hears Chris say something but doesn't bother to listen, just walks calmly to the door.

She doesn't know, Phoenix thinks. This Lisa person doesn't know shit. Sparrow is her boy, looks as much as her sister, the first Sparrow, as he does like Clayton. That means he's both of them. Always. She carried him, birthed him, carried him. You can't break that. He belongs with her. She could get a lawyer. She could get all the lawyers. That Lisa bitch doesn't know shit fuck all.

This is what she thinks as she walks back to her room/cell, what she rages as she walks all calm like the perfect inmate.

She gets in there though, and Chris keeps talking like he does when he's trying to calm her down. She's not even upset yet. She tries to ignore it and walks to her desk. Her old textbook laid open, right where she left off, "delusional disorder, narcissistic disorder, oppositional disorder." She pulls off her fucking stupid useless mask and lets out a scream as she pushes the heavy book off the cheap table they call a desk. Then she pushes that over too, knocking it against the cinderblock wall until it makes a good cracking noise. Then she takes the chair and pounds it against the table, bending its weak metal legs one after the other. She hears a loud beep and some more screaming and knows by her raw throat that it's her but she doesn't want to stop. She turns toward her bed as someone comes up behind, pulling from behind, the plastic of their face shield knocks against the back of her head, the weight of their arms across hers at the elbow. She has known this move her whole life. She bends forward and pushes her elbow back as hard as she can. She feels the plastic fall off and pushes again until she feels the connection to flesh and keeps going. Her strong right elbow going and going. Hard. She feels skin yield. She feels bone. The warm wet of blood.

Someone on her other side, and another, they pin her to the floor. She's half under the bed but starts kicking. There must be someone else too because she feels her ankles bound by something. It hurts like a strap and she can't move them. A quick prick to her shoulder and she thinks, Oh fuck no, and maybe she screams it too. Starts thrashing again, as long as she can. As long as there's something in her.

The last thing she hears before she passes out is Henrietta's muffled voice. "I think she broke my fucking nose."

It makes her want to laugh, but she can't.

—

She knew they'd be moving her before they even said anything. She knew they were fucking done with her.

Henrietta didn't come back, neither did Ben. Chris was still around but only ever said what he needed to. They all let her be for a couple days, and then two city cops came in followed by two other guards. She'd never seen them before and their uniforms were different. Still fucking familiar though. But she knew before that anyway so it was no fucking surprise to her.

She didn't say anything. Not when they asked if she wanted a lawyer, not when they read her her rights. Not when they handcuffed her and led her out, through each beeping door, down each long hall, and out the building. The sun was shining and it felt like one of those super-hot summer days. The kind of day kids wait for all year. She looked up and let the sun warm her face before one of them put a hand on her head and pushed her into the cold, dark van.

The thing had no windows but the air conditioning was cranked to freezing. She shivered and there was nothing to look out of except the front, and that was mostly blocked by a cage wall of thick metal. She could only see a bit, but saw a corner of the brown river as they went over a bridge. They went through downtown. The trees were green. The people tan and smiling.

They pulled up to the old white brick building but she didn't need to fucking look up to know where she was. Lock-up. Remand. She'd been here before. She didn't feel anything about it. Didn't let herself. She only shivered in the cold fucking van wishing she was in the sun awhile. So what if this is where she went when she first went down. Where she was when Sparrow was born. Who the fuck cares.

The guards took their fucking time going around to let her out. It was good though. Enough time to let her get her breathing right, to put her face in order. To stop fucking feeling anything except hard, and cold, all the way through. Again.

Phoenix never made a decision to do anything. There was never a moment when she knew exactly what she was going to do. But if there were one, if she ever did or could look back and say, "there, that's when I knew," it would have been then. That moment when she was led into the Remand Centre for the last time. That was the moment she knew, what she had always known but never wanted to admit. When she knew all that time being good was just something to do to pass the time. It was like jail. Jail wasn't real either. Just something to do.

And that couldn't last forever either.

18

CEDAR

"Hey," Faith says and plops down in the armchair opposite the couch.

After a moment, a stunned moment with my pencil mid-air, I say, "Heeey?" letting the word drag, in wonder.

Faith says nothing more. She sits there and looks at her new press-on nails, inspects them closely. Then checks her phone and gets distracted by something there, so I go back to Pre-Cal.

This is beyond weird. Faith never comes into the upstairs living room, and never willingly talks to me. Something must be up. I don't think she's been alone with me since that ill-fated party outing in grade ten. She spent most of the lockdown at her boyfriend's house, but they broke up a few weeks ago and she sulked back home. Nikki was beyond pleased. She even kept her "I told you so's" to a minimum. I am curious but unwilling to let it show, so I stare down at my book. Like I could concentrate with her here.

But I need to. My provincial exam is only a week away and I am only halfway through my review. My own review. The one I planned on my own. Not to be confused with the weeks of review, or at least the attempted review, my teacher tried in my stupid online class. But everyone seemed to be late or not show up all the time so it was distracting and repetitive. I want to get it all right. I want all good marks after all this struggle.

When I'm done with that one, I have English right after. It's one of those progress exams that lasts a whole week and you can't really study for, but still, I stress the whole time. I'm not as worried about that one. I've always done well in English. And Bio, that's the last big one. But first it's Pre-Cal. That's the one I want to get right. They say they're going to excuse some assignments and forgo some grades but I don't trust it, and I don't want it. I don't want to just be given something everyone gets after I've worked this hard to get something better.

Faith is still on her phone. Hand to her temple like this is all normal. She doesn't look up. Doesn't acknowledge that she's in the space I normally keep to myself when Dad is on his overnights and Nikki is working. Usually these days Faith is downstairs in her room or out at some friend's place. She's not all that concerned with things like bubbles, no matter what Nikki tells her. I take a baby carrot from the bag and chomp self-consciously. Been trying to eat healthy. Not just because I am afraid of this pandemic stuff but mostly 'cause I should be healthier. It's mostly been baby carrots so far. Sometimes salad. I contemplate heating up some of Nikki's cleanse soup, the cabbage kind she makes and eats nothing but that for a few days thinking that it's healthy. I really hate it, but again, trying to be healthy. I'd rather heat up a pizza pop. This is the great debate going on in my head when Faith finally speaks.

"I don't know how you can study that stuff. I quit Pre-Cal in, like, grade ten. That stuff is messed."

"It's pretty . . . intense. Yeh." I take another carrot and try to chomp the thing as quietly as possible.

"You're never going to need that in real life, you know." Faith leans forward. Picks at one of her fake eyelashes with her impossibly long fingernails. Impossible to me anyway.

"Probably not. But it looks good on the university application."

"I thought you already got into university."

"I did. But I still have to finish."

"Seems like a big waste of time to me."

I don't say anything about all the things Faith does that seem like a waste of time to me. That would be rude. And I could tell Faith wasn't trying to be rude. If Faith wanted to be rude, she would be ruthless.

She sighs. "I never wanted to go to university anyway."

"You could always change your mind," I say only because I think it's what you're supposed to say.

"No, I know. Nikki tells me that all the time, fuck. But I don't want to go. Never been interested. It's not like I can't. I just don't want to." She seems so tense. Even more than usual.

I nod and get it. Guess Faith is in an unloading kind of mood, so I say supportively, "It's not for everyone."

"I want to travel. I want to go see the world, you know."

I did know. Had spent nights fantasizing about backpacking through Europe or Southeast Asia. And I've always wanted to go to New Zealand. That's the first place I'd go, as soon as I ever could. If the world ever opens up again. "That's cool. Where'd you go?"

"Alberta."

I laugh but quickly swallow it, realizing she's serious, and pretend to cough.

"But not to Edmonton," she continues. "I want to go where my family is." Faith rubs her temple again, somehow expertly with her long fingernails.

I think a minute, about Nikki's family who I've never met but have heard about endlessly. "I thought they lived in B.C. now." Remembering all the yacking phone calls Nikki had with her sister.

"Not *that* family." Faith looks at me this time. Looks hard so I know this is what she wanted to talk about. The one thing only I would understand. That she couldn't talk to Nikki about.

"Oh," is all I reply.

She seems to go back to her phone but pulls something up and shows it to me. "I've been talking to my aunty. On Insta."

She shows me the profile pic of a nice-looking Indigenous woman, about thirty or so. She's smiling and wearing what looks like a bridesmaid's dress. Her hair pulled up, the sleeves off the shoulder, the dress a pale pink.

"She's pretty."

"She is. Do you think she looks like me? Or I guess, that I look like her?" She takes the phone back and presses a couple buttons.

"Definitely." I smile at her. Even though she's not looking.

"This is my Grandma. My Kookum?" This photo shows an older woman with long grey hair in a braid swooped over one shoulder. A face so familiar.

"Wow!"

"I know, right?" Faith takes the phone back and puts it aside. "Guess Mom was right about one thing. I do look like her."

"Like just like her. That's amazing." I feel something like jealousy.

"She's apparently super nice. An Elder up there. From where they're from. My aunty. Sam's her name. She doesn't live there anymore. She's in a city. Grande Prairie. But it's not far."

"That's great, Faith." And I mean it.

"My aunty manages a Tim Hortons there. She said she could get me a job no problem. Tim's is like essential or whatever, hey? And we can visit my Grand—my Kookum whenever. She lives in the bush so it's like, open, and my aunty goes there all the time. "

I nod again. Trying to be encouraging. I want to ask why now, or what brought this on, but that seems rude and nosy, somehow.

"She doesn't see much of my dad, she says. He lives even further up north. He's doing good though. He's married and has like three kids. Three other kids. My siblings, I guess. Can you, like, imagine?"

I smile. Because I can, imagine it, that is.

"Sam was going to get in touch with him. To let him know she's been talking to me. You know, she didn't know we were over here. Thought we were still in Edmonton."

I try to think of the best thing to say. The thing that won't make her mad or anything. "I guess Nikki didn't talk to them for a while."

"Just took off. That's what my aunty says. Her and her mom never knew where I was. Just knew Edmonton."

I can relate but don't want to talk about me. That would for sure make her mad. So I take another carrot instead.

"It doesn't seem fair, you know. That mom didn't even give them a chance. To, like, know me. They seem like really good people," Faith says. She sounds like she's trying to convince herself as much as wanting to convince me.

"They do." I don't need convincing.

"I always thought they were, like, demons or something."

"I think," I say carefully, "Nikki thinks she's protecting us. Protecting you, I mean."

"But she doesn't know."

"No, she doesn't."

With that, Faith's face changes. Looks more determined. "I'm gonna go there. I already bought a plane ticket. One-way. Sam says I can stay with her as long as I want."

"Wow." I'm super surprised. "When are you going?"

"Next week. I wanted time to pack up my stuff properly. Let Nikki get used to the idea."

It all seems almost sensible. So unlike Faith. Maybe that was the whole point.

"They sound like really nice people, Faith. Good people. And you can always just come home if it doesn't work out."

"Yeh, they do sound like good people. I feel like I should have known them all along." She looks down, so sad. "Wish I did."

"I know," I say slow. "I really do. They're family. They're who you are."

Faith doesn't look up. She cries without a sound. She looks so much younger than all her makeup usually lets her.

"I don't even know who I am," she says finally. "I don't know anything about all that."

I almost want to go hug her. Almost want to cry too. But I don't move. Don't want to spook it. "It's easy to learn. It's already in you. Like blood memory."

"Like what?" Faith shoots me the "what the fuck are you talking about?" look I've seen so many times before.

"Blood memory. Or sometimes it's called bone memory. It's this old teaching that everything that's happened to your ancestors, everything they know, good or bad, is already in you. It's in your blood. So even if you don't know it, or don't think you know it, you do." I check to make sure. "Does that make sense?"

"Yeh, I think so." Faith looks lost in thought, looking out somewhere far away, or maybe just some place inside herself she never thought she knew. I get that too.

She takes a deep breath and leans far back in her chair. "Fuuuck," she draws out the word, and says with a sigh. "Nikki's going to be so pissed."

"Yeh." I grin. "But you're used to that."

"Yeh." Faith rubs at her temple again. "It might even be fun."

"Still working on that Pre-Cal?" Dad calls over from where he's setting the dining table.

I nod absentmindedly. My books are strewn across the coffee table in front of me as I sit on the floor. I'm not really studying anymore, mostly looking out the window. The bright spring light. Still so light out even though it's evening. The leaves just pushing out of the buds on the trees.

I've been so busy, I barely remember the snow melting. Barely remember that May is almost over. Wouldn't know at all if I wasn't so focused on that date, all those dates coming up. Exam, exam, exam, then convocation. I'm so glad everything else is cancelled these days. I wasn't really going to go and it all seemed so pointless anyway.

Instead I'm spending my time getting ready, thinking of what happens next. Planning. I got all my deposit for the dorm ready. Didn't quite have enough, but Dad gave me a few hundred dollars on the condition that I don't tell Nikki. He took me down there before lockdown. He changed his shifts around and everything so he could take me down there. We did a little tour of the dorm. The skinny rooms were mostly full but they let us look in an empty one. It had a tall bed, drawers underneath, a closet, a desk and chair, shared bathrooms, and common rooms with couches and long tables to study at. That was before all this but all the group chats say that they're adhering to the rules, and all the rooms are private anyway.

"Big tall windows," he had said. "It's a nice enough view."

I barely looked at the lit-up downtown and the Christmas decorations still up. We walked through the cutting wind to the accounting office, paid my deposit, and got a receipt-like letter. I stared at it, the logo, the officialness, as long as I had stared at my acceptance letter a month before. It was all real now. All there. Another series of dates, August then September. Registration a week after graduation. So many things to do.

I've never been so happy.

On the way home, we drove past the old child welfare building and I thought of my mom. The visit that still didn't happen even though Dad was looking into it, he had said. Said he would arrange something soon. But everything takes even longer now. All this horribleness made me so fucking impatient. I know I'm lucky and grateful and everything, but I really just want my life to fucking start already.

I hadn't heard from Phoenix either, in weeks. I knew that could happen sometimes. Could always happen even when the world wasn't on fire. Things can change quickly, or my sister could lose phone privileges or something. I knew how these things worked, but that still didn't make it any easier.

"Chin up, C," Dad said as we crossed the bridge back to the south end. "It's a good day."

"I know. I just." I didn't know how to finish. I didn't even know.

But Dad nodded like he did. Know, that is.

Nikki carries a glass salad bowl into the dining room. "Cedar, put that away, it's dinnertime," she says. Then calls "Faith" down the stairs.

Nikki was off her cleanse now. Only ever lasted a couple days and never on the weekends, but she still makes sure she's having salad with everything. I don't mind, but Dad tends to harp on about it. He thinks it's a waste of money and table space. It's a running joke they seem to have. Sometimes I can't tell if they're really annoyed at each other or joking. Dad seems more to be joking but Nikki could be taking it seriously. You never knew with her.

Once we all sit down, Nikki starts talking about her week. Like it's a meeting she always starts this way, like we all don't already know. She's working all the time. They made her, like, "an essential worker basically." She wishes she'd gotten laid off and could collect CERB like everyone else. Being in a call centre already, she didn't have to work at home or anything, they just made her shifts longer, had less workers on the floor, and she never stopped complaining about it.

"I mean, I put my life at risk every time I go to work, but do I get any more money? Yeah, right."

Faith and I just keep chewing, saying nothing as always.

It's Dad who starts talking. "I hear they're opening things up again soon. That they want the school year to go on as normal next year."

"If they can, that would be great," I say.

"I still don't know," Nikki launches in, "why you want to spend all that money on a dorm when you can just live home with us. It's not that long a bus ride. And it's so much safer. Especially now. You should get your licence. Spend your money on a car instead."

I swallow the barbecued pork chop before I say, quietly, "But I want to."

"I just don't see the point. It's not like it's a different city. Usually kids only go to dorms if they're from out of town."

"Actually lots of the kids on the group chats are from here, or near here," I say. "Most of them, really. I think it's just easier."

Nikki shakes her head, still not convinced after all these months. "You would have to live downtown. You don't know what that means, Cedar. If you'd seen half the stuff I'd seen, even before all of this, you wouldn't set foot down there. Ever." She keeps shaking her head. "I don't think you're ever going to convince me this is a good idea."

I look at Dad, who looks back at me with the same look of "oh shit." It didn't even occur to us, to me anyway, that he hadn't told her.

"We already paid the deposit, hon." Dad says between swigs of his beer. "We could get it back, of course, but you know, things are looking up. The spot's hers."

"You what? You paid already?" Nikki's face drops. Her voice goes high.

"C had all the money. Saved it all herself." He winks at me.

"And you wasted it all on . . . ? Oh Cedar." Nikki leans back and gulps the last of her wine. Then leans forward to quickly pour more. "I would have thought you would have told me that."

"Thought I did," Dad says with a mouthful of potatoes. "It's all she's been talking about."

"Yeh but, I thought we were still discussing it. I would have liked, I would have liked to be a part of this discussion." She leans back again, so everyone can tell how annoyed she is.

"Hon, C has always said she wanted to live in the dorm. She's been saving up for two years."

"Yeh, well, when I was seventeen I had crazy ideas too. I wanted to be a model. Was almost going to move to Toronto and everything. But that's what parents are for. To make you see sense." She glares across the table at him. No joke now, all serious.

But Dad, for once, isn't budging. Not yet, anyway. "This isn't something silly, Nik. It's university."

Nikki huffs into her glass, and pushes her food away like she's too disgusted to eat anymore.

I'm annoyed and angry but keep eating. Fucking Nikki making it all about her as usual. I used to think it was my fault when Nikki got upset. Always felt so sorry for her because I didn't know any better. Today, though, I only feel annoyed. And pissed off.

Dad, too, keeps eating, like this is normal. Which it is. Faith is giving me this grin, like she's really enjoying this. At first I think she's making fun of me, but then she almost shouts triumphantly, "I'm going to Alberta." Then smiles over the whole table.

"What!" Nikki leans, almost stumbles, forward again.

"I'm going to Alberta," Faith says a little quieter this time, but not much. She puts down her fork and looks directly at her mother.

Nikki looks genuinely confused. "What for?"

"To see my family," Faith says simply. Sharply.

"Your . . . what?"

"My family. I've been talking to my aunty. Sam. You remember her, right, Mom?" She says "mom" like an insult. "She's doing great and said I can go stay there. So I'm going."

Nikki, so rarely at a loss for words, stumbles. "What . . . when?"

"Tuesday."

"Tuesday!" Nikki almost spits. "You can't be serious. It's too dangerous. You can't travel now. And, and, you can't be serious!"

"So serious. And I didn't tell you this, C." Faith turns to me. "This just happened. My dad is coming down to see me too. Right away when I get there. He's bringing my brothers. I have brothers! We're going to have a picnic at this park by my aunty's house." She looks so gleeful. Happy. Faith is never happy.

"You knew about this?" Nikki shoots a glare at me, then at Dad, who has a dumb look on his face, too.

"There's three of them. My brothers. The oldest is twelve. The youngest is only five, and so cute. Their names are—"

Nikki takes a loud breath. "Faith, honey. You don't understand. They—"

"No, Nikki, you don't understand. They're my family. I'm going to see them." Faith's eyes widen. As much as she's doing this for show, there is truth there. Truth she probably didn't know how to say in any other way.

"Oh honey, it's so . . . Have you even thought this through? The risk in getting there alone. And these people, oh hon, you don't even know."

"I do know. And I'm going."

"You don't even know them, Faith."

"And whose fault is that!" She shoots Nikki a look that could honestly kill.

I think I would honestly die if anyone ever looked at me like that.

Nikki sighs again. "Faith, you just, you don't know. What they're like."

"And again, whose fault is that?" Her voice so hard. Unrelenting.

"Faith, I, I don't know what you think you know or what that . . . woman said to you, but you don't know. I am your mother. I always do what is best for you."

"They're my family too, Mom. And you kept them from me."

"It was for the best."

"Why?"

"What? What do you mean?"

"Why was it for the best?"

"Because, well, your dad, that man, he was, he wasn't a good person."

"To you. Maybe. So you say. But what about everyone else?"

Nikki pours the last of the wine into her glass. She seems as annoyed with this as everything else. "They were. We had my family, your Gran, Grandpa, and your aunt. We were fine."

But Faith is not letting this go. "They didn't even know where I was. She didn't even know we moved here."

"Well it's not my job to keep them up to date," Nikki says, exasperated. "You're my daughter."

"And I'm her niece." Faith's voice cracks now, and she sounds so young. All truth, no show anymore. "And I don't even know them. I just want to know them."

Nikki looks at her as if for the first time and her mouth firms into a thin line. "You don't know what you're asking for. It'll all end in tears, mark my words."

"Nik," Dad finally cuts in, with his same calm tone. "You don't know that."

"Don't I? That guy, that so-called father, didn't do anything for us.

Nothing. We were better off without him, and his—his *family*." Nikki twirls the stem of her glass and looks almost smug. "Once a loser, always a loser."

"Some could say that about me, you know," Dad says, still calm but with a little bit of something else. He looks so old all of a sudden. "But I changed. I turned myself around. Maybe he did too."

Nikki glares at him. A look like the one Faith just gave her. Full of hate. "Yeh and how did you do all that, Shawn?" Her voice grows louder. "Don't act like I didn't help you every step of the way. God, you weren't even employed when I met you. You still had a record. Your kid was in foster care, for fuck's sakes. Foster care! I did all this. Me." She points a finger to her chest.

Dad's hands are up like he's trying to talk to something big and scary, something that needs big and scary gestures anyway. "Nik, I know you're upset, but come on."

"Come on, what?" she yells. "Pretend like I haven't done everything for all of you? All of you! And now, you, now both you girls just go and leave me! Like it was all for nothing!"

Dad's voice is still shockingly unmoved. "They're not leaving you, Nik. They're growing up."

She takes a breath. Says quieter, "I wish to God I had had more children. Maybe some of them would be the least bit grateful."

She pushes her chair back and stomps off to the kitchen. We hear her cry. We all hear her crying because she wants us to.

Faith and I look at each other, stunned. I almost want to laugh because it's so awkward, because I almost feel bad for it all, but my dad puts up a hand to stop me. He looks at us both, Faith and me, one after the other, and gives his half smile. The one I think says "I got this" or "I got you." Both, usually, prove to be true.

He gets up and goes into the kitchen. I can't hear the words but don't have to. His voice is still level.

Then Faith inhales with a wide eyes at me, and then does the most surprising thing of all. She starts to clear the table.

I help her, carry all the plates carefully to the kitchen where Dad has his hand on Nikki's back. He's looking down at her, and she is staring out the window as if watching the sun slowly move through the spring evening. Neither of us say anything, only stack the plates and serving dishes around them. Then Faith gets a cloth to go wipe the table. I think of something I really want to say.

"I am grateful, Nikki. I am grateful for all that you've done." I don't say the "but" and all the other stuff that comes after that. I say only that, to the back of her head.

She doesn't say anything. Or turn around. Dad does though. He nods back at me with a smile, but Nikki's only response is the tink of her empty glass as it hits the counter a little too hard.

Later, I hear Nikki go to bed early. She took a long bath and probably a few sleeping pills too, because I hear her snoring by nine. Faith went out, and the TV blares the news downstairs.

Dad's slouched in his chair when I come down. I know how much he misses sports.

"Are you mad at me?" I finally manage when a dishwashing detergent ad comes on too loud.

"Mad at you? Why would I be mad at you?"

"About Faith. That I knew what she was going to do."

"I'm not mad about that. I get that Faith wants to go back to Alberta. She has to see for herself. She's tough. She's always been super independent. She'll be fine."

"They seem like really nice people." I think for a minute. "She showed me their socials and stuff."

He laughs. "Well, everybody looks good on social media." He laughs a bit. "But what do I know. I don't know these people."

"Only what Nikki told you." I lean back. A death tally runs on the bottom of the TV screen. "You think she's, like, biased?"

"Of course she is. Dude walked out on her and left her with a baby. You don't just get over that."

I don't know what would be the exact right thing to say to this. An explosion of something goes off. It looks big. I feel so tired all of a sudden.

To my surprise, my dad mutes the TV and turns to me.

"I hate that I wasn't there for you guys. All you guys. I will regret that forever. And I love Nikki. She's hard to take sometimes but her heart's in the right place. She did push me. And I thank God she did. I was so full of regret and had no idea how to do any of what I had to do to get you back. I felt completely fu—completely lost in all that paperwork. So I am glad she did. I just wish it didn't take me so long to get my sh—stuff together."

He turns back to the screen but doesn't put the sound back on. We don't need it. The world goes by in flashes. Protests. Placards. Dead people. We're quiet for a long time.

Until something occurs to me. "You never talk about your family."

"Nothing much to say," he says simply.

I can't tell if he's willing to talk but I try gently. "Did you know them?"

"Of course. Well, my dad was never around. But I always lived with my mom, until she kicked me out for getting into trouble." He winks at me like this is funny.

But I know it isn't. "How old were you?"

"Fourteen. I stayed in group homes after that." He'd told me about the group homes before. Or only that he was in some as a kid and they were not the best places to be.

"That's sad. That she put you in there."

"It was rough," he nods and seems to think on this a long time. "But she was all on her own, right? And I was a really bad kid."

I remember another piece and put it together. "And she died when you were young?"

"Yeh, like a year later." He leans forward, rubs his hands like he's anxious. Anxious but not unwilling. The weather starts. Big yellow suns over the province.

"What about your other family? Like her family?"

He gets up and grabs a beer. "I know some," he tells me. "They were always all over, living in different places. I still talk to a couple cousins, but we were never that close. Or no one was close to my mom, really, so I didn't know them that well."

"Why weren't they close to your mom?"

"I dunno. I think she was sad. Never was much for people. Never really went anywhere. Just kept to herself. I guess she just lost track of them. Her parents died young too, so all her sisters and brothers just went their own way. They all came to her funeral though. First time I met some of them was there."

"That's sad," I say again.

"Maybe. Some families are like that. That's why I really like your mom's family. Your family. 'Cause they all lived together in that brown house and seemed so close. I thought that was pretty neat."

"Yeh. I wish they stayed like that."

"Funny things happen when people die. Sometimes things, people, fall apart. I think that's what happened to your mom's family when her Mamere died." He sounds so calm and wise about all this. Accepting.

"My family," I correct him.

He smiles his great smile. "Yeh. Your family."

The rest of my month is very full. Pre-Cal was difficult, English was stressful, and in the end I felt wholly unprepared for Bio. Convocation will undoubtedly be a letdown, as it is only going to be a small group of people in a tent on the football field, and it all has to be pretty rushed to get the next groups in. I don't even know any of the other students in the group but Nikki is going to do my makeup and hair so at least I will have a couple nice pictures.

A week after exams and a week before convo is an ordinary Monday, not as hot as June is supposed to be and cloudy. I put on my old hoodie because I think it might rain, and take the bus downtown. I didn't tell anyone I was going. Didn't tell anyone when it was. Dad knew it was coming. He had handed me the rip of paper with the ten-digit phone number and said, "Call this lady. She's her social worker."

So I did and the rest is pretty easy. I didn't know how to take the bus so I am late, but everything there is the exact same. Even with all the masks and plastic and questions, and even after all these years, it's like I am that same little kid who doesn't know any better. Who is filled with hope and love and fear, especially when I open the door and see her face. Her eyes, anyway, behind a face shield and over a blue paper mask. I get shy all of a sudden. I pull the cuffs of my sleeves down over my wrists just like I used to. I look down and around, everywhere but at those big beautiful familiar eyes and the crazy curly hair just pulled down a bit with the shield's band, more grey but still pretty long. I look at my feet 'cause I don't know what to do and say in a small voice, like no time has passed at all,

"Hi, Mama."

19

ELSIE

Elsie would know her anywhere. She had been afraid. Of everything but mostly that she wouldn't recognize her own daughter. That Cedar would be so different. But she was the same. Same crazy just contained hair. Same permanent pout that doesn't mean she's upset only looks that way. Same way of standing almost leaning forward, like she's trying to hide. Not be seen. Protecting herself. Has had to, Elsie knows. No one else was ever there to do it.

Elsie doesn't want to cry. Doesn't want to ball up in tears and brokenness like she used to. She wants to tear off all this stuff covering their faces and hug her so hard and never let her go. Instead, she stands straighter, and forces a smile that will reach her eyes. Not force exactly. The sight of her daughter makes her glow, but forces away the crying and only shows the smile. She holds out her arms shyly.

"I wish I could give you a hug. Can I?"

Cedar nods, not looking up, and lets Elsie reach out to her. Leans her shoulders into her mom who wraps her arms all the way around and breathes in the smell of Cedar. She can still smell her. And feel her. The feel of Cedar.

Cedar.

They stand there a long time. Too long. Neither pulling away. Elsie waits for Cedar to move first.

The clock on the wall makes its ticks and office people walk by the little room they were put in. Cedar's hair is so long. And she's as tall as Elsie now. Has the shape of Elsie's mom. Looks like her but feels completely different. Margaret, who always held herself stiff with anger, ready to fight. Cedar, though, has no fight. She's like me, Elsie thinks, soft.

Soft soft hair, long sleeves, old army bag that looks like something her dad would've bought, way back when Elsie knew him.

Cedar pats Elsie's back quick and pulls away. Elsie lets her and sits down behind the stupid plastic partition they put up between the chairs. Wanting her daughter to be safe from her. She takes off her mask and Cedar does too. And it's all Elsie can do not to stare at her daughter's face. Her eyes. Still trying to only smile. She can see the age there. Not much of it but the change of Cedar's eyes. In and around them. The hardening of the old child features. Still the same cheeks though. She wants to touch them. She wants so much.

Elsie doesn't talk for a long time. Doesn't know what to say. Then, "Need anything? Like a drink maybe? They have a drink machine down the hall." Like she's the hostess or something.

Cedar shakes her head and wipes her face with her pulled-down cuffs.

"You look so . . . you're so beautiful, my girl. Can I call you my girl?"

She nods, still not looking at Elsie. Not all the way.

"You have the look of your Grandma. Anyone ever tell you that? You look like your Grandma Margaret."

"Dad said." She speaks so quietly. A voice not like her old one. "Shawn said something like that, once." Cedar looks at Elsie, checking. Looking to see how she reacts.

But she only forces the smile harder. Swallows.

"Yeh, I guess he would know." She folds her hands together. Afraid all the touching she wants to do will be too much.

"He's told me stories. About your family. Our family."

"Really? That surprises me," she says only because she doesn't really know what to say.

"Yeh. About your brothers. Well, Joey—well he likes to be called Joe now—and what it was like when we were small." She looks down again. "I didn't remember."

"You were really small." When he went to jail, is what she doesn't say. When it all fell apart.

"I kind of remember the brown house. And Grandma. Margaret, I guess. I remember her making us pancakes."

Elsie laughs. The rare happy memories of her mom. "Yeh, she was good at those. Cooking anything." She pauses. Trying to think of something funny. Something normal. "I didn't get that gene."

Cedar smirks. "Me neither."

Elsie relaxes a little more. It's her beloved Cedar. And it's like it's always been. How they know each other, are each other. It's just them. The rest is only noise.

"Where have you, like, been?" Cedar steps lightly over the words.

Elsie sighs into her hands folded on the table in front of her. Thinks of a cigarette. But then knows she has to be clear. Honest.

"It's been rough. I'm not going to lie. I really fell apart when Sparrow died. I don't know where I went, really. I wish, I wish I didn't and I am so very sorry. So sorry to you, and to your sister, but I fell apart. I checked out for a long time." She nods, at this. At the thought that she can say it now. Can say it without completely falling apart. "I'm feeling better now. I've been staying with my Uncle Toby. Do you remember him?"

Cedar looks unsure.

"He's still kicking it. Still living in that stinky place on Main Street. I'm . . . I'm working now, clean now." She looks up to check Cedar's face. Her girl is unfazed. "I'm working and want to get my own place."

"I remember going there. To Uncle Toby's. I think." Cedar speaks slowly. Not really looking up. "I thought, I thought you might be, or he might know where you were. I thought of that."

"You must have known. Somehow. Felt where I was or something."

Cedar tugs at her cuffs.

"Mamere Annie—your Grandmère, Great-Grandma—she always thought we could feel each other. That we knew, as a family, where each other was, what we were doing, how we were doing kind of thing. Does that makes sense?"

The girl only nods. Her girl.

"I thought of that a lot. Have thought about it a lot over these years. I knew you were safe, with your dad anyway. I knew you were sad. But safe. I knew Phoenix has been struggling." Elsie looks over to the wall. Wants to go really far away. "It's the only thing I've done, been allowed to do." Feel you, is what she doesn't say. Doesn't want to say more.

"I have been safe. With Dad, anyway. The foster homes were, well, different than that." But she stops, doesn't want to say anymore either.

"I hope you, if you want to, tell me about it. Tell someone to, you know, heal." Elsie longs for that cigarette. "I'm sorry you had to live like that."

Cedar wipes her face again. Crying again without a sound.

"It's been good, with your dad?"

"Yeh. I mean, it's not always easy. Nikki, Nikki is his wife, she's a bit, different. But he's cool. It's been good. For the most part." Her words like steps.

"I was so glad when that all worked out," Elsie lies. Then remembers to be honest. "I mean, it wasn't my first choice. I wanted to have you. I never wanted any of this to happen. But they weren't letting me. So I'm glad he got it together, came through for you." Not for me, but for you.

"Nikki did most of that. Or so she tells us." Elsie catches the smirk. "I think it was really hard for him. Back then."

Now it's Elsie's turn to nod.

"Do you know what happened? To him? Like when he went away?"

She shakes her head. "No. You'll have to ask him. He just went away." She checks herself again. "I know he didn't want you visiting him when he was inside. It was hard to get there anyway, but he didn't want you to, like, know him there. And by the time he got out, well, we'd had to move. Mamere died and then things went to sh—went to hell."

Cedar nods like she knows what Elsie is talking about. "We had to move. Out of the brown house, right?"

"Yeh. It was all pretty suddenly." Elsie looks over at the faraway place on the wall. Surprised this is the hard part. "Right after she died. Right then."

"That must've been hard."

"It was." Elsie turns to her sympathetic, smart daughter. "I was . . . Sparrow's dad started hanging around more. I didn't even . . . he was just there, and the only person who seemed to want to care for us, so I let him." She shrugs though she wants to do so much more.

"I remember him," Cedar says simply. Angrily. "I don't want to but I remember him."

"He wasn't the best person. He was a horrible person." Elsie wipes her own tears forcefully. "But Sparrow was . . . she was the best kind of person."

"She was," is all Cedar says.

Elsie feels the wall of things she can't talk about. No matter how honest she is trying to be. "Did you ask your dad? About what happened?"

"No. I, I guess I was too shy."

"I heard something from your Uncle Alex once, that your dad was up in Alberta for a while, with your Uncle Joey. I got the impression he was, like, wandering around awhile."

"He told me that. He said he was up there working for a long time. That's where he met Nikki. They only moved here a few years ago."

"They sound like good people," Elsie says. "And you have a stepsister, right?"

"Yeh. A year older. She's in Alberta now. Back in Alberta, anyway. She's Cree. Didn't know her family much either. I mean, she was never around her family, her dad's family, so she's up there getting to know them. It's going well, I think. She seems happy. She has three little brothers now. Works at Tim's . . ." Her voice fades off.

"And you? Are you working? School, of course."

"Yeh. I'm graduating next week, actually. You should come." She says it quickly and then looks, checks.

"I would love to. Wouldn't miss it."

"I'm starting university this fall. The one downtown."

"Really? That's incredible. I am—I am so proud."

"Yeh. I'm going to live in the dorm, if they'll still let us. I could take the bus home, to Dad and Nikki's place, but I don't want to. I want to live on campus."

"Right over there? I was going to get a place around there! My work is just a few blocks away so I wanted to get, you know, something in walking distance."

"Really? We could, like, live close."

"We'd be so close."

Cedar looks up. "Have you heard from Phoenix?"

"No. Not for, not since all that trouble." A horrible way to describe all the horrible things she did. "You?"

"We were talking, for a while, last year. Up 'til a few months ago, actually. But I haven't heard from her in a while." Cedar looks so sad at this. Elsie knows.

"It goes that way sometimes. When people are inside."

"I guess. But I thought she was going to get out soon."

"Don't give up hope. She'll always find a way to talk to you. You're her Cedar. She loves you." Elsie smiles. Loving that she can do this bit of mothering.

Cedar looks up again. "She loves you too, you know."

"I know. She also, she has every right to be mad. I'm still her mother either way. Can't get rid of me that easy." Then cringes a bit at her stupid, useless attempt at a joke.

Cedar says nothing.

For a moment, Elsie thinks she's wrecked it all, all of it, for good.

But her girl says, "We can talk now. I mean I'm not eighteen but I have a cell phone and it's only mine, no one checks it."

Elsie feels an old wave of shame. But pushes it down. "I don't really have a phone, right now. I use Uncle Toby's. I can give you that number. He never answers it. Pretty sure the old man doesn't know how."

Cedar laughs. "I'll give you mine and when you get one, you can give me that one."

"There's a phone at my work I can use. It comes up as a blocked number, if you have call display or something."

"I'll still pick up."

The social worker comes in when the time is up and hovers like they do. Elsie stands up and puts her mask back on so she can reach out to her girl again. To hug her again. Until Cedar pulls away first.

"I can't believe you're going to be right over there," Elsie says into the top of Cedar's head. "We're going to be so close."

"I know," Cedar says into Elsie's shoulder. "We can visit all the time. Whenever we want."

Elsie can't even imagine, doesn't even know what to say to this, to the optimism in her voice. She manages something like, "yeh." But that's it.

The sky's cleared up when she walks outside. She tries not to think of what that social worker is saying to Cedar now. The lady pulled her girl aside to make sure Elsie walks out first. So she could tell Cedar all the things she'd been thinking. The "don't get your hopes up too high." The "once an addict, always an addict." Elsie knows. She's only been clean, what, a few months this time.

Almost twenty-two days.

Basically no time at all.

She lights a smoke in the shade of the office building and walks down the back lane toward the park. She thought about waiting around outside. Getting to talk to Cedar again when she left for the bus. But it felt too creepy. And she feels too exhausted. Her whole body deflates a little more with each drag. She feels light-headed and wants to sit down.

It's her usual bench in the park. The one she used to keep when mooching cigarettes and change sometimes over office lunch breaks. She doesn't have to do that today though. Today she has five rollies in an old pack and about twelve dollars and some change in her pocket. Today she has a child who is almost eighteen. Almost free to see her whenever she wants. She has a job that she's doing good at. A place to stay tonight that's safe and warm. Almost twenty-two days.

The sun is nice. The day has a wind but it's getting hotter. Summer is so much easier than winter. When winter starts and stretches out in front of you like it could go on forever. Never does though. It always ends. And when it goes it feels like it's never going to come back.

Elsie wants to count the change in her pocket. But not out here. She knows she has a five and three toonies, a loonie, and some more. She knows what she has. But wants to keep checking that it's there. She lights another rollie and tries to remember why she doesn't do anything harder anymore. Tries to remember how hard it was to get clean. How awful she felt when she was using. How the highs never seem to last. And when they go it's like they're never going to come back again. She tries to remember all of this. But she also knows it's one and a half blocks to Portage, and ten dollars for a full syringe. The docs there will have them just ready and can shoot her up behind the building or somewhere. They can do it so she doesn't even have to do it. She doesn't even have to look. Can be in oblivion in about ten minutes. She tells herself she wants to do this for celebration. That she made it through the worst of everything and now everything's going to be okay. And it's been so long. She tells herself it's one last time. Just to see and remember and say goodbye to that life properly. But really, she can talk herself into it no matter what. Things can be good. They're never all the way good. Or things can be bad. She wants it either way. All the time. She thinks of getting some percs to take the edge off. She thinks of all of it.

And really, if she's honest, like she's trying so hard to be today, she wants it because she's scared. Because if her kid knows her then she'll really know her. And then she'll really be disappointed in the end.

What if she lets her girl down. What if Cedar sees who Elsie really is. What if she's not good enough for her university-going daughter. What if, in the end, she loses her again. And can't blame a fucked-up system for it. Only herself.

One and a half blocks. About thirty steps to the crosswalk. She can see it.

Or she can go the other way and see what's happening at that bar down the road. Or at the Nor'wester even. She bets Gary will let her in. It's been a while. She can have a few there. Three with her change. See who's around. Mercy will probably be there. Mercy would have something for sure. Not meth in a syringe but something. A gentler goodbye forever. She could sell someone the rest of her grocery card. Make a night of it.

She butts out her smoke at the filter, not a millimetre before. And thinks on it. Left or right she can find something. She can feel all the way good. She can justify anything. All she needs is a little time.

The last time Elsie saw her mom wasn't supposed to be the last time. It was her moving day and she was very emotional about it. Margaret was still very mad at her. Those last weeks they barely talked, outside of packing and organizing. Elsie didn't know what she was doing. Had never moved before.

"You're doing it wrong, Elsie! You can't put those glasses in the box like that. You have to wrap them."

"They're only going in the back seat of Alex's car. They'll be fine."

"Famous last words," Margaret said in a huff, not looking at Elsie. Never looking at Elsie. Only picking through the kitchen cupboards at the stuff she was willing to give to her. "And then you'll have broken glass all over the babies' dishes."

Elsie wrapped a couple tea towels around the glasses. She said, "What about the other dishes?"

"What other dishes?"

"The green ones. Mamere's ones. Where are they?"

"Already packed for my place."

"But I really wanted those."

"They're the only thing in this house worth a damn thing! I am not letting you take them to some low-rent apartment. What if someone steals them? Or pawns them?"

"They're dishes," Elsie said, heartbroken but not up for fighting. She loved those dishes, not because she ever thought they were worth anything but because she knew them her whole life. They were a powdery shade of green glass, with a flowery imprint along the edges. They had a set of tiny little bowls that they used to eat ice cream out of. She thought they even smelled like Mamere.

Margaret folded a box lid closed. "If you think they're only dishes then that's all the more reason for you not to have them. You can go to Walmart and get dishes. It's not like you need a lot."

"And how am I going to pay for that?" Elsie felt the crying starting again. She felt like she'd been crying since Mamere died.

"Elsie, you're a grown woman. You're already getting the couch, the chair, the kitchen table, all your beds . . ."

"Those are mine!"

"Are they? Who paid for them? It certainly wasn't you!"

"They're not yours either!" She didn't often raise her voice to her mother, and always regretted it as soon as she did. She knew if you got mad at Margaret like a normal person, she'd come back at you like a beast.

"This is how it works, young madam. Those were my parents who died, whose stuff this all is. Now it's mine." Margaret was on a tear now and Elsie knew she wouldn't stop. Wouldn't quiet down. "I was the one who cared for them, cleaned for them, looked after this whole falling-down house. All while you got to be a child. Going out and making more children you can't afford or take care of. Well. The gravy train is over for you, kid. Now you get to work for a change. Not that you won't just sit on welfare and pretend to look after your kids. And don't think I'm babysitting them. Oh no, I am done taking care of everyone else." She got so hoarse she started coughing, but still managed to sputter. "I hate that my mother spoiled you so much. I hate that—"

Elsie knew what she was going to say she hated next.

It was nothing she hadn't heard before. So many times. It was always poor Margaret, sacrificing all for everyone. Elsie didn't mention that Margaret barely raised her, that she shuffled her off to her parents whenever she could, and then for good. But Elsie didn't fight. Didn't have it in her. She knew what her mother would say. That Elsie wanted to stay away. That she was only supposed to be away for a little while but wanted to stay. And she'd be right. Elsie never wanted to be with her. And Margaret had never forgiven her for it.

Elsie let her yell. No one really noticed. Uncle John and Sasha passed by a few times, carrying the mattresses down the stairs to the truck. But they didn't say anything. That is what Margaret did. Yelled at people. Mostly at Elsie.

The girls peeked out from the nearly empty living room where they'd been sitting on the floor watching TV. Cedar's eyes were wide and worried but Phoenix stood with a shrug.

Elsie led them back and away. Asked them if they were hungry, and, of course, they were. But she sat with them a spell before going back to the kitchen. She knew Margaret would be leaning against the counter smoking. Huffing and thinking about how much she hated her own daughter.

Elsie heard Sasha's low monotone. "That's it upstairs, I think. Want me to take this stuff here?"

"It's going in Alex's car, apparently," her mom said sarcastically.

"Alex is coming back?"

"Apparently."

Alex who said he would help had been gone all day. He might have forgotten. He didn't have to move. The rest of them were staying another week.

"There's still room. I'll just take it."

Elsie could hear Margaret's scoff from the living room but didn't get up. Let them decide, she thought. Decide her life. Her stuff. Her everything. Just like they always had. Without even thinking of asking her.

She knew she'd been crying since Mamere died.

She knew she should have planned this all better. Known better. But she didn't think Mamere was going to die. She knew that was stupid. The woman was over ninety. But Elsie really thought she would have been around longer. Or maybe she thought Mamere wouldn't've let this all happen. No one would've ever sold the house while she was alive. No one would've ever put Elsie out either.

She was going to move out once. They had planned it, Shawn and her. He wanted to get a better place. His was only this one room in an old house on Selkirk. He wanted to get something close by so they wouldn't be far from Mamere. They had walked down Henderson all that summer. Looking at the buildings. Choosing favourites.

He got picked up before the end of August.

Elsie knew what they were doing but never thought they'd get caught.

And then she thought she would wait. But he didn't want her to. He cut her off. "For your own good," he'd said, crying over the phone. She remembers thinking that was a pretty big deal because he was in a hall with all these other cons. To cry there must mean he was really upset.

Funny how people always say things are for your own good but never ask you what you think your own good is.

She met Sparrow's dad like a week later. Didn't even want him. Just wanted somebody. And he was willing to be around. Shawn never called. Mamere started getting really sick. Sometimes you just wanted someone around.

She likes to think she never loved him. That she never loved any of them. That she was aware they were no good. But she was never that smart. She wasn't aware of any of it. Until it all blew up in her face.

She heard Sasha leave and Margaret go upstairs. Kissed Phoenix's head and went into the kitchen to make them some sandwiches. She dug out the green plates. Rolled her fingers over them like she was saying goodbye. She had no idea what her mom had packed up for them. Guessed she'd find out when she got to her low-rent apartment. Which would be soon enough.

Alex wandered in as she was putting the dishes in the sink. He looked hungover but happy. "Hey, where's all your stuff?"

"Uncle and your dad took it already," she said, looking around at all the empty spaces.

"Looks different, hey?"

Elsie could only nod.

Her brother put an arm around her shoulders. Pulled her close. "Hey, don't worry. I'll come visit all the time."

"You better." She wiped her face with her sleeve.

"Where's whatshisname?" No one ever bothered to learn Sparrow's dad's name.

"I told him to stay away today. He's going to meet me at the apartment later."

"Probably a good plan."

Margaret stomped down the stairs. Annoyed at something new. "Oh there you are. God, you look awful. Go take a shower."

"I will later. I came to help Else."

"Well too little too late just like the rest of them."

Neither of them bothered to ask who she was talking about. Alex handled their mom better than Elsie did though. He slides easily to the next subject. It also helped that Margaret didn't hate him.

"What's left?" he asks.

"Nothing," Margaret answered. "Just the girls and this one." She glared at her. "You should go too, Elsie. Help your uncle and stepfather move your things."

"I'll take you." Alex smiled.

"Can I leave the girls here?"

"No, ma'am. I told you. No more babysitting."

"But they're going to be in and out with the furniture. I don't even have a TV over there."

"Oh my, you'll have to parent, then. God forbid." Margaret moved over to the sink and scoffed at Elsie's dirty dishes. Elsie ignored her and went upstairs. Just to check, she told Alex. But really it was to say goodbye.

To look around her empty room. The dents in the brown carpet. The curtain pulled back. The tape on the wall still holding the corners of posters she didn't tear off carefully enough. There was a hanger in the closet. An old craft Phoenix had made that must have gotten lost under things. It was a Santa head with a cotton-ball beard. Elsie smiled at it. Smiled around at her room. It had always been her room. Since she'd moved here when she was little. Even before then when she went over for sleepovers. When she stayed as long as she could in the warmth. Grandpa Mac's meat-cooking smell. Mamere's Noxzema skin smell. Everything happened here. Elsie was here when he died. Every horrible thing in between. The deaths were the worst parts though.

She checked over the bathroom. Her shelf in the medicine cabinet was empty. Even all the girls' bath things were gone. Margaret hadn't missed a thing. Anywhere. Like she was trying to erase them from the house. From her life.

She walked down the stairs slowly. The construction-paper Santa in her hand. Like it was the only thing she had left. That and her bag at the door. The girls. Even their jackets were packed and gone. Good thing it was nice out.

She went into the living room and looked around there too. The old, dusty drapes always closed. Sasha's lawnchair where the couch used to be. So he could watch TV for the few days they'd still be there. They'd bought all new furniture for their new condo down Main

Street. Didn't even tell her where it was exactly. Just down past the bridge. In the good part of town.

"Okay, girls, we have to go now."

"No!" they moaned in unison. Only because their show wasn't over. Not because they knew what was happening.

"Come on, girls." Margaret's voice was always a little lighter when she talked to them. But not by much. "You heard your mom. Time to go. To your new home. You can set up your whole new room."

They still complained but started moving.

"Say goodbye to your Grandma."

Alex took Phoenix's hand and Elsie took Cedar's. Elsie didn't look up at her mother. Didn't acknowledge this in any way. She could see Margaret looking at her expectantly. But instead of giving in, Elsie hardened her face and turned to the front door.

She didn't look back. Not when she closed the door behind her. Not when she saw her mother still looking through the window. She knows it was childish. But it was all she had.

Elsie was determined to prove her mother wrong. Or something. She doesn't know what kind of stubbornness she was working on but she was determined anyway. She never asked her for anything ever again. Didn't call her, didn't visit. Didn't even know where they were really. Not even when Alex said her mom asked after them. Not even when Sparrow was born. Not even when she got sick and sad and felt completely alone. When she had nothing and no one to help her. She didn't see her mother at all.

And then Margaret died.

It was sudden. No one thought it was going to happen. It was only a year later. She was only in her fifties. Aunty Genie at her funeral said she probably just couldn't live without her mother. But Elsie knew that wasn't it. More likely she was just too angry. Made sense she had a heart attack. She smoked like a chimney and stressed all the time. There was something to be said for her actually having a heart. But Elsie's never said anything like that out loud.

She didn't think things could get worse after Margaret died. Didn't think her mother could affect her anymore. But like everything, Elsie was fucking clueless. And the deaths are always the worst of it all.

—

She lights another smoke and counts how many she has left. Two. Not enough to spend some time at the Nor'wester. Only twelve dollars and some change so can't buy more. She could go home to Uncle Toby's and roll some more. Then go. She could walk a block and a half and forget everything for a few hours. She thinks of that time. That waking up in a back lane puddle. It's the only thing that pushes her up to standing and gets her walking.

Without her mom around there was no one to take her kids when they took them away. She didn't think they'd actually do it. But of course they did. She was so sick and clued out she didn't know anything was going on. Not really. It was all she could do to stay awake all day. Phoenix never told her. Never told her what Sparrow's dad did. Was doing. Elsie wishes she would have told her. But she doubts anyone would have told her anything back then.

Without an approved relative to take the girls in they had to be separated. Put into the system. Phoenix was in a hotel for a while. Not that Elsie knew that 'til later either. Cedar and Sparrow seemed okay at that lady Tannis's house. Or at least that's what she told herself as she tried to detox for the first time. Detoxed while working. While everything else. If her mom hadn't died, Elsie would have talked to her eventually. Or maybe Margaret would have even talked to her. She would've taken her kids. Elsie knows that for sure. That's the worst of it. She knew Margaret would've done that. She would've hated it, but she would've done it. And they would've been all safe. All cared for. All alive.

Uncle Toby's snoring to Wheel of Fortune when she gets in. His breathing is really awful these days. She wakes him by handing him the Coke she bought for him. Cold in his open hand.

He mumbles, "Oh maarsii. Maarsii, ma fii," he says with his wake-up cough and sputter. When he recovers he asks, "How'd it go?"

"Good," she says. Morose and forgetful. "Great actually. She's so big." Elsie sits on the couch and rubs her hands together. Thinking of another smoke already. "She looks so much like Mom. Smart like her, too. Going to university in the fall."

"Another Margogo, hey?" He smiles. "Your mom would have liked that."

"Nothing like her though. She's like, well, me. She's quiet and sad but looks like Mom. It's weird."

"Yeh, your mother was anything but quiet. Pretty sad though."

"You think?"

"Oh yeh. Margogo? Saddest person I ever knew."

"I don't remember her sad at all. Just angry." At her. All the time.

"She was just being tough. Margogo was sad. She never got over not being a lawyer. Disappointing everyone. Our dad mostly, I think."

Elsie doesn't say anything. Picturing Margaret as a sad person. Maybe.

"Never the same after. And Sasha." He lets the air out from between his teeth. "He's all the way hard, hey?"

They're quiet for a while. Watch the letters ding and turn over. Somebody wins a trip to Paris. Elsie's always wanted to go to Paris. Always thought she'd like to climb the Eiffel Tower or walk over all those fancy carved bridges.

She feels warm. And hungry. Realizes she hasn't eaten all day. Was too nervous before. She could cook up that bacon. Uncle Toby would like that.

"Should we go visit her?" she calls from the table as she rolls another rollie in her fingers. "Her grave, I mean."

"Could," he calls back. "Call Alex."

"Yeh, he'd drive us, hey? Maybe we could even get flowers."

"Margo'd like rollies better," he says with a laugh.

Make sense to her. "Yeh, knowing her, hey?"

She leans back and enjoys the smoke. It's been nineteen today. Nineteen smokes, but no pills. And nothing else. Five cups of coffee maybe. It's been three weeks and a day since she's been all the way clean. Weaned herself slow this time. Everyone said it was the best way. Her knees hurt. Her hip hurts. She inhales long and watches the final puzzle. The familiar music going along. Neither one of them has a clue what it is. But when has that mattered.

20

MARGARET

On the day she moved out of the house she had known had all her life, Margaret woke up with a craving.

The house was quiet. Empty. So much silence she could hear the fridge hum as she brewed her coffee. She leaned against the counter, lit a smoke, and listened to the hum and churn, the bubble and cough of the coffee spitting out. This house had never been empty. Margaret had never lived here without too many family members around her. First all her brothers, then visiting cousins, always visitors, then Genie, Jerome, Toby didn't move out until after she did. Even when she wasn't here there was always someone, Jerome, Renee, and their first baby for a time, and then Elsie, then her babies. There were always babies. Always toys to trip over, baby gates to open, leftovers in the fridge, a pot of too-dark tea going cold on the stove, and her mom, Annie, at the centre of everything, stationed like the sun they all orbited around.

Her mom liked it that way, liked to keep people close, liked to care for them and always have something to do. It was Margaret who always thought something was wrong with it all.

"That's the way it's supposed to be, ma fii," Annie would say. "That's how we lived, with family around. People these days don't know, don't remember. That's why they're lonely." Her mother's body like it was when Margaret was young, bent over some task, cooking something, washing something, never complaining about all that was in front of her.

Margaret had had so many ideas about how things should be.

"That's the old way, Mamere. People don't need to live like that anymore. We don't need to farm land for hay, either."

Annie chuckled. "We never had land for hay. Not for generations anyway."

"You know what I mean. We can live like normal families now."

"And what is normal, ma fii? Isn't our way normal, too?"

Margaret didn't remember giving her an answer. She did remember at a certain point in most conversations, she'd stop to roll her eyes but let her mother be. She thought Annie was old, living in the past she never got over and remembering things as if they used to be good.

They were never good.

In her mother's childhood, they were Métis stuck in a city they had created but now were all but pushed out of. Their home was little more than a shack, and they never had two pennies to rub together, of course. Never seemed to get ahead, keep jobs, or finish school. And then they all seemed to die way too young, and none too normal. No one else in her family got to die old and surrounded by people who loved them. Margaret knew that meant everything to her mother. To Annie. To Angélique. To be able to live that long. That well.

Margaret knew all the other stories like a list she needed to memorize on the way to the store:

Her mother's mother dead of TB before she was thirty, had probably suffered with for years.

Her father, not long after. Annie always said he died of accidentally falling into the river, but crusty Tante Marguerite said he got himself in trouble and thrown in there.

Baptiste, the oldest, was hit by a streetcar, but no one knew how and why, only that it was quick. Someone told them it was quick.

Josephte, the oldest girl and Annie's favourite. Her young husband a bad man who didn't quite abide by the old rule of thumb.

Her other brother Tootie was a heart attack around fifty.

And Tante Marguerite was cancer, but she couldn't've been sixty.

Margaret remembered that one. She had been in university then.

The rest she had only heard, as if they had all just happened. Stories from long nights spent peeling potatoes, making vats of stew for other relatives grieving other tragedies. Stories whispered over cigarettes while tea steeped to black. Still moments when Annie couldn't keep the ghosts away any longer.

"My dad was never the same after Maman died. That's what everyone said. He couldn't help himself after that, they said."

"Everyone loved Baptiste. He could have had his pick of girls to marry. He got a job on the trains. A good job. He even went all the way to Montreal one summer. He would have kept it too. Good money, that."

"Josephte should have never married that one."

That's what everyone became, small stories, tiny really, to explain their whole lives. Those too-short lives.

Margaret used to think this was normal, that all families were made up of so many sad stories. But as she got older, it seemed only Indians, Métis, who had sorrow built into their bones, who exchanged despair as ordinarily as recipes, who had devastation after devastation after dismissal after denial woven into their skin. As if sad stories were the only heirloom they had to pass on.

She doesn't know when she stopped being affected by it. All she seemed to do is nod and listen to her sad mother. Sometimes she wonders if she ever was affected at all. Annie was. Annie shed tears her whole life. Margaret would catch her mother crying quietly, quickly, before sighing and going on with all the work she had to do. Margaret never seemed to feel it though. Only thought of all the things she wasn't going to let happen to her. Only thought of all the ways she would harden herself against the inevitable onslaught.

To think she was almost free of it. She had almost overcome the sad Indian stereotype. She'd almost become an example. She used to try and tell herself she was only Métis, not a real Indian, as if that could spare her from it. Even though it never spared her family. It never made any difference at all to anyone on the outside looking in.

She tried to hide it, kill it in her, be as white as possible, pass, but it didn't much matter what she did. To the world she was still a squaw. Trying to reason that she was only half a squaw didn't matter much to anyone else, not even her.

And here she was now. Alone in a big empty house. Her family useless—every last one of them. Nothing to look back on but a bunch of shameful stories. No successes to speak of. Nothing to show for a life of hard work. Until now.

Margaret butted out her smoke and waved away the self-pity. Who cares about the rest, she was going to finally get something. A condo in the good part of the north side was waiting for her. All brand-new furniture too. Things she picked out of a catalogue, exactly as she pleased. And this house, this fucking tired house, was going to be just another bad memory. She was going to keep all the bad memories here and only take what she wanted into her new life.

She wanted new everything. Determined to buy new clothes, new appliances, she didn't want anything second-hand or used for once. The only old stuff she wanted to keep was a couple photos, framed ones of her dad looking sharp, her mom looking happy, and those fucking green dishes. She'd bought them for her mom, over two winters when she was working at Eaton's. Bought plate after plate, cup after cup, one or two each paycheque, checked each off the list until she had the whole set, twelve of everything. Jerome had broken a small saucer so there were only eleven of those, and one of the cups had a chip on the lip, but it was still a lot. Almost enough. Annie was so proud of them. Kept them in the china cabinet, the only actual china in there. For years she only brought them out for special occasions, and barely then. But of course Annie indulged Elsie so damn much, and the girl got to use them more than any kid before her. To think the girl was going to take them. Ungrateful and spoiled, that girl, Margaret was still fuming over it. The girl didn't see how valuable they were, not like Margaret did.

That was it, really. That's all she wanted. The rest could go fuck itself. The rest of them too. She only wanted to do this one last thing, this one last time. Then she would finish packing, make Sasha his roast because it was Tuesday, and damn if that man could miss his Tuesday roast. Tomorrow he would get the truck and John and Toby would be by first thing and they would be moved out. But today she had some time, for this one last thing.

She got out the flour, put the lard on the counter to soften, beef drippings from the freezer to thaw, and dug out the big pot that always smelt of grease and scrubbed the dust off it. She was drying the big, nasty thing when someone knocked on the back door. She wasn't expecting anyone and was annoyed, wasn't going to answer it. But the knock kept going.

Margaret put the pot down and stomped to the door, swung it open more forcefully than she'd intended. That Shawn stood on the other side of the screen, ragged and messy looking. He held his head down and let his long hair fall over his face, just like the shameful letch she always took him for.

She stood looking at this one, her mouth a thin line. Then finally, "Well, look what the cat dragged in."

"Hello, hello, Margaret," he had the nerve to say. "Is Elsie here?"

If he had a hat, he'd have it in his hands. But of course his hands were empty.

"No. No, Elsie's moved out, Shawn." She bit over his name. "We sold the place. Finally."

"Oh." He looked surprised. "I wouldn't think, I never thought Mamere Annie would do that."

She cringed at his using her name. "My mother is dead. She died three months ago." She was almost sorry when his face fell like it did. The boy looked ready to cry. "I would have thought you knew."

The fool boy only shook his head. Wiped an empty hand over his greasy hair. Margaret contemplated him through the greying of the screen. She would have felt sorry for him if she didn't know him.

"You best come in, then." She didn't know if she was moved out of pity or resignation.

Shawn followed her through to the kitchen then sat without waiting to be asked. She poured him a cup of coffee and smacked it down in front of him. Black.

"I came," he stumbled, "I wanted to come after the girls went to daycare or something. I, I didn't want to confuse them."

But she didn't respond. Didn't think she needed to. Only moved the flour and bowls to the counter and pulled out a chair across from him. She lit up and tossed her pack over to him. Might as well be hospitable.

"I would have sent something, if I had known." He lit up with shaking hands. "How'd she die?"

"She was ninety-three," Margaret spat out. "How do you think she died?"

He smirked, his feigned coyness. "I thought she was going to live forever."

Margaret made a sound that was more grunt than anything else.

"I'm sorry for your loss, Margaret."

She stared at him and his gall. The stink of jail still on him. That wary look in his eye. The one in every man's eye when they first get out, when they don't know where they are or what they're doing. Where the next fight was going to come from.

"When'd you get out?"

"Two days ago. I'm at a halfway house in Point D. I would have called . . ."

"Had you known. I know."

He had the nerve to smile. One of his smirks anyway. "No, I, well yeh, that too. But I told Elsie I would call when I got out, but it was, I wanted to get settled first."

Have a good drunk was more like it. But she only half grunted again.

"I guess you know I, I told Else to, to stay away." He was back to stumbling his words around. No fight left in him, this boy.

She huffed. "I figured something like that had happened."

"I didn't want her to have to go there, see me there. Didn't want my daughter going there either. Or Phoen." He looked down, trying to rouse more pity, Margaret figured. "I thought it was a just a short stretch."

"Two years is a lot for a young child." A young woman too.

"It feels like it's been like forever. Twenty-eight months but forever."

Margaret didn't have to answer. Not that she would.

"I got a, I'm getting set up with a job. I only have to be in the halfway house for a few months. I want, I'd like to see them. Where did they move to?"

"Over up on Henderson," she said vaguely, sizing him up. "You should know she's got another man in there already."

"Really!" He seemed genuinely surprised.

"Well what did you think was going to happen?" she scoffed.

"I don't, I don't know what I thought." He made a show of butting out his smoke, taking a gulp of coffee. "But if she's happy . . ."

"Of course she's not happy," Margaret blurted. "She's Elsie. When has Elsie ever been happy?"

He was quiet for couple beats. Maybe he was sizing her up too. No doubt making a show of it anyway. "Is he, good to her?"

Margaret exhaled long. "I think his only redeeming quality is he's not in jail. From what I can tell anyway."

He leaned back, defeated. "Still, I can . . . Can you give me the address?"

She cleared her throat first. Then leaned in, looked right at him. "I don't think that's a good idea, Shawn."

He tried to look all sorrowful. "But I'm her dad."

Margaret was unmoved. "What sort of dad have you been? You've been away longer than you've been around. She doesn't even remember you. And Phoenix, well, Phoenix now with this new change? And another man around? You should leave them be."

"But I want," he mumbled. "I can help."

Margaret's voice grew, filled the whole room. "Help what? Her? Them? You can barely help yourself by the looks of it. Showing up here in the middle of the day, stinking of who knows what, like you haven't even showered the penitentiary off of you? Tell me, Shawn, what do you have to offer them? If you ask me, you should stay away. Don't make promises you can't keep and just stay away. Get yourself in order and forget about trying to be all things when you can barely stand upright. Go look after yourself."

"But she's my daughter."

The fool really was going to cry. Margaret recoiled from him but didn't it let go. "And you're her father. But what kind of father are you being?"

He couldn't even look at her. His eyes wandered around trying to find something to hang on to. The bowls on the counter, the window, anything but her. She could feel him getting angry but knew he wouldn't do a damn thing about it. "Do you have a number for her at least?"

Margaret scoffed again. "I don't even know if that girl has a phone. Wouldn't surprise me if she didn't. Didn't even so much as say good-bye, never mind leave me a way to reach her." She went on, wanting to drive her point home. "She's been, for months now she hasn't been herself. Losing her Grandmother. The girl never had to work for anything in her life and now has to live on her own. Spoiled thing. I don't know how she's going to be a mother. I bet she'll find a way to have me take those children by Christmas, mark my words. Phoenix, Cedar, and now this new one too, I bet."

Fool boy didn't know what hit him. "New one? She's having another baby!"

"Oh yes. Elsie wastes no time. Not even twenty-three, that one, and three kids by three different fathers." Margaret really grunted this time and pulled her pack over to light another cigarette.

He only nodded now. He looked like Elsie usually did, deflated and defeated.

Her voice softened, a bit. "As I said, you should leave them be. Go try and take care of yourself while you're young and still can. They won't even remember you."

The boy didn't look up. He looked so pitiful Margaret pushed the pack back across the table. He took one. His hands still shaking. Margaret only hoped he didn't actually cry. She couldn't stand it when men cried.

They were silent for a long while before he finally got up. "I guess I should be going, then."

"Okay, then." Margaret didn't have anything more to say.

"When you see her, can you just. Tell her I love her." This time he really was whimpering. It was pathetic.

She didn't even know which "she" he was talking about, but if it got him to leave.

He went out with an almost soundless click of the door. Well at least he knew how to do that.

Margaret sat there for a while longer. Stuck in her thoughts, huffing with everything. Her daughter's shamelessness, the boy's pure gall, their utter uselessness. The pair of them couldn't raise a chicken to slaughter. Margaret knew, just knew Elsie was going to come crawling back and she'd be saddled with those kids before the girl even grew her belly. Mark my words, she thought, pointing her smoke at no one, mark my fucking words.

She was still mad when she started putting everything together. She slammed the pot on the stove and wacked the frozen dripping container until the icy brown chunk released. She turned the element on low, let it all melt and fill, and got the other ingredients ready.

Her mother never slammed things around. Annie never took her anger out on the world, only herself. Margaret read once that depression was only rage pointed inward. That comforted her. She couldn't relate to her mother if the woman didn't have rage. If Margaret had had to live Annie's life, she'd have killed someone a long time ago. Probably more than one. As it was, Margaret never saw the point of suffering in silence. Or pointing it at herself. She was usually the only one not doing something wrong.

She cut the lard into the flour with a vengeance. Laughed at how her mother taught her to always make dough with love.

"You can taste the love in it, ma fii. Have to be gentle." Annie's breaded things were always light and fluffy. Margaret never made anything that way. Hers were heavy, flat, and she liked it better that way. She crammed the floured mash harder.

She didn't get the letter until she came home from work one summer evening. A rainy one, she remembers, the wet soaked through her little plastic cap, the kind ladies used to wear to protect their hair. It was such an uncomfortable thing, the plastic cutting into her cheeks and the little polyester tie tight under her chin. She hadn't brought an umbrella and had to walk home all the way from the bus on Main Street. She grabbed a newspaper as she passed a stall and held it over her head, not that it did much, and ran.

"You look like a drowned rat!" Annie exclaimed when Margaret burst through the door. Then laughed as she helped her with her coat, shaking it out as close to the mat as possible. "Ma fii, you have a letter."

"From the school?" But Margaret knew immediately what letter.

Excitedly, girlish-like, Annie nodded. And picked up the galoshes and useless plastic hair cover Margaret had thrown on the wood floor as she raced to the kitchen.

The letter was there on the table next to her mother's cutting board and half-made dinner. It was thick.

Margaret ripped the thing open. The opening line, opening half of a line, the only thing that registered: "We are pleased."

"I got in!" she whispered, in disbelief and delight.

When her dad came home, he called everyone over. Joseph, Genie, young, fat Jerome, and just-out John all came over. Toby came down from upstairs. Mac opened up the Crown Royal, the bottle wrapped in its purple flannel bag and kept above the sink for Christmas and maybe, maybe, New Year's. But today he pulled it down, opened the drawstring, and told Annie to get all the shot glasses out, even one for young Jerome.

Warmed by the golden syrupy rye, they laughed around the table. Annie apologized for the boring soup and bannock she'd made because she didn't know it would be a celebration, and it was Wednesday. Margaret said she didn't care and it was the best meal she could have hoped for.

After dinner they pushed the living room furniture against the wall, and Mac called all the cousins, many of whom came over right away. He went down the street and next door to get the neighbours. He got out all his records and put the Redbone one on over and over, like he had for years after he got it.

"These guys, my girl, they're Indians!" Mac said in his third tiny glass of rye. "Real ones from California! And they had a hit on the radio! Indians on the radio! Real ones!"

Mac was as proud as if he'd done it himself, was always so proud of any Indian actually "making it." He had every Buffy Sainte-Marie album, three worn copies of Prison of Grass, and half a dozen biographies of Riel, even though they were all written by racist Easterners. He watched every John Wayne movie, "for the Indians," even though they always died and most of the actors weren't even Indian, but he watched them for the odd one that was. He was heartbroken when he found out his favourites were Italians in prosthetics.

Sometime near eleven, when Genie was still giggling and young Jerome was asleep upstairs, Mac gathered everyone around.

"Come on, come on, if there was ever a time to make a speech," he called to the room. His face reddened with singing and talking. "I wanted to say, well, only things you all know, but I'm going to say it all again anyway because I feel like talking.

"My Maman, my dear Maman was born on the side of a road in the bush, lived her whole life on land that she couldn't own. Driven out of too many places to count. She was in, she was a widow living in Ste. Madeleine when they burned it down. Burned it all down and forced the Métis there from the homes they had occupied for decades. Decades.

"They never wanted us. They never acknowledged us, or included us. They all just wanted us to fade away. To die. But we didn't. You didn't. I didn't. We all fought for anything we could have. We all worked for everything, every little thing. My Maman, your dear Aunty and Mamere Rosary, always said we had to work twice as hard to get anything. I always thought that was what it meant to be a halfbreed. That we were only ever going to be half as good, no matter what we did.

"But today. Today we celebrate. We don't have many celebrations, so those we have we have to use. Today, my daughter got into law school. Law school, can you believe it? She's going to be a lawyer and she's going to change the laws that our people have fought so long to change.

"Me, I am just a working sap. I have only ever known to work with these two hands. It's got me all I have. My beautiful wife, Annie, this house, this house that I bought with my own money. No one ever gave us anything. We had to work. But now Margaret, our little Margogo, our Maggie Muggins here, is going to work with her head. She's going to wear her fancy suits like she does at her job at Eaton's and she's going to be something in the world. Something we can all look up to. Something we can all tell our friends, our bosses, and neighbours about. Then they won't be able to say we're all useless. They can't say we're all just the same, that we're all worth nothing, because she is going to be worth something." He got all choked up and stopped. He pulled Margaret close and raised his half-empty little glass. "To Margaret!"

"To Margaret!" the room shouted.

Margaret saw her mother wipe a tear from her eye, quickly, before she took up her cloth again and picked up a few stray glasses.

It was the moment of Margaret's life. The moment she'd been working for and made. It didn't even make her sad now. It only made her ashamed. And then angry. Very, very angry.

"Morning, Ma." Alex burst in, the door slamming behind him. "Oh frybread. Yes, please." He grabbed a piece of pain croosh right off the paper towel.

"Careful. It's hot," Margaret said, not turning from the pot.

She could hear him huffing with a full mouth. She knew it'd be too damn hot. "So where'd you get up to, then? Or should I even ask?"

"Just a friend's," he said with his mouth full.

She knew he'd been spending nights at that Angie's place. Why his father got him a car the second he turned sixteen she would never know. She pricked another done piece and turned it over on the paper towel. She rolled it a few times to get the grease off.

He looked around. "This place is so empty."

"Well, that's moving for you."

"You didn't pack my room, did you?"

She pricked another. "There're boxes on your bed. But you better get moving. Trucks are coming first thing tomorrow."

"I will. I will."

She put her fork down and opened the window to let the greasy air out. Then lit up and looked at her son. He was a good boy, or used to be. Now she wasn't so sure. He wasn't going to school much, she knew that. He wanted to work for his dad now, be a man and all that stupid stuff. Alex looked older than his sixteen years, he looked hungover and slack-faced as he crammed another piece of frybread into his mouth. Another child who was not even going to graduate high school. She drew her lips into their thin line.

"Did you hear from Elsie yet?" he said, like he knew it'd press her buttons.

"Her? No," she puffed.

"She told me she'd call here and leave her new number."

Margaret scoffed. "I doubt that girl even knows how to get a phone."

"Maybe I'll go down there. Just to check."

"Do your packing first. Your sister's a grown woman." She butted out her smoke. "She can manage. She has whatshisname to help her."

"Waste of space that guy," Alex said matter-of-fact. "I doubt he's any help at all."

"Well, she made her bed." Margaret turned back to the last of the batter. Made two more large pieces, to get it all over with.

"She's not like you, Ma. She's not even like me."

"What's that supposed to mean?" She turned and pointed her fork at him. "What am I like?"

"You know," he said with his mouth full again. "Tough."

"Well then, she needs to toughen up real quick, or the world is going to chew her up and spit her out." Margaret looked out the window as she said this, at the sunny afternoon, at the overgrown grass in the backyard.

Alex eventually stomped up the stairs and made a show of playing his stupid music too loud while hopefully packing up his things.

Margaret pulled the last piece out of the oil and turned off the element, took the pot off so the grease could cool faster.

She sat at the table and picked at a couple pieces. She didn't want to indulge in them too much. Never did like the greasy frybread as much as everyone else did. Sasha would eat some when he got home. John and Toby would appreciate them in the morning.

She pulled out her cell phone and clicked on her new game. Elsie was not as stubborn as Margaret's waste of a son Joey. She wouldn't have the nerve to cut her mother off completely. Elsie needed her too much. She'd call any day now, come crawling back with her tail between her legs the second she realized how hard it was to actually be an adult.

This was what Margaret thought as she finally pushed the pain croosh aside and made some fresh tea. As she lit up another cigarette and returned to her game. This new flashy game where she made row upon row of shiny candies. Where the screen filled with flashing lights and bonuses and silent cheers. She played until her eyes went squirrelly, until it was time to start Sasha's roast. As she thought about her grandbabies and daughter, and waited for Elsie to call, certain she would.

But in this, of course, like in so many things she did or thought, Margaret was very, very, tragically wrong.

21

CEDAR

The summer flew by, just like everyone said it would, and even though I didn't believe it and really didn't do anything or go anywhere. Before I knew it, there I was, standing in my bedroom trying to think of everything I needed to take with me.

I'd left packing too late, and now I had to get it all done as quick as possible. Dad was already waiting to take me across town because I want to get there in time to set up before supper was delivered to my room. Not that it was mandatory or anything, but I had to quarantine for two weeks and wanted to start that right away. Classes were all online and all my books were getting delivered too, so really, there was no rush. But still, I just wanted to get there.

Dad appears at the door, eyeing the cardboard boxes. "You ready for me to start loading the car?"

"Think so." The room nearly as empty as it was when I first moved here. Not that there was ever much in here to begin with. I never managed to get more than the odd poster on the walls. Never had much for clothes. Hated too much clutter or mess. The new emptiness feels different though. Before it was blank and waiting. Now it's more like emptied out and spent.

As Dad grunts over a box of books, I go into the bathroom with a box. But there's already one waiting for me. Taped closed and marked with "C bathroom" and a happy face. I open the medicine cabinet anyway, and sure enough, all my stuff is out of there. Not that I had tons of creams and hair products, only one or two buried among Nikki's hundreds, but still they made little holes along the shelves.

But that still didn't make me sad. Nothing did. Not today. Not Nikki's long texts telling me how proud she is and how much she loves me. I reply with the odd emoji but can't seem to get all emotional about it. Or as emotional as Nikki thinks I should be. I also can't shake the thought that if Nikki really did care, she wouldn't have taken an extra day shift. Would have been here for such a "big day."

"It's hard for her," Dad had explained when he took me to Sal's for breakfast and we ate the takeout in his car. "She didn't want to get you down by crying or something. You know she's a crier. You wouldn't have wanted her there."

"She didn't want to go downtown, you mean."

"Maybe a bit of that too," Dad said like it was no big deal. "She worries. It's how she cares."

I didn't say anything, just picked at my bacon.

It's not like I wanted Nikki around, but I didn't want her not around either. She was all over everything when Faith went away. Took a couple days off. Made all her favourite meals. Made sure she packed everything she needed. All trying to make her change her mind, I knew, but at least she was there. At least she made us all drive Faith to the airport even though she only blubbered in the passenger seat the whole time.

Guess I don't get a send-off like that. But then again, I'm only going across town.

"You can come home whenever you want," Dad told me for like the hundredth time. "You don't have to call or anything. Just come. Or I can come get you. If you have laundry or something."

Dad tells me, again.

"They have a laundry room, you know."

"Naw, save your money. I can get you on Saturdays. How else are you going to keep up with hockey?"

"Um, the internet? My laptop?" I say, thinking of my graduation present. The beautiful black slim thing I now cherish more than anything.

"That's no way. You need a big screen!"

I swirled the last of my blueberry pancakes in the syrup drippings left on the styrofoam container and smiled.

I heard from Phoenix finally, sometime in July.

"Hey, Cedar-Sage," my sister's voice boomed over the phone.

"Hi, hey, where you been?" And hope it doesn't make Phoenix feel bad for not calling.

"Got into a bit, got a bit delayed, I guess." She was upbeat but obviously trying to be. She explained she was at adult prison now, in Headingley, but that she'd be out in less than two years.

"I'll be eighteen soon. Then I can come visit you," I told her.

"That'd be, that'd be nice, Cedar-Sage. But I think you gotta get approvals and shit."

I told her it didn't look so bad but I'd double-check. I'd already researched the application process online. Things were backed up, of course, but it could happen. Maybe by Christmas. It might not be as easy as it seemed, I knew. I knew how these things went.

Not even two years more. The timeline echoed long after our short call. It's twenty-one months now. Twenty-one months and Phoenix will be out. And I'll be living on my own. Well, in the dorm anyway. Will come and go as I please soon. Doesn't seem all that long a time, considering.

I haven't heard from my mom since my convocation but didn't really expect to. I know she's working on things. Things that take a lot of time. I keep my phone charged. Check it often.

She'll only be blocks away from me now. Phoenix will be close enough, too. All three of us. All the time. I can barely believe that either.

Thirteen months.

"Well, that's the last of it," Dad announces as he sets down the last box in the narrow room. The tall bed stacked high with my stuff. Not that it was that much stuff but it looks like a lot in here.

I look around this other empty room. It doesn't make me sad either.

"Wanna go grab a coffee or something? Are you hungry?" He itches the top of his mask on his nose.

I shake my head. "I kind of just wanna, organize everything."

"Nuff said, nuff said." Dad waves his hands up. "I'll get out of your hair."

"You're not in my—"

But Dad gives me one of his famous smiles. "Don't worry about me, C. I can be the uncool dad, no problem."

I roll my eyes at him and toss the last duffle bag on top of my new desk.

He nudges me with what looks like a bunch of twenties.

"You don't have to give me money, Dad."

"Yes, I do. That's what dads do. Take it."

Shyly I take the little roll. It's a hundred dollars.

"Freshly sanitized and everything. Don't spend it all in one place. And lock this door, all the time!"

"Yes, Dad."

He pulls me in for a hug. Usually he just pulls me from the side, like a half hug, shy and reluctant, or nudges my knee or something, but this was a real hug, warm and long. "I am so proud of you, C." His mask muffles hot on the top of my head.

"I know," I say to his shoulder.

He pulls away and gives a final wave as he's out the door. His eyes red-rimmed with tears.

It's the only thing that's got me emotional all day.

Faith is doing super good in Alberta. At least that's what her socials say. Every photo a smiling girl, usually with a fancy drink in her hand, or her hanging with her little brothers. They are three very cute little kids. All of them looking a bit like their older, long-lost sister. And in all of them, Faith's smile is wider than I have ever seen it.

We've messaged a bit over the summer. She's busy with work, bros, and this bar she likes to go to. She's feeling at home, she had said. She is home, I had thought. And didn't feel as jealous as I used to be.

I've also gotten pretty close to Nevaeh. She still sends me funny memes, nearly every day these days, and likes to chat late at night sometimes. She's on her own now, working at some takeout and not very far. I'm going to go visit her once I get settled. The thought makes me more anxious than I want to admit. I don't like to think about all that. How sad I was, where I was, when I knew her. My time with Nevaeh at Luzia's house was by far the best of the rest. But it was all connected to the other stuff too. It was easy living at Dad and Nikki's. Being busy with school and stuff. Easy to forget there was a time when I was too sad for words. When no one checked to see if I was all right. Or gave me money. Or even passive-aggressively tried to show they cared. When I was stuck in places where no one really cared about me at all. Easy isn't the right word but I try not to think about it anyway. I know that's not the right way to go about it, but it's been working so far.

Actually I've been thinking about starting therapy or something like that. Whatever it was called. The university has stuff like that. I always liked the idea of speaking to someone willingly, and not because they were forcing you to talk or had to make sure you weren't that bad off because then they would be in trouble. I am going to be eighteen in a month and then I can do whatever I want. No matter what.

When everything has a place, clothes in the closet, books on the shelf, all my shower stuff in a caddy, I look around the room and smile. I should find a poster, a good one or two, to fill the walls. I left my Harry Styles one rolled up in my closet at home. I didn't want to bring it to the dorm just in case it wasn't cool enough. Or just in case I could find something new. Something more adult. More appropriate for a university dorm.

I eat supper bent over my Intro to Psychology textbook. Going over the chapters and all they talk about—brain, senses, memory, learning. I don't know how I'm going to remember it all.

Afterwards, I take the book down to the dorm's common room and sit by one of the big windows. The sun is going behind the buildings. I curl into a corner chair self-consciously. Trying to look and be as relaxed as possible. There are a few people here and there on the floor, but it doesn't look like everybody is here yet, and everyone is quiet behind their masks. Some seem to know each other already. I try not to stare. Not sure if I am supposed to be introducing myself or not. No one is really paying attention to me, so I keep reading.

A group of girls come in and they look so fun and cool. I don't mean to eavesdrop, but they're pretty loud so it's hard not to. A couple of them look Indigenous. One stands at the edge of the cluster looking definitely Indigenous and kind of perfect. She has these great oversized glasses, ACAB in marker across her red fabric mask, and her jeans slouch just the way jeans are supposed to. She's wearing Converse running shoes. I have always wanted a pair of Converse running shoes.

I am absolutely mortified when the girl looks over, catches me looking, and I look down quickly. Even more mortified when she walks over.

She stands over me. "Hey, why you studying? You got plenty of time to do that."

I can't even think of a thing to say. Even if my throat worked. So I just sort of shrug and hope it comes off right.

"We're going to sit outside, if you wanna come? It's not much but it's the only place we can, like, go."

"I'm, not," I stutter, actually stutter. How fucking embarrassing. "I haven't quarantined yet."

"That's okay, none of us have. We all just got here." She literally sparkled. "We'll be safe, don't worry. Masks, distancing, everything."

I look over at the other girls. A couple look over at me but don't seem mean or anything. Seem normal. Seem like the kind of people I would want to talk to, if I talked to people.

I decide with a nod and a close of my textbook. And try not to stumble as I stand up. "I just have to get my sweater."

"Groovy," the girl says. Without a hint of irony. Only smoothness. "What's your name?"

"C-Cedar." I push my hair behind my ear and try to keep eye contact.

"A great Nishnaabe name!" She looks elated. I know she's not too close but she feels so close. "I'm Ziggy."

ACKNOWLEDGMENTS

Maarsii to my agent Marilyn Biderman, who always has my back, and my Canadian editor Nicole Winstanley, who helped make this story whatever it is. Maarsii to everyone at the University of New Mexico Press, Native Edge series editor David Heska Wanbli Weiden, and the great Erika T. Wurth.

Maarsii to Nicole LeClair for letting us use her stunning piece of art for this cover.

Maarsii to Aunty Esther for the story of pain croosh. Uncle George for showing me all the old photos and sharing stories (Rest in Power, Uncle).

Maarsii to my dad, my brother, and all my superhero nieces. To my husband and all my insanely good-looking children.

Maarsii to those generous enough to read and give feedback: Aubrey Jean Hanson, Jordxn Pepin, Dr. Marcia Anderson, Anna Lundberg, Ela Vermette-Furst, and Jewel Vermette.

Maarsii to all the storytellers—traditional, non-traditional, and everyone in between. Stories are medicine. Stories are magick.

Many of these names came from my Vermette family: Eugenie was my dear Great-Aunty; Toby was my Great-Uncle; Joseph was my Great-Grandfather (and his Grandfather and Great-Grandfather—really, there are so many Josephs!); and Angélique Laliberté was my 3rd-Great-Grandmother (1810–1905), mother to at least fourteen children, including another Joseph, who died at Batoche, and Pierre, my Great-Great-Grandfather.

Maarsii to all you readers. It is my honour to do this work.

© Vanda Fleury

KATHERENA VERMETTE (she/her/hers) is a Red River Métis (Michif) writer from Treaty 1 territory, the heart of the Métis Nation in Winnipeg, Manitoba, Canada. She holds a Master of Fine Arts from the University of British Columbia, an Honorary Doctor of Letters from the University of Manitoba, and has worked in poetry, novels, children's literature, and film. Her father's Michif roots run deep in St. Boniface, St. Norbert, and beyond. Her mother's side is Mennonite from the Altona and Rosenfeld area (Treaty 1). Vermette received the Governor General's Literary Award for Poetry for her first book, *North End Love Songs*. Her first novel, *The Break*, won several awards, including the Amazon First Novel Award, and was a bestseller in Canada. Her second novel, *The Strangers*, won the Atwood Gibson Writers' Trust Fiction Prize and was longlisted for the Scotiabank Giller Prize and named Indigo's 2021 Book of the Year. She lives with her kids (fur and human) in a cranky old house within skipping distance of the temperamental Red River.